SWEET CHARITY
by Rachel Wilson

Sweet Charity

Rachel Wilson

JOVE BOOKS, NEW YORK

SWEET CHARITY

A Jove Book / published by arrangement with
the author

PRINTING HISTORY
Jove edition / August 1997

All rights reserved.
Copyright © 1997 by Alice Duncan.
This book may not be reproduced in whole or in part,
by mimeograph or any other means, without permission.
For information address: The Berkley Publishing Group,
200 Madison Avenue, New York, New York 10016.

The Putnam Berkley World Wide Web site address is
http://www.berkley.com

ISBN: 0-515-12134-7

A JOVE BOOK®
Jove Books are published by The Berkley Publishing Group,
200 Madison Avenue, New York, New York 10016.
JOVE and the "J" design are trademarks
belonging to Jove Publications, Inc.

PRINTED IN THE UNITED STATES OF AMERICA

10 9 8 7 6 5 4 3 2 1

A dear friend, Susan Oliveau, asked me once why I never wrote a book with a minister hero. So I did. *Sweet Charity* is dedicated to Susan; her father, the Reverend George Heck (Great name for a minister, isn't it?); Mrs. Heck; Grandma Oliveau, who lives in Geneva, Switzerland; and, of course, Susan's husband, Don. Don's read every single one of my manuscripts, even the first, most ghastly ones. Talk about a hero!

Sweet Charity

1

New Mexico Territory, 1880

*H*ER HEART HAMMERING so hard it hurt, Grace Molloy stood at the door of the small adobe house, hugged little Charity to her breast, and prayed hard. Desperation made her knees try to wobble, but she wouldn't let them, stiffening them hard and managing by force of will to keep them motionless. She wouldn't show her fear to the baby. God and Gracie both knew she was the only hope Charity had, and she owed it to her to be strong. Gracie would die before she failed Charity.

Where on earth is he? She wanted to shriek her question to the heavens. To do so would have frightened the baby, though, so she didn't.

The tang of pine and ancient forest mingled with the scent of dust, and something in Gracie's rattled brain registered appreciation of the combination. Allowing herself a short peek at her surroundings, she decided they seemed quite pretty, in a wild sort of way.

This New Mexico Territory was like nothing she'd had anything to do with before—which was almost as frightening as her purpose. She'd heard dire tales about the perilous landscape and the lawless men who dwelled on it.

Neither novelty nor violence would stop her, though. Gracie knew herself to be resourceful. She also had no choice. She made a mental note to study this milieu later, when she wasn't so worried.

Oh, dear God, please let him be here.

She shut her eyes tightly, afraid she'd begin to cry before anybody answered her knock. She wouldn't allow herself to cry. The only thing tears had ever done for her was make her eyelids swell unbecomingly and give her a headache. Right now she needed her body and mind to function properly in order to carry out her plan. Her plan was the only thing that might save Charity.

After what seemed like ten minutes but must have been only a second or two, she sucked in another resolute breath and rapped on the door again.

Footsteps. Gracie's eyes flew open and she strained to hear. She was sure she'd heard footsteps. *Please, Lord. Please let him be home.*

When the door opened abruptly she looked up, startled, and beheld that face, the face she'd loved since she was four years old—more weathered now, but no less dear. Her heart soared like a hawk and her lips trembled in spite of her determination. With a strangled *"Jake!"* she burst into tears and threw herself at his chest, baby and all.

Jake Molloy had an impression of soft blond hair under a green calico bonnet, of a faintly remembered innocence and an entirely new womanliness, before his arms closed around the female who'd just flung herself at him. Good God, it couldn't be! Could it?

Flabbergasted, barely able to speak, he mouthed, *"Gracie?"*

The name left his lips in an incredulous puff and seemed to hover in the atmosphere above them.

Good God. The thought shot through his mind again.

He'd been writing tomorrow's sermon when he'd heard a knock at his door. The rapping had interrupted his train of thought and he didn't appreciate it. He still found that particular task, as much as he valued it, burdensome.

He'd yanked off his half-glasses and set them on the Bible resting open in front of him, risen from his chair, and stretched. Another knock had propelled him toward the door, frowning and wondering who the hell it could be. Nobody knocked in Diabolito Lindo.

His arms full of woman and baby, scarcely knowing what he was about, he tested the name again, a little louder, not quite believing the evidence of his senses. "Gracie?"

Laughing and crying, in a state in the likes of which Jake had never seen her, she pushed away from him.

"Yes. Yes, Jake, it's Gracie. It's Gracie, and I've come to you because you're the only person in the whole wide world who can help me!"

Jake still gripped her shoulders, a maelstrom of emotions rioting in his breast. He peered down into her upturned face, ragged with tears and worry. Gracie! Great God Almighty, it *was* Gracie!

His arms went around her again, naturally, as if they'd been crafted to do so. A lifetime or so ago he'd sometimes thought they were, although they hadn't been called upon to perform the service for more years than he cared to remember. He'd resented the duty back then; now he was so stunned, he could hardly think at all.

He was in trouble, though; he knew *that* for a rock-solid certainty. Gracie had always meant trouble. But at the moment, he couldn't make himself care about it to save his life. In spite of her dramatic declaration, ancestors of which had plagued him during his youth, lightness filled his soul and he smiled.

"My Lord. Gracie. I swear, I never thought I'd hear you say those words again."

He squeezed her tightly, astonished by the miracles God could perform in one poor sinner's life. Then, even though he knew Gracie's sudden reemergence into his life boded something strange—at the very least—he shut his eyes and offered up a prayer of undiluted gratitude. Gracie! Gracie was here!

When he looked down again, his gaze drifted past her face for the first time. His smile faded. "Good God! Is that a baby?"

He knew it was a baby, of course. The tiny child stared at him from Gracie's arms, wide-eyed and solemn. Its big brown eyes seemed to take up half its face. Jake, who had no experience with babies, felt a pang of fear. His reaction was absurd and he knew it; he'd faced infinitely worse things than babies in his life. All he had to do was look in the mirror, in fact.

Gracie pushed herself away from him and wiped her eyes with the back of her hand. Jake found his lost smile. Same old Gracie. Never prepared for anything. Some things never changed, he guessed, and thanked God for that as he handed her his clean bandanna.

"Oh, thank you, Jake. Thank you so much. Yes, it's a baby. Her name is Charity. And—and Jake, she's mine!"

"*What?*"

Little Charity, startled by Jake's booming exclamation, cringed in Gracie's arms and began to whimper.

"Oh, poor love. Don't cry. I'm here. I—Mama's here, dear." Gracie looked up at Jake, her expression as stern as Gracie's expression could get. "Don't shout at my baby, Jake."

Raking a hand through his hair, his brain awhirl, Jake muttered, "Sorry, Gracie. Listen, you'd better come inside. We can talk there."

"All right. But—but first I'd better tell you . . . um . . . something else."

Why didn't this surprise him? A little warily he asked, "What else?"

"I have my husband's coffin with me, too. It's in the wagon."

"Husband! Coffin?"

Jake looked past the woman and baby filling up his front doorway and beheld the wagon parked in front of his gate. The Mexican man at the reins of the two sorry mules grinned and tipped his hat. Jake nodded at the man mutely, too bewildered for words. Gracie married?

No. It wasn't possible. The Gracie he remembered was a heedless, aggravating, scrape-kneed ten-year-old who'd dogged his every step and made his life a misery—when she wasn't making him laugh.

But Gracie, a wife? A widow? He took another look at the baby. A mother?

As if in answer to his unspoken questions, Gracie hurried on. "Aunt Lizzy said you lived here and that you're a minister now, Jake."

He blinked and murmured numbly, "She did?"

"Yes. And I could hardly believe it when she told me, 'cause the last I heard you were in jail."

"You did?" He felt an absurd urge to deny the truth, even as he knew it would be useless. Somehow the very word *jail* seemed impure in Gracie's presence.

She nodded. "But I always knew you had a good heart even when you were running wild and getting into mischief, and you were always the only person who ever seemed to be able to help me when I was in trouble, and since you're a preacher, I reckon you can bury the cof—my hus— my—my Ralph. You know, perform a service and all."

Gracie sucked in a huge breath at the end of her impassioned speech. If Jake hadn't been so unnerved by her bursting into his life—complete with accoutrements—after fourteen rough years, he might have smiled at how little she'd changed. Her mouth still ran on like a fiddlestick. Gracie had never needed another person in order to carry on a conversation in all the years he'd known her.

She still seemed to have been put on earth to torment him, too. That's another thing that hadn't changed at all.

And, as he was extremely unnerved, he stammered, "You—you brought your husband's coffin here? All the way from St. Louis? Because you wanted me to bury it? Him, I mean?"

Giving him a great big smile, Gracie said brightly, "Yes. Because you're a minister and all, Jake, and the only person in the whole wide world who—"

"Yeah, yeah, I know all that." He peered down at her, his brow wrinkling. Something was odd here. Ancient, troublesome incidents began to dance around the edges of his memory, and he asked cautiously, "How long's he been dead, Gracie?"

"Four months."

"Four months?"

She nodded again, a shade less brightly. "I wanted *you* to bury him, Jake. Because you're kin, and I didn't have anybody else."

"What about Aunt Lizzy?"

"Well, I mean, I didn't have any other *men* kin, Jake. And besides," she pointed out as if to put a period to the discussion, "Aunt Lizzy isn't a minister."

He stared at her hard, trying to determine exactly what was going on here. Granted, he hadn't seen Gracie for fourteen years and they hadn't corresponded for five or six—more's the pity—but still, he hadn't entirely forgotten the twisted paths her mind could travel. Uneasiness began to nibble at him. "Last I heard you were living in St. Louis and teaching school, Gracie."

"I was, Jake, yes."

"You mean you left your teaching job, your friends, and your entire life behind and brought your dead husband here to the Territory from St. Louis? Because you wanted *me* to bury him?"

She nodded again, and smiled that innocent smile he'd never been able to resist. Or trust. His uneasiness swelled until it stampeded around his insides like a herd of wild horses.

"Because Aunt Lizzy said you were a minister and I needed to be with somebody kind." She buried her face in his bandanna. "I thought you'd understand, Jake. You always used to understand me."

"No, I didn't, Gracie. I never understood you at all." He heaved a sigh as big as he was and, with some difficulty, remembered his calling as a man of God. "But I'll help if I can."

Her face reappeared from his bandanna, looking remarkably dry-eyed. Jake wasn't surprised.

"Oh, thank you!"

He shook his head, gave up his lingering reserve, decided that whatever this meant he could handle it, and chuckled. Good old Gracie. Life sure wasn't dull around her, whatever else it was.

"Take Charity into the house, Gracie. It's not much. Diabolito Lindo itself isn't much, I reckon. But if you've come all this way to visit and to have me perform funeral services—well, I'll go take care of your coffin."

"Thank you, Jake."

"You have anything else in the wagon?"

"Well, yes. I have my bags and the baby's things."

He nodded, resigned to his fate. "I'll take care of them, too." Shaking his head, he strode off to deal with Gracie's bags. And her dead husband. Good God. He looked back once to see Gracie at the door, watching him.

Then he heard her say, "Come on inside, Charity. We'll be all right now. Your Uncle Jake will take care of us. Jake always took care of me when I was little."

Jake almost groaned.

Fifteen minutes later, he reentered his once-peaceful home to discover Gracie and her baby playing pat-a-cake on the braided rug on the parlor floor.

Gracie still had curly blond hair, darkened with the years into an almost-brown color, with wisps escaping from underneath her bonnet. She'd never been able to keep her hair in place. Those big hazel eyes of hers still leaned toward green, and her dark brows and long lashes made her eyes look even bigger than he remembered. Today, with a jolt, Jake realized they were bedroom eyes if he'd ever seen any. And he had. Plenty, God save him.

Charity, on the other hand, had reddish-brown hair. What he could see of it under her tiny little sunbonnet looked straight and thick, too. It had been pulled back from a forehead wider than Gracie's. Her face looked as round as a pumpkin, although that might just be her babyishness expressing itself, Jake reckoned. What did he know about babies? Her eyes were as brown and soft as melted chocolate, and her complexion was a creamy ivory, not at all like Gracie's peaches-and-cream. She was solemn as a bishop and stared at Gracie as if she were the adult and Gracie the child. Jake shook his head, grinned, and decided that Charity was a smart kid.

They didn't look much alike, Gracie and Charity, but they were both like spots of bright sunlight in a world of shadows. He watched, nearly transfixed, for several seconds, unwilling to break the spell of peace and domesticity these two remarkable creatures had cast around him.

He hadn't realized how much he'd missed a home and family until right now, and wondered if it was a good thing to have been reminded. Especially since it was Gracie who'd reminded him, and he couldn't make himself forget exactly what diabolical schemes that sweet facade of hers could conceal.

When she looked up and smiled, though, he almost forgot to remember that this was the grown-up edition of the same female who'd once made him rescue an entire litter of puppies she'd claimed were being abused, fight the town bully on behalf of the crippled Osborne boy, and pay a whiskey-boat oarsman five whole dollars for a broken-down mule she'd claimed he was mistreating. It had taken him half a year to pay for that damned mule. And the stupid thing was too ornery to be of any use to anybody except Gracie, whom it occasionally condescended to allow to pat its neck and feed it carrots.

And then there was the time she'd made him climb a tree to rescue a raccoon Zebulon Foster had wounded with his slingshot. Jake shook his head, the memory returning with a resounding thump. Not only had he been severely bitten by the victim during that particular escapade, but the branch had broken, and with it, eventually, his arm, when he and the raccoon had hit the earth. If he recalled correctly, all Gracie's sympathy had gone to the raccoon, too. His arm gave a twinge as if in warning.

Her smile was as winning as ever, however, and Jake discovered that the memories, for all their prickles, couldn't hold a candle to its lure. For a second he had a mad impulse to fall on his knees and thank God for this invasion. He didn't, because his gut told him it boded ill for his future peace of mind. He smiled back at her, though, because he couldn't help himself.

In order to shake off his strange feelings, he said, "The baby must look like her daddy."

She peered critically at her daughter. "Do you think so? I always thought she looked like her mama."

This time Jake laughed outright. "Gracie, Gracie. She has brown hair and brown eyes, a round face, and a much darker complexion than you have. Now you tell me how much that looks like you."

He saw her big hazel eyes open wide and her pale cheeks blossom into pink. She swallowed. "Oh. Oh, well, I reckon you're right, then. I was thinking of her . . . her features, you see."

"I see."

Still chuckling, suppressing his urge to sweep her into his arms and swing her around as he used to do when they were growing up—when he wasn't wanting to wring her neck— Jake strolled to his desk and sat in the chair he'd recently vacated. He glanced at his unfinished sermon and decided that, once again, God had demonstrated in no uncertain terms how the fragile designs of man were nothing compared to what He had planned. At least for this man, Jake Molloy.

Trying to sound severe, he said, "All right now, Gracie. Suppose you tell me why you're here, and this time tell the truth. It can't be just because you want me to recite the verses over your poor dead husband's coffin."

Picking Charity up from the floor, Gracie carried her to a chair and sat, too. Jake realized he hadn't heard the baby utter more than that one tiny whimper when he'd frightened her outside, and wondered about it. Granted, he'd not had much to do with babies, but he didn't expect one to be this quiet.

Before she could respond to his earlier query, he asked, "How old is Charity?"

Gracie's smile for the baby was one of absolute love. Jake recognized it, and his heart responded. She used to look at him that way. He hadn't appreciated it then; now it made his heart do funny things in his chest.

"She's twenty-six months old, Jake. A little over two years old."

"Why didn't you write me, Gracie?"

He wished he hadn't asked when she gazed at him, her ever-honest soul in her eyes. He'd forgotten for a minute how she used to be able to puncture his densest emotional walls with one of her looks . . . and then use it to her advantage.

"I used to write to you, Jake. You never wrote back."

Unable to hold the soulful stare piercing him like a beam of light and threatening to illuminate the ugly trash at his core, he dropped his gaze and mumbled, "I know it, Gracie. I had some hard years."

She was doing it again, blast it all. If he didn't watch himself, he'd be agreeing to whatever she wanted. Jake gave himself a firm mental shake and told himself to get a grip.

"I'm awfully sorry, Jake. I knew you'd have written if—well, if you could. I guess I should have kept writing anyway."

She was genuinely contrite; Jake knew it. Same old Gracie. To his knowledge, she'd never deliberately hurt anything or anybody in her life, no matter how much chaos had seemed to follow in her good-hearted wake. After clearing his throat, he said, "I'm surprised Aunt Lizzy didn't let me know, though."

Gracie said quickly, "Aunt Lizzy didn't know. It—you see, it was a sudden marriage, and then the baby was born nine months later."

"And you didn't write Aunt Lizzy?"

"Oh, well, my husband didn't . . . want any visitors at first. You know how Aunt Lizzy can be. She'd have swooped down on us for sure." Her laugh sounded forced, and she stopped abruptly and licked her lips. "Anyway, Charity was just a little over a year and a half old when her daddy died. She'll never know him now."

"Too bad," Jake said.

"Yes. Isn't it."

She seemed to have to fight a smile, though, and Jake felt his eyes narrow. "Go on, Gracie. Tell me your story."

"Well . . ."

She appeared to droop for a second. Jake detected an air of desperation in the slump of her shoulders and it surprised him. He couldn't even imagine his sunny little Gracie in despair. Her manner provoked something primitive in him. Every single one of his protective instincts surged to the fore, and he experienced the same urge to slay dragons for her that he'd known in their childhood. That chivalrous feeling had managed to ensnare him in one perilous adventure after another, and memory made him grin again.

Good old Gracie. In the years since they'd been separated, he'd begun to think of her as a benevolent whirlwind, never heeding the tumult she created, but leaving it to him to pick up after she'd done her worst—with, of course, the best of intentions. And he always had, more the fool he.

"Well . . ." Lifting her head, Gracie stared at him, her eyes pleading for understanding. "Well, Jake, we've come here to ask you to take us in. To let us live with you. Everything I have in the world is in those bags. We aim to move to the Territory and make a life for ourselves here." She added, plaintively, "If you'll have us."

His eyes widened and his mouth dropped open, and Jake could only stare at her for a moment, stunned. "Live with *me?*"

She nodded.

"But, Gracie, this is Diabolito Lindo. This is the New Mexico Territory. There aren't any women here, except for a Mexican woman who works in the saloon and doesn't speak hardly any English. Even if she could, she's not the sort of female you're used to. This is a rough, wild place. It's violent. You're used to pretty things and peace and luxuries and—and besides, I'm a single man. You can't live with me! It's unheard of!"

"But you're my brother, Jake."

Every one of his senses trumpeted an alarm, and he rose

from his chair so fast its legs clattered against the rough wooden floor, making the baby jump. "I am not!"

Gracie's arms tightened around Charity, and Jake was sorry he'd startled the child. Still and all . . . Gracie's sweetly uttered comment presaged disaster. He knew it, because he knew her. Striding to the streaked window, he raked his hand through his hair again before he turned and faced her.

"I'm not even your real stepbrother, Gracie. Not even your real *foster* brother. There's no tie of blood between us. You know that. When your ma and pa took me in because I was your pa's dead partner's son, we became sort of like kin. That's all. It would be improper for you to live here with me. I'm a minister. I have a moral obligation to my congregation here in Diabolito Lindo." Because he anticipated she'd object if she ever got to know exactly who composed his congregation, he added, "No matter what they look like to outsiders."

"I grew up thinking of you as my brother, Jake, whether or not we're kin by blood or law."

"You were only ten when I left home, Gracie. That was fourteen years ago!"

She lifted her chin, the same stubborn chin she used to lift when they were kids. Jake began to have a sinking feeling in his middle.

"I don't care how many years ago it was, Jake. I *still* think of you as my brother!"

"Well, that's just too bad, Gracie. I'm a minister now, for heaven's sake. I can't be taking in single ladies and their babies, even if you do think of me as your brother."

"But even Mama and Papa used to treat us as if we were kin. You even took our name! I've *always* called you my brother. To everybody. Besides," she added with piercing simplicity, "you're the only one on earth I trust."

Hearing the ring of truth in her words, Jake eyed her sharply. She sat stiff as marble on the edge of the chair, clutching Charity. Both females stared at him as if their very lives depended on his decision.

He felt like groaning even as a grin tugged at the corners

of his mouth. Gracie's exterior hadn't changed much at all over the years. She still had that sweet air about her, and the impression of innocence. Hell, she *was* innocent. No matter how much of a pain in the neck she'd been all those years ago, there wasn't one of her scrapes that hadn't been instigated out of goodness. For some unfathomable reason, Gracie believed herself to have been placed on earth to right the world's wrongs. He didn't suppose it was her fault that she considered him the tool with which to do it.

Something odd was going on here, though. He knew it even though he couldn't quite put his finger on it. But she was still Gracie, the same Gracie who'd alternated between being the scourge and the salvation of his youth. If anything, marriage and motherhood had softened her buoyant prettiness and matured it.

Which was definitely not a good thing. She appealed to him now in a way that was very different from the grudging affection he'd had for her when they were growing up, before he'd escaped home to see the world and make his mark.

He'd made his mark, all right. But that was another matter entirely, and nothing to the purpose. Jake searched Gracie's face as if he'd find an answer there. He didn't.

Still . . . Something was not right about this strange flight of hers. All the way from St. Louis, a civilized city in a civilized state where she had friends—where she taught school, for heaven's sake—to here, an outlaw town in outlaw territory. It didn't make sense to him. Not even for Gracie, who, if he recalled correctly, made less sense than most people.

"Why is your trust in me so important, Gracie? What aren't you telling me?"

Her eyes opened up so wide that he knew she was going to lie even before she opened her mouth. He'd always been able to tell.

"Nothing, Jake. There's nothing I'm not telling you. It's just what I said. My husband—my husband—my husband—"

"Your husband?" he prompted, torn between amusement and exasperation.

"Yes. My husband—Ralph! He died, and I brought him here. To you. Because you're my—well, I think of you as my big brother and I love you and you're a preacher, and I wanted somebody I trusted to perform the burial service."

"That's all?"

"Yes. I—I loved Ralph and wanted somebody else I loved to—to lay him to rest."

"You're lying to me, Gracie."

He remembered the practiced pout that met his bald declaration, and might have smiled if the circumstances had been different.

"About what?"

"You've got to tell me about what, because I don't know." He added gently, "You were always a terrible liar, Gracie. You know that."

Her gaze dropped again and she squeezed the baby tighter. Her whispered "I know" was so tiny he barely heard it. When she lifted her head again, she wore an expression he'd never seen on the face of his lighthearted, happy-go-lucky, pesky little Gracie. She looked inflexible, as though no matter what he said, she knew what she had to do and aimed to do it.

She didn't speak for a minute, and Jake saw her take a big breath. "I loved Ralph, Jake. I really did, but—but—well . . . my marriage was—was a mistake. It wasn't very happy."

Foreboding sucked any hint of humor out of Jake. No matter how annoying she was, no matter what scrapes she'd plunged him into over the years, Jake had always been willing to fight battles for her.

Willing, hell. He'd gone out of his way to seek them. He still didn't understand the compulsion he'd always felt to protect her. Right now, everything in him compressed into one intense question. "Did he hurt you, Gracie?"

She looked up, surprised. "Hurt me?" She shrugged. "Oh, well, not very much."

The pain hit Jake so suddenly he winced. Gracie saw, and

continued hurriedly. "He really didn't, Jake. But, still, we weren't happy even though—even though we loved each other, you see. Ralph's family blamed me. Now they're trying to take Charity away from me. He—his brother is the one. He's mean and spiteful and—and he used to come over to the house after Ralph died and shout at me." She looked at him, her eyes huge and earnest. "He used to swear something awful and threaten me. He—he drinks, Jake."

He drinks. Jake suddenly felt as though somebody'd punched him in the stomach. Gracie had come here, to Jake Molloy, the worst drunkard God ever created, and expected him to save her. If only she knew. He leaned against the wall and put a hand over his eyes as what seemed like an eternity of fuzzy years staggered past his mind's eye and reeled out of sight. *He drinks. Oh, dear God.*

Fussing with the baby's dress ribbons, Gracie said, "I couldn't give my baby up, Jake. I just couldn't do it. But Ralph's brother has lots of money, and he kept threatening, and I was afraid he could do it, because I'm just a woman and everything. I wanted to come here to you, because you're the only person on earth I love—besides Mama and Papa, and they're dead. Please help us, Jake."

When the sheltering hand left Jake's eyes, Gracie was crying. Not like she used to cry when she was a kid, because she knew he'd give in to her if she cried, but because she couldn't help it. These were the silent, terrible tears of a woman, and they shook Jake like nothing ever had before.

And suddenly he knew why God had sent Gracie here to him, and it wasn't just for Gracie's sake. This was a test; probably the first real test he'd encountered since he'd gotten out of prison five years before and taken the pledge and the cloth. The last few years had merely been training. They were nothing compared to what the test of Gracie was going to be.

Not only would he have to deal with Gracie herself, around whom trouble mounded up like snowflakes in a blizzard, but he was going to have to deal with his own reaction to the grown-up Gracie. He suspected that reaction was going to be pretty far removed from brotherly. Suspected, hell. It already was.

And then he was going to have to share his three-room adobe shack with a baby. A baby! In Diabolito Lindo, for the love of God!

This was a test, all right; God planned to see exactly what Jake Molloy was made of. Something cynical in him wanted to laugh, but such a laugh would have been a blasphemy in the presence of Gracie's distress and the purity of baby Charity.

Silently, he prayed for strength to the God he'd begun to take for granted recently, when all he'd had to deal with were drunken cowboys, Indian incursions, border bandits, desperadoes, and guns and knives. He said roughly, "All right, Gracie. You can stay here with me."

Her face lit up like Christmas and the years fell away. She was his Gracie again. His sweet little, pretty little, irritating little Gracie. He'd die to protect this girl—this woman. He wondered if Gracie, and not the bottle, might truly be his fatal flaw and reckoned he'd find out fairly soon.

He dreaded it.

"Oh, Jake, thank you!" With Charity in her arms, she hurtled out of her chair and threw herself at him for the second time that day.

As his arms closed around her, Jake shut his eyes and prayed again. Hard.

His prayer was interrupted precipitately when baby Charity screamed as if somebody had just pinched her.

2

STILL LAUGHING AND crying intermittently, Gracie soothed the baby and unwrapped her while Jake rearranged his living quarters to accommodate her and Charity. She'd known he wouldn't fail her. No matter how cranky he got, Jake had never failed her.

The very first time she met him, when she was four years old, she'd recognized him as the hero of her life. The only thing she even remembered about being four was meeting the lanky twelve-year-old Jake. He'd taken her hand and smiled down at her, and she'd known then and there that he would never fail her.

When she contemplated the string of lies she'd just told him, though, her heart battered her insides like a wild animal trying to get out. She wondered if he'd have taken her in if he'd known the truth. The Jake of her childhood would have—grudgingly, complaining and scolding her all the while—but she wasn't sure she even knew this Jake. She slid him a glance as she fussed over Charity.

He sure didn't look like the Jake she used to know. Oh, his features were the same, but he seemed much craggier now. Weathered. There were lines around the beautiful dark brown eyes she used to love, and gray streaks tinted his dark, dark hair. He had scars, too, and he was taller than she remembered. And bigger. Those broad shoulders were used to hard work; she'd bet money on it. There was certainly nothing boyish left in him. However he'd spent the fourteen years since he left home, he'd evidently not had an easy time of it.

Gracie chided herself. Of course those years hadn't been easy. He'd ended up in jail, hadn't he? Her heart gave an enormous tug at the thought of her Jake behind bars, and she wondered what dreadful miscarriage of justice had thrown him in there. Surely he'd done nothing bad enough to deserve it. Not her Jake.

Suddenly guilt slapped her hard. Her wonderful Jake. She'd loved him for as long as she could remember, and she'd just spent the last half hour pouring a pile of rubbish into his ears. She had a dismal feeling that he deserved better from her than all those awful lies, even if she didn't dare tell him the truth.

Merciful heavens, she'd never had to improvise so fast in her whole life. How stupid of her not to have thought of a reasonable story before she got here. He was right about her inability to lie; lying was a skill she'd never practiced, and she wasn't any good at it. But she guessed she'd learn. If it was the only way to keep Charity safe, Gracie would walk through the fires of hell. She wouldn't let Martha's baby— *her* baby—down.

"What's your name now, Gracie?"

Jake's voice—roughened with years and she knew not what else—sliced through her thoughts and startled her. She turned and looked at him, wondering if he was teasing. "What do you mean what's my name? I'm Gracie, for heaven's sake. Gracie Molloy. Your sister—well, at least, I think of myself as your sister."

His bark of laughter made her smile. "You goose," he said, so lovingly that the last remaining knot of fear in her breast melted, turned into steam, and wafted away. "I mean your married name."

"Oh! Oh, of course! I—I reckon I'm so glad to be back with you, I didn't think."

Good grief, how could she have forgotten to provide herself with a last name? Cursing inwardly, wishing yet again that she had more practice in deceit, Gracie's brain scrambled for a name. The first one to pop into her head was that of a town they'd passed through on their way here, and she blurted out, "Trinidad. It's Trinidad now."

"Trinidad? Strange name."

"Is it? I don't know. There were lots of Trinidads in St. Louis." Lies, lies, lies. Gracie hastily turned toward the baby because she didn't want Jake to see her face and know she was fibbing.

Names. You have to remember the names, Gracie. Ralph was your husband and Trinidad is your last name. What a stupid last name.

She vowed to endow her imaginary dead spouse with an imaginary family tonight—a family with more fitting names—before she went to sleep. Especially the evil brother; she couldn't forget about him. While she folded baby things, she decided grimly that his name would be John. That should be easy enough to remember. She'd practice smiling innocently, too.

"Never met any Trinidads back home myself." Carefully setting his Bible on a chair, Jake said, "All right, Gracie. There are only three rooms in the house, but I can get busy building another big room for you and Charity. There are lots of men in town who'll be glad to help me."

"You don't have to do that, Jake." Now Gracie felt guilty for putting him through all this. Another glance at Charity, who was as grim as a high priest on Judgment Day and sitting entirely too still for a child her age, firmed up Gracie's grit, which had sagged momentarily under the weight of her guilt. Jake was strong. He was a sight stronger than Charity and undoubtedly a whole lot stronger than Gracie. He could handle it. "But we'd surely appreciate it."

He winked at her, and her guilty heart fluttered like a

feather in the wind. "I'll make it up to you, Jake. You'll see. I'll cook and clean and make your life comfortable. You just wait."

"I'm sure you will, Gracie."

His voice held a laugh and she knew he didn't believe her. He used to call her the most uncomfortable girl he knew, back when they were growing up and he'd had to extricate her from predicaments all the time. But she'd changed, just as he had. She really would make him comfortable. She'd show him.

With a grunt, Jake shoved his desk across the floor, then straightened and wiped the sweat from his forehead. Picking up his Bible, he placed it gently back on his desk, patted it as if it were a dear friend, and said, "There. That should about do it. I'll just keep my bedroll in the chest and then when the new room's finished, I'll move you two into it and take my bedroom back."

"Thank you, Jake. You'll never know how much this means to me."

She didn't quite trust that squint of his.

"Oh, I expect I will one day, Gracie. When you trust me enough to tell me the real story behind your move here."

"Jake!"

He laughed. "Oh, I don't aim to pry, Gracie. I still have my sermon to write for tomorrow."

He walked over to where Gracie had begun feeding Charity a biscuit and water. The baby flinched when his shadow blocked the light coming through the window, and Gracie quickly cooed to comfort her.

"She's skittish as a new colt," Jake observed. "I never knew babies were jumpy like that."

Aiming for a nonchalant laugh, she said, "Well, I reckon most of them aren't. Poor little Charity's been through a lot in her life, what with losing her daddy and traveling all this way to the Territory." She looked up and wasn't pleased to see Jake's soft frown. Then he shrugged, and relief made her shoulders sag momentarily.

"Reckon you're right. I don't know a thing about babies."

"You'll learn, Jake," Gracie said, smiling. "You'll learn."

*   *   *

So great was Gracie's relief, now that she'd been accepted into the sanctuary of Jake's home, that she overslept the following morning. It was Charity, stirring softly at her side, who finally nudged her consciousness and made her yawn and stretch.

She smiled, recalling the events of the prior day, and felt safe for the first time since leaving St. Louis. She and Charity were in Jake's care now. Nothing could hurt them. She opened her eyes to see dust motes dancing like tiny gilt fairies in the sunbeams pouring into the room.

Then a terrible thought shattered her calm, and she sat up, startled. *Oh, criminy, I forgot to fetch the bag of money out of the coffin!*

Berating herself as an irresponsible, scatterbrained fool, Gracie scrambled out of bed only to find Jake standing beside the window, watching her. He smiled and her insides turned to slush. Shaken, she smiled back. "Morning, Jake."

"Morning, Gracie. Didn't think you'd ever wake up. You must have had a hard trip of it."

Snatching up her robe and groping for the sleeves, she said, "Yes. Yes, it was kind of rough."

Charity's hand grabbed a chunk of her robe, and Gracie wanted to scream at herself for being so stupid. How could she have forgotten the money? Almost frantically, she searched her brain for options, only to crash up against the iron wall of reality every time one popped up. There was no way on earth she could open that coffin in broad daylight without attracting an audience.

Shoot. Frowning, she scooped Charity off the bed. Well, there was nothing to do but accept the consequences of her irresponsibility. Anyway, she decided philosophically, if there was one place the money would be safe, it was in that coffin and six feet under.

Her frown melted into a grin when she remembered the piece of meat she'd thrown inside so nobody would even think about lifting the lid. The coffin didn't stink quite as much as it used to, but it also wouldn't hurt to leave everything safely underground indefinitely. By the time it became absolutely necessary to use the money, maybe she'd have figured out how to confess everything to Jake.

"Did you get your sermon finished?"

"I did."

"I'll be really interested to hear you deliver it." Gracie sailed Charity across the room and plopped her on a blanket she'd spread over the kitchen table.

His chuckle was warm and deep and rich and slithered through her like honey over warm toast. "I don't expect you've ever been to a church the likes of which we have here in Diabolito Lindo, Gracie. Hope you aren't easily shocked."

"Shocked?" She shot a peek at him over her shoulder. "Why on earth should I be shocked?"

He shoved himself away from the wall and came over to watch the action. Gracie was sorry when Charity saw him, shut her eyes, and turned away. Jake apparently didn't realize there was anything unusual in the baby's attitude and actions.

"For one thing, during the rest of the week, it's a saloon."

"What?"

"Told you you'd be shocked."

"You hold church services in a saloon?" Gracie couldn't not laugh at the absurdity of it. Her cheerful giggle apparently soothed Charity, because the baby dared look at her again, even though she offered no responsive smile.

"Pablo Fergus's place. He's my best friend, and he runs the Devil's Last Stop here in town. We sweep it out Sunday mornings before church."

"Good heavens."

"But I'll come back to get you and the baby if you want to attend services. I'd rather you not walk in the town alone until I introduce you. The men around here aren't like those back home. They might get the wrong idea."

Now Gracie was shocked. "For heaven's sake, Jake, I know this is the frontier and a little rough, but it can't be that bad."

Unsmiling, he said, "It is, Gracie, and I don't aim to have you prove it for me."

He sounded so very serious, so very like the Jake of yore when she'd bucked his authority, that Gracie's little laugh leaked out again spontaneously. When he looked exasperated, she said hastily, "All right, Jake. We'll wait until you come to get us. Don't want to be snatched off the street or anything in your outlaw town."

"It *is* an outlaw town, Gracie, and it's not funny."

His eyes twinkled, though, and Gracie's heart went *pitter-pat* in response. She wondered if she'd ever get over loving Jake Molloy. Sometimes she thought she'd loved him since the beginning of time.

"I'll wait for you, Jake," she said softly. And she would, too. Already had, in fact.

She heard the door shut quietly when he left the house, and she picked Charity up. "Let's get some breakfast into you, young lady. Then we're going to church with your Uncle Jake."

For the first time since the wagon had rumbled them into Diabolito Lindo, Charity smiled. She said, "Beffas," and Gracie's eyes filled with tears.

"Didn't know you had no sister, Jake."

Jake saved his breath and didn't answer until he and Fergus had hoisted Harley Newton up from the floor where he'd been snoring off his Saturday-night excesses. Hoisting Harley wasn't a new experience, but it never got any easier, as Harley wasn't a small man. After propping him against the back wall next to two other overnighters, Jake straightened and sighed, wondering how Gracie could have him prevaricating so soon after reappearing in his life.

He also wasn't at all sure what he felt about having suddenly acquired a sister. Especially a sister who looked like Gracie. Unfortunately, she was no longer the skinny, flat-chested kid who used to harass the life out of him. The cuteness he recalled from her childhood had blossomed into full-blown womanly loveliness that seemed to call to him like a siren's song. He still hadn't quite recovered from watching her wake up this morning. He'd have to remember not to do that again.

He'd been almost sorry when her eyes opened. He'd been so busy watching her sleep, he'd not wanted her to stir. She'd looked so sweet and so pure, so much of what she'd always been and he never had, that he'd wanted to go on looking at her forever. His own thoughts hadn't been pure in the least. Still, he reckoned he'd store the memory up anyway, and take it out and examine it during black moments in years to come. His little Gracie, grown up at last. Lord, Lord.

Deciding to play it Gracie's way for Fergus, he said, "Yup. Gracie. She's eight years younger than I am."

Fergus thought hard for a minute. "Hell, Jake, that must make her near to thirty."

Delivering a light punch to Fergus's shoulder, Jake muttered, "She's twenty-four, Fergus. Don't make me any older than I am. I already feel like Methuselah."

"Look it, too." The usually stony-faced Fergus *hee-heed*.

Even Jake chuckled, although he feared his friend's assessment was more accurate than funny. As he'd shaved this morning, he'd stared into his mirror and wondered how on earth Gracie's big almost-foster brother had gotten so lost since she'd seen him last. Had it really been only fourteen years?

The once-innocent, once-unlined face had stared back at him, now sporting not merely a variety of creases, but also a scar running from his left eyebrow to mid-cheek. The wound had been delivered by a man wielding a broken whiskey bottle some nine years earlier. The scar reminded him of others he couldn't see, but which were there nonetheless—the marks on his body only fractionally echoing those on his soul. Jake's dark brown hair was silvered around the edges, and his dark eyes held weariness and wariness—two qualities collected during a whole raft of experiences. They were experiences different from any he'd had when he'd lived with the Molloy family and adopted their name. He hoped Gracie would never have to know about the half of them.

Maybe he should never have left St. Louis. Shaking his head as he took the broom Fergus held out to him, Jake acknowledged that it didn't matter. Contemplating the what-might-have-beens in life was a useless occupation, a waste of time; he knew it—but he couldn't stop himself from doing it anyway.

He remembered those days in St. Louis with something akin to reverence. Even when he'd been in the very thick of hashing up his life, memories of St. Louis and Gracie had seemed almost holy to him. All the annoyances and uncomfortable situations Gracie had visited upon him had softened over the years until they'd begun to shine in his memory, as precious as gold.

His introduction to God had come to Jake in an unlikely way and through an unlikely agent, but even that he could lay, indirectly, at Gracie's feet if she only knew it. He wasn't sure he wanted her to. His was an ugly story—too ugly for Gracie, he feared. When most folks spoke of being saved, they didn't mean it nearly as literally as Jake Molloy did.

"She a spinster lady, your sister?"

"Widow."

"Hmmm. Any kids?"

"A little girl. Charity."

Fergus folded his wrinkles into a smile, liberating his face from its granitelike hardness. Most of the time Fergus looked like what he was: a tough-as-old-cowhide barkeeper who'd lived a life rougher than sandpaper. When he smiled he looked like what he also was: a man with a heart as big as the sky sheltering the little hellhole of Diabolito Lindo. That sky was as infinite as God's love, and Jake often thought Fergus's heart was, too. Jake loved Fergus like the brother he'd never had.

"Good name, Charity. We could use a bit o' charity around these parts. Good name." Fergus *hee-heed* again.

"It is, Fergus. It is indeed." So was Grace.

Jake wrinkled his nose as he plied the broom. No matter how much sawdust and filth they swept up every Sunday morning, nothing could rid the place of the stench of stale whiskey, spilled beer, tobacco smoke, too many men, and not enough grace and charity.

He guessed it was all right, though. Jake loved this place because it reminded him every day of what he'd risen from. Most of his flock wouldn't know what to do if they happened to find themselves in a tidy church in an orderly society. They'd undoubtedly run away, embarrassed, and then they'd never understand what redemption was all about.

That's one of the reasons he stayed here—or at least that's what he told himself. Since his own experience, Jake had felt the need to share, and he wanted to share with these men because they needed it; not because they were bad, but because they were lost.

He was sure they'd be more apt to accept God's grace from him than from some big-city, hellfire-and-damnation preacher. Why, they'd laugh a regular, turned-around-collar preacher out of town. Probably make him dance first. The poor man would be lucky to get out with his toes still attached to his feet.

Jake patted the pistol tucked into his waistband and shook his head again, grinning. Lord, what a man of God *he'd* turned out to be. Still, a rugged preacher was the kind he'd needed and, therefore, he reckoned the men who lived here could probably use one, too. It had taken him a long time to admit it—and he hadn't liked the truth even then—but he guessed he wasn't all that different from the bulk of those fellows.

"Be kinda nice to have us a lady in town," Fergus offered as he straightened chairs into neat rows.

"You think so?"

"Sure. A female might give the place some polish."

Jake laughed as he watched Fergus wipe off various deposits his customers had left on the chairs and tables during the week. "You think so, do you?"

"Couldn't hurt, anyways."

"I reckon not." Jake propped the broom up against the bar. "Say, Fergus, you want to go to a funeral after church?"

"Who got kilt? Don't reckon I heard nothing about it.

Must've been a knife fight, 'cause I don't recollect hearing no guns."

"Nobody got killed here in town. It's Gracie's husband. She brought the coffin here from St. Louis."

It didn't surprise him any when Fergus looked at him as though one of them were crazy. "She brung a corpse here from St. Louis?"

"She did."

"What in hell'd she do that for?"

Chuckling, Jake said, "You don't know Gracie yet. She's always been fairly single-minded about things. She claims she wanted me to bury him, so she brought him here."

"Hell, if she wanted to watch you plant a corpse, she could've just hung out here for a while and waited for the next fight."

"Reckon she figured this was a sure thing."

Fergus grimaced, an activity that did ghastly things with his wrinkles. "Well, it sounds *loco* to me, but then I reckon your whole family must be fair off their runners, if you're any example."

Jake almost retorted that there were no blood ties between himself and Gracie, and caught himself just in time. Lord, this new arrangement of hers was going to be difficult in more ways than one. How typical. He sighed and said instead, "Reckon you might be right about that."

"She comin' to church this morning?"

"Yes. I told her to stay at my place until I go to get her. Don't want her walking around town until I've introduced her and everybody knows she's off limits."

"Might not make no difference, Jake, 'specially when the fellers get to drinking. Better watch her."

"I aim to."

Then he smiled. By God, in spite of all the complications, it felt good to be watching out for Gracie again. Felt almost like old times, in fact. The thought cheered him up and kept him cheerful all the way back home, until he looked at his reflection in the glass window of his house and saw the face of the man he'd become since he'd last had to slay dragons for Gracie.

* * *

Gracie finished feeding herself and Charity and wondered when Jake would come back to get them. She could hardly wait.

Now that she'd done it, it scarcely seemed possible that she could have come all this way to Jake's tiny little territorial town without anybody stopping her, and that he should have taken her in with barely any argument at all. With an enormous sigh, she guessed she might have known Jake would come through for her. No other man she'd ever met had measured up to her Jake. She'd loved him forever; he'd always come through for her.

And she'd better just shove those improper feelings for him away, too, at least for the time being. She was supposed to be his sister, and his sister she would be. Charity's very life could depend on her deception.

Gracie possessed a fidgety disposition, however, and idleness did not sit easily upon her. While they waited for Jake's return, she played with Charity, at last coaxing the baby into singing with her.

As they sang and Charity kept time to the music, banging on the floor with the wooden spindle Gracie had given her, she searched through the things in Jake's kitchen, ultimately finding a scarred wooden bucket, some rags, and some vinegar. Then, filling the bucket with water and vinegar, she set to work on the windows. There were only four of them.

What a mess they were, too. Gracie smiled as she sang and scrubbed. Jake needed a woman around the house to help keep him civilized. He might be tidy and he might have reformed from what Aunt Lizzy had called his hell-raising days, but his bachelor's quarters seemed awfully bleak and cold to Gracie. Why, there wasn't a hint of personality here. Not a decoration anywhere. Everything was neat and plain and about as colorless as a foggy morning.

She'd fix them up, though. She knew she could. Why, pretty soon Jake would be so happy, he'd never be able to leave her again.

"Shoo, fly, don't bother me! Shoo, fly, don't bother me! Shoo, fly, don't bother me, 'cause I belong to Comp'ny G!"

Charity sang with her, although her words were some-what different. "Soo, fie, doh bodda bee! Soo, fie, doh bodda bee!"

She could hold a tune, though, and Gracie considered her quite a remarkable child because of it. The baby's tuneful-ness sometimes gave Gracie hope when she despaired of ever healing her manifold hurts.

She didn't see Jake silently push the door open.

When Charity saw him, she shut up like a clam, curled herself into a ball, and hid her head in her arms. Jake stared at her, mildly troubled. This reaction of hers didn't seem right to him, even if he didn't know anything about babies.

Suddenly finding herself singing solo, Gracie turned around, her vinegar rag dripping. "Jake! You're back!" When she saw the baby, her smile faded, and she dropped the rag into the bucket. Wiping her hands on her apron, she hurried to Charity.

"She's a little nervous, Jake. She's not used to you." Gracie picked the baby up and cooed to her. Charity buried her head in Gracie's shoulder.

"Are all babies like that, Gracie? I don't recall ever hearing they were."

Gracie kept her smile deliberately cheerful. "Oh, I reckon Charity's somewhat more bashful than most, but she'll get over it when she's used to things around here."

A little doubtfully, Jake said, "I expect so." He looked around his tiny home and said stupidly, "You washed the windows."

"I sure did. It's brighter in here, too, isn't it?"

"It certainly is, Gracie. It certainly is."

He was looking at her and not the windows when he said it, and Gracie felt a flush spread across the back of her neck. To cover her reaction, she said pertly, "Well, I suppose I can finish them later. Let me just make sure Charity's all tidy and fetch my bonnet, and then we can all go to church. Just like a real family."

Just like a real family. She felt a catch in her chest as soon as the words hit the air. They used to go to church together: Mama and Papa and Gracie and Jake. Oh, how she missed those days. She'd get them back again now, though. She'd do it or die trying.

When they stepped outside, Gracie inhaled the scents she'd noticed yesterday, liked what she smelled, and looked around. She'd been too nervous to examine her surroundings then. Now her gaze encountered a raggedy scramble of tumbledown adobes mingled with a spatter of wooden buildings, all lined up like scruffy schoolchildren behind a walkway that sagged here and there. Beyond the short main dirt road proclaiming Diabolito Lindo a community of man, other structures pocked the countryside sporadically. There seemed no rhyme or reason to their placement.

Jake's small house sat at the end of the main road and off to one side. A split-rail fence surrounded it on three sides and, although it boasted neither lawn nor garden, it looked tidier than the rest of the buildings, in spite of a dilapidated wagon listing against the fence.

Diabolito Lindo squatted in the foothills of the Capitan mountain range. Gracie saw the big mountain itself rise grandly behind the shabby village, its sides bristling with junipers, mesquites, piñons, and oaks.

The town was silent as a tomb this Sabbath morning, and Gracie wondered why Jake had been so adamant about her staying indoors until she'd been properly introduced.

"Is it always this quiet, Jake?"

His crack of laughter caught her off guard. "Only on Sunday mornings, Gracie. I'm surprised you could even sleep last night, what with the ruckus going on."

"Really?"

She looked up at him from under her sunbonnet brim. His face was harder than that of the boy she used to know. This face had creases around the eyes, and its mouth seemed grim in repose. She didn't remember Jake's mouth being austere like that, and she had an urge to smooth her fingers over it, soften it, and mold it into what it had once been. Then he looked down into her eyes, smiled, and she forgot all about the changes and saw only the person he had always been.

"Yes, really. And until I introduce you to the people in

town and recruit them to look after you when my back's turned, I'm not letting you or Charity out of my sight unless I know exactly where you are and that you'll stay there until I say so."

Gracie grinned, recalling countless times in her childhood when Jake had given her peremptory commands, which she'd obeyed or disobeyed as the fancy struck her. Another glance at him now persuaded her to go along with him this time. At least for today. It wouldn't do to be setting his back up until she was sure of her place.

"All right, Jake. We'll do as you say."

With a touch on her shoulder, Jake stopped her. "I mean it, Gracie. No fooling this time. This town isn't like St. Louis. It's rough and the people in it can be violent, not to mention crude. There's shooting all the time and drunkenness and lots of other things you don't want to know about."

Hugging Charity to her bosom, Gracie said solemnly, "All right, Jake." And, she decided suddenly, she meant it, too. It was well past time she began behaving as an adult.

Charity, still subdued since Jake's interruption of her happy song, seemed to catch the seriousness in the air around her and hid her face against Gracie's shoulder once more.

"It's all right, Charity, dear. I'm right here," Gracie said softly, thinking that if for no other reason she had to do as Jake told her for Charity's sake. She had somebody besides herself to take care of now, and she'd do it. Whatever it took.

"Howdy, Preacher Jake."

Turning to see who had addressed Jake thus, Gracie opened her eyes wide and stared, until she caught herself being rude and glanced quickly away.

"Morning, Bart. How're you holding up?"

Unable to help herself, Gracie peered again at the man Jake had called Bart. He spat out a disgusting stream of tobacco juice, hitched up his trousers, and said through the gap in his front teeth, "Fair. Fair. Got me a head. Who's the li'l gal?"

Since Bart was grinning at her and Gracie had been

reared to be polite to strangers no matter what they looked like, she smiled and gave a little curtsy even as Charity buried herself more deeply in her arms. Gracie knew she was trying to hide from Bart and understood completely. She wished she could hide herself.

Shorter than Jake, Bart must have outweighed him by a good fifty pounds. The right side of his face was quite bristly, as if he hadn't shaved for a while. For the first time in her life, however, Gracie had the opportunity to observe that a gentleman's beard didn't grow on scarred flesh. The left side of Bart's face was a shiny, wrinkled sheet of hairless scars.

That would have been alarming enough, but the rest of him was equally disconcerting, particularly the several weapons he had residing in various places on his person. The large gun sticking out of his waistband was the first to catch Gracie's eye. The knife stuck into a sheath near his boot then captured her attention, which shortly drifted to a second knife holstered on his thigh, then a third, a very small model, stuck into his hatband. She swallowed hard when she noticed the derringer peeking out of a pocket in his grease-spotted leather vest.

Good grief, she'd never seen a less promising individual in her life, save as illustrated in the bloodcurdling potboilers she used to devour in the comfort of her bedroom in St. Louis. And Jake had just greeted him as he would a friend.

"Bart, this is my sister, Grace. She and her daughter, Charity, just arrived from St. Louis and plan to stay a spell. I expect you to watch out for them, y'hear?"

"I hear and obey, Preacher Jake." Turning to Gracie, Bart stuck out a hand minus pieces of two fingers and said, "How-do, Miss Grace. Any kin to Preacher Jake's like kin to us. Ain't no man in town won't go to the wall for you."

Worried about Charity's reaction to the remarkable Bart, Gracie offered him a tentative smile and shook his hand. Charity slithered so far down Gracie's shoulder, she almost curled up double. "Thank you very much, Mr.—er—Bart."

"Ragsdale's my handle, ma'am."

"Mr. Ragsdale," Gracie amended conscientiously.

Bart nodded and jerked his head toward Charity. "Kid's skeered of me. Don't blame her none. I ain't a pretty sight."

Gracie thought about protesting, but to do so would be a blatant lie and she sensed Bart wouldn't be flattered. Or fooled. Instead, she stammered, "Oh, well, she's—she's a little shy around strangers. Especially men."

"Is that what the matter is?" Jake peered at the hiding Charity. "I wondered if it was just me."

"Oh, no. She's real scared of men."

"Smart kid," observed Bart.

Gracie, remembering things from St. Louis she wished she could forget, silently agreed with him.

"She's smart to be a little leery around the ones who live here, at any rate," Jake muttered.

"It'll be all right once ever'body gets to know you, though, Miss Grace. Don't nobody mess with nothing belongs to Preacher Jake."

With a wave, Bart loped off to the saloon, leaving Gracie to lift her hand in a salute of good-bye. She was sure he didn't hear her whisper, "Good."

Jake's chuckle surprised her.

"Don't see too many folks like Bart in St. Louis, do you?"

She investigated his expression and decided he was being deliberately ironic and not merely inquisitive. "No, I certainly don't. My goodness, Jake."

"Bart's a good man, for the most part."

"I'm glad." Astounded, but glad. Bart had looked like a mountain-dwelling pirate to Gracie. A mean mountain-dwelling pirate. "How on earth did he ever get those dreadful scars?"

"Fight in a saloon." Jake sighed heavily. "Somebody tipped over a lamp and the place caught fire. I was there and managed to drag poor old Bart outside before he could burn up. Burned his face pretty badly, although I reckon the fire cauterized the knife cut."

Gracie shuddered. "My goodness." She rubbed Charity's back lightly, hoping the gentle massage would soothe the baby's damaged spirits. After a second or two, she said, "It's a good thing you were there to help him."

His laugh sounded harsh. "Good thing? I reckon it was, for poor old Bart."

"Did you get hurt, Jake?"

"Me? Lord, no. I used to lead a charmed life, Gracie. Couldn't get myself killed no matter how hard I tried."

It hurt her to hear him sound so cynical. He hadn't been cynical when they were children, and she wondered what had made him so. She guessed she shouldn't ask; at least not yet. "Well, I'm glad you weren't hurt."

She peered up to find him watching her with a strange expression on his face. Then he grinned and said, "I reckon I am too, Gracie. Now."

She reached up and touched the scar adorning the left side of his face. "But you have scars."

His smile flickered briefly and died. "Oh, yes, I have scars, all right."

They entered the saloon together, and Gracie blinked at the darkness after so much sunshine. Then she looked around and her mouth dropped open.

"Scared yet?"

Darting a glance at Jake, she realized he was teasing her. So she stood up straighter and lied. "Certainly not."

She was, though. She'd never seen anything to match this congregation of Jake's. At least she hoped that's what they were. If they weren't his congregation, then the three of them were about to be attacked by a herd of wild *banditti*.

The most predominant feature of the people seated in front of her was their gender. Next to the unrelieved masculinity came facial hair, then scars, eye patches, dirt, and the absence of body parts.

Cheeks pooched out, filled, Gracie was sure, with wads of tobacco. Guts pooched, too, except on those men who looked nearly cadaverous. The very air around this group of humans bristled with something savage. Charity felt it; Gracie could tell because she began to whimper very softly.

"There, there, Charity. Everything will be just fine. Your Uncle Jake will take care of us." Gracie knew she told the truth, although she knew not how to impart her faith unto Charity.

"Gentlemen," Jake said, "let me introduce you to my sister, Grace Trinidad, and her daughter, Charity. Grace has come to stay with me for a while, and she's brought her dead husband's body along with her. We'll have the funeral directly after church, if you'd like to pay your respects. Grace and Charity would take it as a kindness, as would I."

Every single one of those hard, hard eyes was upon her, and Gracie felt heat creeping up her collar. Charity began to moan.

Taking a resolute breath, Gracie smiled and said, "Good morning, gentlemen. It's a pleasure to be here with my brother, Jake."

Although she detected varying degrees of skepticism on several faces, they all muttered words of greeting.

"You and Charity sit here, Gracie," Jake murmured, seating her in a chair in the front of the room facing the men.

Gracie wished she weren't so blatantly on display, but guessed it would be unwise to request a change. Maybe next time she'd get to be inconspicuous. Another glance at her fellow parishioners disobliged her of the notion. As the only female in the room, she figured she'd be conspicuous even if she hid in a corner. For the very first time, she wondered if she should have come here.

But she'd had no choice. The knowledge made her sit up straight and lift her chin. In spite of her trepidation, she boldly stared into the crowd of desperadoes lined up to hear Jake preach. To distract herself from the visual charms of the congregation, she began to take note of the room itself.

The saloon, although it had obviously been tidied up recently, retained a rank odor. Gracie, who had never been inside a drinking establishment before, could only guess at the smell's origin. The walls might have been painted once, but whatever color they'd been had faded into a pasty ocher. Gracie suspected that tobacco smoke had contributed a good deal to their present unhealthy color.

A piano rested in a corner—a battle-scarred upright. She wondered if it had always lived in a saloon or if it had resided in more elegant surroundings during its youth. She also wondered how on earth anybody had managed to move it to Diabolito Lindo in the mountains of the New Mexico Territory, where the only way in or out was over rough, winding dirt roads via the bumpy freight wagons folks hereabouts called jerkies—or the way she'd done it, in an armed and guarded wagon hired especially for the purpose.

A long, polished bar curved along the other side of the room, and Gracie saw rows and rows of bottles lined up against the wall. A large painting loomed over the bottles.

Gracie took one look at its subject matter and immediately looked away again, embarrassed. Good heavens, it was a painting of a naked lady! Well, she amended mentally, perhaps not a lady. Whatever she was, she wasn't wearing a stitch, and Gracie felt not only shocked, but profoundly out of place.

She wasn't sure she liked being the only woman in a room full of villainous-looking men, loomed over by an unclad female. She slipped another tiny peek at the picture and decided that she and the barque of feminine frailty depicted bore very little resemblance to one another. Anywhere.

Oh, dear. She forced her attention away from the painting and began to examine her companions once more. They certainly didn't look like any men she'd ever seen in St. Louis. She wondered if any of them were the mountain men she'd read so much about. Mountain men were reputed to be a rough lot. These men certainly seemed to fit that category, and these were, after all, mountains.

Every one of them wore a sidearm. Sneaking a peek at Jake, she noticed his gun for the first time. He had it tucked into the left side of his waistband, butt forward, as though it were simply an article of clothing he'd donned in the morning along with his boots.

She wondered why, if he had to carry an instrument of death, he didn't wear it in a holster. Those same bloody chronicles with which she used to amuse herself back home in St. Louis, and which presented illustrations of gentlemen of Bart's stamp, always depicted their tidy lawmen and depraved outlaws with their guns residing neatly in leather holsters. She decided to ask later.

When she saw the snoring men propped up against the back wall, she forgot all about Jake's gun.

Then she forgot about them, too, when Jake began to preach.

3

"ALL RIGHT, BOYS, I'm preaching from another psalm today. You all like the psalms."

Jake grinned and his congregation chortled. Bart, in the front row, stamped his booted feet on the floor in a gesture Gracie recognized as one of approval, although she'd never encountered it in a church before.

"It's from the hundred and thirty-ninth chapter, verses seven and eight: 'Whither shall I go from thy spirit? or whither shall I flee from thy presence? If I ascend up into heaven, thou art there: if I make my bed in hell, behold, thou art there.'"

He looked solemnly out over his unprepossessing flock. "Remember that, boys, and don't ever forget it: 'If I make my bed in hell, behold, thou art there.' It's the most important thing you'll ever have to know about anything, because most of us in this room are going to be in hell at one point or another before we're through here on earth.

"When Black Pete Banner bought a bullet in Lincoln last

winter, shot all to blazes, God was with him at the end. He knew it, and I knew he knew it, because we prayed together. It wasn't a pretty end—gut-shot never is—but it was an end a lot of us can expect, living the lives we do. Just don't ever forget that wherever you are and however you live and die, you're not alone. You may not have another man in a hundred miles to call your friend, but God is with you."

Gracie stared at Jake, confounded. He hadn't raised his voice, but she'd never heard a more compelling presentation. She could tell he believed every word he said, too, and she paid close attention. His words obviously meant a lot to him, even though they meant virtually nothing to her. She guessed she'd been pretty sheltered in her life.

Up until a few months ago. She tightened her arms around the baby on her lap and swore she'd learn from Jake.

Keeping a finger in his Bible to mark his place, Jake went on, "We're all sinners, boys. We're all weak and we all miss chances to do good in our lives."

Murmurs of agreement rose from the congregation, and Gracie turned, astonished, to scan the crowd again. The men were all staring at Jake, their concentration seemingly absolute.

"There's not a one of us in this room who probably doesn't deserve hanging for something or other."

Another, louder, swell of agreement. Gracie swallowed hard to hear her beloved Jake speaking of himself as though he were one of these ruffians.

"We're not a pretty lot," Jake said, and Gracie guessed she agreed, except about him. Jake wasn't pretty, either, but he was the standard of masculine beauty to which she'd held all other males her entire life. And not another man had ever even come close. She loved the way he looked.

"We've hurt people: people we've loved, people we've hated, and people we didn't even know. There's lots of folks who'd call us—and rightly, too—the scum of the earth."

Gracie felt her eyes open wide to hear those words come out of Jake's mouth. Scum of the earth? Jake? No. Maybe some of these other men. She glanced at the congregation and was dumbfounded to see some of them nod. One of them even yanked out a red bandanna and wiped his eyes. *Mercy sakes!*

"But you know what, friends? God loves us anyway, and He's with us all the time. If you don't believe it, just take a look at me, your own Preacher Jake. Sure as hell, if God didn't love me, I'd be dead instead of standing here talking to you. If God hadn't intervened, I'd have killed myself, one way or another, ten times over by this time.

"I've been down so low, I couldn't see the top of the hole anymore. I've been down so far, I had to crawl and eat dirt. I've been down so bad, no man alone could have helped me. It took a man and something more than a man to help me. It took God through that man. God was there with me, even in the pit, and He rescued me through the agency of a man nobody else on earth would have called good and most people wouldn't even talk to if they could avoid it. I don't know why God chose to come to me the way He did, or even at all. But if God, through that man, thought I was important enough to save when I didn't care myself, then He sure as hell won't quibble about any of you. There's no man in this room worse than I was."

Never in her life had Gracie heard such language in church. On the other hand, she'd never been in a church the likes of this before, either. Maybe this was the only kind of language these men understood. Her heart felt heavy and she thought, *How sad.*

But Jake? Her Jake? No. He wasn't like these other men. Was he? He couldn't be. Could he? The Jake she used to know wasn't. She shook her head, puzzled and a little melancholy, wondering yet again if she even knew this Jake.

There was something rhythmic about the way Jake spoke to his flock. A cadence or something. Gracie felt Charity begin to relax, and smiled down at her. She found the baby watching Jake, her eyes big, her attention intense. For the first time since Gracie could remember, she didn't look scared in company.

Jake kept the sermon short. When he asked his congregation to stand for a final prayer, Gracie eyed the piano in the corner and wondered if he had ever considered singing hymns in his church. She'd heard it said more than once that music had charms to soothe the savage breast. With another glance at her comrades, she decided that if these breasts weren't savage, she'd eat her hat.

Besides, Charity loved music. The only times she seemed completely happy were when she and Gracie sang together. Why, she could even handle the words of most songs, more or less. Maybe music would help her get over her fears and terrible memories.

She looked at her unpromising surroundings again, but this time a bubble of excitement began to dance in her middle. She was the only proper woman in this whole town. Perhaps she could fix it. Oh, maybe not the whole town, and maybe not a lot. Still and all, she *was* a woman, and, therefore, absolutely suited to bring the light of civilization into the dark reaches of this wild frontier. No matter what the world thought, Gracie knew women were strong. Shoot, just look at what she'd done. A little grimly, she thought that if any female should fit into this lawless town, it was she.

Heaven alone knew, too, that she had sins for which to atone. Maybe she could begin to do so here. Maybe she could help Jake bring a little softness into these hard men's lives.

She could at least help Jake and his friend Mr. Fergus fix up the saloon on Sunday mornings. Jake had said something about a woman working in the saloon. Perhaps Gracie could recruit her to help. Maybe a pot of flowers here and there would be nice. She'd be happy to play the piano. That was about the only thing she'd ever been good at. And she knew a slew of hymns. She'd love to be able to sing again, too.

A choir. Oh, wouldn't that be something, if she could get together a choir! A men's chorus, made up of these ruffians who seemed to need something besides liquor and violence and emptiness in their lives. She wondered if Jake would go along with her.

She felt a little guilty when a growly rumble of "Amens" assaulted her eardrums and she realized she hadn't paid attention to the closing prayer. They passed a hat around and everybody in the room plopped in a coin or two.

The man called Bart brought the hat to Jake, saying, "Here ya go, Preacher Jake. Reckon you'll be able to buy yer grub for another week or two."

The two men grinned at each other, and Jake said a sincere "Thanks, Bart." Gracie wondered how much money the hat-passing had garnered, then wondered if Jake had to supplement his income by doing tinsmith work. She forgot about Jake's income when he spoke again.

"All right, boys. We're going to bury Mr. Ralph Trinidad now, in our own Boot Hill." He smiled at Gracie. "The cemeteries are prettier in St. Louis, Gracie. You really sure about this?"

"I am, Jake. This is what I want."

"So be it. Anybody who wants to pay his respects, follow me."

The entire congregation apparently decided they wanted to pay their respects, because they swarmed around Jake. Gracie looked at him and then at Charity, who was withdrawing again.

"Why don't you all go on outside, Jake, and I'll follow with Charity." She smiled at the milling men. "She's sort of shy around strangers."

The men seemed to respect Charity's sensible attitude in the presence of their villainous selves, so Gracie quickly found herself alone in the saloon with Charity. As soon as the swarm of burly men left, the baby relaxed, and Gracie took a deep breath of relief. It tasted of the stuffy, sour air of the saloon, and she glanced at the windows, thinking she should bring her vinegar water in here. And then air the place out.

"My goodness, Charity. When Aunt Lizzy said your Uncle Jake was a preacher, I expected something a little different." All at once she considered how absolutely astonishing Jake's congregation was, and she giggled. Aunt Lizzy would die if she knew. "Want to get down and walk a little, baby?"

She slid Charity to the floor, not letting go of her hands. The little girl never tried to walk a lot, although she could toddle when she wanted to. Gracie knew why she was so restrained, and never forced her. But since they were alone together now, she figured it wouldn't hurt to let her spread her wings, as it were.

Slowly, with Gracie allowing Charity to set the pace, they walked over to the piano. The baby limped a bit and, watching her, Gracie's heart ached. She made her voice extra cheerful to make up for it.

"For heaven's sake, Charity. This looks like it might be a fine old instrument."

She plinked a key, watching the baby all the while. When it didn't look as though the sound frightened her, she played a chord. Charity smiled and Gracie, relieved, smiled, too.

"She likes music, I see."

Jake's voice came from the door of the saloon, and Gracie cursed herself for starting in surprise when Charity folded up like a concertina and sat, *plunk*, on the dirty floor, her arms folded over her head.

Gracie swooped her up and hugged her.

"Gracie, what's the matter with Charity, really? It can't be normal for a baby to be so scared like that."

Looking up from little Charity, Gracie saw Jake walking toward her, an expression of concern on his face. She swallowed, and her brain scrambled for a convenient lie. Then, disgusted with herself, she gave up and said truthfully, "She's had some frightening experiences. I—I'd just as soon tell you about them later."

Jake chucked her under the chin, very gently. "Are you sure that husband of yours didn't hurt you, Gracie? He wouldn't have been the first bastard to abuse his wife."

She got lost in his beautiful, somber, dark brown eyes for a minute. "No. No, I know that, Jake." Taking a deep breath she continued, still truthfully, "But Charity's father never hit me. Not once. Honest."

He searched her face closely before he said, "Well, all right. But we'd better get his bones planted now, Gracie. The boys are all ready. Fergus and Fat Julio have the grave all dug."

"That was nice of them."

"Yeah, and Fergus needs to get back here and open up for

business pretty soon, too, so we'll have to make it a short ceremony."

"You mean he runs the saloon on Sundays?"

With a deep chuckle, Jake said, "Oh, Gracie. There's a whole lot about Diabolito Lindo you don't know yet. Until recently, the saloon was never closed at all. You know what a *diabolito* is?"

"A—a little devil?"

"Yep. Only in this case, it's an understatement."

"Oh."

They walked side-by-side out the door of the saloon. Looking back, Gracie was startled to see the face of what appeared to be a very young woman peering at her over the second-floor railing of the saloon. She shot a surprised smile over her shoulder, but the face offered no smile in return.

She sighed, wondering who the face belonged to, but decided to save her questions for later. Jake steered her down the dusty street toward a rise topped by a couple of straggly trees. Gracie could see some crosses, too, leaning this way and that, and a row of men, black shadows against the noonday sun. A lazy wind rustled the trees' branches, making them seem to reach for the men. The stark, skeletal outlines were eerie, even in full daylight.

She shook off her fanciful thought and looked around. What a beautiful place this was. A deep azure sky spread overhead, and clouds stretched across it in sheets, reminding Gracie of pulled taffy, only sparkling white—which reminded her of something else.

"I would have started supper, Jake, but I wasn't sure what kinds of supplies you have. I didn't find much in the kitchen but some beans and salt bacon."

His ironic grin warned her, and she braced herself.

"That's about it, Gracie. This isn't St. Louis, remember."

For some reason, his constant jibes about the luxuries she'd left behind were beginning to irritate her. "I know it," she said sharply. "And that's just fine. I left St. Louis because I wanted to. What I need to know now is what kinds of provisions you have here so I can begin earning our keep."

Jake's grin faded, replaced by a look that started Gracie's bones to melting and her heart to slamming around in her breast like a demented bird.

"I'm sorry, Gracie. I reckon I don't have to rub in our lack of civilization quite so much."

"That's all right, Jake." In order to circumvent the lightheadedness Jake's tender look had engendered, she asked, "Are—are those men who came to church mountain men?"

"Mountain men?"

She nodded. "Yes. I used to read books about mountain men back home. They were depicted as a—a sort of rough type of men. I just wondered if these men were mountain men."

Jake didn't answer; when she looked up at him, his expression seemed puzzled. By way of explanation, she expanded in a small voice, "These are mountains, aren't they?"

Suddenly his expression cleared. "Oh, mountain men. You mean trappers and miners and so forth."

"Yes." She smiled.

"Good God, no. I reckon most of these men never set out to accomplish anything of that sort. They just got lost along one of life's twisted roads and ended up here by accident."

"Oh." She remembered the gist of his sermon. "Is that what happened to you, Jake? Did you get lost?"

"I did, Gracie. And with a lot less reason than some of these fellows have, too. Some of these men—Bart and Fergus and Black Pete—"

"The man who died?"

"Yes, that's Black Pete. Well, they fought in the war, and something about the fighting and the killing and the destruction seemed to—oh, I don't know—damage them somehow. When Pete got shot last fall and I went to Lincoln to help ease him out of this life, he told me about it. He was on his deathbed, and I reckon knowing you're going to die makes a man want to talk if he has the time. He told me that after the war, it was like he lost his way, like nothing meant anything to him anymore; not his family or his friends or his old job; not even his own life.

"It was the first time I even knew Pete had a family—a wife and two kids back home in Tennessee. I wrote them but never heard back. I reckon they didn't even care by that time. Can't say as I blame them, even though Pete didn't set out to hurt them. He did hurt them, though. He knew he did and hated himself for it, but he couldn't seem to help it."

Sobered, Gracie whispered, "That's pitiful, Jake."

Jake shook his head sadly, as if he agreed with her. "A lot of these fellows are pitiful, Gracie. They might be able to help themselves if they'd give God a chance. I reckon most of them don't believe it yet."

Gracie nodded in agreement, even though she felt rather at sea. She'd never encountered individuals like those Jake described, and was far from understanding them. Since she wasn't sure what else to say, she murmured, "I—I saw a girl in there, too, Jake. When we were leaving."

He nodded. "I expect that'd be Clara."

"Does she—does she live in the saloon?"

"Yep."

Trying to think of a diplomatic way to phrase her next question, Gracie stumbled a little. "Does—is—well, does she like living there? I mean—well—isn't it kind of noisy? Or something?"

She knew she was in for another jolt when Jake gazed down at her somberly. That look of his boded ill, she knew it.

"She's a prostitute, Gracie. She earns her living there, selling her body to the men in town, probably some of the men I just preached to, in fact."

Gracie opened her mouth, but nothing came out.

"And I know popular morality holds that she's sinning and that what she does is evil and she's going to hell for it, too, so don't preach to me about it." He gave her one of his wonderful smiles, but she recognized the steel underneath. "About the only thing I've learned since I came to know God is that we mortal creatures who walk this earth, for the most part, do what we have to do in order to get along.

Life's not fair, Gracie, and it doesn't treat everybody the same. Some people have to do things that others can't even begin to imagine."

After a moment during which Gracie scrambled to gather her fluttering thoughts together, she said, "And that's what she has to do?"

"That's what she has to do. For whatever reason. But this I do know—and I'll tell you free of charge—no female would ever live that life if she believed she had a choice in the matter. And I'm sure as hell not going to condemn her for it."

Gracie, who'd never *had* to do anything sinful in her life—and was only sinning now because she'd made an admittedly hard choice—could think of nothing at all to say. They walked the rest of the way to Boot Hill in silence.

The same congregation of desperate characters that had lately graced Jake's saloon-church now stood around a rectangular hole in the ground. They'd dug the hole under a spreading oak whose scantily leafed-out branches let drops of sunlight dribble in and dapple the coffin's wood. The shiny mahogany box Gracie had paid a fortune for in St. Louis was probably the most elegant feature not made by nature in the group. It rested on two long ropes. Gracie supposed the men planned to lower it into its hole on the ropes.

Because she had always had a soft heart, and because Jake's explanation about how some of these fellows—and Clara—had come to be what they were had touched her, Gracie smiled at the men and said softly, "Thank you all for coming." She received an assortment of shuffles and incoherent rumbles in answer. Charity didn't whimper, but she clutched Gracie's arm more tightly.

"All set, Jake," a tall, bristly individual said.

"Thanks, Fergus."

Gracie looked more sharply at Jake's best friend, curious to know just what sort of man could fill such an important position in her Jake's life. Her first impression dismayed her.

Fergus was one of the gaunt ones, a tall scarecrow, his

whiskery face a map of wrinkles. Gracie wondered where the map led, then decided she didn't want to know because it didn't look like anywhere she wanted to be.

Good grief, whatever could Jake be thinking of, holding this terrible, hard man in affection? Then he smiled and her heart discerned what her eyes hadn't. She smiled back and felt a stab of shame for having judged the man by his packaging.

"All right, boys, reckon we'd better get this poor soul planted. Gracie's brought him a long way and he's been waiting to be laid to his final rest for four months."

A chorus of shocked noises issued from the clump of men.

"It's all right, boys. Once you get to know Gracie, this won't seem odd at all, I promise." Jake laughed and Gracie blushed.

Then Jake got serious, and the men respectfully removed their hats. A whole orchestra of headgear, from once-tidy derbies to wide sombreros, swept from a variety of heads, from bald to grizzled to . . . good heavens! Gracie had to look twice to make sure her eyes hadn't deceived her. Yes, she was sure of it. Those were the two long black plaits of an Indian man.

Gracie glanced from the men to the coffin and shook her head. Even though she couldn't foresee any immediate need for the money, much less the jewelry or the papers, she wished she'd at least peeked inside the blasted coffin once more before it had come to this. The fact that she'd missed her opportunity because she'd overslept was what really galled her. She had no business oversleeping when Charity's entire future still lay in jeopardy.

All her life, Gracie had taken the easy road and let other people do the hard work and the thinking. Even teaching school had been easy. Her mother had pointed the way and she'd followed happily, without once deciding anything for herself. Now she had somebody whose entire well-being depended on her, and she had to shape up pretty blasted fast if she aimed to fulfill her obligations. And she did. She'd promised Martha that.

Oh, sweet Lord have mercy. What would happen if anybody found out which way she'd gone and came after her? They'd take Charity away, sure as blazes. Gracie didn't expect that the authorities allowed convicted thieves to keep their children with them in prison. Especially children who weren't theirs.

But she'd been given the money; she hadn't stolen it. Or Charity. Even as the excuses chimed in her head, Gracie knew that no law in any state or territory would look at it that way.

Squeezing her eyes shut, Gracie ignored Jake's requisite funereal words and prayed, *Oh, God, please help us.*

4

$\mathcal{G}$RACIE WHISPERED A last "Amen" along with the clump of scruffy men gathered around the hole in the ground, and watched solemnly as the coffin was lowered into the red-brown earth. The last note of the song she'd just sung seemed to echo in the still air. It didn't feel quite right to her that she had no flowers to lay on the coffin—even that coffin.

Her heart clutched painfully as she saw clods of dirt strike its beautiful, shiny wooden surface. So this was it. She'd really done it.

Oh, God. Oh, God. Please, please help us.

Rocking Charity gently in her arms, Gracie blinked back her tears. If anybody'd asked her, she wouldn't have been able to account for those tears. They certainly weren't from any grief over Charity's father. Maybe they were for Charity herself. Or Charity's mother.

Yes. Gulping a big breath of dusty, piney air, Gracie decided they were undoubtedly for Charity and her mother.

Making a huge effort to stifle her emotions, she smiled at Jake when he lifted his head and glanced at her.

"You all right, Gracie?" he asked quietly, and she wanted to bawl again.

But because she knew she had to be strong, she braced herself and said, "I'm fine, thank you, Jake. It was a beautiful service."

Jake's mouth kicked up in an ironic half-smile, but he didn't say anything. Gracie figured he chose not to mention their rough surroundings in order to spare her feelings. Oh, if only he knew what he'd really just laid to rest! Gracie hadn't believed she could feel any guiltier until that minute.

Since she wasn't sure what protocol prevailed after one's almost-foster brother buried one's nonexistent husband's coffin, as she fell into step between Jake and Fergus, Gracie murmured, "It surely didn't seem to take as long as funerals in St. Louis."

"We've had lots of practice planting corpses in Diabolito Lindo, Gracie."

Gracie looked up into Jake's face and wondered if he expected a response to that. If he did, he was bound for disappointment, because she couldn't think of a thing to say. Which was most unlike her.

Fergus spared her the effort. "Ain't that the truth? Don't take no time at all fer a man to die, do it, Jake?"

"Nope."

"Don't take much longer than that to plant him, neither."

"Nope."

As Gracie walked between these two rough men, she felt about as out of place as a pigeon in a lion's den. Even the glory of her surroundings and her happiness at having found Jake again couldn't quite wipe out the unsettled feeling Fergus's words fostered in her. He'd sounded so terribly matter-of-fact about death and its aftermath. If he'd offered her platitudes about the sanctity of human life, or even if he'd given her gory examples of death in her new home in an effort to shock her, she didn't think his observations would have seemed as terrible. She'd heard people talk about life being held cheaply here and there; she hadn't understood what they meant until this minute.

She held Charity close, hoping with all her heart that she'd done the right thing. Then she commanded herself to stop being wishy-washy; she'd had no choice and that was that. She'd made her decision and now she had to take the consequences.

That didn't sound right. Reap the rewards. That's what she meant. Consequences resided in St. Louis. Rewards belonged to her new life.

Frowning, Gracie reminded herself that she and Charity were in Diabolito Lindo now, and in Jake's care. They just had to trust that Jake would guide their path from here on out. If anybody could do it, Jake could.

"That was a right pretty song you sang at the end there, Miss Gracie."

Fergus's kind words startled Gracie out of her grim contemplation of her problems. She was annoyed with herself when Charity winced. Deciding to pretend Fergus was just another man like any of the other men she'd known—which she could probably do as long as she didn't look at him for too long at any given time—she smiled winningly, mostly to settle Charity's nerves. "Thank you, Mr. Fergus. 'Abide with Me' is one of my favorite hymns." She looked away again quickly. These men were *so* different from what she was used to.

Then she looked up at Jake and smiled at him, too. "Thank you, Jake. That was exactly the sort of service I'd been hoping for."

Jake's bellow of laughter made her smile crinkle up. "Don't you laugh at me, Jake Molloy!"

"I'm sorry, Gracie." He was laughing so hard, he had to stop, stamp his feet, and bend over. "I'm sorry!"

Jake couldn't help it. He knew Gracie was irritated and didn't mean it, but his laugh had sneaked up on him and burst out without warning. He hadn't meant to laugh at her.

"I'm sorry, Gracie," he choked out again.

"You should be," she said, obviously miffed as all get-out.

Making a valiant effort to control the tickle in his innards, Jake said, "It's . . . it's just really difficult for me to imagine you having longed to have your beloved husband laid to rest amid a host of dead outlaws, and prayed over by a group of men most folks wouldn't invite into their parlors."

He started to sling an arm over her shoulder in a companionable manner, only to notice little Charity's gasp and withdrawal. Recalling the baby's fear of men, he removed his arm and stopped laughing.

Looking down at Gracie and seeing her again as the woman she'd grown up to be, Jake decided maybe it was best that the kid did have this aversion to men. Since Gracie didn't seem inclined to let the baby out of her sight, Charity would be very effective in keeping him at a distance should he ever forget himself. Knowing himself, he feared he *would* forget. The thought troubled him a lot and he cast up a quick, silent prayer for strength.

"You just stop laughing at me this minute, Jake Molloy."

It sounded to Jake as though she were trying her best to sound severe. He exchanged a glance with Fergus. Fergus, too, looked amused, and Jake couldn't help himself; he grinned again.

"Jake ain't laughin' at you, Miss Gracie. He's laughin' at us fellers here in Diabolito Lindo. Reckon we never thought to have to mind our manners before a couple o' ladies afore now. You'll teach us some manners, though, I'll warrant."

"Oh." Gracie looked thoughtful. "I didn't mean to disrupt your lives. We'll stay out of everybody's way. Promise."

Both men chuckled again and Jake shook his head. "I'd like to see you try to do that, Gracie."

Her brows dipped over her pretty eyes; Jake despaired of ever being able to think of her as a sister again. Right now he had the urge to wrap his arms around her and kiss that miffy expression right off her face. This was bad. It was really bad.

"Well, Mr. Jake Molloy, if you'll just give me a chance, I bet I can make your life more comfortable. And the rest of you fellows, too," she added, glaring at Fergus. "Why, this place needs a woman's touch!"

A woman's touch. Jake peered down at her as a wistful feeling curled around his heart. That sounded so peaceful: a woman's touch.

Fergus rubbed his scratchy chin. "Don't guess nobody'd argue with you there, Miss Gracie. I told Jake that this very mornin'."

"And the very first thing we're going to do to prove it is fix your place up, Jake." She poked him in the chest. "Right after you figure out how to get milk for Charity. Babies need milk."

Jake felt his smile dim. "Milk?" It came out sounding as if the word were new to his vocabulary. Which it very nearly was. Jake hadn't so much as thought about milk in a dozen years or more.

Fergus repeated pointlessly, "Milk."

"Yes, milk. Are there any cows in town? I can buy milk."

Digging into his memory and recalling everything he'd ever heard about mothers and babies, Jake said, "Er, can't you . . ." Even as he stopped speaking, he felt himself flush.

Damn! He wished he hadn't implied that Gracie might still be nursing Charity. He was already having to fight with his impulses. Gracie was no longer the child he'd left behind in St. Louis. She was a lovely, entirely too-appealing woman, and it would be extremely unwise of him to begin thinking about her breasts in any connection at all.

Gracie frowned, puzzled. Then her face flamed and she ducked her head. "No," she said shortly. "Good heavens, Jake, the child is more than two years old. She's too old for . . . that."

Feeling about as stupid as he probably looked, Jake cleared his throat. "Right." He glanced hopefully at Fergus. Fergus was an enterprising fellow. Jake expected he could find even milk if he put his mind to it. He was, after all, in the liquid refreshment business.

As so often happened, the look of befuddlement on Fergus's face faded into one of deep thought. He rubbed his chin again, a sure sign he was concentrating. Jake's heart lightened.

Scratching at his whiskers, Fergus said, "Reckon there's a Mexican settlement in Hondo where we could get us a goat."

Gracie brightened right up.

Jake asked, "Can you get milk from goats?" Then he guessed feeling like a fool was a small price to pay for one of Gracie's glorious smiles.

"Of course you can, Jake! A goat would be perfect, Mr. Fergus. Do you need some money? I've got plenty of money back—" Her eyes went round as saucers when Jake's big hand clamped over her mouth.

"Shhh, Gracie. Don't talk about having money anywhere. Not out loud in the middle of the road." His whisper grated in the air. He tentatively let up on her lips, not quite trusting her to do as he'd told her. He well remembered the Gracie of old.

When she merely seemed chagrined and said, "Oh," he guessed she was at least going to try to do things his way for once without fighting him about them first.

"Don't do to bait the devil, Miss Gracie," Fergus told her. "Not around here. The town's earned its name honest, ma'am." Jake silently blessed him for the gentle lesson.

Gracie squeaked out another little "Oh," and added, "I didn't think."

Jake suppressed the comment that immediately leapt to mind and was proud of himself. "It's wise to keep it in mind, though," he said mildly.

He hoped to hell she hadn't left any money lying around his house in plain sight. For the most part, the residents of Diabolito Lindo wouldn't dream of touching anything belonging to their Preacher Jake. The town sat in Lincoln County, though, and on a road passing as a thoroughfare and leading directly to Lincoln. Every desperado in the territory rode through Diabolito Lindo at one time or another. Even the nominally reformed citizens of the town itself might not be above borrowing from a newcomer.

"Anyway, I'll send Ramón to Hondo as soon as I open up,

ma'am. If he can find you a goat, we'll talk about payin' for
it later."

"Thank you very much, Mr. Fergus."

"And I'll explain the food situation as soon as we get
back home, Gracie."

"Thank you, Jake."

She sounded so subdued, Jake was tempted to apologize
for his somewhat brutal lesson. He didn't, though. He'd
rather have her alive and unhappy than dead. Lord, he didn't
think he could stand it if anything happened to Gracie. Even
when he'd believed he'd never see her again in this life,
he'd felt better knowing she was alive and decorating the
earth somewhere. Gracie dead didn't bear thinking of.

"After you explain supplies and I get supper going, may
Charity and I go outside and pick flowers, Jake?"

He glanced down to find her looking very humble, her big
hazel-green eyes shimmering suspiciously, as though she
were trying not to cry. His heart plunged violently, and he
had to bite his tongue to keep from begging her forgiveness.

"Of course you can, Gracie. I'll come with you."

Silently, he thanked God when she smiled again. "Thank
you, Jake."

As Charity was yawning and rubbing her eyes by the time
they got home, Gracie settled her down for a nap on the bed
they'd usurped from Jake.

"There. Now you just sleep for awhile, sweetheart, and
I'll fix some supper for us all."

Charity didn't seem inclined to let Gracie out of her sight,
so Gracie sang several songs until the baby drifted off to
sleep. Jake watched the operation with a gentle ache in his
heart. There was something about Charity that touched him,
something a little . . . not right about her. He found
himself feeling sorry for the tyke, and he wasn't sure why.

"You expect she'll ever get used to me, Gracie?" he asked
softly after she'd finished a sweet rendition of "Aura Lee."

Gracie's smile, Jake decided, should be captured in a jar
like a lightning bug, to take out during those times when a
body felt low. It could cheer the bleakest of souls and warm

the frostiest of days. Jake wished he could keep it with him forever.

"I'm sure she will, Jake."

Jake suspected she was only being nice. Still, he had the ridiculous notion that he might like being some little girl's hero again. A wave of painful nostalgia washed through him, and he sighed.

"I sure hope she does."

There was something almost holy about the way Gracie gazed at Charity. It was too pure for Jake; he had to turn away and pick up his Bible. After clearing his throat of an aching lump, he said, "Well, I reckon I'll do some Bible study until she wakes up."

"All right, Jake," Gracie said sweetly.

Jake thought he'd better not look at her again until he shook off this odd mood of his.

After Charity finally went to sleep, it didn't seem to take Gracie long to find the dried beans and put some on to soak. Nor, apparently, did it take her long to realize she was going to have to do something drastic about the food supply in her new home.

Jake heard her muttering about how she wondered how some bachelors got on in the world if they had to live like this. He grinned and tried to concentrate on the Bible verses he'd set out for himself.

She clucked in irritation. "It's a wonder you haven't taken sick from having so little good food to eat, Jake Molloy."

Since she'd muttered the words to herself, Jake guessed he didn't have to answer.

"I'd never have forgiven you if you'd died before I managed to find you."

He couldn't help chuckling.

"We need a garden, Jake."

He straightened in his chair and turned to find her scowling at the tidy, and very small, row of canned goods in his cupboard.

"What's the matter, Gracie? My kitchen not good enough for you?"

Her scowl deepened. Jake hadn't known she could look so

fierce. He wondered when she'd glance his way and discover he was teasing.

"Well, I expect it would be good enough for *me*. It's Charity I'm thinking of."

She did look at him then, and when she noticed his grin, her frown lifted. "Do you think I can plant a garden, Jake?"

"Of course you can, Gracie. We'll probably have to go into Lincoln for seeds and so forth."

"Would you mind?"

"Not at all. In the meantime, Fergus or Ramón might be able to show you how to use some of the plants that grow around here naturally. Maybe that Mexican family in Hondo can sell us some vegetables, too."

"That would be wonderful. Then we can have fresh greens and I can put up preserves for the winter."

"You know how to do all that?"

She looked at him as though he'd asked if she knew how to be female. "Well, Jake Molloy, I'd like to know what you think they taught me at school and what I've been teaching all those other young girls for five years now. Can I do all that indeed. I may not be the world's best cook, but I know how to preserve and to plan."

"Sorry, Gracie."

He guessed she'd forgiven him when she asked, "Can we get some chickens?"

"I reckon we can. I'll have to make a coop."

"Would you mind?"

"No."

She clasped her hands in front of her and began plucking at her apron. "I'm really sorry we barged in on you like this, Jake. I guess I didn't even consider how much trouble we'd be."

Without thinking, Jake rose from his chair and moved to take her in his arms. She felt like refuge to him, and when she threw her arms around him, he knew he was home at last.

Then she said, "I love you, Jake. I've always loved you," and he said, "I love you, too, Gracie," and he wondered suddenly if they were talking about two different things.

*   *   *

Gracie just about swooned when Jake said he loved her. Almost immediately, she told herself not to be a fanciful fool. He loved her like a sister, not the way she loved him, as a hero, as the ideal she'd held up as an example to other men. She knew he didn't think of her in those terms. Romantic terms.

None of that mattered, anyway. She couldn't afford to become distracted from her primary purpose. She had to be strong and stay alert because she still wasn't sure she was safe. And if she wasn't safe, Charity wasn't safe.

Reluctantly, she loosened her arms and tried to step away from Jake. After a second, he let her.

"Can we pick flowers when Charity wakes up, Jake? I want to pretty your place up some."

He laughed, but it sounded like it cost him because it came out husky and forced. She hoped he wasn't regretting his kindness in taking them in. "You've already prettied it up, Gracie."

Giving him a playful pat, she said, "You know what I mean, Jake Molloy."

"I reckon I do."

They heard a knock, and Jake went to see who had come to call, muttering, "*Now* who's knocking? Until you showed up here, nobody ever bothered to knock."

Gracie wondered if she should apologize and then decided not to. It wasn't her fault if the people who lived in Diabolito Lindo didn't have any manners.

Speaking of manners, she noticed he picked up the sidearm he'd set in a holster hanging by the door and stuck it into his waistband before he opened the door. Mercy sakes. Life was *so* different here. She sighed, wondering if it was really as rough as that, or if Jake only wanted her to think it was. Maybe he was trying to frighten her so that she'd behave herself. She wouldn't put it past him.

"Brung you some goat meat, Jake."

"How come you knocked, Fergus? You never bothered to knock before."

"You never had no lady livin' with you before, neither, Jake."

"Yeah. I guess not." Jake took a step back and opened the door wide. "Thanks, Fergus. Bring it on in. Gracie's just been nagging at me about supplies."

"I have not!"

"Reckon that's what females is for, is to nag us menfolk."

"So I've heard."

Gracie stopped fuming when she realized the men were teasing her. Adopting the gracious manner she remembered as having come naturally to her mother but which she had to consciously put on like clothing, she smiled at Fergus.

"Thank you very much, Mr. Fergus. I was wondering what we were going to do about meat."

Fergus nodded. "Most of us galoots eat beans and bacon and tortillers, ma'am, but I 'spect a female with a baby'd want something more."

Gracie wondered what a "tortiller" was. Then she gazed down at the stringy hunk of goat meat Fergus had handed her and wondered how in God's name to cook it. "Thank you very much."

As if he'd read her unspoken thoughts, Fergus said, "Just dump it in with the beans, Miss Gracie. Throw in an onion or two and mebbe one of them chili peppers folks grow around here, and you're likely to have a pretty fair meal if'n you don't watch out."

Gracie said "Thank you" again; this one came out sounding much more cheerful.

"I can get you some chickens, too, ma'am, soon as Jake here gets off his lazy butt and builds you a coop."

Gracie stopped being shocked by Fergus's disparaging comment as soon as she realized the two men were grinning at each other. Wondering if she'd ever get used to the customs prevailing in her new home, she said, "Thank you very much. Jake and I were just discussing chickens."

Fergus nodded. "Interestin' conversations you folks have."

She couldn't help giggling, and decided it wasn't such a surprise that this man was a friend to her Jake after all. "We never got a chance to discuss eggs, but they'll come in handy, too."

"Eggs ain't no problem, ma'am. They's chickens runnin' loose all over the place in back o' my saloon. The gal workin' there, she boils 'em up and pickles 'em."

"My goodness." Gracie had never heard of a pickled egg before—which didn't surprise her a whole lot. In truth, the culinary arts were not her strong suit, although she knew the basics and had a whole shoebox full of recipes. When it came to domestic matters, she was much more skilled at needlework and gardening. She expected she'd better learn to cook pretty quickly if she wanted to fulfill her goal of being useful to Jake, however.

Since Fergus and Jake seemed to be chatting, she went to the kitchen and began cutting up the goat meat. It seemed rather tough, but that didn't stop her. If goat meat was what her new home provided, then goat meat she'd cook. Looking around, she didn't see an onion. Well, they'd just have to live without one this time.

"There's wild onions growin' up by the crick, ma'am."

"Really?"

"Wild onions and some other stuff that makes fair eatin'."

"Up by the creek, you say?"

"Yes'm. You can find wild onions and garlic and sage and mint and bitter root and pepper grass, popotillo, and probably some dandelions and lamb's-quarters."

"Really." Gracie stared with dismay at Fergus. She'd never even heard of most of those things, and she had absolutely no idea what to do with any of them. She felt horribly inadequate all of a sudden.

Once again Fergus surprised her. "Don't reckon you never had nothin' to do with most o' them things, ma'am, but I can teach you."

If Gracie had run across Fergus in St. Louis, she'd likely have crossed the street in order to avoid him. Now his kindness almost overset her composure. "Thank you very much." Until this moment, Gracie had never had occasion to examine her own unwitting intolerance of people different from herself. She found her character sadly wanting.

"Don't think nothin' of it, ma'am. Hell, this place takes some gettin' used to, I reckon."

"Yes," she said. "Yes, I guess it does."

After Charity awoke from her nap, Jake led the two new women in his life up the hill and farther into the woods, until they came to an opening in the trees. As she stepped out into the sunlight, Gracie beheld a perfectly beautiful scene.

A small stream bubbled merrily through a meadow. Cottonwoods and a couple of weeping willows sprang from the grassy sward of green, and verbena, globe mallow, yellow mustard, and other flowers of which Fergus would undoubtedly know the names dotted the riverbank. Robins sang in the willows. A dove cooed, and a mockingbird answered. Gracie was delighted.

"Oh, Jake, this is very pretty."

Looking around, Gracie wondered why this landscape should appeal to her so much. It wasn't as lush as the woods back home in Missouri. Maybe it was because everything else around here was so primitive and desertlike that this tucked-away Eden seemed especially idyllic. Besides, back home in Missouri, she hadn't had Jake with her.

She decided not to think about that, but to make this excursion out of doors as pleasant for her baby as possible. Poor Charity had seldom been allowed outdoors in her short life until now. Gracie decided not to think about *that*, either, as it only made her sad.

Since it was a warm day, she decided to make the most of the experience and took off Charity's shoes and stockings. Then she took off her own shoes and stockings, set the baby on the riverbank, and plunked down next to her.

"You can stick your toes in the water, Charity sweetheart. See?" Gracie demonstrated by dipping her toe into the creek and lifting it out again. Sparkling droplets of water dripped from her foot and plinked into the stream.

Charity looked at Gracie's foot and then glanced uncertainly at her face, her big brown eyes attesting eloquently to her state of constant vigilance. Gracie recognized the baby's uncertain expression for what it was, and her heart ached.

"Come on, sweetie," she whispered gently. "Don't be scared."

She reached into the cold stream and dribbled a few drops of water on Charity's own bare feet. The little girl's eyes opened even wider as she stared at Gracie. Then she peeked at the water, then at her dripping toes, then at Gracie again. With extreme caution, she pointed her big toe at the water and carefully touched it. Then she giggled.

"There you go, sweetheart. That's the way."

Gracie praised Charity's boldness for several moments without even thinking about Jake. When she glanced up to find him watching her, a quizzical expression on his face, she wished she'd been more discreet.

She cleared her throat and said, "Charity's never seen such a pretty stream, Jake. She's used to the city."

"I see."

He didn't see at all; Gracie could tell. She was casting about in her mind for another excuse for Charity's odd behavior when she learned why Jake wore his gun the way he did. No sooner had they heard a terrible thrashing noise coming from the woods than Jake jumped up, reached over with his right hand, grabbed the forward-facing butt of his pistol, and aimed it at the sound. It happened so fast, Gracie didn't have time to be scared. She only blinked, astonished, and reached for Charity, who had jerked in alarm and was folding up on the riverbank.

"Qué quieren?"

Jake's voice was soft and deadly. Alarm speared Gracie much more painfully than it would have if he'd shouted. Carefully, she picked the baby up and set her on her lap. Only then did she look at the woods to where Jake's gun pointed.

Her mouth went dry when she saw three mounted men, looking for all the world like villains out of *El Hombre de Muerte, Border Bandit,* her favorite dime novel. From the safety of her bedroom in St. Louis, the book had seemed exciting. Right now, Gracie would have wished herself back home were it not for other considerations.

"No queremos nada, señor," the leader of the pack said

with a careless shrug and a glittering grin Gracie didn't believe for a second.

A longer look confirmed that these fellows were clad exactly as she'd expect border bandits to dress. They even wore ammunition belts crossed over their chests, a phenomenon she'd originally chalked up to the dime novelist's overactive imagination. Unfortunately, she knew better now.

"*Váyanse*. Get out of here." As soon as the implacable command hissed from his lips, Jake's piercing whistle tore through the air and Gracie's eardrums. Charity cringed, and the bandits looked mildly outraged.

"We don't want nothing, *señor*. Just water for our horses."

"Forget it. Go downstream if you want water."

"But, *señor, los caballos necesitan agua, bien*?"

"Too bad. Get out. Now."

As if to underscore Jake's command, a disembodied voice sang out, "*Váyanse, todos*. Get the hell out of here, Miguel."

Gracie recognized Bart's voice. Then she heard crashing noises as men hurried through the underbrush, and spared a moment to hope these unknown newcomers were friends. Miguel, the fellow whom Gracie assumed to be the bandit leader, looked disgruntled and she took heart.

With a good deal of shock, she saw him drop a wicked-looking knife back into a thigh holster. She hadn't even noticed when he'd reached for the knife, and she gulped, wondering if he'd planned to fling it at Jake. The thought made her insides crinkle up, and she squeezed Charity more closely to her breast.

Suddenly the woods disgorged six or seven of the men Gracie had seen in church that morning. She suspected Jake's whistle had called them thither, and could only thank God for it. Then she allowed herself a brief moment of surprise that she should be glad for the advent of these men whose appearance had, only hours earlier, frightened her.

Miguel's teeth glittered as the sun's rays struck them, and Gracie wished he hadn't smiled. Somehow, he looked much more sinister when smiling than when merely grinning.

Perhaps this was so because the expression was patently false. The gold glinting from his front tooth didn't add to his appeal any.

When she'd read accounts of New Mexico Territory before she moved here, she'd envisioned rough accommodations and few luxuries. She'd been prepared for those conditions and had steeled herself to endure them without complaint. She hadn't given a thought to the people and realized she hadn't been ready for them. They terrified her.

"Drop your weapons before you leave, gentlemen," Jake advised in a voice of silk.

Miguel's smile vanished instantly amidst mutterings and stirrings from his companions. Gracie knew no Spanish, but she expected she might be shocked if anybody translated these words for her. They sounded perfectly vile.

"We leave. You don' need our guns. We won' bother you no more."

"Drop the damned guns."

As if to add emphasis to Jake's command, six or seven of his friends cocked their weapons. The clicks seemed to echo in the clearing, sounding like twigs snapping underfoot to Gracie's untrained ear. She hugged Charity more tightly still and began to scrunch back against a nearby boulder. Poor Charity looked as if her eyes might bulge out, and Gracie could have shot Miguel herself for causing the baby this distress. Why, Charity had even been giggling before he'd shown up!

Miguel squinted at the group of armed men as though calculating odds, then shrugged and grinned again. Slowly, he drew a rifle from his shoulder scabbard. Gracie held her breath when it slid into his palm until the barrel pointed directly at Jake's chest. She heard another click and saw a tiny flash of irritation cross Miguel's face. Then, with an indolent chuckle, he allowed the firearm to slide to the ground. His companions also rid themselves of their rifles.

"Keep going," Jake advised in a steely voice.

Miguel chuckled again, an ominous, ugly noise in a day formerly filled with birdsong and good cheer. Another gun plopped to the earth. It was joined by similar weapons from his friends.

"Now the knives."

Miguel heaved a big sigh, as though sorely aggrieved by Jake's mistrust. He flung the knife that had earlier frightened Gracie into the dirt at Jake's feet. The blade was so sharp and Miguel's aim so good that not so much as a puff of dust followed the *chunk* as the point slid through the soil. The thought of that honed steel slicing through Jake's flesh made Gracie shiver. Other knives joined it.

"We'll leave 'em at the foot of the hill, Miguel. You can pick 'em up tomorrow sometime." Bart sent a stream of tobacco juice through the gap in his teeth.

Jake's friends surrounded the three horsemen, who seemed quite peeved. Bart spoke for all of them.

"If'n you want to get them sidearms back someday, *váyanse ahora, Miguel.* Else you won't never need 'em again. We told you before not to show your brisket in Diabolito Lindo. You don't learn easy, do you?"

"Lo siento mucho, señores. Vámanos ahora."

"You better vamoose now, 'less you wanna see your hearts and livers on a spike."

Appalled by Bart's savage suggestion, Gracie gaped at the assortment of men aiming a miscellany of arms at the horsemen, then at the horsemen themselves. She'd read the colorful phrase *bristling with weapons* a couple of times in novels. She hadn't understood what it meant until this minute.

Miguel muttered something in Spanish Gracie figured to be impolite.

"Vámanos." Miguel wheeled his horse around and headed back through the woods. His *compadres* did likewise.

Just before the tail of the last horse swished out of sight, one of Miguel's men whirled suddenly in his saddle and Gracie screeched when a knife came whistling through the air. Then she saw a puff of smoke from Bart's shotgun. The explosion from the weapon followed almost instantaneously, along with a scream and a crash in the woods.

"Bastards," the disgusted Bart snarled. Gracie's ears were ringing so loudly, she barely heard him.

Jake didn't put his gun back into his waistband until the sound of galloping horses had faded into the trees. Then he said, "Better see if he's dead, Bart."

Expelling the spent shell from his rifle, Bart grumbled, "I'll see if his damned horse is still around, too. Them dogs gen'ly have pretty good horseflesh."

"They should," another fellow said harshly. "They steal 'em from Chisum, and he's rich as God."

With an apologetic look at Gracie, Jake said, "Nobody's as rich as God, boys."

Fergus, standing next to Bart with his gun still aimed at the woods, grinned. "Welcome to Diabolito Lindo, Miss Gracie. Reckon this is your real introduction."

Still shaking, Gracie whispered, "Oh, my."

They buried the outlaw on Boot Hill not far from the grave marked with a rude wooden cross bearing the name "Ralph Trinidad." Gracie didn't sing at this, the second funeral of the day.

5

*J*AKE HAD BEEN chewing for entirely too long. Gracie gave him a sidelong glance as she spooned another drink of broth into Charity's mouth. Her heart hurt. She'd always been a mediocre cook, even back home where she was familiar with the foodstuffs. Here, where all she had to work with were beans and goat meat, she knew she'd failed utterly in this, her first trial.

She offered tentatively, "Maybe I didn't soak the beans long enough, Jake."

She saw him try to swallow, fail, and stuff the mass into his cheek so he could speak.

"Maybe."

"I'll start them early in the morning tomorrow. Or maybe soak them overnight."

He'd begun chewing again and only nodded.

"I expect goat meat might be a little tougher than beef or pork, too, Jake."

"Mmmmmph."

"It probably should have cooked longer."

Jake gave a shorter "Mmmph" this time.

"At least it made up a pretty good broth for the baby."

He nodded and finally managed to swallow his first bite.

Suddenly the enormity of her sins seemed to explode in Gracie's heart. Here she was, thrusting herself and Charity on Jake, disrupting his life, lying to him—and lying and lying and lying some more. He was so good to her; so kind to Charity; so understanding. And she couldn't even serve him a decent meal. This last, most miserable deed of hers grew in significance until it loomed like a mountain in Gracie's mind. How could she do this to Jake?

She blinked furiously to hold her tears at bay; she didn't want to cry and frighten Charity. Because of her past experiences, the baby would undoubtedly lay Gracie's unhappiness at Jake's feet, and Gracie couldn't abide giving her such a patently false impression of Jake.

She said cheerfully, "Here's another bite for Charity. Charity's such a big girl."

After giving Jake a wary glance, Charity dared offer up a tiny smile and took another slurp of broth.

Striving to keep her voice level, Gracie said, "I'm really sorry, Jake. I don't know the first thing about the food you have available here in the territory. Or anything else, either. If I'd known, maybe . . . maybe I wouldn't have come out here."

She knew she'd just lied. She'd have come if she'd known it would be twice as bad. She'd had no choice.

Looking at his beans and meat as if contemplating whether or not to tackle another bite, Jake muttered, "Well, it's rough all right. That's why I don't want you roaming around by yourself."

"I'll learn, Jake. You just wait and see. I'll learn, and then you won't have to eat tough meat and hard beans ever again, I promise."

Jake heaved a big sigh. "It'll be all right, Gracie. It just takes time to adjust, is all."

When she braved looking at him again, he was cutting his meat up into mince and the urge to weep assaulted her anew.

"I reckon you think I was pretty rash to come out here without knowing what I was getting into, don't you, Jake?"

His lopsided smile almost broke her heart. She remembered that smile from when they were children.

"Gracie, I've never once known you to think a problem through before you acted. I don't reckon things have changed all that much." He smiled at Charity who, miracle of miracles, didn't immediately look away. "The stakes are higher now than they were when we were kids, though. You might want to take your baby into consideration before you do things other people advise against."

A retort bubbled up in Gracie's throat, and she swallowed it back with difficulty. She wanted to shout at him that she'd undertaken this perilous move *because* the stakes were high; that her only concern in the world for months now had been Charity.

But she didn't, because for the first time in her life she had something to fight for. And something to hide. And something to fear. And everything to lose.

Also for the first time in her life, she had to bear her burdens alone; she couldn't dump her responsibilities onto Jake's shoulders, no matter how broad those shoulders were or how much she might long to do it. Not only would relinquishing her burden be unfair, but it might get Jake hurt. Gracie already had enough on her conscience; she couldn't bear to see Jake get hurt because of her.

Also—although she didn't want to think about it—if Jake knew, he'd probably say she was wrong to have done what she did and try to make her undo it.

Besides that, he was right. It hurt to admit it, but everybody had always told her that the truth hurt. She'd been rash and irresponsible all her life. She'd also always been hot to leap to her own defense, no matter what her folly.

This evening she said meekly, "You're right, Jake. I'll try my best to remember that." The words almost choked her.

"You know I'm not just being mean, Gracie," Jake said gently. "Life here in the territory is real rugged. I reckon you saw that today."

Remembering the corpse of that bandit—who only seconds before had been a living, albeit worthless, human being—lying on the forest floor with his chest a gaping, bloody hole, Gracie shuddered. "Yes, I did," she whispered, and forgave Jake a little for bringing up her feckless youth.

"And I expect you'll get used to the food here pretty soon, too." After looking at his minced goat meat and beans for another second, he added, "At least, I hope so."

She shot him a look. He lifted his head and peered at her with such a tender expression on his face that she had to glance away again quickly. "Here, Charity, drink some more broth. Tomorrow I'll try to find some greens."

"Fergus will probably bring you the chickens pretty soon, too, and then you can have eggs. And the goat, for milk."

"Is there a mercantile where I can get flour and corn-meal?"

"I'll take you there tomorrow, Gracie. It's in Lincoln. We can get seeds for your garden there, too."

"What about fruit? Are there any fruit trees around here?"

"I think we can get some apples."

"Thank you."

Charity lost interest in her broth, and Gracie handed her a rock-hard biscuit to gnaw. Taking a tip from Jake, she cut her own goat meat up into tiny pieces before daring a bite. It was tough as an old boot and tasted like rancid lamb. Biting into a single bean, she guessed she should at least be glad it didn't break her teeth. She'd never eaten a crunchy bean before and had to fight her urge to curl up in a corner and sob.

Extravagant emotional displays belonged to the St. Louis Gracie, though. The New Mexico Gracie was tough—at least as tough as this stringy old goat meat. There was no room for hysterics in this Gracie, any more than there was room for false pride.

As if he could read her mind, Jake repeated softly, "It'll be all right, Gracie. You'll get used to things. You'll learn. You never ran from a fight that I can remember."

She had to blink several times and swallow her bean. "No, I never did."

"Of course, you always used to drag me into them, too, but I reckon that was then."

She looked over at him and found him grinning. She'd never felt so guilty in her life.

They ate, or tried to, in silence for several minutes. Gracie's spirits were bruised as much by Jake's kindness as by the miserable meal she'd fixed. It was her first one here in her new home, and it was about as dismal a failure as she'd ever tasted.

Deciding that self-castigation would lead her nowhere, she sat up straighter and scrambled furiously for something to deflect her mind from her deficiencies. It didn't take her more than a minute or two to remember the piano.

"Jake, do you think the men in your congregation would mind if I played the piano at church?"

He glanced up from his plate, where he'd been hashing up some more meat. "They'd probably love it."

"Really?" She suspected it was irrational to take such joy from Jake's simple declaration, but she did anyway. "Do you know if any of them like to sing?"

"Sing?" Jake looked at her as if she'd asked if they liked to ride elephants. "Well, I don't know. Why?"

Feeling herself flush, Gracie muttered, "I just thought maybe your church could use a choir, Jake." She felt like an idiot.

It didn't make her feel any better when he burst out laughing. "A choir? Oh, my God."

A curl of resentment slithered into Gracie's innards. "I don't know what's so funny. Lots of churches have choirs."

"Lots of churches in St. Louis, maybe. Or even in Albuquerque. It's hard to imagine getting a church choir together in Diabolito Lindo."

"They say music has charms—"

" 'To soothe the savage breast, to soften rocks, or bend a knotted oak.' I know, Gracie. Your mama read that same poem to me when I was a boy."

She didn't appreciate his sarcasm one tiny bit, and frowned at him. "Well, maybe she was right."

Jake looked at her steadily. "Maybe."

She didn't appreciate the expression on his face, either. Or his tone. They hit her wrong. "I thought you loved Mama, Jake."

"I did."

"How come you're talking like that, then?"

He was silent for a minute, then gave a big sigh. "Oh, Gracie, I did love your mama. She was a sweet, pretty woman. But she was like a blade of grass, you know. She was no knotted oak for music to bend; she bent all by herself. You're too young to remember, I reckon, but Gracie, she was a weak woman."

In spite of her noble resolve, Gracie's eyes filled with tears.

"And don't you go crying on me, either. You know she was weak. She kept your father dancing around her like a wind-up toy soldier. He spent so much time taking care of her, he didn't have any to spare for you. Or me either, for that matter." He sounded almost bitter. "If you don't remember, I sure do."

"I guess I don't remember, Jake," Gracie said in a small voice.

"No, I don't suppose you do, although you learned how to play the game pretty well, all things considered."

Shocked and mortified, Gracie exclaimed, "Jake! Do you think I'm manipulative?"

He shook his head, obviously annoyed with himself for saying more than he had intended to say. "All I know is you always had me dancing to your tune when we were kids. You played me like a fiddle, Gracie." His sudden grin almost took her breath away. "And it looks like you're doing it again."

She was trying so hard not to cry that she couldn't say a word. His assessment of her mother and herself wounded her to the very core. Pain lumped up so thick in her throat that it felt like somebody had stuffed a rock down her gullet. Denial rose within her and battered against the rock, but feebly. Those awful words of Jake's rang of truth, and they crushed her.

"I didn't mean to hurt your feelings," Jake said. "I never

minded taking care of you when we were kids—well, not much anyway—no matter what nonsense you got into. And I don't mind now. I'm glad you came to me for help."

She managed to whisper, "You are?"

"I am. Sort of. It's just . . ." He took his dish over to the kitchen sink and stood there with his back to her. "It's just that the stakes are real high now, what with you and Charity, and the territory being so rough and all. I'm afraid I'll fail you."

Since he wasn't watching, Gracie wiped her eyes with the edge of her apron. "You won't fail me, Jake."

With a laugh, he turned around. "Now how can you say that, Gracie? You don't know what's in store for us."

Reality pierced Gracie's consciousness like the sting of a wasp. Memories of her mother and father chased each other through her brain with the speed of lightning. She could almost hear her father telling her mother not to trouble her pretty head, that he'd take care of her. She even heard her mother utter a few feeble protests, only to be overridden by her father, who had loved her, almost literally, to death.

Her mother had been helpless; Gracie admitted it to herself starkly, refusing to deny the truth any longer. But Gracie wasn't her mother. And she wasn't like her, either. Not in the least.

All at once she discovered herself resenting Jake's attitude; he was treating her just as her father used to treat her mother. As if she were too stupid and helpless to do anything for or by herself.

Well, by gracious, it wasn't going to work with Gracie Molloy. She might not know a lot about the Territory, and she might not be a great cook. She might not even know as much about being a mother as she needed to know. But, by all that was holy, she aimed to learn. And she wasn't about to let Jake Molloy make her feel any more useless than she already felt.

Anger bubbled up in her, miraculously melting the rocks in her throat. "Well, neither do you, Jake Molloy. You don't know what's in store for us any more than I do!"

She sucked in a deep breath and tried to calm down some. It wouldn't do to let her anger show and frighten Charity.

Jake looked surprised. Gracie didn't much blame him; she was a bit surprised herself. She wasn't used to standing up for herself; she'd learned to be meek and sweet-tempered at her mother's knee, and had been an apt pupil.

"You keep telling me life's rough in the Territory. Well, so what? Life was rough all over until people tamed it. *People*, Jake. Not just men. Men and women together are what tamed the stupid, rough world. And if I want to put together a choir in Diabolito Lindo, I think it's mighty mean of you to laugh at me for it."

"Gracie, I—"

"No. No, you just be quiet for once, Jake." Gracie stood and gathered the rest of the dishes. Although she was fuming inside, she gave Charity a sweet smile and kept her tone calm. "All you've said so far is about how awful it is around here. You keep telling me all the men are criminals who'd as soon shoot me as shake my hand."

Jake shrugged, as if to say the truth wasn't his fault.

Gracie swept past him and over to the sink. She came up only to his shoulder, but she felt tall as anything right then. "Well, maybe they *are* rough and tough. Or maybe they're like a little boy I used to know who liked to act rough and tough. Maybe if somebody treated them like civilized men, they'd *act* like civilized men."

Jake shrugged again, more helplessly this time.

Gracie swirled around and waved her wooden spoon under his nose. "You men! You're always trying to show people how big and bad you are. Well, by gum, nobody's going to be big and bad with Gracie Molloy! If I want a choir in Diabolito Lindo, Jake Molloy, I'm by gum going to do my best to make one, and I'll thank you not to get in my way!"

She'd about run out of bluster by this time, and couldn't believe she'd actually spoken to Jake, the champion of her entire life, in anger. She'd never done such a thing before. This behavior directly controverted every single thing her mother had ever taught her about the proper way for a lady to behave. Shocked by her own boldness, she began to shake in reaction and turned to grip the sink so her legs wouldn't fold up under her, bracing herself for Jake's angry retort.

Oh, Lord, what had she done?

He didn't answer for the longest time, and Gracie wanted to scream. At last, he said softly, "By God, Gracie, maybe you're right."

She nearly fainted dead away.

Jake hoped to God Gracie would learn to cook pretty soon. He wasn't sure how many more experiments like her beans and goat meat he could survive without withering into a wisp and blowing away on the winds that whistled through Diabolito Lindo. He sat at his desk staring out into the starry night for a long time after Gracie and Charity went to bed, contemplating things.

She was right. After giving a good deal of thought to the relationship between her father and mother, Jake realized Gracie's father had helped her mother be weak. After what he'd been through, he understood how people, with the best intentions in the world, assisted others to be weak. The good Lord knew, plenty of people had helped him along his path to ruin.

Not that he blamed those people any more than he blamed Gracie's father. Or her mother, either, if it came to that, because they didn't recognize what they were doing when they did it.

Gracie's mother and father had loved each other, too, and their love had set an example Jake would never forget or regret. Genuine love provided a lot better example of how to live than most folks ever got, he reckoned.

He wondered if there might be a way for a man to love a woman without smothering her or allowing her to run roughshod over him. With a grin, he expected Gracie would show him if there was, although he wasn't too sure about the running-roughshod part. He couldn't believe the feelings he was having for her. He'd never thought of her as anything but his irritating, albeit endearing, younger sister before she'd showed up at his door yesterday.

Right now, he longed to go over to the bed and simply gaze at her. Just being able to see her face made him happy, although it also made him want more. Of course. He shook his head. Good old Jake Molloy. Always wanted more.

Bitter memories made him frown. By the light of the single tallow candle flickering at his elbow, he thumbed through his Bible, seeking help. Ah, yes, there it was, in Proverbs.

Jake read very softly to himself, "Before destruction the heart of man is haughty, and before honor is humility."

If Jake had learned nothing else in the last five years, he'd learned that. With a sigh, he acknowledged it was going to be mighty difficult, living here in the same house with Gracie and not touching her. Yet he couldn't touch her. He had neither a moral nor a legal right to her body, no matter how much he might want to have one.

Besides, he'd lied to the boys about her. He couldn't unlie now and tell them she wasn't really his sister; his own hard-earned sense of honor wouldn't let him. He'd broken his own code of conduct by lying and now had to abide by whatever the result of that violation turned out to be.

"Before destruction the heart of man is haughty, and before honor is humility."

Jake read and reread the familiar words, praying for strength. He wasn't, perhaps, the holiest of ministers, but he'd be willing to bet there was no other man of the cloth anywhere who loved the Lord's Word more than he did. It had saved his life, God's Word had. And before he'd let it save his miserable soul, he'd been haughty as hell. He'd needed to be humbled in every way possible before the Word had been able to penetrate his thick skull and thicker heart.

After reading for several minutes, Jake decided he'd become entirely too complacent in recent months and had forgotten the humility that had saved him in the first place. Then and there, he got down on his knees, shut his eyes, pressed his face into his hands propped on his chair, and humbly begged God to guide him.

By the time he finally went to bed, he guessed he'd survive living with Gracie. At least for a while.

"I think I read a book about Lincoln once, Jake."

Chuckling, Jake said, "Wouldn't surprise me much. The dime novelists had a field day with the troubles that went on here a couple of years ago."

The day was as clear and pure as Gracie and her daughter, and Jake exalted in both it and them. Until Gracie had shown up and made him examine his surroundings, he'd liked them all right but his liking had to do with things other than physical beauty. Looking around now and breathing in the clean scent of the pine woods, he caught some of Gracie's enthusiasm. This place was downright pretty. By God, it was.

"Did you know Billy the Kid?" Gracie asked breathlessly.

"Who?" Her question interrupted his contemplation of God's glory, and he frowned, puzzled.

"What on earth do you mean, 'Who?' Why, Billy the Kid is who!"

"Who the hell is Billy the Kid?"

Gracie's exasperated huff tickled Jake's funny bone and he smiled at her. Since she was holding Charity on her lap, his smile included her. To his astonishment, she gave him an almost infinitesimally small smile in return, then turned her head around and tried to bury her face against Gracie's shoulder. Gracie patted her absently.

"'Who was Billy the Kid!'" she mimicked, as if she'd never heard such a silly question in her life. "Billy the Kid was the hero of the Lincoln County War, Jake Molloy! All the newspapers said so. And now he's escaped again, too. I read all about it back home."

Jake shook his head, a little peeved that Gracie was so insistent upon something that was, to him, an obvious falsehood. Good grief, he'd been living in Diabolito Lindo when the so-called Lincoln County War was going on. He didn't remember any Billy the— All of a sudden, enlightenment struck.

"Oh! Good God, Gracie. Are you talking about Billy Antrim? That rotten little skunk?"

It was Gracie's turn to look puzzled. "I don't think his name's Antrim, Jake. The newpapers called him William Bonney—Billy the Kid."

Jake flicked a fly away from his mule's ear with his whip, disgusted. "The newspapers ought to be burned down if they're calling him a hero, Gracie. Why, the boy's a cold-blooded murderer. And when he was running around killing people in these parts, he went by the name of Antrim, whatever they're calling him now."

"Oh." Gracie looked disappointed. "Well, the papers didn't say that."

"No doubt." Jake sounded as fed up as he felt. What was the world coming to, he wondered, when people made heroes out of scum like Billy Antrim?

"Well, anyway, I'll be interested to see where all the excitement took place."

It appeared as though Gracie was trying to sound subdued, but Jake wasn't fooled; he could feel her excitement. The air around them fairly quivered with it. With a resigned sigh, he said, "All right, Gracie. I'll show you where everything happened."

Peeking at her slantwise, he saw her lovely eyes light up, and was glad he'd come down off his high horse.

"Oh, thank you, Jake!"

"You're welcome, Gracie." He shook his head, wondering how he could have come to love her so much in so short a period of time. With luck, he'd get over it.

He wished he believed in luck.

"Well, here we are. This is Lincoln."

The weather was unseasonably warm this sleepy April day, and Gracie had been dozing, holding the sleeping Charity on her lap. When she heard Jake's announcement, though, she snapped to attention in a hurry, eager to see the

famous Lincoln, New Mexico Territory, where the cel-
ebrated outlaw, Billy the Kid, had earned fame and glory.

She blinked, surprised, and tried to hide her disappointment. In fact, if she'd done much more than blink, she might
have missed it entirely. As she gazed at the dusty little
clutter of buildings dozing under the noonday sun, she was
hard-pressed to reconcile the vision before her to the
romantic tales of rivalry, deceit, honor, villainy, and may-
hem she'd read.

"This is it?"

"This is it."

"This is where all the excitement happened?"

"Well . . ." She could tell Jake was trying to smother
his laughter at her reaction and was having a hard time of it.
She was too curious to resent it. "Not all of it, I reckon.
People were killing each other all around the countryside
hereabouts. But see down there? That big white building?
That's the courthouse, where Antrim broke out."

Gracie had to squint in order to see the unprepossessing,
boxy-looking building at which Jake's gloved finger pointed.
She said, "Hmmm."

"That's where Antrim and his friends murdered the
sheriff."

The way Jake said it, all stark and unadorned by flowery
adjectives, struck Gracie oddly. She shivered and wished
she could run her hands over her arms, which had suddenly
sprouted gooseflesh. Since she was holding Charity, she
couldn't. She opted for another small "Hmmm."

"That's where McSwain's store was before they burned
him out."

The pile of rubble looked like—well—a pile of rubble.
Gracie frowned and pointed at another structure. "What's
that, Jake?"

"The *torreón*. That's where the earliest settlers—they
were all Mexican—used to take shelter during Indian
attacks."

"Oh." Gracie's eerie feeling vanished in a puff of irritation.

Well, now, wasn't this just the way things always turned

out? The most interesting thing in the whole stupid town wasn't connected with the much-vaunted "war" at all. Gracie had a mind to write to a couple of dime novelists and tell them what she thought of their overblown accounts of the Lincoln County War.

"Just because the town doesn't look like much doesn't mean a lot didn't happen here, though," Jake said, surprising her yet again.

"No?"

"No. But it wasn't romantic, Gracie. It was grim and ugly and a whole lot of people died. I'd venture to say whiskey played a bigger part in the action than anybody wants to admit, too."

"Whiskey?"

Jake slanted her a wry look. His face seemed hard and jaded when he looked at her that way; his expression made Gracie feel uneasy.

"You don't suppose gents shoot each other up for the hell of it on a daily basis without inspiration, do you? Not even the Territory's that colorful."

"I don't expect I ever thought about it."

"Well, take it from me, liquor's inspired more meanness in more men, good and bad, than about anything else human beings have ever invented."

His words struck a chord that vibrated of truth in Gracie. She believed him. She also sensed that the words meant more to him than they did to her. Unable to account for her strange impression, Gracie wasn't sure what to say.

"Have—I mean—" She took a deep breath, annoyed with herself for being so jumbled in her thinking. "I mean, did liquor ever make *you* mean, Jake?" She couldn't imagine it.

He was silent long enough for Gracie to get a sick feeling in her middle. Nor did he look at her.

His expression was about as remote as the moon when he finally said, "I killed a man drunk, Gracie."

6

GRACIE THANKED HER lucky stars and the good Lord when, almost immediately after he'd made his astonishing confession, Jake said, "Here's the mercantile. Hold on to Charity, and I'll fetch the both of you out of the wagon."

Her mouth was about as dry as the earth under the wagon's wheels when she said, "Thank you, Jake."

He seemed not at all disconcerted when he reached up to grab her around the waist and lift her to the ground. Since he didn't seem inclined to elaborate on his words, Gracie decided she wouldn't pursue the subject. Certainly not here, at any rate, on a public street and with Charity in her arms.

"Thanks," she said, smiling up at him. Then she checked to see if the baby had been frightened by being so close to Jake. She was pleased to discover her looking at him, her large, always-cautious eyes curious but unafraid.

"I think she's getting used to you, Jake."

"You think so?"

He gave the little girl a friendly smile, and Gracie's heart fluttered hard. *Oh, my.* His smile was as warm as the sun above them. From the remote, icy man who'd just confessed to killing another human being, Jake was back to being himself. At least, he was back to being what Gracie remembered him being.

An unexpected shiver shook her, and she wondered if she knew anything at all about anything at all. Reminding herself that it was too late to worry about such things, she squared her shoulders and marched next to Jake and into the crude wooden building he claimed was a mercantile establishment.

"Not like the ones you're used to in St. Louis, I reckon."

Gracie almost sagged in despair when she glanced around the store. There was nothing here! Nothing that she could use, at any rate. Everything was hardware and lumber and tack and—oh, there was flour, at least. And cornmeal. Were those bolts of calico in that corner behind the dusty barrels claiming to be filled with nails?

Telling herself to buck up, she renewed her determination to make the best of things and began a businesslike inspection of the goods available for purchase.

By the time she'd peeked into every nook and cranny the store possessed, she had cheered up considerably. In fact, as Jake drove her back toward Diabolito Lindo, she actually felt rather proud of herself. Things might be different here, and they might be backward and rather rough, but by gum, if other women could do it, so could she. Gracie Molloy possessed at least as much grit as her pioneer ancestors.

Gracie considered the next several weeks an education. Every day she learned more about her new home. Every day Jake introduced her to new people, all of whom were men and all of whom were not the sorts of fellows her mother would have approved of her even speaking to in St. Louis. But this was not, Gracie reminded herself over and over again, St. Louis. And if she didn't, Jake did.

She discovered with some surprise that she liked her new home. Life was freer here. Occasionally it was a little too free, in fact. There were certainly no stuffy matrons frowning down their noses in disapproval at disorderly behavior. And although Jake kept her locked up tight after sunset, Gracie could hear the shouts and shots resulting from such behavior almost every night, and witness the results of it in the morning.

Very few days dawned during which she didn't find herself picking up bottles and debris scattered during the previous night's hard revels. Many mornings, men who'd been perfectly sound the day before greeted her with blackened eyes or bandaged limbs. Almost invariably, those same men complained of aching heads and queasy stomachs, even as they headed back to Fergus's place.

Gracie began to appreciate the power of social disapproval for the first time in her life, and wondered if these men would behave in so rowdy a manner if they had neighbors to frown at them for it. On the other hand, perhaps that's why they lived here instead of, say, St. Louis, where rules were set in stone and one did what one was supposed to do or suffered the ostracism inherent in daring to defy convention.

Freedom or restriction, which was better? It was a difficult question, and one Gracie found herself unable to answer. Not only that, but her feelings on the matter wobbled considerably from day to day—sometimes even from hour to hour.

Still, she found herself settling right into her new environment. There was something exciting about abiding in a place into which civilization had yet to sink deep, permanent roots. A body could improvise freely without fearing censure. Those same stuffy matrons who weren't here to disapprove of Diabolito Lindo's citizens' penchant for violence were also absent when Gracie's meals didn't measure up. Given the state of her mastery of the culinary arts, she considered that a real blessing.

Life in Diabolito Lindo was good for Charity, too. Every day, the little girl seemed to relax her guard a bit more. Gracie knew better than to expect her to blossom into natural, easygoing childhood any time soon, but she considered it encouraging that the baby at least smiled more often. Also, she began sleeping through the night after only a few days. She'd been troubled by nightmares ever since Gracie could remember. Now, two or three days would pass without Charity waking up crying in the middle of the night.

She seemed to enjoy being outdoors, too, and Gracie liked to take her for walks in Jake's yard. They even planted a small vegetable garden. Occasionally, and only when Jake accompanied them, they'd go up to the creek. Charity loved the water, the flowers, and the soft green grass.

A couple of weeks after their trip to Lincoln, while Jake was out visiting one of his parishioners who'd taken ill—"lead poisoning," according to Jake—Gracie bustled down the one dirt road in Diabolito Lindo toward Pablo Fergus's saloon, with Charity balanced on one hip. In the hand not occupied with the baby, Gracie clutched a pretty embroidered sampler.

When she'd made it to the saloon, she paused for a moment, nervous as a mouse about to boldly enter a room full of tabbies. Then, with a muttered "It's up to us, Charity," she squared her shoulders and forged onward. She was going to civilize this place if it was the last thing she did.

"Miss Gracie, I don't think Jake'd want you bein' out in town on your own."

Fergus had looked horrified when he saw her swish through the splintery batwing doors of his business establishment with the baby in her arms. Now that she stood before him at the shiny bar, he still looked horrified.

Gracie gave Fergus one of her most charming smiles. "He said it would be all right as long as it's daylight and morning, Mr. Fergus. He said afternoons tend to get a little ticklish." She frowned, still unclear as to what he'd meant by that. "Anyway, he's visiting Mr. Clifford, who must have eaten something that disagreed with him."

Fergus rolled his eyes, a gesture Gracie didn't understand. She began to feel uncomfortable again and her smile faded some. "I brought you something for your wall, Mr. Fergus."

"Fer my wall?"

"Yes. I thought it might be a nice touch and just the thing

to perk up your place of business, since Jake preaches here on Sundays." She held out the sampler. "I made the frame myself, out of piñon pine wood. The piñon trees around here are so pretty. Jake sanded and painted it and showed me how to stretch the fabric so that it fits."

Fergus sucked in a big breath. Given the state of the air in his saloon, Gracie wasn't sure it was a wise thing to do, but she wasn't about to admonish him for it.

"Miss Gracie, this is a saloon."

"Well, of course it is, Mr. Fergus. I know that. Charity and I thought we'd pick you some flowers, too, come Sunday. They'll be really pretty sitting on Jake's pulpit. We always had flowers in church back home on Sunday mornings."

She couldn't account for the way Fergus seemed to puff up. His face was turning red, too. At least, she thought it was. It was so dark in here, it was hard to tell.

"Would you like me to wash your windows for you, Mr. Fergus? That would brighten the place up a good deal. Then those men would be able to see their cards better."

She swept an arm out to indicate a table full of men who had been playing poker when she waltzed in. They seemed to have forgotten their cards momentarily and were staring at her as if they'd never seen a female with a baby before.

They all looked extremely surprised to find her here, so she gave them a sunny smile and said, "I'm Gracie Trinidad, Preacher Jake's sister." She'd heard many of the men in town refer to Jake as Preacher Jake. She figured calling him by his nickname, especially one that had apparently been bestowed in affection, would help her fit in.

One of the men removed a fat cigar from between his teeth, opened his mouth as if to say something, shut it again, then jammed the cigar back in. He looked at the man across from him. Gracie saw the other man lift his shoulders in a helpless shrug. Then they both commenced to stare at her some more. Feeling even more uncomfortable, she turned back to Fergus.

"Miss Gracie," Fergus said in what sounded like a very strained voice, "Jake's pulpit is a beer keg."

She nodded. "Yes, I noticed that. And I think it was very enterprising of the two of you to have made such good use of the materials available in your drinking establishment."

Fergus drew in another breath and tried again. "Gents like the light in a saloon to be sorter dark, Miss Gracie."

"Oh." Since Fergus still hadn't taken her sampler, Gracie set it on the bar and shifted Charity to her other hip. She was glad Charity didn't seem to be shrinking in fear from Fergus, as she'd done when she'd first met him. Maybe she was getting used to her new situation in life. "Well, I'll be glad to make you up some curtains. Jake and I bought some pretty chintz and some gingham and calico when we went to Lincoln."

"Chintz?" Fergus shut his eyes. He looked like he might be praying. Gracie thought that was sweet.

"If you really want to keep the atmosphere dim, perhaps the calico might be better because it's thicker. I could at least wash the windows and walls and scrub the floor. I could make a pretty cover for the pulpit, too. A little paint might not hurt, either. Jake is really handy about things like that. He's a tinsmith by trade, you know, and very good with his hands. Why, he and that nice Bart Ragsdale built a chicken coop in one single afternoon. Those chickens you brought seem quite happy there. They've been laying up a storm. Thank you very much for your kindness in bringing them to us. They're going to start building another room any day now, too—Jake and Mr. Ragsdale, not the chickens." She giggled nervously.

"Miss Gracie—"

"And that goat you brought over is just perfect. Now Charity has milk with all her meals."

Gracie paused to give the baby a hug. Fergus watched, looking thoroughly baffled.

"And you know something else, Mr. Fergus?"

After a fairly long period of silence, Fergus said, "No, Miss Gracie. Why don't you tell me."

This next part was touchy. Gracie licked her lips before she plunged ahead. "I think it would be wonderful if we were to have a choir here in Diabolito Lindo."

Fergus's eyes opened so wide, Gracie realized for the first time they were blue. Fancy that. Fergus had quite nice eyes, if one could get past his wrinkles and his whiskers to notice them.

"Do any of the men in town like to sing?"

"Sing?"

Laughing a little at the way Fergus had spoken the word—which was very strangely indeed—Gracie said, "Yes. You have that lovely piano in here. Wouldn't it be nice if we were to sing songs in church? At first Jake thought I should sing alone, but I think it would be much nicer if we were to get up a real choir."

Fergus had been standing behind the bar, looking at Gracie as if she'd lost her mind. Suddenly he snapped to attention, slapped his rag on the counter, and lifted his head. Over Gracie's bonnet, he hollered, "Anybody in here wanna join this here li'l gal's church choir?"

The silence that greeted Fergus's question was almost as thick as the tobacco smoke. Gracie gazed out over the men sitting at the various tables—in the middle of a glorious spring morning, for heaven's sake—and felt a small shaft of disappointment. Not a single, solitary one of them looked interested in her choir.

Her eyes drifted to the staircase and she saw the girl Jake had called Clara watching her. She stood next to a young man who had his arm slung over her shoulders. Gracie gave Clara the friendliest smile she had in her repertoire. She was disconcerted when Clara, after staring at her insolently for several seconds, tossed her head and deliberately pressed her bosom against her companion's arm. Then, rubbing her hand over the front of his trousers in an outrageously suggestive manner, she led him up the stairs.

Gracie knew she must look like a ripe tomato, she was blushing so hard. She couldn't recall ever having been rebuffed so thoroughly. Or so embarrassingly.

"I like to sing, Miss Gracie."

Shocked, Gracie turned away from her latest failure to determine who had spoken. She almost fainted when she realized it was Bart.

"You—you do?"

Bart scratched his shiny, scarred cheek. Gracie had to suppress a grimace. "Well, t'be honest, I ain't sung nothin' since the war, but we used to sing around the fire at night."

Straightening, trying to thrust the image of Clara and the young man—and what they'd undoubtedly gone upstairs to do—out of her mind, Gracie smiled at Bart. "Did you enjoy singing, Mr. Ragsdale? I think it would be lovely to have hymns in church."

"I did like it, yeah," Bart acknowledged, as if the truth of his declaration surprised him.

"Don't reckon I know no hymns, ma'am," another voice said.

Gracie looked at the speaker. She recognized him as one of the gentlemen propped up against the wall during last Sunday's service. And the Sunday service before that. *Mercy sakes.*

Remembering her manners, she said, "I beg your pardon, sir. I don't believe we know each other. I'm Gracie Trinidad, Preacher Jake's sister."

"Harley Newton, ma'am."

"Well, Mr. Newton, I should be happy to teach hymns to Jake's choir."

"It'd be Preacher Jake's choir?" another man asked suspiciously.

"Why, certainly. He's your minister, after all."

"I recollect my mama singin' to me when I was a young'un. She used to like them church songs," another fellow said.

The men who had been playing poker tucked their cards close to their chests and bent forward to consult among themselves. Gracie hoped they were discussing hymns. She heard Fergus sigh heavily.

"I'll hang this here sampler up above the pianner, Miss Gracie." He sounded resigned. Gracie recognized the tone of his voice from her childhood. Jake used to sound like that when, he claimed, she'd pestered him nigh unto death. No wonder Jake and Fergus were friends.

"Thank you, Mr. Fergus." She smiled brightly, feeling a little better. "I thought the motto was appropriate."

Fergus looked at the sampler's words for the first time. "Waste Not, Want Not," he read aloud.

He didn't sound as pleased as Gracie had hoped he would. In fact, this whole expedition wasn't going as she'd planned. If she hadn't been holding Charity, she might have wrung her hands. "Do you like it?" she asked anxiously.

With another gigantic sigh, Fergus said, "Yeah. Yeah, it's real nice, Miss Gracie."

"Do I got to, Preacher Jake?"

Chauncy Clifford peered at the jar of soup sitting on the table next to his bed. His face registered extreme doubt.

"Gracie made it especially for you, Cliff."

"She made it for me, did she?"

"Yup. Said you needed nourishment. Said chicken soup is supposed to be good for what ails you."

"It's good for gettin' shot in the leg?" Chauncy looked unhappy.

Jake shrugged. "Can't hurt, I reckon."

Even more unhappily, Chauncy said, "I don't know, Preacher Jake. I like your sister a whole lot, but Fergus told me about her cookin' already."

"She's getting better, Cliff. Anyway, what can anybody do to ruin a chicken?" Jake lifted the pretty cloth cover Gracie had made to decorate the jar lid and sniffed. Then he cleared his throat and choked out, "Well, I reckon I've heard onions are good for an ailing body, too."

"Lots of onions in that there soup of her'n, huh?"

Jake had to wipe away a tear that had leaked out of his left eye. "Yep." He coughed. "Cleared me right up. It's bound to be good for you."

After what seemed to be a gigantic internal struggle, Chauncy apparently resigned himself to his fate. "Well, I 'spect I'd better eat it. Reckon I like onions all right. Don't want to hurt your sister's feelings, Jake. She's about the purtiest thing we ever seen here in Diabolito Lindo."

At Chauncy's words, a surge of primitive rage exploded in Jake's middle. He knew his eyes were squinting up.

So, evidently, did Chauncy. He hurried to say, "Not that any o' the boys would ever do nothin' to her, Jake."

Not quite willing to relax yet, Jake said ominously, "That so?"

"Hell, yeah, Preacher Jake. There ain't a man in town'd do nothin' to any kin o' your'n. You know that."

Exhaling a deep breath, Jake commanded himself to calm down. "I hope so."

"Oh, hell, Jake. You know it's true. 'Specially not Miss Gracie. She's somethin' special, Miss Gracie is."

Jake managed a small grin. "She's something special, all right." He wasn't sure exactly what, but he knew she was something. And whatever it was, was special.

"I heard where she bought some o' them moccasins off'n Red Willie fer her kid. Red Willie says as to how she was right nice about it, too, sayin' as to how the kid can use 'em 'cause they're soft and she has trouble walkin'. Red Willie—well, I reckon he's used to white ladies screechin' or preachin' when they see a red Indian."

Finally relaxing into a full-fledged smile, Jake murmured, "I suppose he might be right there."

"She sings purty, too."

"Yes, she does."

"So I reckon I'll eat her soup. If it kills me, I 'spect it won't hurt no more'n another bullet." Chauncy sighed deeply.

"Speaking of your bullet, how about we pray a little, Cliff? Maybe it'll help Gracie's soup go down."

With a grin, Chauncy said, "Mebbe. Thanks, Preacher Jake. I don't know no other preacher who'd give a crap about the likes of us here in Diabolito Lindo."

A wave of sadness wafted through Jake. He feared Chauncy was right. "Well, I'm one of you. You know that."

Chauncy looked away, embarrassed. "I do know it, Jake. We all know it. And we appreciate it, too." He heaved a small, defeated-sounding sigh. "Wish I knew how you do it, too. I can't leave off the bottle no matter how hard I try."

Although he suspected his words would go unheeded—because the truth was both too simple and too difficult for most people to comprehend—he said, "You might want to stop trying, then."

Chauncy whipped his head around, shocked. "You mean you think I should keep drinkin'?"

"No, I don't mean that. What I mean is, trying doesn't do any good. The only thing that ever helped me was admitting the bottle was stronger than I was. I gave up."

"Yeah?" Chauncy looked unconvinced.

Jake wasn't surprised. He gave Chauncy a smile, a sort of melancholy ache building in his heart. "Maybe sometimes, when a man gets down as low as I got and gives up the struggle, a door will open in his heart and the good Lord can finally sneak in." He shook his head, feeling helpless. "I don't know how to explain it any better, Cliff. All I know is that's what happened to me."

"Well, it don't make no sense to me, Preacher Jake. No offense meant."

"No offense taken. And if it makes you feel any better, it doesn't make any sense to me, either. All I know is that's what happened."

"Sounds kinda strange."

"It was."

Ever since he'd felt his calling, Jake had adhered to one strict policy. He never pushed his message of redemption. He didn't push now. More than most folks, he knew that shoving messages down people's throats—no matter how important the messages were—did little good, and probably did harm. The sweet Lord above knew such tactics hadn't done him any good.

Now he knelt beside Chauncy Clifford's bed and prayed with the gun-shot man, asking God to bless every one of the sinners in Diabolito Lindo and keep them safe. He lingered over his pleas for Chauncy's renewed health.

When he rose from his knees, he smiled. "You going to make it, Cliff?"

"Reckon I am, Preacher. If'n Miss Gracie's soup don't kill me."

Laughing, Jake said, "It won't kill you, Cliff. Hell, I've been eating her cooking for a month now, and I'm still alive." He added, with little conviction, "She's getting better at it."

Chauncy grunted.

When Jake strode back to his own house, his heart felt light, and his step was eager. It seemed perfectly astonishing to him that he should have become accustomed to the presence of those two females so quickly that he didn't like to be away from them for any length of time. Now, every time he left his tiny abode, he counted the minutes until he could return.

His life was so pleasant with Gracie in it. The little girl who used to torment and bedevil him until he thought he'd go crazy had actually grown up to be a delightful companion, even if she couldn't cook worth a heap of cow patties. She still chattered away like a runaway wagon, but she'd learned enough sense to be quiet when he was working on his sermons, trying to memorize Bible verses, or writing to bereaved relatives.

During those quiet times she sewed tranquilly—she'd made up several pretty samplers and embroidered dresses and things for the baby—or read the books she'd brought with her from St. Louis. Sometimes she and Charity worked outside in the tiny kitchen garden she'd planted. Jake often found himself lonely during those periods. A couple of times he'd even left off his sermon writing to go outside and join his girls. He missed them when they weren't around.

Charity seemed to be warming up to him, too. He still suspected there was more to the baby's unnatural wariness than Gracie had told him, but he didn't probe. The same understanding that prevented him from hectoring his flock about their dissolute habits also kept him from prying into matters with which Gracie didn't yet trust him.

He expected she'd tell him Charity's story one of these days. Until then, he tried to be even-tempered, friendly, and unobtrusive around the little girl. His strategy-that-was-no-strategy seemed to be paying off, too. Charity had actually taken her wooden spindle from him this morning when he'd offered it, instead of crumpling up on the floor and covering her head with her chubby arms.

He opened the door, eager to hear one of Gracie's cheery greetings, only to be met by silence. He stepped into his house, puzzled. "Gracie?"

Nothing.

Uneasy, he strode through the three rooms, looking right and left. He knew it was no use. If Gracie were inside, she'd have answered him; there was no way she wouldn't have heard him. He peeked into the backyard to see if she and Charity were working in the garden. They weren't, and he went back inside.

"Aw, hell."

Jake stood in the room that served as parlor and dining room and scratched his head, frowning. Now where in God's name had she got herself off to? He'd kill her with his bare hands if she'd walked up to the creek without him.

"Not even Gracie could be that stupid."

He said the words aloud in order to make himself feel better. They didn't work. He knew her too well. Just because they'd almost been murdered by Miguel and his gang at the creek didn't mean Gracie wouldn't go back there alone if she took a fancy to.

"Damn it all to hell and back again."

Furious, Jake stomped across the road, tramped up the hill, and marched through the woods to the creek.

No Gracie. Thank God. He was relieved. And mad as hell. He removed his hat and raked a hand through his hair. Where in blazes else could she have gone off to? A thought occurred to him, and he said, "No. She wouldn't have."

Then he recalled her saying how well that sampler he'd framed for her would look in his church, and muttered, "Aw, shit."

And, cramming his hat onto his head, he loped back into the woods, down the hill, and through the swirling dust to the Devil's Last Stop saloon.

"That was perfectly lovely, gentlemen."

Gracie didn't figure a tiny fib would be inappropriate

under the circumstances. They were all working awfully hard, and they were definitely improving. "Would you like to try it one more time? Then I have to get home and start supper."

"One more time'd be good, Miss Gracie," Bart said.

Beaming at him, Gracie decided that her mother, for all her weakness of character, had been right about music. Bart looked almost cuddly under the influence of the beautiful hymn they'd been singing for the past half hour or so. It was difficult for her to reconcile this sweet man with the desperado she'd met on her first Sunday morning in Diabolito Lindo.

"Yeah, let's try it once more. That there's a pretty song."

"Yes, indeed. 'The Old Rugged Cross' is a beautiful old tune. I'm glad you like it so well."

"Yes, ma'am." Harley Newton nodded several times for emphasis. "I like it real swell."

"And you have a perfectly splendid bass voice, too, Mr. Newton. You hold the bottom line very well."

Harley blushed like a schoolboy and had to suffer the teasing of his friends. He was pleased, though. Gracie could tell.

So she played the introductory chords of the hymn. This time her raggedy choir all started at the same time. And on the same relative note, what's more. She felt quite encouraged, particularly since Charity, sitting next to her on the piano bench, hadn't folded up once since the several large, intimidating men had gathered around them. In fact, when the men began to sing this time, Charity did, too. Gracie almost cried.

"What in the name of holy hell is going on in here, Fergus?"

Jake was mad enough to spit railroad spikes, but he didn't shout because he was too confused. And he didn't want to scare Charity, who seemed to be enjoying herself over there next to Gracie on the piano bench.

Fergus stood behind his bar, under the painting of the naked lady, and continued wiping his glass as if his saloon weren't filled to the peeling plaster ceiling with church music. "Choir practice," he said phlegmatically.

"Choir—" Jake gulped in a huge breath, then expelled it with a cough when his lungs objected to the tobacco smoke.

"Miss Gracie come in and brung me a sampler. Then she got some of the boys together." Fergus jerked his head toward the piano. "Fixin' herself up a choir, she says. Fer your church."

Jake couldn't recall ever having heard Fergus's voice sound so strange. He hardly blamed him. Remembering both his vocation and a promise he'd made to himself years before not to blurt things out while angry or befuddled, he shut his eyes and prayed for a moment before he opened his mouth to speak again.

Then he said, "She really did it, huh?"

"She really did it."

Pinning his best friend with a searching look, Jake asked, "You mind, Fergus?"

After a small pause, Fergus said, "Don't reckon I do."

"You sure?"

Fergus released the biggest sigh Jake had ever heard. "Naw, I don't mind. Even if I did, ain't nothin' I could do about it. Look at them fellers, Jake."

Jake looked at the men and then back at Fergus.

"You gonna tell 'em they can't sing with your sister? I sure as hell ain't." Fergus sounded somewhat peevish.

Jake eyed the men again. This time, he noticed their expressions. They looked happy as they warbled away to Gracie's piano playing. He couldn't recall seeing so many members of his congregation looking happy at the same time in the same place before. He took off his hat and scratched his head.

"By God, I think they like singing, Fergus."

"Seem to."

"I thought she was crazy when she suggested a choir."

"So'd I."

"Reckon she wasn't."

"Reckon not."

"Who'd have thought it?"

Fergus only shrugged.

When Gracie and her choir hit the final note of the song—more or less together and quite tunefully—Jake could hear her happy sigh from where he stood. After exchanging one more look with Fergus, he walked over to the piano.

"That sounded real pretty, boys."

The men all turned to greet him. If he didn't feel so odd about the whole thing, he might have been tempted to laugh. They looked like a herd of happy puppy dogs.

"Did you hear them, Jake?" Gracie asked, obviously pleased as punch. "Weren't they wonderful?"

Wonderful wasn't the first word that had sprung to Jake's mind when he'd heard the hymn, but he wasn't about to argue with her. "It sounded real good. Really very good."

His attention had been on Gracie. Now he looked down at Charity and was amazed to find her smiling at him. He smiled back and said, "Hi, there, Charity. Did you sing, too?"

His amazement trebled when, after a tiny hesitation, the little girl nodded. Then she turned away and buried her head in Gracie's skirt. Jake saw tears in Gracie's eyes when she picked the baby up and cooed to her and told her what a brave, good girl she was. Jake didn't blame her; he was a bit choked up himself.

"How'd we sound, Preacher Jake? Did it sound good?" Bart looked at him, eager as any five-year-old.

"It sounded real good, Bart."

Gracie's ramshackle choir slapped each other on their backs and chortled gleefully. Jake couldn't remember the last time he'd seen these men look so pleased with themselves.

"Kin we practice again tomorrow, Miss Gracie?"

"I expect we can, Mr. Newton. If it's all right with Mr. Fergus."

They all looked expectantly toward the bar. Fergus nodded with what looked to Jake more like surrender than agreement. He knew just how Fergus felt. Gracie's choir members thanked him happily. Then they thanked Gracie.

Then they thanked Jake. It took another ten minutes or so before Jake could herd his womenfolk out of the saloon and head off toward home.

She'd done it. By God, Gracie had done it; she'd gone and organized herself a choir. He ate his supper that night without a single thought for its deficiencies.

7

THE NEXT MORNING, Gracie was thoughtful as she took another bite of her breakfast biscuit. This biscuit wasn't quite as wretched as the results of her prior forays into the art of biscuit making had been, but she had to acknowledge it wasn't great. If one allowed the sausage gravy to soak in long enough, she supposed it wouldn't break anybody's teeth. The gravy itself was kind of tasty. Floury, maybe; a little gummy perhaps; but tasty for all that.

"At least you can't offer to take these to the soldiers at Fort Stanton to use as cannonballs, Jake," she murmured.

"You're getting better, Gracie," Jake said kindly as he sawed off another piece of biscuit and gravy with his hunting knife.

She chuffed impatiently. "It seems to me as though cooking should be one of the simpler things to do in life. I mean, I must be the only person in the world who can't make a decent biscuit. Even *men* make biscuits."

Jake chuckled and took a sip of coffee. Gracie had never

drunk coffee at home, preferring tea as a rule. Until she dared write anybody in St. Louis, however, such gentle practices as tea drinking would just have to remain a fond memory. She knew for a fact that her coffee this morning tasted like axle grease. She didn't know how Jake could stand it.

"Now how do you know that men can make biscuits, Gracie? I can't."

"Well, *you* might not be able to, but I've read plenty of books about cattle drives and so forth, and the cooks on the chuck wagons are always men."

"Dime novels again?"

Gracie began clearing off the table and mumbled, "Yes."

"You might consider serving tortillas, Gracie. They're pretty tasty, and you can buy 'em from Old Man Ramirez."

"I'm sure tortillas are fine in their place, Jake, but I aim to civilize this place. And by gum, biscuits are more civilized than tortillas." She considered the biscuit residing on her plate and honesty compelled her to amend her vehement declaration. "At least they are if a body can make them right."

"Dime novels and biscuits. Oh, my." Jake chuckled again.

Gracie decided it would be imprudent to voice her indignation at his laughing at her. She resolved to broach another subject that had been nagging at her instead.

"Jake, do you suppose Clara would like to attend church services? Maybe join the choir?"

"Clara?" Jake looked up from his breakfast, puzzled. "Who's Cla— Oh. You mean the girl at Fergus's?" He frowned.

"Yes. It occurred to me yesterday that she might enjoy the company of another woman. After all, it can't be easy for her to be doing—" Embarrassment overtook her and Gracie felt herself blush. Squaring her shoulders and telling herself to stop being prudish, that Clara was simply one more poor creature in the world who needed her, she went on. "It can't be easy for her to do what she has to do for a living and never have another female to talk to."

She'd been scraping plates and hadn't looked at Jake until

now. When she glanced over her shoulder, she found him gazing at her with an extremely skeptical expression on his face.

"You don't think so?" She was disappointed.

After her resounding success with the choir yesterday, a crusading zeal had settled into Gracie's heart, and the urge to help the poor scarlet Clara had attacked her with a vengeance. She wanted to do it: to make a friend of her, to lead her away from the path of wickedness and into the light. Besides, this wouldn't require any effort on Jake's part. It wasn't at all like the time she'd made him rescue the puppies or the mule or the raccoon or the little Osborne boy. This was something Gracie could do all on her own.

"Well . . ." Jake took another sip of coffee and sat back in the creaky, straight-backed chair he used at mealtime. "I'm not sure, Gracie. What makes you think she'd appreciate your interference?"

Interference? Gracie blinked at him, not having considered her proposed trek as being in the nature of interference. "I don't mean it that way, Jake," she assured him.

"No?"

"Of course not. I just wondered if she'd like a friend, is all."

"And you think she'd like you to offer her your friendship?"

"Well, I don't know why not. After all, maybe if we become friends, she'll see that she doesn't have to sell herself for a living anymore."

"What do you propose she do instead?"

"*I* don't know, Jake! I'm sure there are lots of things that need doing in this town." Recalling the fragrance of her new choir as they'd gathered around the piano yesterday, she muttered, "Laundry, for one."

"Hmmm."

He didn't sound convinced. Nor did he sound as if he believed her. Gracie's evangelical spirit, never far from the surface, bubbled over. She wagged her finger at him.

"Why, Jake Molloy, I'd like to know what kind of

preacher you think you are, if you condone that woman's occupation."

"I never said I condoned it, Gracie."

"Well, then," she said, and didn't know what to say next, his gentle tone having taken the wind out of her sails.

"What I said was that I don't judge her for it. If that's what she has to do to put food in her mouth, I'm not going to tell her she's bad for doing it."

Patience had never been one of Gracie's primary virtues. It snapped now in the face of what looked to her like Jake's abdication of his responsibility as a man of God. "Well, I just like that! You sure don't mind preaching at the men in this town of yours. What about the women? Woman, I mean. That poor female's being exploited, Jake! What she does to put food in her mouth is demeaning to herself and to all women! It should be outlawed!"

"I reckon it is in a lot of places, Gracie."

"It should be here, too."

Jake said "Hmmm" again, and lifted his hands in a gesture betokening his inability—or unwillingness—to agree or disagree.

"You mean you won't go with me to talk to her?"

"Sorry, Gracie. You're on your own this time."

She sensed she couldn't budge him, and was grumpy about it. Gracie couldn't recall Jake ever being so reluctant to take up the cudgel of righteousness with her. Actually, she amended, she couldn't recall herself ever being unable to persuade him into it. She guessed he'd grown stubborn over the years.

"Well, if you don't think it's important to set that poor woman straight, I certainly do, Jake Molloy."

With a lopsided grin, Jake said, "Somehow that doesn't surprise me much."

Gracie harrumphed. Then she went over to the bed to see if Charity had awakened yet. She had, so Gracie scooped her up, sponged her off, put on a pretty new dress she'd just made up for her out of a sprightly yellow calico, brushed her shiny brown hair, and sat her in the new raised seat Jake had fixed up for her. Then she brought over the biscuit she'd been soaking in milk and began to feed her breakfast.

"We're going to visit your Uncle Fergus this morning, Charity, and see if we can have a chat with a lady named Clara. Will you like that?"

As Jake watched, Charity nodded. He smiled. Every day, it seemed the little girl was allowing another tiny shred of her reserve to fall away, and he hoped she'd eventually trust him enough to let him hold her hand when they walked up to the creek. He remembered another little girl's hand in his and how good it had felt to know she trusted him.

He sure couldn't work up much enthusiasm for Gracie's mission this morning, however, even though he knew better than to argue with her anymore about it. It had taken him long enough, but he'd finally learned that it did people more good to discover their own lessons than to tell them anything. And if Clara responded to Gracie's gesture of goodwill the way Gracie hoped she would, Jake would be every bit as happy about it as Gracie was sure to be.

Since he'd had a good deal more experience with the world and with sinners than Gracie, however, God save him, he expected she'd be disappointed. He wished he could spare her, knew he couldn't, and felt kind of sad about it.

She didn't bother speaking to him again as she prepared herself and the baby for their assault on sin. He watched her bustle about, certain of the righteousness of her mission, and remembered when he'd been so sure of things. It seemed a lifetime ago. He guessed it was. With a sigh, he went to his desk and picked up his Bible.

"I'll be here, writing tomorrow's sermon, Gracie. Let me know how your mission prospers."

He heard her say, "Humph. Some ministers seem to pick and choose their targets, don't they, Charity?" as she sailed out the door.

He shook his head and decided he could use a brief chat with God before he tackled his sermon, so he got down on his knees and prayed. Most of his prayers were for Gracie. And Clara.

*   *   *

Gracie arrived at the Devil's Last Stop a good twenty minutes before choir practice was set to begin. She'd let the men choose the time for practice, since she wasn't sure what hours prevailed in a business of this nature. They'd selected a morning hour. As Harley Newton had phrased it, "Better get us whilst we're all still standin', Miss Gracie." Gracie hadn't argued.

"Good morning, Mr. Fergus," she called out cheerily when she pushed through the swinging doors. Then she had to stop and blink several times in order to accustom herself to the dismal atmosphere inside the saloon. She couldn't understand what men found so appealing about not being able to see anything.

"Mornin', Miss Gracie. You're early." Fergus didn't sound especially pleased about it, either.

His voice hadn't come from the bar, where Gracie had aimed her greeting. Turning her head, she perceived his vague form over by the staircase, where he appeared to be dusting the banister rails.

Consoling herself with the knowledge that she was on a reforming mission, Gracie bucked up and said, "I know, Mr. Fergus. I wondered if it would be possible for me to speak with Miss Clara for a moment or two before rehearsal begins."

Fergus looked blank for a moment. "You wanna talk to Clara?"

"If possible." Gracie nodded firmly. In truth, she felt quite nervous about this. She'd never tried to redeem a prostitute before. She wasn't altogether sure how to go about it.

"Well . . ." Fergus murmured, and got no further.

"What you wan'?" a woman's husky voice asked from the far end of the bar.

Surprised, Gracie turned again and realized Clara was sitting there dressed in a ragged wrapper. Her face was puffy-eyed and she appeared blowsy. Her hair was a mess. She looked as if she'd just risen from bed—somebody's bed. Gracie refused to speculate further. She cradled a cup of something in her hands. Gracie hoped it was coffee.

"Good morning," she said cheerfully.

"What you wan'?" Clara repeated, not at all cheerful.

Although Gracie wasn't sure how she had expected to be welcomed by the fallen woman, she hadn't expected the blatant hostility Clara exuded. Even Charity felt the woman's antagonism. She scrunched down in Gracie's arms, a reaction she generally reserved for the male of the species.

Telling herself that Clara's very soul might be at stake here, Gracie braced herself and strolled over to where she sat in her solitary state on a barstool.

"Good morning," she said. "My name is Gracie Trinidad, Preacher Jake's sister."

"I know who you are." Clara looked her up and down; Gracie got the distinct impression that she didn't like what she saw. "What you wan'?"

Gracie cleared her throat. Suddenly she didn't feel quite so brave. "I—I just wondered if you'd like to join us for church services Sunday morning."

For a good thirty seconds, Clara said nothing. To Gracie, it felt like hours. Then the prostitute took another sip of whatever was in her cup, propped her elbows on the bar, directed her attention at the wall, and said, "No."

No? Just *no?* Gracie opened her mouth, shut it because she wasn't sure what to say, and then told herself to stop being timid. Plunking herself down on the stool next to Clara—which earned her an irritated scowl—she asked, "But why not? Wouldn't you like to hear my brother preach?"

After another few seconds—Clara said more with silence than anybody Gracie'd ever met—she said "No" again.

"Why not? Jake's a wonderful preacher. Why, the men in town love him."

Gracie saw Clara's lips lift in a snide smile and wondered what it meant.

Then the girl turned her head fractionally and said, "I'm Catholic."

"Oh." Gracie guessed that put a different slant on things.

"I didn't know that. Do you go to Catholic services then?"

"No."

Oh, good grief. The woman was being deliberately provoking, and Gracie didn't appreciate it. "Well, then, why don't you join Jake's church? Or at least the choir. Since you live here anyway, it might be fun. I—I'd enjoy having another woman to talk to." At least she thought she would. At the moment, Gracie wasn't at all sure about Clara.

Suddenly Clara turned on her stool to face Gracie. She paid not the least heed to Charity, who was trying her best to hide in Gracie's armpit, but stabbed Gracie on the knee with a needlelike fingernail.

"Listen, lady, I don' like you. I don' wanna join your brother's church. I don' wanna sing in no choir. I don' wan' nothing to do with you or him. You unnerstand?"

Gracie understood. Very well indeed. In a small voice, she stammered, "But—but, I'm only trying to help you."

Clara lifted insolence to a fine art. She turned it on Gracie, full bore. "I don' wan' your help. I don' need your help." Her gaze raked Gracie again, her expression one of utter contempt. "You come prancin' in here like some gran' lady with your baby an' your fine ways and think you better than me. You act like some kinda queen or somethin'. Well, you not better than me. You go 'way and leave me 'lone. I don' like you."

"Oh, but I didn't mean—"

"You did, too," Clara said flatly. "Why you think I need your church? You gon' save my soul?" She put her hand to her breast and fluttered her eyelashes. "'Cause I'm a sinner-lady? 'Cause I sleep with lotsa men?" She turned toward her coffee cup again and ended with a concise "Shit."

Utterly crushed, Gracie couldn't even move for several seconds. She stared at the back of Clara's head, sick at heart. And humiliated. And—worse than anything else—having been put firmly and solidly in her place. Clara's interpretation of Gracie's mission made it seem like an act of pompous arrogance. Gracie hadn't meant it as such.

Finally finding the wherewithal to climb down from the

barstool, Gracie gulped and blinked several times. So much for her noble motives. Jake had been right. Again. She went over and sat on the piano bench, bowed her head, and tried not to cry.

She watched miserably as Clara sauntered past her and on up the stairs. She still felt awful ten minutes later when her choir showed up.

Gracie, Charity, and Jake lounged beside the creek. The afternoon was beautiful and serene, as peaceful as Eden must have been, before those fools began eating apples. The air buzzed with insects and was filled with birdsong. If he didn't know better, Jake would never consider even the possibility of outlaws or bandits invading the placid glen.

The stream sounded happy as it babbled along, and Jake felt happy, too. In fact, his level of contentment astonished him. Although he'd undergone a remarkable transformation several years ago, internal devils still plagued him more often than not. He wasn't sure where those pesky devils had got themselves off to today, but they weren't tormenting him at all. He appreciated their consideration.

He leaned against a big, graceful cottonwood. He and Gracie had taken off their shoes and stockings and were cooling their feet in the water. Gracie had pointed out polliwogs under the water's surface to Charity, and now the little girl lay on her tummy, giggling, while she tried to touch the wiggly creatures with her tiny fingers as they darted about. Jake hadn't heard her giggle before. The gleeful sound made him smile.

"Powwywah," she said, and giggled again.

"Those are polliwogs, all right, Charity," Jake said softly, hoping his deep voice wouldn't startle her and spoil her fun.

It didn't seem to. She just giggled again and repeated, "Powwywah."

Gracie and Jake had already determined that the word *polliwog* tickled Charity's funny bone. Until today, Jake hadn't even known she possessed one. He was pleased to learn that she did.

"She talks real well, Gracie. I didn't know kids that young could talk."

"I think girls generally learn to talk earlier than boys."

"Figures. And once they start, they never seem to stop, either." Jake smiled at Gracie, expecting his teasing comment to draw one of her quick retorts. It didn't.

In fact, Gracie seemed rather subdued. Jake hoped her choir hadn't misbehaved. Or, worse, not shown up. Yet she'd indicated the practice had been successful. Maybe she was just sensitive and didn't want to tell him if the boys had been profane or drunk—or had lost interest.

"Anything the matter, Gracie?" He tried to sound casual, watching her face as she gazed pensively at her daughter.

She dipped her head slightly in a gesture speaking of a degree of defeat. Jake didn't like seeing his happy-go-lucky Gracie defeated, and couldn't recall seeing her thus before today. As far as he could remember, she never gave up until she'd whipped whatever goal she was aiming for into submission—or made him do it for her. Something in him ached briefly, and he wanted to take her in his arms, hold her close, and kiss her unhappiness away. He didn't do anything so clearly idiotic, of course.

After a moment, she said, "You were right, Jake."

Well, that was a first. Jake didn't consider himself to be right very often. "About what?"

"About Clara."

"Oh." He understood now, and the urge to hug Gracie grew. Poor Gracie. No wonder she seemed so downcast. She wasn't used to failing in her attempts to rescue people. "Clara wasn't interested in your offer of friendship, huh?"

To his dismay, a silvery tear crept down her cheek. She wiped it away, obviously embarrassed. "It was worse than that, Jake."

"Worse how?"

Gracie took a big breath. "She said she didn't like me. She said that she didn't want me coming in there, acting better than her and telling her how to live." She groped in her pocket. Since he knew she was never prepared for anything, Jake handed her his bandanna and she blew her nose. "But I didn't mean it that way, Jake. I didn't!"

"No?" Even though he expected he was making a big mistake, Jake put a comforting hand on her back. She looked so small and disconsolate, and her pretty face was all pink with trying not to cry, and he couldn't seem to help himself.

"No."

Poor little Gracie. In Jake's experience, she'd never wished another human being ill in her life. He thought it was pretty mean of Clara to have rebuffed her so soundly, even though he understood why she'd done it.

"I'm sorry, Gracie."

Shaking her head impatiently, Gracie said, "You told me what would happen, Jake. I didn't listen, as usual."

"It's all right. You meant well."

She lifted her hands and dropped them in her lap. Jake read anger, hurt, and frustration in the gesture. "But I didn't *do* well, Jake. All I did was insult her. I didn't mean to insult her. Honest, I didn't."

Unable to hold back another second longer, Jake pulled Gracie over to his side and slipped his arm around her. Her head settled onto his shoulder and she sighed deeply. Trying to keep his mind on Gracie's despondency instead of on her soft breast pressing into his ribs, he hesitated for a few seconds.

Then he said, "Please don't get mad at me, Gracie, but I think you're still dealing with life in terms of St. Louis."

"I am not!" She sounded more hurt than angry.

For several more seconds, Jake thought about how to say what he meant. He didn't want to hurt Gracie's feelings any more than they'd been hurt already.

"Well, maybe you could look at the situation this way. Suppose somebody from back East moved into St. Louis, next to where you lived. And suppose that person was from Beacon Hill or New York City or someplace really, really rich. Maybe she seemed to you to be even a little snooty, and was used to things being a certain way. Suppose that person didn't hold with ladies teaching school, but believed the only people fit to teach were men, and that women who taught school weren't ladies."

"Oh, but Jake . . ."

"Just supposing now, Gracie. I know the two professions—yours and Clara's—seem as different as night and day to you, but other people might not look at it that way. Why, it wasn't too long ago that the very thought of a woman voting made people laugh out loud. Nowadays, the suffrage movement is going great guns. From what I hear, Wyoming Territory's even given women the vote. Yet there are still people—men and women—who consider a woman voting nigh as sinful as whoring—er—doing what Clara does."

Gracie didn't say anything. Jake hoped it hadn't offended her. For at least two or three minutes they sat in silence, Gracie cradled against him, Jake wishing they could stay here forever, just like this.

He figured that his fumbling attempts to explain why Clara might have taken exception to her benevolence had disgusted Gracie into silence. He was just wondering why she hadn't pulled away from his embrace in a snit when she finally spoke again.

"You mean Clara thinks I asked her to come to church because I look down on her?"

"I expect that's exactly what she thought."

In a very small voice, Gracie asked, "Is that what you think, too, Jake?"

He considered softening his answer, but decided against it. If Gracie deserved anything, he reckoned she deserved his honesty. "Well—yes."

To his horror, Gracie hiccuped three times, then turned to press her face against his shirtfront and began to cry. "I didn't mean it, Jake! I swear I didn't mean it that way! Oh, why can't I ever learn to mind my own business?"

"Shhh. Shhh. It's all right, Gracie. You didn't do any harm. You were trying to help." In spite of his dismay at having her weeping in his arms, he smiled. Gracie had never been able to mind her own business. Ever.

"But I didn't help! I made that poor girl think I think she's dirt, and I didn't mean it that way, Jake! I didn't!"

Jake had never held a sobbing woman before. He wasn't altogether sure what to do. But this woman was Gracie, his own darling Gracie, and he closed his arms around her, buried his face in her soft golden curls, and whispered, "It's all right, Gracie. It's all right, sweetheart. Everything will be all right."

He wasn't sure how long she cried, or how long he continued to hold her after she quit sobbing. All of a sudden, however, he realized that Charity had stopped playing. When he lifted his head from the heavenly cushion of Gracie's curls, it was to encounter two of the largest, most horrified brown eyes he'd ever beheld.

Oh, criminy. He'd forgotten all about the kid and her fear of men. Although he didn't know for sure, he had a gut-deep feeling that Charity believed Gracie was crying because he'd hurt her. Unsure what to do, Jake put every gentle impulse he could come up with into his smile. Then, although it nearly killed him to release Gracie, he held out one hand to the baby.

"Charity?" he said as quietly and in as friendly a manner as he could. "You want to come over here and join us? Your mama's a little upset right now. She'll be just fine in a minute. I think she could use one of your hugs, too."

His words had a startling effect on Gracie. She cried, "Oh, my Lord, how could I?" and pushed herself away from Jake's chest. He was surprised by how desolate he felt—and she'd only been in his arms for a few minutes.

"Bring her here, Gracie, and maybe she'll realize you're not trying to get away from me."

Gracie shot him a startled glance. "You're right," she said, obviously shocked by his acute perception of the situation. "Of course, you're right."

Jake was proud of her when, in an instant, Gracie chucked her own problems aside. With her attention focused entirely on the baby, she said, "Come here, Charity honey. Your Uncle Jake will hold us both for a minute."

She turned to him. "Do you mind, Jake?"

Mind? Jake considered telling her he'd gladly hold the two of them for the rest of their natural lives, but decided he'd better not. Instead he said, "I don't mind at all," and that was the truth, too.

When Gracie held out her arms, Charity crawled into them as if they were her personal refuge from life's storms. Then Gracie settled back into Jake's embrace again, and the three of them sat under the big cottonwood tree for a long, long time.

After a few minutes, Charity leaned over from her perch in Gracie's lap and resumed dangling her fingers in the water, playing with the polliwogs. Her concentration seemed quite remarkable to Jake, who'd always understood very small children to be on the order of flibbertigibbets, always dashing here and there and wearing their parents out with their energy. Not Charity.

They saw a hummingbird chase a finch away from a long stalk of Indian paintbrush, then watched, fascinated, as the tiny bird's long beak sipped nectar from the flower's bright scarlet cups. They saw a fish leap from the stream and splash back into the water, its shimmering, scaly body shooting silver streaks under the sun's reflective rays. A dragonfly glimmered peacock-blue in the sunlight and looked like a mobile jewel as it darted here and there above the water, which itself sparkled like diamonds in the late afternoon.

Jake didn't know how long they relaxed there in the beautiful spring day beside the creek, Charity on Gracie's lap and Gracie in Jake's arms. He only knew it wasn't long enough.

Gracie had never considered herself particularly vain. She knew she wasn't the most beautiful woman in the world; nor was she the smartest. She sure as check wasn't the world's best cook.

Until her encounter with Clara, however, she'd never doubted her own motives. She'd always tried to do the right thing. She'd never paused to consider how she knew what the right thing was; she'd always just *known*.

She didn't know any longer. Clara's rebuff had stung. What had stung even more were Jake's words. No. What had really stung was knowing Jake's words to be the truth. She *did* think she was better than Clara. Everything she'd ever been taught in her life pointed out to Gracie that her ways were the right ways and that people who didn't conform to her ways were wrong. Particularly those like Clara, who performed work Gracie considered not merely beneath her, but downright sinful.

But Jake, in his gentle, compassionate way—and in remarkably few words—had hashed up everything Gracie had ever known as "right" and served it back to her as the provincial, narrow-minded dish of opinions it truly was.

For the first time in her life, Gracie felt properly humbled. She hoped the feeling would last, not because it felt good; it didn't. She hoped it would last because she realized she had a lot to learn, and not just about her new home. She had a lot to learn about life.

If what Aunt Lizzy had told her was true, Jake had transformed his life from one of—of—well, Gracie didn't know from what, although if he'd truly killed a man, it had been pretty bad. But he'd changed and turned his life around.

Today Jake was the best man Gracie had ever known. From the kindhearted, impatient boy she'd loved in her childhood, he'd grown into a man possessed of a wisdom and an understanding of his fellows that left Gracie breathless.

She loved him today, too, but in an entirely different way from her childhood adoration. When he'd held her in his arms, she'd wanted to stay in them forever.

The problem with the love she had for him now was that she knew she didn't deserve him. She aimed to, though. Somehow, some way, she aimed to. When the time came to tell Jake the truth about everything, Gracie swore to herself that she'd have earned his love.

8

AFTER GRACIE AND Charity retired to their bed that night, Jake's mood remained unsettled. He'd stepped over an invisible boundary today, and in many ways he was sorry. The problem as he saw it was that in many other ways, he wasn't sorry at all.

He never should have touched Gracie. He knew it with a certainty that ate into his guts like acid. Yet he wasn't sure he'd ever sufficiently regret having held her and comforted her and felt her delicious body pressing against him. After having had a tiny taste of what Gracie had to offer, he wanted more. In fact, at this moment, Jake hungered for Gracie in a way he hadn't known was possible, one that far surpassed mere physical desire.

God save him, he loved her. Not the way he used to love her when they were kids—as a pesky, charming sister. He loved her today the way a man, if he was very lucky, loved a woman. He'd never expected to love a woman this way. He'd believed himself incapable of it.

Lord, Lord, why did he have to learn the lesson now, when there was no way in the world to express his love or assuage his hunger? With a deep sigh, Jake reminded himself that God's ways were mysterious to poor sinners like him who fumbled around blindly here on earth.

Of course, if she hadn't talked him into lying for her in the first place . . . But no. Thoughts of that nature led nowhere. He *had* lied for her, and now he had to live with the consequences. Not for the first time since Gracie and Charity had come to live with him, he got on his knees, propped his elbows on his chair, pressed his fists to his forehead, and prayed. Hard.

"What are you doing, Jake?"

Gracie's husky voice drizzled into Jake's consciousness like an extension of his prayer. He didn't know how long he'd been meditating, but when he opened his eyes, he found her staring down at him. She looked tousled and sleepy and more enchanting than a woman had any right to look—especially this woman. Especially given the state of his body's hunger and his soul's thirst.

In spite of, or perhaps because of, his violent physical reaction to her nearness, Jake grinned and mentally tipped his hat to God. Gracie's presence in his life and in his house was a test, just as he'd known it would be—a powerful test. Jake could appreciate the humor in it, even if it was hard on a man.

"I was praying, Gracie."

She looked apologetic. "I didn't mean to interrupt you. I just needed to use the—you know. And I forgot to bring in the chamber pot after I washed it."

Even by the light of the one small candle, Jake could see her cheeks darken as she blushed.

"I'll walk you outside, Gracie."

"Oh, please, you don't have to. Unless it's dangerous. Will some desperado try to shoot me?"

She gave him a saucy look. He expected it was to counteract her embarrassment about admitting having to use the privy, although it sent a savage urge to ravish her through him. He suppressed it rigidly.

Chuckling softly, Jake got up from his knees. He towered over her—his little Gracie. She had a big heart in spite of her tiny stature. Too bad Clara had driven a spike through it today. "I don't expect so. It's pretty quiet out tonight. I'll just tag along to make sure you don't fall in."

She giggled, and everything in Jake's nether regions clenched. He shook his head and picked up the candle, wondering if he would survive this test of Gracie's presence in his house with his mind intact.

He opened the door for her to precede him and then almost knocked her flat as she stopped stock-still in front of him. At first he thought she'd been frightened by something.

Then she whispered in a small, amazed voice, "Oh, Jake, it's magnificent."

She stared at the sky spread above them like black velvet sprinkled with glass chips, and Jake recalled the first time he'd seen one of these ink-and-sparkle territorial skies. He didn't wonder at Gracie's reaction.

"It's pretty awe-inspiring, all right."

Actually, he was looking at her when he said it, and it took a good deal of effort for him to pry his gaze away from her uptilted face, soft with wonder. Hers was the purest, most perfect face Jake had ever seen. She wasn't faultless, his little Gracie; far from it. For some reason Jake couldn't fathom, though, she was the first female he'd ever loved; he expected she'd be the last.

His fingers clamped more tightly around the candle holder, and he managed to rip his gaze from Gracie's face and direct it at God's heaven. He prayed some more.

Gracie couldn't seem to pull her attention away from the sky. "I don't think I'll ever be able to drink my fill of that sky, Jake. I've never seen anything like it."

Jake wasn't surprised. Except for his candle, the only light anywhere around them came from up there, from what seemed like millions of brilliant stars and a shimmering quicksilver moon. It was almost new, that moon, and its tiny crescent glowed like something magic. The new moon's glow wasn't enough to dim the stars, though; they had the entire unimpeded firmament in which to twinkle, and they did.

"Why does it look like that, Jake? I've never seen a sky look like that before."

"I don't reckon you have, Gracie. You've always lived in a city. I think the city lights and the smoke from chimneys and so forth get in the way of the stars and the moon."

"Really?"

It sounded as though she was having trouble finding her voice. Jake understood; he'd felt like that before. The first time he'd felt real reverence in the presence of nature was when he'd come to the Territory and seen his first night sky. Sober. Drunk, he'd never noticed.

"Is this what made you turn to God, Jake? This amazing sky? It's enough to do it, all right."

"'Fraid not, Gracie. It wasn't anything as noble as the infinite heavens that made me realize I needed God's help, believe me."

Laughing softly, Jake took her arm. Only five minutes before, he'd have been afraid to touch her. His interrupted prayer and his voyage outside and into the presence of infinity seemed to have renewed him, though. With God's help, he knew he could suppress his masculine urges and be strong for Gracie and her daughter.

"It wasn't anything noble at all, in fact."

Gracie didn't like Jake to sound like that. He sounded acerbic, and his tone troubled her because she couldn't believe he had reason to be. Her Jake was so wonderful, so giving. And she was so selfish. Since she'd thrust herself into his life, she'd done nothing but lie to him and partake of his generosity, and she was ashamed of herself.

She wished she had somebody to talk to about it all, but the only person around was Jake. Heaving a weary sigh, she wondered if Jake ever felt the need to talk to another person, as she did. The very least she could do for him, she guessed, was offer her services. "If you ever want to tell me about it, Jake, I'd be glad to listen to your story. I don't mean to pry. Just, if you ever feel like it, I'd be honored."

She stumbled when she started walking again and was grateful for his hand on her arm. It was difficult for her to stop looking into the heavens.

"We used to tell each other our secrets, didn't we, Gracie?"

"We sure did, Jake. I remember you told me you were going to see the world someday. I pretended you didn't mean it because I didn't want you to go away. And then you went away anyway." Suddenly she felt like crying and was irked with herself. She figured that astonishing sky had knocked her senses around. She hadn't meant to tell Jake that, ever.

"You always were pretty good at seeing only what you wanted to see."

The way he said it made it seem like not so dreadful a fault, and Gracie appreciated his forbearance. She even managed a soft laugh. "I reckon I did generally see only what I wanted to, at that."

When she wasn't being very careful she still did, in fact. Clara's face, surly and ironic, thrust itself before Gracie's mind's eye. Subdued, she kept her eyes on the ground. She couldn't see it very well, but knew that if she concentrated very hard on what lay in her path, she wouldn't fall. There must be a lesson there, somewhere.

When she'd finished at the privy, she couldn't find Jake. After searching the darkness for a minute or two, she saw him standing beside the skeleton of the old broken-down wagon, staring into the sky. Carefully, picking her way over weeds and clumps of verbena and saltbush, she joined him. She wanted to put her arm around him and have him put his arm around her, the way they'd done at the stream earlier in the day. Then she wanted to stand still and stare into heaven with him.

Sometimes when they were kids, they used to sit on the front porch steps and just be quiet together. She wanted to do that again now. They weren't kids anymore, though, so she kept her hands to herself.

He heard her and smiled when she approached. "All done?"

"All done."

Neither of them spoke for a minute. Then, a little hesitantly, Gracie said, "I know this is a rough place, Jake. I mean, I've seen it over and over again, what with the bandits and the men at Fergus's place and Clara and all. But it's still really pretty. This town could be quite nice with a little love. I guess I'm trying to give it some."

He smiled down at her, taking her breath away. Jake by the light of the moon and stars was a sight that made her heart stumble. The ghostly silver glow washed over the planes of his face and softened them until he looked almost like the Jake she used to know. Only this Jake was more precious somehow, perhaps because he was a man with a man's experiences behind him, and with a man's heart and soul.

"You may be right, Gracie. A little love can do a lot." He swept a look around. Gracie could barely make out darker shapes against the night, and figured them for other buildings. "It might take more than a little to fix this place, though."

She gave him a playful swat on the arm since she couldn't hug him as she wanted to do. "Now, Jake Molloy, what kind of preacher are you to doubt the power of love?"

His laugh curled through her and made her tingle.

"I reckon I'm a no-account preacher, Gracie, and I need you to keep me on the straight and narrow."

"You're not no-account, Jake. You've never been no-account, no matter what mischief you got into. I know you better than that."

They stared at each other for what seemed like a long, long time. Gracie couldn't tear her gaze away from Jake's face. He looked so serious; she wanted to reach up and smooth the harsh, tired lines from around his eyes and mouth. She wanted to see him smile freely, without the wariness and constraint that seemed to be a part of him now.

Why not ask for the earth and sun, Gracie? And for poor little Charity to have another start in life? And for Martha back?

Sighing, she returned her attention to the sky. She might

just as well ask for all those other things; they were as attainable as Jake Molloy. "I guess I'd better get back inside, Jake. Charity gets scared if I'm not there when she wakes up at night."

"Someday you'll have to tell me the real story behind Charity, too, Gracie," he said softly. "I know you haven't told me the truth."

She didn't answer for a minute, trying to come up with a plausible lie. She was sick to death of lies, though, and eventually settled on, "Sometimes the truth can be frightening, Jake. Sometimes it can even be dangerous."

He sounded a bit impatient when he said, "I'd just as soon know what dangers await me as be surprised by them, Gracie."

Thinking about the possibilities scared her. Even though she'd sworn to be adult about her life ever since she'd decided to do what she had to do, she shrank from revealing too much, even to Jake. She murmured, "I'm just teasing, Jake. I've told you everything, really. Charity's just—she's just shy around men is all."

Jake said, "Humph," as he opened the door. Gracie was glad to be inside the adobe where she could go back to sleep and forget the truth and her worries and Charity's problems. She started tiptoeing over to her room, only to be stopped by Jake's hand on her arm.

"I'd like to tell you about it now, Gracie, if you aren't too tired to listen."

Turning, surprised, she said, "Tell me about it? You mean about your life?"

She saw him nod in the flickering candlelight.

"It's not an edifying story. I'm not sure you'll like me much once you hear it. But I think you'd better know who I am, to whom you've given the care of your life and that of your baby. I'm not the boy you used to know."

She couldn't help it; she reached up and pressed her palm against his beloved cheek. "You're still my Jake, and I still love you."

For just a second he shut his eyes and seemed to lean into her hand. Her heart thumped hard when she thought he might kiss her. His eyes opened abruptly, however, and he stepped away from her.

"Thanks, Gracie." His voice sounded rough. "But I still think you ought to know, and it's a hard story for me to tell, so you'd better hear it now before I run out of nerve."

"All right, Jake."

Jake sat at his desk. Gracie saw him finger his Bible and had a shrewd suspicion that he was gathering courage there. She sat on a nearby chair and folded her hands in her lap.

For several minutes, Jake just fidgeted with his Bible and looked sad. Then he began. "I left home to see the world, Gracie. I was going to do great things and have exciting experiences. Maybe head out to the silver mines in Virginia City or the gold mines in California."

"I remember you saying that."

"Before I left home, though, I'd already started down the road I aimed to take, even though I didn't know it at the time. I don't suppose you remember when I used to be friends with Carl and Tom."

Gracie had to think for a minute. "Oh. Yes, I think I do remember, Jake. Mama used to say they were a bad influence on you."

He chuckled without humor. "We were a bad influence on each other. I'm afraid your mama just hoped it was all their fault. The truth of the matter, even then, was that I was a drunkard."

"Jake!"

"It's all right to be shocked, Gracie, because I don't guess people are usually so blunt about their problems, but I won't lie to you. It took me years to admit the truth, but I finally did it and I'll never lie about it again. Drunkenness—the kind I had—is a sickness. I don't know what the cause is—or the cure, either, for that matter—but I've got it."

Shaken, Gracie said, "But—but you're not a drunkard now."

"That's only because I'm not drinking."

Gracie frowned. "That doesn't make any sense, Jake."

"Yes, it does. If I took a drink right now I doubt that I'd

be able to stop until I passed out. I just wouldn't be able to. That's the sickness part."

"I don't think I understand. Why can't you just not drink too much?"

He shrugged and shook his head. "Damned if I know. All I know for sure is that I can't. And neither could Carl or Tom. We were all drunks, near as I can assess the situation from here." Peering at his fingers as they slowly turned the pages of his Bible, he murmured, "I wonder whatever happened to those two."

In a very small voice, Gracie said, "I think Carl got run over by a milk wagon, actually."

She heard his sad, short "Damn," and cringed. "I'm sorry, Jake."

Shaking his head again, he said, "It's not your fault. Reckon I might have guessed something like that would happen. Poor old Carl. What about Tom?"

"I don't know. He left St. Louis after you did. I don't think his family's heard anything from him for a few years."

"Figures."

Jake bowed his head and Gracie wasn't sure, but she thought maybe he was praying. It hurt her to hear him call himself a drunkard. Jake couldn't be a dipsomaniac. Not her Jake. If she knew nothing else about him, she knew he possessed a noble soul. Not the soul of a dipsomaniac. It was such a disparaging term: *drunkard*.

Gracie had known a real drunkard, and that man was nothing like Jake.

"Well, anyway, I drank my way from St. Louis west and then into the territories. I didn't do much for a living; just earned enough here and there to go out and get drunk again."

"But—but you were a tinsmith."

"I was trained to be a tinsmith. During those years, I couldn't hold a job with both hands."

"Jake . . ."

He looked at her and she wasn't sure what she'd been going to say. She guessed she wanted him to stop. At first she'd wanted to listen to his story, but she hadn't anticipated anything like this. This was painful; she didn't like it. Her Jake possessed a noble soul. He was better than this tale he was telling her.

"I told you it wasn't an edifying story, Gracie. I wish I could say I joined the army and did heroic deeds, or made a fortune panning for gold in California, or something. Anything. But I can't say any of that because they're not the truth. The truth is I'm a drunk, and I did nothing worthwhile with the years God gave me. I don't even remember half of them."

"Oh, Jake."

"I buddied around with some men and we moved from place to place. I was with Bart when he got into that bar fight."

"You saved his life, Jake. That was heroic."

His teeth flashed white in the candle's glow. "You think so, do you?"

"I imagine Bart does, too."

"He might if he remembered. *I* don't remember, to tell you the truth. Fergus is the one who told me I dragged Bart out of the place."

He didn't remember saving a man's life? Gracie had an almost ungovernable urge to cry and found herself swallowing convulsively and blinking hard.

With a heavy sigh, Jake said, "I'm ashamed of the mess I made of my life, Gracie. I ended up in prison because of the drink. Fergus and I'd been working on a spread in Texas. Fergus used to take care of me: prop me up when I passed out, carry me home, give me coffee when I was sick."

"Jake . . ."

"Do you want me to stop? If you can't stand it, I won't burden you with it, and I understand. Like I said, it's not pretty."

Yes, she wanted him to stop. She couldn't bear to hear about her Jake behaving like the kind of man he was speaking of. She'd seen men like that, staggering around, being carried out of saloons, raising hell, causing trouble. She'd always been disgusted by them. The idea of being disgusted by Jake was more than she thought she could stand.

She'd seen another kind of drunkard, too: mean, vicious, as malignant as a cancer, destroying anybody and everybody he touched. Shuddering, she wondered if Jake had been like that.

No. No, she wouldn't allow it to have been so. Not Jake. If he told her he was like that other drunkard, she was sure she wouldn't be able to stand it. Yet he'd already told her he'd killed a man. *Oh, Lord.*

Then she looked at his face, thinner than she'd remembered it, more gaunt, sadder than the Jake she used to know should be, and she decided that if he could stand the talking, she could stand the listening. She realized her hands were almost strangling each other and made a conscious effort to relax them.

"No, I want you to finish, Jake. I want to know you." That was the truth; she hadn't lied, and was proud of herself.

"It was in prison that I hit a low so low, I didn't think I'd ever see up again." He looked at her without lifting his head. "I'd killed a man, Gracie, just like I told you. I reckon he was another drunk like me, but he was a living human being until I killed him."

Against her will, her hand flew to her mouth. This is what she'd been dreading.

"It was a drunken barroom brawl. Nothing notable, believe me. I don't even know what we were fighting about, but I somehow managed to punch him, he hit his head when he fell, and he died. The judge said it was involuntary manslaughter, and I got five years.

"Knowing I'd killed a man was a burden, Gracie. Knowing I'd killed another human being senselessly, for no better reason than because the whiskey had fogged my brain, was about more than I could take.

"I was sick, too. God, was I sick. I don't know if you know what liquor does to some men, Gracie, but it made me sick as a dog. I had the shakes and saw things crawling on me. Bugs and spiders. I knew I didn't want to live like that anymore, but I didn't know what to do about it. I knew myself for a weak man when it came to the booze. I couldn't not drink. I needed it, like an opium addict needs opium. I didn't know how to stop. I knew it was killing me, but in order for the shakes and bugs to stop, I needed it.

"It's hard to describe. It's worse than a compulsion. It's . . . well, it's a sickness. A disease. And, since I didn't know a cure, I began looking for ways to escape. Not jail. Life."

"Oh, Jake." Gracie's shoulders began to shake with the effort to keep from crying.

"Yeah, well, it's not easy, killing yourself in prison. They don't let you have things like guns and knives. The bed sheets were so thin, I couldn't even hang myself, because they wouldn't hold me. I know, 'cause I tried. Where I was, which was in Texas, they throw you in with anybody. I got to share a cell with an old Indian, Gideon Elkhorn. He was a drunkard, too. Lots of Indians are. Don't know why."

Gracie had read that it was because their morals and character were weak, but after listening to Jake, she couldn't make herself believe it was true. Not if Jake was a drunkard, too. She still didn't quite believe him.

"Anyway, old Gideon had been in there for a while. He was over his shakes by that time, although I think the drink had already got to him. His skin was yellow and he was in a lot of pain. I understand that's what happens after a while. The alcohol eats your liver. He liked to sing, though, and sometimes when it was dark and we were lying on our bunks trying not to sweat to death or get eaten alive by bedbugs, he'd get up an old hymn. He says some missionaries taught him the songs and he'd always liked 'em.

"One night when I was at my worst, shaking and sick and wanting to die, we were lying there and he began to sing a hymn."

Jake looked up from his Bible and smiled at Gracie. She was ashamed of the tears dripping down her cheeks. Jake reached over and wiped them away with his fingers.

He was looking at his damp fingertips when he said, "Old Gideon sang 'Amazing Grace,' and something in me snapped."

He took a deep breath that shuddered in and out, and Gracie wondered if he was having trouble keeping his own tears confined.

"I thought about you, Gracie, and about how you used to look at me as if I could solve all the world's problems, as if I were the most wonderful person in the world. I thought about what I'd made of myself since those days, and I started to cry. I don't think I'd cried since my own pa died, but I cried then and kept it up until I didn't think I had any more tears left inside me."

She had to wipe her cheeks on her robe. "I'm so sorry, Jake."

"Well, actually, it's a good thing it happened, Gracie, because I realized my life was hopeless and gave up."

He shrugged and grinned, and she felt at a total loss. "I—you—I'm sorry, Jake. I don't think I heard you right."

"I think you did. I said I realized everything was hopeless and I gave up. I gave up everything I'd been doing for so long: fighting, struggling, thinking—everything. I realized there was nothing I could do about my sickness, that I was helpless to fight it, that my will was useless, that my craving for whiskey was bigger than I was, that there was nothing I, as a man, could do about it, and that it would take some kind of unearned divine intervention to save me. I realized the only thing that could possibly save a wretch like me from my sickness was grace."

He smiled at her.

She whispered, "Grace?"

"Grace."

She looked at him for a full minute before she could ask, shakily, "And it did?"

He nodded. "And it did."

"And you stopped drinking?"

"Haven't had a drink since."

"Do—do you ever think about drinking?"

With a shudder so eloquent Gracie felt it in her own chair, Jake said, "Only with gratitude to God that I don't have to anymore."

"I'm glad, too, Jake."

His smile broadened. With a shock of awareness, Gracie realized that his smile held real amusement. She didn't understand that smile. She herself still felt like crying. In fact, she still was crying. She wiped her eyes with her robe once more, and swallowed.

"What—what happened then, Jake?"

He shrugged again. "I paid my debt to society. While I was there, I took to studying the Bible. A Baptist minister used to come in and preach to us, and I asked him to help me understand the Bible. Reverend Gaylord Pike. I'll never forget him. I'd never paid much attention to the Word before then, but I was really grateful to God, even though I wasn't sure at the time that I could stay sober. Reverend Gay did help me, bless his heart.

"While I was in there, I began to feel an urge to preach God's grace to other men like me. At first I thought I was crazy, but Reverend Gay encouraged me. Said it was God calling me to help my fellow man. Eventually, I came to agree with him. When I got out, I was ordained." He chuckled. "I could hardly believe it myself."

Gracie could believe it. There was something about Jake tonight, this instant, that seemed as close to holy as anything she'd ever witnessed.

"I've been doing it ever since, preaching to my flock." He looked at her, an intense expression on his face. "I love them, Gracie. I'd do anything for these men in Diabolito Lindo. That's one of the reasons I don't tell them they're wrong for being the way they are. Because they aren't wrong; they're lost. I know that, because I was lost myself, until God's grace saved me."

Because she didn't feel able to express herself adequately on the subject, she asked, "What happened to Gideon Elkhorn?" It sounded like a stupid question once it was out in the open, but it was important to her. In a way, the old Indian had saved Jake's life; she wished she could repay him somehow.

"I don't know. He got out before I did, and I never saw him again." Jake turned to stare into the darkness and his face appeared very sad. "I tried to find him, though. I owe him my life," he said, speaking Gracie's thoughts aloud.

Gracie didn't know what to say. She knew Jake's salvation had had nothing to do with her; yet to her there was something very personal about his belief that grace had saved him. She figured she was just being selfish again, and wished she were as good a person as he was.

The silence stretched out, encompassing both of them in its soothing stillness. They were so silent for so long that the crickets they'd scared when they trekked outdoors began to chirp again. A coyote yipped in the distance. An owl hooted from a treetop in the yard. Something—probably a field mouse, Gracie expected—rustled through the underbrush outside.

They sat without speaking for so long that the quiet took on a life of its own, until the very idea of breaking it seemed a profanation.

After what felt like a lifetime, Jake shrugged off what had become a heavy atmosphere. Then he grinned the grin she loved so well and said matter-of-factly, "So there you have it, Gracie: the story of my life."

Gracie couldn't help herself. With a sharp "Oh, Jake!" she shot out of her chair and into his arms.

9

*I*F THERE WAS one thing Jake hadn't expected to do, it was to hold Gracie in his arms again today. He'd anticipated her dismay; that hadn't surprised him. But he'd expected her to be repelled by his dismal recitation. He considered his story to be at least faintly shameful, if not downright disgusting.

As his arms closed around her, he wondered if she merely felt sorry for him. He found it difficult to care when her warm, luscious body, unimpeded by corsets and stays, crushed against his.

"Ah, Gracie, how I love you. How I missed you."

"I love you, too, Jake. I love you so much!"

When she kissed him, he felt a moment of absolute shock. Then, even knowing nothing could or should come of it, he kissed her back. His little Gracie. Her lips were as soft and delicious as any heavenly fruit. More succulent than wine. The intoxication he felt while kissing Gracie was nothing like any he'd experienced from a bottle. This was perfect.

He'd like to have kept the kiss chaste and pure; to endow it with the nobility of motives the occasion warranted. After all, he'd never opened his heart or exposed his soul to another human being before, barring the Reverend Gaylord Pike in the Dallas jail. And that had been a long time ago; he had been a different person then.

He was only a man, though, and a poor excuse for one at that. So he couldn't keep this kiss chaste. His love for Gracie was too human and his reaction to her nearness too carnal. In half a minute, his body was as ready for consummation as it had ever been.

He felt her breasts flatten against his chest, her nipples puckered with her own excitement, and he wanted to roar like a lion and take her like the base animal he was. In defiance of his brain's lecture, which hummed a faint background chord of caution, he cupped her round, beautiful bottom with his two hands and pressed her against his arousal.

Great God above, he wanted her. He wanted her more than he'd ever wanted another woman in his whole miserable life, and he knew it was because this was Gracie. His Gracie. The Gracie he loved as he'd never expected to love a woman. He wanted to take her into his bed and into his life; to marry her and make her his; to protect and cherish her forever. And her daughter, too. He wanted to be a family with Gracie again; to have her in his life for however long his life lasted. All the sunshine and gladness he'd tried to drown for years and years in the bottom of a bottle had coalesced in this one woman, and he wanted to keep her by him.

And if he did such a blamed fool thing he'd lose everything he'd made of his life. Like a bucket of cold water, reality sloshed over him. Although his body ached for her, he gently broke their kiss.

"J-Jake?"

Taking her tenderly by the shoulders, Jake pushed her slightly back. She looked like she might fall down if he let her go, so he didn't. With every ounce of self-control he could muster, he resisted pulling her back into his arms. To do so would have been wicked. Jake Molloy was done with wickedness in this life if he could help it. And, with the grace of God, he could help it. Still gripping her shoulders, he stood and looked down into her lovely eyes.

"I'm sorry, Gracie. I shouldn't have done that."

"I—I—" She looked perfectly stunned. "Why not?"

In spite of his physical and emotional misery, Jake couldn't keep from chuckling at her question. Good old Gracie. Some things never changed, thank God, and Gracie was one of them.

Because she looked about as confused as he felt, he decided to keep the explanation simple. And honest. "It would be wrong, Gracie, that's why."

"Wrong?" she repeated, as if she'd never heard the word before.

"Wrong."

Good Lord on high, she was adorable. If he didn't know that his entire spiritual life—and maybe hers, too—was at stake, he'd chuck his morals and take her here and now, and to hell with it all. But his reformation had come to him the hard way, and he couldn't make himself violate his own moral code.

"Why—" She had to clear her throat. "Why would it be wrong?"

He stared into her eyes for a minute. They were so big and beautiful. And so guileless. There was something absolutely pure about Gracie. Always had been. He suspected there always would be. Suddenly he felt like a brute—a big, ugly, dissolute, disgusting brute.

Since his mouth had gone dry, his words didn't come easily, but he forced them out. "We're not married, Gracie."

"But—but—"

He shook his head, stopping her before she could speak. He knew her too well to dare listen to whatever she planned to say. Remembering all too well how Gracie could make the most insane request sound reasonable, Jake hurried to explain.

"No, Gracie. Listen to me. You and I are living here—in the town in which I serve as a minister of the Gospel—as brother and sister. If we were to carry on an illicit affair, it wouldn't be fair to anybody—not to you, not to me, not to Charity, and not to the men I preach to."

"But—"

"I love them, Gracie," Jake interrupted mercilessly. "I love them and they depend on me. I have a duty to them. And to you and to Charity. If we went to bed together—and God knows I want to make love to you—it would be a betrayal of your trust in me, their trust in me, and Charity's trust in us both. I couldn't live with that."

She stared up at him as if he were speaking a foreign language, and he wanted to shake her. This was hard enough without her playing stupid.

Immediately, he chastised himself. She wasn't acting stupid; she was shocked. He knew the difference; he also knew that his contemptible nature was trying to lay the fault on her. But the blame belonged solely to him. No matter how long she'd been married, Gracie would always be innocent in the ways of a sinner like Jake.

"I think I could live with it, Jake," she said in a very tiny voice.

The pure Gracie-ness of her confession shattered Jake's last lingering doubt about his ability to stand firm against his lust and Gracie's wants. With a stifled bark of laughter, he pulled her to his chest, this time in an embrace he made sure he kept brotherly.

"Oh, Gracie, Gracie, Gracie. I don't know how I ever lived without you."

"But you want to live without me now." This time her voice was a bit louder. She sounded even a little irked.

"I don't want to live without you, Gracie. But you know I'm right. You have a daughter to rear and I have a position in Diabolito Lindo to uphold, and I aim to uphold it. Until five years ago, I'd let people down all my life. I'm not about to start letting them down again."

"What about Charity and me?"

Now Jake knew she was peeved.

"I'm not letting you down, Gracie. I'm doing this *for* you and Charity, as well as for me," he said gently.

She sniffled. He let her go again because he didn't quite trust himself not to trick his baser nature into comforting her in inappropriate ways. Deciding it might be a good idea to put a few more articles of furniture between the two of them, he headed into the kitchen and poured them each a glass of water from the pitcher he kept at the sink. Gracie skirted around the table and followed him. With a feeling of defeat that she should have circumvented his tactics so easily, Jake decided he wasn't surprised. She'd always been able to circumvent his tactics.

He did not, however, touch her again, but leaned back against the sink and crossed his arms over his chest. He drank his water with his arms crossed. It wasn't the easiest way to drink water, but it kept his hands busy and, therefore, away from Gracie.

"But, Jake," she said after she'd downed her own water, "we already live together. Do you really think your flock would object if we—if we—well, if we . . . um . . . got married or something?"

She ducked her head, and Jake knew she hadn't even thought about marriage until right this minute. Which just went to show how much she needed his protection. For Pete's sake, she'd have given him her love and her body without one single thought for the consequences. Thank God for—well, Jake thought with gentle irony—thank God for God.

If he'd been the man he was six years ago, he'd have taken her up on her generous offer without so much as a twinge of conscience. And without an inkling of the treasure he'd have been ruining. Lord, Lord, what he'd come from. Contemplating the many ways in which he'd changed from the contemptible creature he had been was a worthwhile occupation, he decided, and one that would undoubtedly come in handy when he was tempted in the future. He knew he'd be tempted.

"No, Gracie. The boys think we're blood kin. They think we're brother and sister. I've already lied to them, and I don't aim to undo the lie with a truth that would shock them and probably make them wonder if I've been lying to them about everything else all these years."

"But—"

"No!" He felt wrung out all of a sudden. "No, Gracie. These men are my flock. That may not mean anything to you, but it means the world to me. And to them, too. They trust me, because I've earned their trust. Nobody's ever trusted me before, because I never deserved it. But I deserve the trust of these men, and I'm not about to violate it."

"I always trusted you, Jake."

"You didn't know me, Gracie. If you had, you'd have been a plain fool to trust me."

For the first time since the day of her arrival in Diabolito Lindo, Gracie pouted. Jake saw her lower lip pooch out and he grinned because he couldn't help it.

He knew his grin aggravated her. She even went so far as to stamp her foot, although her slipper didn't make much noise. "I think you're being mean, Jake Molloy."

"I'm not, Gracie. And you'll know it, too, in the morning. You may even thank me."

"I won't!"

She dashed a tear away, and Jake did begin to feel the tiniest bit mean. "Aw, Gracie, please try to understand. I'd have to leave here if we had an affair or got married. I couldn't stay in Diabolito Lindo after having proved myself a liar to the boys. Where would we go? What would happen to us? To Charity?"

"Couldn't you just explain everything?"

"Explain what? That I'd been lying to them? Think for once, for heaven's sake!"

"Don't talk to me that way, Jake Molloy."

"Oh, Lord, I'm sorry." He heaved a big sigh. "And I didn't mean it that way." Because he'd resolved to be honest with her and with himself, he amended, "Well, I guess I did mean it, but I didn't intend for it to be unkind. It's just that, well, you tend to act before you think. You always did, and you're doing it again now."

She looked as though she was going to huff out another

angry retort, so he forestalled her. "You are, Gracie. Think! Think!"

Her lips pinched up like a prune and she looked as mad as a wet hornet while she took Jake's advice and thought. After several seconds, her lips unpinched and her eyes unsquinched. She dipped her head and Jake got the feeling she had done exactly as he'd requested and, what's more, that she was beginning to be a little embarrassed, if not ashamed.

It obviously cost her a great deal to say, after several more moments, "Well, maybe you're right."

"You know I'm right, Gracie."

Jake wanted to kick himself when she lifted her head angrily. "I *don't* know you're right! I said *maybe* you're right, and maybe you are. I still think you're being silly, though. And mean. I love you, Jake, and I don't think there's anything wrong with that!" Another sniffle overtook her. "I guess if you don't love me, then, well . . . well, I suppose that's another matter."

"I *do* love you, Gracie. I love you more than anybody else on the face of the earth."

"Then I don't understand!"

She was dreadfully frustrated by this time, and raised her voice. They heard Charity stir, and with an irritated exhalation, Gracie raced into the bedroom to comfort her. Jake just hung his head and prayed for this scene to be over with soon because he wasn't sure how much more he could take.

What miserable irony, to be forced to refuse the only woman he'd ever loved, precisely because he loved her. It was beginning not to make sense to him and he knew he'd better keep himself clear on the subject or they'd both be in big trouble.

Charity quieted almost at once, and Gracie stalked back to the kitchen, loaded for bear. Jake knew it, and decided he couldn't handle any more of her arguments tonight.

Holding out his hand, he said, "Don't fight with me about it anymore, Gracie. I've said what I had to say and don't know what else to say. If you can't or won't or don't understand, there's nothing else I can do. I only know it would be going against every principle I've managed to adopt in the last five years to make love to you or to marry you, and I won't do it."

She opened her mouth and began to say something, but he talked right over her words as if they weren't there. He didn't dare listen to her contentions for fear he'd weaken.

"I won't argue anymore. In fact, I won't talk about it at all anymore. This is it. I've said my piece. I'm sorrier than you can imagine if I hurt your feelings, Gracie. God knows, I didn't mean to. I love you too much ever to hurt you on purpose."

Gracie must have understood that he spoke in earnest; she clamped her mouth shut abruptly. He could almost see the words piling up against her teeth and battering to be let out. He ached for her because he knew how hard it was for his little Gracie to keep her mouth shut when she was passionate about something. How paradoxical that it was he about whom she was passionate this time. And how he longed to feel her passion. And how he couldn't.

Groaning, "Oh, God, this is impossible!" Jake turned to grip the sink, bracing himself with his outstretched arms. They wanted to be wrapped around Gracie.

He was glad he couldn't see her face. He heard her turn abruptly and head back to the room where Charity slept. Then he heard her climb into the bed and settle herself under the covers. He had a feeling she was crying, but he didn't dare do anything to comfort her.

He couldn't remember ever feeling this miserable without being able to lay the blame on whiskey.

Gracie lay next to Charity for a long time, shivering. She wasn't cold; she was mad and hurt and frustrated and wanted to scream. If she'd been home in St. Louis, she would have, too.

She wasn't in St. Louis, though, and for the first time since she'd arrived in Diabolito Lindo, she wished she'd never come. Almost immediately, she realized she was being selfish. Again. All she had to do was feel little Charity, sleeping peacefully beside her, to know she'd done the right thing in coming here. Even if Jake had rejected her.

Loved her, did he? Ha! If that was the way he expressed his love, then Gracie wanted to know how he treated people he *didn't* love. Why, he'd shoved her away as if she were poison! Her throat ached with the effort to keep from crying, and Gracie wished Charity were awake so she could cuddle her.

And that was another thing: Why should *she* be the one trying not to cry? *She* wasn't a nasty old dipsomaniac! It wasn't *her* fault Jake had to stay pure for his stupid old flock! They were nothing but a bunch of raggedy old sinners anyway. Why did he care more about them than he did about her, whom he claimed to love?

It wasn't fair! Nothing was fair! *Life* wasn't fair! At last her self-control forsook her, and Gracie turned over as carefully as she could so as not to disturb Charity, and let her tears soak into her pillow. She tried not to make any noise because she didn't want Jake to hear her and know how much his rejection had hurt.

Gracie awoke with a headache on the morning following her orgy of misery. Small wonder. She'd never cried so much in her life, and felt a little silly about her self-indulgent wallow. She was still miffed at Jake, though. In fact, she was mad as fire.

Fortunately, he had already left the house before she arose. Holding Charity close, she climbed out of bed, her grievances against Jake simmering. He'd rejected her! Humiliation ached in her heart and burned her eyes.

After she'd been awake for a few minutes, though, common sense began to filter through the muddle of emotions balled up in her heart. It wasn't long before she realized it was probably a good thing he hadn't accepted her offer when she'd all but flung herself at him.

"Criminy, Charity," she muttered as she bathed the little girl in the kitchen basin. "Maybe Jake's right, after all. Maybe I wasn't thinking very clearly."

You're lying to yourself again, Gracie Molloy. You weren't thinking at all. Jake was right. Gracie spared

Charity her sudden and unflattering moment of self-discovery.

Charity, taking in the gravity of Gracie's countenance and the tone of her voice, looked worried. A pang of shame assailed Gracie for getting so caught up in her own concerns that she'd forgotten the little girl whose safety had become her purpose in life.

She put on a happy face for the baby and tickled her tummy. Charity, not being one to take anything on faith, waited a while before she dared trust Gracie's apparent change of mood. After a minute or two she began to respond, first with a faint smile and then—when Gracie blew a raspberry on her belly—with a giggle.

Gracie's eyes almost filled with tears again—this time with gratitude. "Well, I suppose it doesn't matter, sweetie. Your Uncle Jake was smarter than I was. Again. If we'd made love last night, he'd have found out I'm still a virgin. And _then_," she said, swooping Charity up and swinging her around, "he'd have known for sure I've been lying to him all this time." She wrinkled her brow in thought. "I imagine men can tell. I've always heard they can."

She fought her frown as she considered how she'd almost exposed herself to Jake. Not for the first time, she wasn't proud of the tale her rash behavior told about her character. Nor was she proud of keeping the truth from Jake. Yet she still didn't dare reveal everything. Later. When she knew for a certainty that they were safe.

"I have you now, Charity. I have to think of you." God knows, nobody else ever had. Well, Gracie amended, Martha had, for all the good it had done either of them.

With the morning to herself in which to think, Gracie also had lots of time to consider Jake's story. A drunkard. He'd been a nasty, disgusting drunkard.

"I don't understand it, Charity." With breakfast over and her energy high, she scrubbed the floor with fury. She'd given Charity a rag, too, and the baby sat beside her, swiping it across the floor. Her little face puckered up with concentration as she did her level best to imitate Gracie.

"How can your Uncle Jake be an old drunk like he said he was? The only drunkard I've ever known before wasn't anything like Jake." She found herself scowling over ugly memories, and made an effort to smile for the baby. "I mean, he doesn't seem at all like—like that other one."

Before she'd ever set out for the Territory, Gracie'd made a vow never to speak that name again, and she didn't do it now. That name belonged to another life. If Gracie had anything to do with it, Charity would never hear the name spoken; would never know the name had anything to do with her; would never even read it in print.

"The whole thing doesn't make any sense, anyway. Jake was never a bad boy. He was a wonderful boy, and he's a wonderful man. At least he seems to be. How can a body allow himself to sink as low as he claims he did?"

Since she was in danger of succumbing to another indulgent mood, Gracie reached over and chucked Charity under the chin. The baby squealed with glee and clamped her chin down to trap Gracie's finger. It was a favorite game with them, and infinitely more important than Gracie's muddled emotions or Jake's muddled past.

Recalling her determination to create a new life for Charity, Gracie thrust her doubts and hurts aside. Charity was her priority now. No matter how much Gracie loved Jake—had always loved Jake—no matter what misadventures Jake had endured in his past, Gracie had no business losing sight of her goal. And her goal was keeping Charity safe. The good Lord knew, there was nobody else to do it. The only person in the world Charity had was Gracie.

"I won't let you down, sweetheart," she murmured as she pretended she couldn't get her finger out from under Charity's chin. "I swear I won't let you down."

When Jake opened the front door, he discovered Gracie on her back, laughing with pure joy. Charity sat on her stomach, and Gracie was pretending to be unable to pull her finger out from under the baby's chin. Jake's laugh caught him by surprise. He hadn't felt the least bit jolly when Fergus had called to fetch him to the saloon this morning.

As soon as he stepped inside, of course, Charity swung her head around to see who had invaded her privacy, her face exhibiting all the fear Jake had come to expect in her. He knew her extreme reaction was unnatural and wished Gracie would trust him enough to tell him the baby's story. At least Charity no longer folded up like a collapsing fan every time somebody surprised her. This morning, once she recognized Jake, she even managed to reward him with a tentative smile.

"Howdy, Charity," he said softly, giving her one of his best, least-threatening smiles in return. "Good morning, Gracie," he added, a shade more formally than usual since he wasn't sure what to expect from her.

"Hello, Jake," Gracie said, sounding less chirpy than usual.

"Ho, Jay," came from Charity, shocking Jake nearly to death.

Apparently the little girl's greeting took Gracie by surprise, as well. Forgetting her restraint, she immediately turned her attention on the baby.

"That's right, Charity, sweetie. That's your Uncle Jake. Can you say Uncle Jake?"

The baby still sat on Gracie's stomach, and Jake was impressed that Gracie didn't immediately sit up and strive for some kind of dignity, particularly in light of what had passed between them the night before. Instead, she paid attention only to Charity. He watched and listened, enchanted. Lordy, how he'd love to take both of these females into his life. He stamped down hard on the notion, knowing it to be impossible.

Charity said, "Unca Jay," and immediately tried to hide her face against Gracie's bosom.

"What a good girl you are! Why, you said that beautifully." Gracie turned to look up at Jake. "Didn't she, Uncle Jake?"

Because he couldn't seem to help himself, Jake squatted down next to Gracie so that he could be nearer the action. "She sure did. You did a real good job, Charity."

The baby turned her head on the cushion of Gracie's breasts and peeked up at him. Her expression seemed trapped somewhere between abject terror and pleasure, and he tried to demonstrate with his big grin how much he appreciated her. Out of nowhere, he found himself holding out his arms and saying, "Want to come visit your Uncle Jake for a minute, Charity?"

"Oh, Jake, I don't think she—" Gracie shut up in shock when Charity, after a brief hesitation, actually reached for Jake. "My God," she whispered.

Because he was so surprised—and so glad—Jake plunked himself right down on the floor next to Gracie. He wasn't sure, but he had a feeling that if he'd picked Charity up and walked off with her, she'd have been scared. So he sat smack down on a newly washed, damp spot on the floor of his tiny adobe home and lifted her onto his lap.

"I never thought she'd ever do it." He was a little embarrassed by how much emotion sounded in his voice.

"Me, neither."

Gracie suffered no such masculine scruples about showing her feelings. Although she was obviously fighting her tears of joy, some of them leaked out. Sitting up slowly, she wiped her cheek and said, "I didn't think she'd ever trust another man again as long as she lived, Jake."

"Really?" He searched her face and she looked away.

"I—I'll tell you about it one of these days, Jake. I promise."

"Thank you, Gracie."

Jake felt humbled by the baby's trust. And Gracie's. The good Lord knew he wasn't a man to inspire trust. Not until recently he hadn't been, at any rate. Now people trusted him, and he didn't aim to let them down. No matter how much it hurt him.

Charity was a sweet, small bundle. Jake had never held a baby before, and was amazed to discover how plump and pokable they were. Her arms were chunky and as pliable as uncooked bread dough. Actually, he thought with a grin, Charity's flesh was a good deal more flexible than any bread he'd eaten since Gracie had begun cooking for him.

Pressing a finger against the baby's chubby cheek, he asked, "You take and store acorns in there, chipmunk?"

Her eyes went round and, shaking her head, she drew

away from him. "Charity not take corn." She sounded scared to death.

Shocked, Jake shot a swift glance at Gracie, who looked as though she wanted to cry again. She shook her own head, hard.

Turning his attention back to the baby, he smiled and hugged her. "I know you didn't take anything, sweetheart. But you've got real cute cheeks." He pressed her plump cheek again, playfully.

After a moment, during which she assessed him with the wariness he'd begun to expect from her, she seemed to relax. Then she grabbed his finger in her fist. Her tiny fingers looked pale and fragile against his larger, darker ones. Watching him carefully, she dared a grin.

Making sure he kept his tone jolly, he teased, "You stole my finger, didn't you?"

This time, apparently realizing he wasn't going to hurt or scold her, she broadened her grin and nodded. Jake's heart cried for her, even as he kept a smile on his face.

Gracie couldn't seem to stop staring at the two of them. Or stop swallowing, as though she were trying to get rid of a lump in her throat. She kept shaking her head as if she knew she was being silly and couldn't help herself. "I swear," she said. "I swear." And she grabbed the bandanna out of Jake's pocket and blew her nose.

Attempting to keep his tone untroubled because he didn't want to spoil Charity's mood, he said, "Fergus came and got me early this morning, Gracie. There was some trouble at the saloon last night. Clara was hurt."

"Hurt?" She glanced sharply at his face, her precarious emotions forgotten.

"Yeah. Somebody got out of hand and pushed her. Clara fell down the stairs."

"Oh, my goodness. How badly was she hurt?"

"I'm not sure. She won't let anybody near her. Fergus thinks she might have a broken rib or something, but she's hysterical and just keeps screaming at him to keep away."

"Oh, dear."

"Anyway, he wondered if you'd come over. Maybe she'll

let you tend her because you're a woman. He's sent Ramón for some fellow who doctors horses in Lincoln, but God knows when he'll get here."

"I don't know, Jake," Gracie had uncertainly. "Clara didn't want to have much to do with me when I tried to be friendly."

"I know that, and I told Fergus so, but he seems to think she needs a woman's touch. And I expect he's right. Poor Clara's had a pretty hard life, you know."

"Has she?" She sounded unconvinced and not entirely sympathetic.

Jake couldn't much fault her, but he tried again anyway. "Well, what kind of life do you think would make a woman take to the kind of work Clara does?"

Gracie's big hazel-green eyes reminded Jake that she possessed the biggest heart he'd ever known a human being to possess.

"You're right," she murmured. "I'm sorry, Jake; I was being selfish again. I know you're right. And I suppose I have to try."

"Thanks, Gracie."

Scrambling up from her seat on the floor, she said, "Just let me fetch my medical supplies, and we can run right along."

"You brought medical supplies with you from St. Louis?" He chuckled. Good old Gracie. She had more tricks in her bag than anybody else he knew.

She shot him one of her looks over her shoulder. "Well, Mr. Jake Molloy, I may not be good for much, but they did teach me how to splint broken bones, wrap sprains, and administer salicylic powders in school. And, I might add, I knew enough about your precious Territory to know doctors wouldn't be perched on every street corner. Of course," she muttered under her breath, "I didn't know there wouldn't be any street corners."

Jake laughed.

Pulling the strings of her bag together, she said, "I have a bottle of laudanum in my bag. I suppose Fergus will have some brandy over there in case we need it, won't he?"

"Oh, I expect he's bound to." Jake couldn't help himself. "Do you doctor folks as well as you cook?"

She giggled. "You stop that right now! You know I'm getting better at cooking."

"I know it, Gracie."

Very carefully, he rose from the floor, too, Charity still in his arms. "Will you stay with your Uncle Jake while your mama tends a sick lady, Charity?"

The baby didn't answer. She did, however, utter no protest about remaining in his arms while Gracie bustled around the house. She even giggled when Gracie played hide-and-seek with her sunbonnet and then plopped it on her head.

"There you go, sweet little Charity. Let Mama tie your bonnet ribbons, and we'll go over to the saloon to see your Uncle Fergus." She gave Jake a look that spoke volumes. "I'd just like to know how it's become perfectly natural for me to be telling my daughter we're going to a saloon as if it's of no more moment than going to the corner mercantile, Jake Molloy. This is some kind of place you live in, is all I have to say."

"Told you so." And he laughed with her, even though his heart squeezed so hard it hurt.

As the three of them walked to the Devil's Last Stop, Jake's heart still hurt. He was pleased, though, that Gracie seemed to have recovered from last night's anger.

Of course, he reminded himself, this was Gracie. Gracie had never been able to hold onto a snit. Besides, she was on her way to help somebody in need. Remembering the crippled Osborne boy, the raccoon, and that mean-tempered old mule, he shook his head and grinned.

10

$\mathcal{G}$RACIE HAD BEEN more shocked than she'd wanted to let on when Charity reached for Jake. Even though she'd been telling herself for months now that, in time, Charity would heal, the baby's acceptance of Jake rattled Gracie to her toes.

She'd reached for him! Not only had she reached for him, but she'd actually seemed comfortable with him as he'd held her. Well, there you go. Gracie had always heard that babies could tell, naturally, when a person possessed a good heart. Babies and dogs.

Well, by gum, she thought, Charity was right. No matter how low Jake had fallen, he'd picked himself up again. He was a good man now, and no mistake. Maybe he was right, too, when he said his problem was a sickness and not merely a sign of moral degeneracy.

He'd said he conquered his drunkenness through God's grace, and Gracie wasn't about to second-guess him on the matter. She'd never had much to do with God's grace before, but she certainly respected it now. Her respect for Jake shot up a notch, too. Anybody who could subdue the demons he claimed to have wrestled with—and conquer Charity's fears—was worth paying attention to.

She'd watched him deal with the baby and had been fascinated by how he went about it. He was quiet and friendly and didn't force attentions upon her that might require Charity to respond in ways that were uncomfortable for her. Rather, he allowed the baby to guide his own behavior. As she'd watched, Gracie's heart seemed to grow. This way of acting was new to her. The Jake she used to know had always been too impatient to take time with people.

As the three of them traveled along the dusty, far-from-well-kept road leading to the Devil's Last Stop, she considered everything she knew about Jake Molloy, and realized the boy she'd known long ago didn't exist any longer. He'd really changed. He'd *made* himself change, and the knowledge touched Gracie and made her want to learn from him, to change herself, to become the woman she wanted to be—needed to be—for Charity's sake.

"Howdy, Preacher Jake. Howdy, Miss Gracie."

"Morning, Bart."

The scar-faced, good-natured Bart strolled over to join them on their walk. "We goin' to have us a choir practice today, Miss Gracie?"

"I certainly hope so. This morning all right? Same time?"

"Sounds good to me, ma'am." Bart nodded at Jake. "Baby's took a shine to you, looks like, Preacher."

Jake smiled at Charity, who didn't appear especially pleased to have acquired company on her trip out-of-doors. Ignoring Bart, she gazed up into the sky as if studying the composition of the atmosphere.

"This is the first time she's let me hold her, so don't you scare her, hear?"

Gracie gave Jake a good glare for saying something she considered as being mean to Bart, but Bart himself didn't seem to mind a bit. In fact, he chuckled with honest pleasure. "Wouldn't dream on it, Preacher. Don't hold with skeerin' kids. Ain't right. Ain't no fun, neither. All's I got to do is look at 'em and they run off screamin'."

Bart and Jake shared a laugh, and Gracie decided she'd never understand men—not even relatively good ones like Bart and Jake—as long as she lived.

"Well, ma'am, I'm lookin' forward to singin' this mornin'. That there choir you got together's a damned fine idear, if you don't mind me sayin' so."

"Er, no. I don't mind you saying so at all, Mr. Ragsdale. In fact, I'm glad you're enjoying it."

"I think I got us another bass, too, ma'am. Old Red Willie says he'd like to sing with us. You don't mind havin' no red Indian in your choir, do you?"

Merciful heavens. A choir filled with desperadoes and Indians. Gracie wished she dared write her Aunt Lizzy about it; Aunt Lizzy had always been ripe for a good laugh. "I think that would be wonderful, Mr. Ragsdale. Please tell Mr. Red Willie he's as welcome as can be."

"Will do. See you later, ma'am. Preacher Jake." Bart tipped his hat and pushed open the broken-down gate leading to Old Man Ramirez's place, where he rented a room.

Gracie wondered if Bart would like to take supper with them some night, then decided maybe she'd better wait until she'd learned to handle biscuits better first. She didn't expect he'd favor the cannonballs she'd been serving poor Jake lately. If she ever mastered biscuits, Bart could at least sop up the gravy with them if she managed to ruin the stew.

Glancing up at Jake now, she realized he was whispering soothing words to Charity. She forgot her cooking deficiencies as she felt her throat tighten. He'd understood that the baby was afraid of Bart and wanted her to know she was safe. And he'd done it without offending Bart, too. A strange, not entirely welcome understanding began to edge its way into Gracie's consciousness.

It suddenly occurred to her to wonder how Bart and his cronies in Diabolito Lindo would have treated her had they not believed her to be Jake's sister. Would her arrival in town have been greeted so happily? Would they have assimilated her into their fellowship as quickly? Would they have joined her choir so readily?

Would they have believed her to be another Clara?

With a jolt, she realized there would have been no choir at all but for Jake. There would have been no church. Looking around, she saw the place to which Jake had brought his version of God's word as a stranger might view it.

Good Lord above, this place was the end of the world. Without Jake and his message, inviting these men to partake of God's grace, there would have been nothing at all here but rough masculinity unmitigated by any softening influence at all. Diabolito Lindo would be a wild, uncivilized heap of broken-down buildings populated by savage men who did nothing but drink and gamble and fight each other.

Even Fergus, for all his basic kindness, had no thought for the betterment of his fellows. He served their needs as he saw them, but the needs he served were the sordid wants of the flesh.

The only person in this whole place who ministered to these men's better natures—to their souls—was Jake Molloy. Probably because he was the only person who realized they *had* better natures and souls. An unpleasant sensation of almost unbearable loneliness seized her, and Gracie wondered if there was anybody else in the entire territory besides Jake who saw goodness in these men and endeavored to nurture it.

With a funny feeling in her middle, Gracie guessed maybe she had a lot yet to learn about her fellow sufferers on this green earth. Perhaps it wouldn't hurt to study Jake a while longer; he seemed to have a handle on it.

"Maybe you'd better take Charity for a minute until we get you up to Clara's room," he said when they reached the saloon's front door.

Gracie agreed to it, and they entered Fergus's place, Jake leading the way. Gracie realized he'd done so in order to scan the place for possible danger. A sharp dart of repentance for having thought ill of him last night and this morning assailed her. Jake was the best man she'd ever known in her life; the best man she'd ever even met. And she'd been stupid enough to doubt him.

Why on earth did she have to act like such a fool all the time? Everything Jake had done ever since she and Charity had thrust themselves into his life had been for them.

She wondered if she could ever achieve such real, honest-to-goodness generosity of spirit. It seemed unlikely, and Gracie regretted her shortcomings.

Fergus had been waiting for them. He looked grim when he came over to greet them. "She's still upstairs in her room, Jake. Won't let me near her. Screeches fit to kill every time I even knock at the door. I expect she'll at least talk to you, 'cause she done it before."

Gracie looked at Jake with surprise. "Did she talk to you earlier? I didn't think she'd let you near her, either."

"She didn't let me near her. I stood at the door and she asked me to pray for her. So I did."

"Oh. My goodness."

Shaking his head, Fergus said, "Now she's askin' for a priest. Thinks she's gonna die, I reckon."

"Oh, dear. Do you think she'll let me examine her, Mr. Fergus? I've had a little bit of medical training, but not enough to help if she's badly injured."

With a big huff, Fergus said, "Hell, Miss Gracie, I don't think she's dyin'. She's probably got her a busted rib and if she'd let somebody bind it up, she'd be all right. But if she don't let nobody near her, it might punch through her lung."

"Good heavens." Even though she was trying to be brave for Charity's sake, Gracie couldn't quite suppress her shudder at Fergus's ghastly prognostication. "I suppose I'd better at least try to talk to her."

"I'd take it as a real kindness, ma'am. Here's a bottle of brandy. Figgered you might need it."

"Thank you."

As she took the bottle, Gracie thought with self-mockery that it was about time she did something to repay these people for their own kindness to her. She'd never seen a less savory-looking set of people in her life, but she had yet to have an unpleasant encounter with any of them, save Clara.

Diabolito Lindo might not be much of a place, but this morning it and Jake had humbled her in no uncertain terms.

"Why don't you hold the baby until we see what Clara's up to, Gracie."

"All right."

She padded up the stairs behind Jake. He knocked softly on Clara's door.

"Who's there?" a querulous female voice called out.

"It's Preacher Jake, Clara. I've brought my sister, Gracie, to look at your injuries. She's had medical training."

"Go 'way! I don' want no sister lookin' at me."

For a quarter of an hour, at least, Jake talked to the prostitute. Gracie stood in the hallway, mesmerized. He didn't lose his patience once, not even when Clara called him—and then Gracie—horrible names. Gracie knew she'd have gotten mad and stomped off after the first five minutes.

Not Jake. He never once lost his temper or the evenness of his calming voice.

Continuing the process that had begun as she and Jake walked to the saloon, Gracie's understanding expanded, and she began to have an inkling of what the people in this town meant to him. And what he meant to them. He was right: he hadn't been mean when he'd refused her. He had a bigger stake in his life here than Gracie had fathomed up till now.

After what seemed like an age, Clara, sounding ragged and teary, gave up. With no show of gratitude, she growled, "Oh, God, come in, then."

Jake opened the door and quietly entered. Gracie stepped inside after him and looked around with interest. So this was where Clara plied her trade. It was a plain, dull little room, with no decoration anywhere, except for a cross hung with a beaded crucifix tacked to the wall over a splintery dresser. The cross seemed an incongruous accompaniment to the activities that went on in the room, and Gracie might have shaken her head in derision except that she managed to catch herself in time.

"May Gracie take a look at your injuries, Clara?" Jake asked kindly. "Fergus said you might have cracked a rib. If it's not bound, you may have trouble with it."

"Does *she* got to do it?" Clara asked ungraciously. "I don' wan' her touchin' me. I let you do it."

"She's the only one who knows how. I have no training in these matters."

If Jake had let Gracie respond to Clara, she'd have spat out something uncomplimentary and left in a huff. Which meant, she guessed, that it was a good thing Jake was doing the talking.

Gracie only smiled with what she hoped bore at least a resemblance to kindness, and kept her mouth shut.

"Well . . ." Clara scowled at her. Gracie fought for and managed to maintain her smile.

At long last, the prostitute let out with a grudging, "Well, all right. But don' you hurt me."

Gracie hesitated for a moment while she strove to gather up some of the residual goodness she knew must be piled up around Jake, and take it into herself. It didn't help, but she decided to pretend. "I'll try very hard not to hurt you. If any of your ribs are cracked, though, binding them will hurt. I brought some laudanum which should numb the pain, and Fergus sent up a bottle of brandy. That should help, too."

"You gon' put that baby on my bed?" Clara didn't appear to find the idea very appealing.

"Jake will hold Charity, although he'll have to stay in the room. The baby is afraid to be away from me."

"Spoiled," Clara spat. "Damn kid's spoiled rotten."

For Jake's sake and the sake of her new home, Gracie was willing to take any abuse this awful woman had to dish out if it was directed at her. A slight against Charity, however, was more than she would tolerate from anybody.

First handing Charity to Jake and making sure both of them were comfortable, she strode to the bed, her hands fisted, her arms rigid at her sides. Almost savagely, she whispered to the prostrate woman, "Miss Clara, I won't listen to anything *you* have to say about spoiled children. Talk about spoiled! I understand you've been lying here crying and screaming and giving everybody fits all morning long. I'll have you know, that baby has endured more pain than you can even *imagine*, without uttering a single sound.

And you call *her* spoiled! You take it back this instant, or I'm leaving you to the tender mercies of whoever did this to you."

It was apparent to Gracie that Clara didn't quite know how to react to her outburst. Her words must have penetrated, though, because after scowling murderously at her for another minute, Clara said, "I din' mean nothing." She sounded sulky.

Gracie sniffed. "Then let's get on with it, shall we? I don't want to waste any more of my morning than I have to."

It was nasty and she knew it, and she didn't care. Calling her baby spoiled! Gracie wanted to spoil Miss Clara the way Charity had been spoiled.

Ignoring her patient, Gracie set her bag of tricks on the stand next to the rumpled bed. The covers exuded a musky smell; Gracie, of course, had no experience with these things, but she suspected the odor had something to do with Clara's employment. She decided to attempt to ignore the smell, too.

She'd had the foresight to bring a spoon, and she trickled two drops of laudanum into it now. Then she stirred the drug into a glass half-filled with water. "Here, drink this," she said in a peremptory, nursish voice.

Clara drank, making a face. Because she was mad at her and knew the stuff tasted vile, Gracie made her take another couple of drops. "It's laudanum. Maybe it'll keep you quiet when I examine you."

Jake's gently reproving "Gracie!" came from the corner. Gracie only sniffed again.

Clara made another face, but didn't say a word.

She did, however, let out a sharp "Ow!" when Gracie tried to ease the wrapper from her shoulders.

"I'm trying to be gentle. This is going to hurt, though, so you'd better just get used to it."

Clara muttered, "All right," and kept her mouth shut from then on.

Although she wouldn't say it because she was still mad at her, Gracie was actually rather impressed with the prostitute's stoicism once she got a good look at her injuries.

Somebody had done more than merely push her, and Gracie experienced a reluctant tug of sympathy. She hadn't seen anybody that badly beaten since she'd had to take care of Martha and Charity in St. Louis.

The thought that she ought to be embarrassed to be doctoring a naked woman in front of Jake and Charity occurred to her, only to be thrust firmly aside. Gracie wouldn't allow Charity to be frightened unnecessarily, which she certainly would be if she had to wait outside Clara's closed door.

And if the sight of the nude Clara's small breasts excited Jake's carnal urges—well, so be it. Gracie couldn't afford to worry about that right now. Or to be jealous. Besides, she guessed she deserved a good deal more than mere discomfort or jealousy if she ever hoped to atone for her earlier nasty thoughts about Jake.

"There's not much we can do about these bruises, I'm afraid, although that one on your leg looks bad. In a day or two, I'd better have another look. If the blood's building up under the skin, we may have to lance it."

Although she didn't much want to feel sorry for Clara, she couldn't help but sympathize with the look of fear on her face. "Do you understand what lancing is?" she asked, more kindly.

Clara shook her head.

"It means we might have to drain the blood out of the wound. It probably won't hurt very much, and we may not have to do it."

"All right."

Gracie was pleased that her show of firmness had stifled Clara's foul temper. Or perhaps it was the laudanum. Whichever it was, Clara didn't object to Gracie's further examination. Even when she tenderly palpated the discolored, swollen area around her ribs, Clara clamped her teeth together and didn't utter much more than a muffled moan or two.

"These ribs will have to be bound. I don't think any of them are broken, but they're undoubtedly cracked and will need to be kept immobilized."

"All right."

So Gracie got the tape out of her bag and bound the ribs as well as she could, trying to remember Miss Pinchot's instructions about how many wraps were required, how tight they should be, and how to wrap them so as to give ultimate support to the sufferer. She hoped she'd done it right.

"There. That should do it." Gracie knew her face had gone red when she added, "I expect you won't be able to work for a couple of weeks."

When she heard the prognosis, Clara's self-control deserted her. "A coupla weeks? I can' not work for a coupla weeks! How I gonna eat?"

"Don't be silly," Gracie snapped. "For heaven's sake, I'll bring you food."

"No you don'! I heard about your cookin'. I don' wan' nothin' you cook."

Gracie's first impulse was to defend herself and her cooking. Her second impulse was to stomp away and leave Clara to her own devices. Another look at her patient, however, stilled the sharp retort she'd been about to deliver.

The woman was crying now; Gracie sensed her tears weren't merely on behalf of her physical ills or her inability to earn a living for two weeks. Perhaps it was Jake's goodness rubbing off, but Gracie thought she could discern a degree of shame and misery behind those tears of Clara's.

So, instead of returning Clara's meanness with meanness of her own, Gracie said, "You're right. I have a lot to learn about cooking in the Territory. Poor Jake has been suffering through my cooking ever since I got here. I imagine you know much more about how to deal with the foodstuffs here than I do. I'd be happy to learn, if you're willing to teach me."

Clara eyed her dubiously, as if she didn't trust such a mild return to her deliberate insult. "I don' know how to write nothin'."

Striving to remain calm, Gracie said, "Perhaps you can give me instructions orally and I can write them down."

Clara's eyes slitted up in mistrust. "What you mean, orally? What that mean?"

"That means you can tell me how to cook things. I can write down your instructions and then follow them in Jake's kitchen. Then I can bring you your meals and you won't have to go hungry."

"You do that for me?"

"I said I would."

"Why?"

Good question. Gracie said, "Why not?" and knew she'd fallen short of her goal, even if she wasn't sure what her goal had been. To be as kind as Jake? She didn't stand a chance. She knew it, and shrugged to make up for it.

Clara looked down at her blanket and began pulling lint balls from it. "Thank you," she said in a voice so low, Gracie barely heard it.

"You're welcome."

There! Gracie felt as though she'd scored a thrilling victory, although she wasn't sure why. She didn't even like this woman; she certainly didn't relish the idea of carting food to her for two weeks while she recuperated. Then she glanced over to find Jake and Charity watching her. Jake's soft smile almost robbed her of breath, and she knew why she felt good. It was because she'd done the right thing; she'd behaved like an adult.

That night, Gracie decided she'd watch Jake and see just exactly how he acted. She planned to emulate him because he was the best human being she'd ever known in her life. For Charity's sake, she could stand to improve herself. And for her own sake, as well.

Jake's unrelenting goodness slapped at her, and Gracie knew she should tell him the truth. She should. With every breath she took, she knew she should. He deserved nothing less from her.

Hating herself, knowing she was failing yet again, she couldn't make herself do it.

11

$\mathcal{A}$FTER GRACIE TOOK Clara a breakfast of cornmeal mush and bacon—not even Gracie could ruin mush—Jake, Gracie, and the baby trekked up to the creek.

Since their arrival in Diabolito Lindo, Charity had become more expansive than Gracie had ever seen her. The baby no longer cringed any time something surprised her, and she seemed to want to enlarge her experience of the world. At the moment, Gracie was helping her toddle along the riverbank, happy as a lark to hear Charity's tiny voice lifted in one of her favorite songs.

"Yankee Doodoo wen to town a-widing on a pony," sang Charity.

"Stuck a feather in his cap," chorused Gracie, "and called it macaroni."

On the word "macaroni," the requisite accompaniment was a tummy tickle on Gracie's part, and it made her insides light with joy to see the baby anticipate being tickled with a sly look and a sparkling grin. As much as a month ago, if anybody had told her Charity would be singing happily in the clear light of a new spring day, being watched over by so large and frightening a creature as a man, Gracie would have told them they were crazy.

Today, almost anything seemed possible when she considered the progress Charity had made toward achieving a normal childhood.

Jake had flopped himself down on the grassy sward and now leaned against a boulder, randomly picking some of the small yellow daisylike flowers that abounded in the meadow and stringing them into a necklace. Gracie realized his progress was slow because he spent most of his time watching her and Charity. His lazy scrutiny heated her insides and made her long for things that couldn't be.

She refused to allow herself to dwell on what wasn't, however. She aimed to concentrate on what was. The morning was magnificent, for instance, and she truly appreciated nature in all its glorious splendor.

Bees buzzed, robins chirped, cottonwood leaves rustled together in the gentle breeze like fairy wings. And if the little town spread out beyond and below them looked more like a blot on the earth's otherwise placid surface than paradise, who cared? If Diabolito Lindo's remarkable assortment of denizens were an unhandsome lot, it mattered not. If Miguel and his bandits lurked close by, Jake would protect them. At the moment, all that mattered were the day, the baby, and Gracie's abiding—and, of necessity, pure— love for Jake Molloy.

"Why does Charity limp, Gracie?"

Gracie whipped her head around. "What?"

The question took her by surprise. Not that she hadn't prepared herself for it; she'd been practicing a plausible lie to account for Charity's limp for weeks. Which, all things considered, was undoubtedly precisely why she felt uncomfortable now. Continuing to lie to Jake in the face of his unrelenting goodness seemed more and more evil as the days went by.

For perhaps ten seconds, she considered confessing everything. Another glance at Charity, her round cheeks pink with pleasure, a big grin on the face that had smiled too seldom during her short spell on earth, sealed Gracie's lips. Her heart ached, though, with the weight of her lies.

Keeping her head down so Jake couldn't detect the betraying flush of shame on her cheeks, Gracie said, "She broke her leg when she was just a baby, Jake."

"Broke her leg?"

It seemed to take him a moment to digest the information. Gracie didn't dare watch him while he cogitated. Instead, she guided Charity around so that they were edging away from where he sat. She decided not to elaborate unless he asked.

He did. "How on earth did she break her leg? Did you drop her or something?"

"Of course I didn't drop her!" Gracie drew in a breath, knowing she had no reason to be indignant. "The poor thing fell down the stairs."

"Fell down the stairs?"

"Having trouble with your ears this morning, Jake?" Gracie wished she'd held back her acid comment, and chalked up the lapse to nervousness.

As she'd had occasion to notice before, however, Jake possessed an angelically tolerant disposition. He only chuckled and said, "No, my ears are fine, thanks. I just can't picture a baby falling down a staircase, is all. I mean, she sure couldn't walk to the stairs and step off, could she? How'd it happen?"

This was what she'd dreaded. "Her father . . . dropped her," she said, and hoped he wouldn't notice her slight hesitation.

"Good Lord. He must have been horrified."

"He was," Gracie lied quickly. "It was awful." That was true, anyway.

"How did you treat the break?"

"The doctor splinted it. She was too small for anything else."

Jake let that one sit for a spell before he said, "Well, I'm glad she's better now, at any rate."

"Me, too."

"You expect she'll have that limp forever?"

"I don't know. At first the doctor was afraid she'd never walk at all, to tell the truth."

"My God. I'm sorry, Gracie."

"Thank you, Jake. So was I."

"You're doing a real good job with her, too. She's a sweet little girl. And she's not so shy anymore, either."

"No. No, she's not." *Thank you, God,* Gracie added silently. *And thank Jake, too.*

"And I," he announced, rising from his seat on the grass, "have just the thing to make a pretty little girl even prettier."

Charity's big brown eyes opened wide when he settled his daisy chain over her head. She looked down to view Jake's handiwork, fingered the flowers gently, and carefully lifted the chain so that she could see it better. Then she looked up into Jake's eyes and said, clear as a bell, "Tank-u, Unca Jay."

Gracie felt like an idiot when big tears rolled out of her eyes, down her cheeks, and splashed on Charity's bonnet. She felt even worse when Jake—wonderful, good, kind-hearted Jake—reached over and wiped them away.

Jake felt traitorous when he found himself wishing that somebody other than Gracie would cook him and Bart dinner today. He didn't mind Gracie's cooking, really. It was just that building this additional room onto his adobe was a lot of work, he was hungry as a horse, and he wasn't sure he could continue working if his stomach ached as much as it had after last night's supper.

He sighed and didn't say anything, resigned to his fate. It was the least he could do, he reckoned, in penance for the unbrotherly feelings for Gracie that threatened to engulf him every day.

"Hey, Jake. Wanna see if Old Man Ramirez has some of them burritos of his made up? We kin eat 'em fer dinner."

Laughing at Bart's tone, which was so innocent it couldn't possibly be sincere, Jake said, "Better not, Bart. I don't want to hurt Gracie's feelings by making her think her cooking's not good enough to eat."

He thought he heard Bart grumble "Well, it ain't," but he wasn't sure. More loudly, his fellow room-builder said, "Course not, Jake. I didn't mean nothin'." He didn't sound very cheerful about it, though.

"I really appreciate you helping me, Bart. And Gracie truly is getting better in the kitchen."

"I don't mind helpin' ya, Preacher Jake. And I don't reckon I mind eatin' your sister's cookin', neither. Not very much, anyhow."

"She really is getting better, Bart. Honest." Jake hoped God wouldn't get him for one more tiny fib. He wished to heaven it wasn't a fib; he could use a square meal.

His surprise was genuine, therefore, when he took a bite of the dinner Gracie set out for him and Bart that noontime and found it quite tasty. "This is *good*, Gracie."

"Well, you don't have to sound so surprised, Jake Molloy," she said tartly.

"Sorry, Gracie. But, well, it *is* good. What is it?"

Gracie spooned a bite of the chicken-and-rice concoction into Charity's mouth. The baby chewed happily, too, as did Bart and Jake. With a small frown, she said, "Well, I'm not sure. Clara calls it *arroz con* polo."

Bart choked on his laughter and grabbed for his water glass.

Jake said, "I think you mean *pollo*, Gracie."

She glanced at Bart and her frown deepened. "Yes, I guess that *is* how she pronounced it. But Fergus spelled it for me, and he said it has two *l*'s. I can't imagine how two *l*'s can end up sounding like a *y*."

"Reckon that's just the Spanish way, Gracie. It's a real good recipe, though. I think you ought to keep this one."

"I aim to." With a sigh, she continued, "I expect *you're* happy about this new arrangement, anyway, with me feeding Clara and all, and her telling me all her recipes."

Jake managed to stuff his mouth full of chicken just in time to be spared rendering a possibly too-enthusiastic response.

Bart, however, said, "If *he* ain't, I sure as hell am, ma'am.

This here chow's a hell of a lot better than anything else you ever give me to eat."

Jake watched Gracie's eyes squint up, and was proud of her when she only said, "Thank you very much, Mr. Ragsdale."

Sighing happily, Bart said, "Think nothin' of it, ma'am," and shoveled another bite into his mouth.

Gracie watched Jake and Bart eat and felt a stab of something very close to jealousy. She truly enjoyed seeing the two big fellows savoring her cooking; she only wished it had been her doing and not Clara's that caused their sighs of satisfaction and happy expressions.

Recognizing her reaction as being small-minded and not one befitting the new Gracie—or at least the Gracie she was trying to become—she told herself to stop sulking. If this recipe was anything by which to judge, her cooking was improving and however the result had come about, that was a good thing.

She probably ought to thank Clara. Maybe by tomorrow morning she'd have worked up the spirit to do so. Clara's jibes about this morning's lumpy cornmeal still rankled at the moment, and she was glad Jake would be taking the prostitute her supper.

That afternoon after she'd cleaned up the dinner dishes, she took Charity outside to weed the garden and watch the construction. Jake and Bart had shed their shirts, and Gracie almost wished she were more bold; she'd offer to do Bart's laundry for him. From the looks of his undershirt, it sure wouldn't ever wear out from being overwashed.

Jake, on the other hand, was a work of art. His shoulders gleamed under their sheen of sweat, and his chest looked solid and hard as a rock. She itched to feel the sprinkling of dark hairs on his chest, to rub them and find out if they were as springy as they looked. She also had a yen to feel the muscles that bulged in his arms. Mercy sakes, her Jake had grown up well. Very, very well indeed.

She wondered if he'd ever lain with Clara in a carnal manner, and hoped not. Not that she expected he'd been pure as the driven snow. He'd apparently been wild as anything before he met up with that Indian in Texas, bless the man for a saint. The idea of him tumbling around on that messy bed with Clara, however, didn't sit well with her. The idea of Clara knowing Jake better than she did—in that way—rankled.

Still, experience wasn't a bad thing, she guessed. Especially in a man. If she were to become Jake's lover, for example, it would be well for one of them to know how to go about things.

Oh, good grief! Gracie snapped her attention away from the man who was supposed to be her brother, annoyed with herself for succumbing to such indelicate thoughts. Charity sat beside her on a square of cloth, tugging for all she was worth on a pecan seedling that had decided to sprout among Gracie's carrots. She wasn't having much luck, as the nut was clinging like a leech to the heavy soil in which a squirrel had planted it.

Watching her baby's valiant struggle with nature, Gracie told herself in no uncertain terms to keep her mind on her business. And to remember with every waking breath that her business was Charity's well-being.

She ultimately helped the little girl dig the seedling out. This gardening nonsense was difficult here in the Territory. The soil was certainly nothing like the rich, soft, dark loam back home in Missouri that God unfailingly watered with His life-giving rain. If Gracie and Charity didn't carry water to this garden every single day, things began to wilt. Charity enjoyed watering with the can Jake had bought for her in Lincoln. Gracie would just as soon skip the back-breaking labor, but she never said so.

She did, however, mutter, "This ground is hard as a rock, Jake."

"Yeah, I expect it is. They make bricks out of it, you know."

"Bricks?" Gracie turned to glare at Jake's back. She realized her mistake immediately and turned back to her task again, swallowing. Good Lord Almighty, Jake Molloy was a handsome man. Even when she couldn't see his face.

For the first time since her arrival in Diabolito Lindo,

Gracie thought to be grateful that no other woman—except Clara—lived here. Another woman would be a fool not to snatch Jake for herself. If that happened, Gracie feared she'd die.

"Yeah. Adobe bricks. They mix it with straw and make it into bricks."

"Hell, Miss Gracie," Bart added, "Jake's whole house is made of adobe bricks. That's what we aim to make them walls with after we get the framin' done."

"Oh." Concentrating on her carrots for all she was worth, Gracie said, "No wonder it's so hard to dig in."

"It's like clay," Jake said on a heavy chuff of breath. Gracie decided not to see what he was doing; she didn't trust herself. "When you get it wet, it's real slippery."

"I noticed that. I almost broke my neck yesterday when I spilled some water and then stepped in it."

"Have to be careful, ma'am," Bart said. "Ain't no doctors in these parts. Don't want you breakin' your leg or nothin'."

"Lord, no. We'd have to call in the horse doctor from Lincoln." Jake laughed.

Gracie frowned harder, then remembered the baby and smiled for her. "All right, sweetheart, why don't you get your watering can and sprinkle the carrots now. I think we have all the weeds out."

With the greatest of goodwill, Charity pushed herself up from her gardening cloth and toddled over to fetch her watering can. Gracie watched her, knowing it was unnatural for a child to be so amenable, but glad that Charity was now willing to leave her side without examining her face for motives first. When they'd first arrived, Gracie couldn't step more than a foot away from the baby without causing Charity real anguish.

Shaking her head, Gracie prayed for strength to fight her urges and to continue healing Charity's hurts. Actually, she guessed, if she paid more attention to Charity, her own problems probably wouldn't seem so insoluble.

"Well, I still don't like Clara, Jake, but I must admit

something good has come of having to cart food to her every day."

Jake looked up from the verses he'd been studying for the forthcoming Sunday's sermon and smiled. When they were alone together, Gracie still exhibited some reserve. Her stiffness of manner had been going on for the past week, ever since she'd doctored Clara. She sounded more normal today.

They still hadn't discussed his midnight confession about his past life or their subsequent kiss and conversation. He knew they should, if only to clear up any lingering misunderstandings, but he couldn't face such a discussion yet. He wasn't sure he could resist if Gracie decided to offer herself up to him a second time.

At any rate, he was glad Gracie was back to chattering as she worked. He could pretend nothing had changed between them when she was acting normal, even if his carnal urges still threatened to burst forth and consume them both ninety-nine times a day. At least.

"What's that?" he asked, although he already knew the answer.

Ever since his first taste of Gracie's *arroz con pollo*, he'd been eating relatively decent food. He expected he should pay a special trip to Clara's just to thank her. They never talked when he took her supper. The whore just gave him a grudging "Thank you," he offered a noncommittal "You're welcome," and he left.

"Clara's given me lots of good recipes, even though I don't know what she's talking about half the time. Thank heavens for Fergus. He translates for me so I can write them down properly. Even if I can't understand the words."

"What's not to understand?"

Gracie threw her arms out in a dramatic gesture, making Charity giggle. Jake noted with a pang that Gracie paused to tickle the baby before she continued her explanation, and decided that was one of Gracie's most endearing qualities. She might believe passionately about any number of things, but she never forgot her baby. And she never took herself so seriously that she couldn't laugh at herself.

Recalling their midnight conversation, he amended his assessment slightly, but not entirely. He reckoned some things just weren't funny.

"Why, the *names* of things, Jake! I didn't know alyssum was called pepper grass out here. *Or* that you could use it in cooking. And I didn't know that a *manzana* was an apple, a *pollo* was a chicken, or a *conejo* was a rabbit. For heaven's sake, in St. Louis a rabbit's a rabbit."

"Well, I reckon a rabbit'd be a *conejo* to a Spaniard, even in St. Louis, Gracie," Jake offered with a chuckle. His heart did a funny leap when she crossed her arms over her beautiful breasts and grinned at him saucily.

"Well, I expect you might be right. Still, I'm really glad Fergus is there to explain all this stuff to me." She frowned as she tied the bonnet ribbons under Charity's chin. "I still wish I could figure out how to make decent bread, though. My tortillas are as bad as my biscuits ever were. How come all I can ever fix are cannonballs, Jake? Everybody else seems to be able to make bread. It's the staff of life, for pity's sake!"

Jake tore his attention away from Gracie's bosom and laughed. "You'll get the hang of it one of these days, Gracie."

"Humph. Well, I don't know about that. I'll keep trying, though. In the meantime, this rabbit stew is pretty tasty. I'll stop by Old Man Ramirez's place and buy some tortillas for supper, so you won't have to eat mine."

Jake took off his half-glasses, stood up, and stretched. "Need any help with Clara's dinner, Gracie?"

"No, thanks. I can take care of it. Anyway, Charity and I are going to stay for choir practice."

Jake was disappointed. He hated it when Gracie left him for any length of time. Nevertheless, he acquiesced because to do otherwise would have been a damnable weakness, and he reckoned he had enough damning behaviors on his record already. Besides, he could use some of the time Gracie spent with her choir in talking to God. He'd felt a tremendous need for the good Lord's guidance during the past few days.

He said, "All right," and sat himself back down, picked up his glasses, and reread the Bible verses before him. He tried to keep his mind on his work, but when he heard Gracie open the front door, he couldn't stop himself from looking.

She'd finished another sampler and was taking it to Fergus's place. It fluttered from the hand holding a can of rabbit stew. Charity perched on her other hip. Amusement battled a pang of despair in Jake's heart. She'd embroidered this new sampler with Clara in mind, he could tell: "A Soft Answer Turneth Away Wrath." The baby held a jar of wildflowers she and her mama had picked earlier in the day.

Jake knew Gracie was pleased with herself for continuing to cater Clara's meals. Clara wasn't an easy patient; Fergus had told him about the grief the whore gave Gracie. Jake figured Gracie looked upon the duty in the light of penance. He knew she felt guilty about having all but thrown herself at him the other night.

"Oh, God." The exclamation leaked out past Jake's sense of humor, and despair assumed precedence over cheer for a second. Sinking his head to his hands, he whispered, "Oh, God, please help me."

Because he felt a particular need for God's good graces this sunny Saturday morning, he leafed through his Bible until he came upon one of his favorite psalms. It sometimes seemed funny to him that he and the boys should take such comfort from the psalms, but they were everybody's favorite here in Diabolito Lindo. The good Lord alone knew what the rest of the world thought about them, but for Jake and his flock the psalms appeared to offer salvation, without reservation, to even the worst of the planet's sinners.

Even a no-good, low-down skunk like Jake Molloy could find comfort and at least the hope of redemption in the psalms. He read softly to himself, praying that the words would ease the hollow pain in his heart.

"Out of the depths have I cried unto thee, O Lord. Lord, hear my voice: let thine ears be attentive to the voice of my supplications. If thou, Lord, shouldst mark iniquities, O Lord, who shall stand? But there is forgiveness with thee, that thou mayest be feared. I wait for the Lord, my soul doth wait, and in His word do I hope. My soul waiteth for the Lord more than they that watch for the morning."

Jake was sick to death of waiting.

Clara glowered at Gracie when she knocked and pushed open the door to her ugly, unadorned room. Accustomed by this time to the woman's surliness, Gracie smiled, keeping in mind Jake's goodness as her example. Charity, unable to appreciate Gracie's motivation in the presence of the dour Clara, hid her face against Gracie's shoulder.

Even terrified, she held the jar of flowers well away from her so as not to spoil them or spill any water from the jar. Charity was the most careful child Gracie had ever known, and for good reason.

Someday, Gracie hoped, Clara would regret showing that mean face to the baby. Until that day, she kept her own voice soft and pleasant, unwilling to allow Clara to goad her into upsetting Charity further.

"The recipe you gave me for rabbit stew is quite tasty, Clara. I hope you like it."

Clara sniffed with contempt. "Anybody can make *olla de conejo*. Anybody. Even children make it."

"Isn't that nice." With a smile she hoped would curdle the nasty woman's gizzard, Gracie set the can of stew beside the bed.

Since Jake wasn't with her to hold the baby, she pulled the room's one chair close to the bed and carefully settled Charity upon it. Speaking very kindly to the baby, she said, "You stay right there now, Charity dear, while I check Miss Clara's bandages."

Clara sniffed again as Gracie waited to make absolutely sure Charity wouldn't object to being left in the chair while she performed her medical duties. Gracie attempted to ignore the invalid's obvious scorn for Charity's shyness. Clara just didn't understand, she told herself, striving to achieve even an ounce of Jake's magnanimity. Failing utterly, she pretended.

"All right now," she said in an agreeable voice at great

odds with the ill will festering in her heart, "let's see how you're getting along." She poured out a couple of drops of medicine and stirred them into some water.

"It hurts," Clara said flatly.

"Of course, it hurts. You were badly injured. Here you go." Gracie guessed she was a weak woman with a black heart, because she took entirely too much pleasure in making Clara sip the horrible-tasting laudanum-laced water. "As soon as that settles, I'll check your bindings. In the meantime, Charity and I brought you a little jar of wild-flowers. I'll just set them over here on the dresser."

She smiled sweetly at Charity when she took the jar. Charity folded her chubby hands in her lap and watched Gracie, eagle-eyed and tense, until she returned to the bedside.

Clara drank her medicine, making a sour face. She didn't thank Gracie for the small bouquet of verbena, mallow, and bindweed, but scowled at it as if it were a jar of snakes. Gracie was neither surprised nor upset. Well, not too upset, at any rate. She was getting used to Clara; she considered her service to the prostitute as a daily exercise in benevolence.

Since the day she'd been called upon to attend to Clara, Gracie had been striving to achieve a fraction of Jake's integrity and generosity of spirit. Every day she fell short, but she didn't aim to stop trying. In a way, she was grateful for this opportunity. She thought—maybe—kindness to Clara was becoming easier with each passing day

"Don't let that baby wet on my chair," Clara grumbled.

Gracie's heart, which seconds earlier had seemed on the way to expanding, slammed shut immediately. She snapped, "My baby will not hurt your stupid chair," and knew she'd failed again. *Drat!*

Clara uttered a derisive snort, and Gracie sucked in a deep breath. She didn't know how Jake did it; she only knew she could merely strive to emulate him. For Charity's sake, for her own sake, and because Jake himself deserved no less from her, she would continue to strive—no matter how blasted often she failed in her dealings with this miserable, ungrateful, horrible witch of a woman.

In spite of her uncharitable feelings, she maintained a polite expression and unbound Clara's ribs carefully, trying not to hurt her unnecessarily.

"You're healing up quite well."

"When I be able to work again?"

Shaking her head, Gracie tried not to blush when she said, "Not for another week at least, I expect."

Clara said "Humph" again. "You keep feedin' me?"

Was it her imagination, Gracie wondered, or was there an edge of fear to Clara's words? She gave a little sideways glance at Clara's face and decided it had been her imagination.

"Of course, I shall." Because it was the truth and she was trying to be good, she added, "I appreciate the help you're giving me with my cooking. Jake—that is, my brother— appreciates it, too. My cooking is improving."

Clara let out with yet another "Humph," and Gracie experienced a tremendous and un-Christian urge to slap her silly.

She didn't, of course, but she still felt crabby when she rewrapped the prostitute's damaged ribs.

Maybe this was what Jake did, she thought suddenly. Maybe he did the right thing in spite of his inner feelings. Maybe this is what being a responsible adult entailed.

Whatever it was, it almost killed Gracie to be pleasant for the remainder of her nursing duties. She was still smiling, however, when she bade Clara *adieu* for the day. Jake would bring the prostitute her supper. He wouldn't allow Gracie anywhere near the saloon at night.

"Well, Charity," she murmured sourly as soon as she shut the door and made it to the top of the stairs, "thank God that's over with. At least I didn't shout at her today like I did yesterday."

It was, perhaps, a small victory, but given the provocation, Gracie considered keeping her voice well modulated a significant one. She had just grasped the banister, intending to practice hymns on the piano for a few minutes before her choir arrived, when Fergus's voice stopped her cold. Dread clamped its icy claws around her heart and squeezed until she could barely breathe.

"A woman and a baby, you say?"

12

FERGUS MUST HAVE heard Gracie's involuntary gasp, because he shot a sidelong glance at the top of the staircase. She shook her head frantically. With his usual indifferent expression in place, Fergus scratched his stubbly chin as if he were merely considering the stranger's question.

"Don't reckon we have us no recently arrived females and babies in town, young feller," he said after a moment. "This here town's not a real big draw for the ladies."

Gracie offered up the most sincere prayer of gratitude in her life. While she was at it, she asked God to heap blessings upon the kindhearted barkeeper.

"No? I heard tell a lady and a baby were living in Diabolito Lindo."

Gracie was sure she saw Fergus's eyes slide toward her again. She shrank away from the stairs and hugged the wall, listening for all she was worth. Since her heart was hammering as loudly as a military drum, hearing the conversation taking place at the bar several yards away was no small feat.

"Well," said Fergus, sounding to Gracie's ears as though he were stalling for time, "I reckon we got us our preacher's sister and her little kid here. But they ain't new to town."

Tears stung her eyes, and Gracie silently begged God to ignore Fergus's lie and to bear in mind the reason he'd had to tell it. Tiptoeing back to the head of the stairs, she peeked over the banister to see who was talking to Fergus.

She'd never seen the man before in her life. For a split second, her heart soared. Then it plunged sickeningly. Of course, John Farthing wouldn't have come searching for Martha's baby himself. He'd have hired people to do the searching for him. God knew, he had enough money to hire any number of people. Except for the cash and the few trinkets Martha had given Gracie, John Farthing currently possessed everything Martha had ever had.

"Thanks for your help, mister," the stranger said. His voice sounded pleasant. In spite of that—or perhaps because of it—Gracie didn't trust him for a minute. "You got any rooms to rent in your saloon here? I'd like to sort of make Diabolito Lindo my headquarters while I look into the other towns in this area. I'm positive they headed out this way."

Oh, God! Oh, God! Her heart racing, Gracie plastered herself against the wall again, scrambling to think of something to do. If this man planned to stay in Diabolito Lindo, for no matter how short a time, she'd sure as heck have to do something. And fast.

"Reckon I have a room you kin rent if you have to stay here." Fergus sounded fairly grudging.

"Thanks," the stranger said. "I know Lincoln's a bigger place, but there's so much trouble in that town, I'd as soon skip it."

Fergus muttered something Gracie didn't catch. Commanding herself to rein in her rampaging emotions, she leaned against the wall and prayed hard. Then, sucking in a deep breath, she grabbed the banister again and whispered,

"Hold on tight, Charity. Your mama's going to put on a show."

The stairs in Fergus's place of business were uncarpeted. As Gracie was wearing her leather-soled shoes, it wasn't difficult for her to make a sizable racket as she descended them. Pasting on her brightest smile, she pretended she didn't see the man standing at the bar with Fergus and kept her attention focused on the piano.

"All done, Mr. Fergus!"

Her tone sounded intolerably perky to her own ears. She hoped it wouldn't strike an insincere note with the stranger. Jake was always telling her she was sunny; maybe this man would chalk up her cheery tone to sunniness. She wanted to run out the door and not stop running until she and Charity were safe. Which might be never. The unpleasant truth kept her pretense alive, even as she prayed for a bolt of lightning to strike the man now staring at her from the bar in entirely too curious a manner.

"She any better today, Miss Gracie?" Fergus asked, as if her sudden appearance under the circumstances didn't boggle his mind. Gracie knew his mind was boggled because his eyes were bugging out.

"I do believe she is, Mr. Fergus. She still needs to keep very quiet, though. I know she's pretty bored, but at least I don't expect my cooking will kill her." She tried for a trilling laugh, failed, and coughed instead. She hoped the stranger didn't notice anything amiss.

Because Gracie had always believed in grabbing the bull by the horns and wrestling it into submission, she pretended suddenly to notice the stranger, adopted an astounded air, and chirped, "Why, goodness gracious sakes alive! Welcome to Diabolito Lindo, sir. We don't generally get visitors here in our little town."

Bracing herself, she walked boldly up to him and stuck out her hand. Charity looked away and cringed, and Gracie almost—but not quite—regretted her audacity. Audacity might be all that lay between them and absolute disaster, however, so she stood firm and smiled the smile of her life.

"My name is Mrs. Trinidad, sir. This is my daughter,

Ch— my daughter." She decided not to give him any names in case he had more information than she wanted him to already. "We moved here a while back when my husband died, and now we live with my brother, Jake Molloy. Jake's the minister here."

The stranger blinked several times, Gracie's fluttering exuberance apparently having caught him off guard. Sneaking a glance at Fergus, Gracie found him staring, too, his mouth gaping open. She didn't much blame either of them. Nor did she drop her exaggerated manner.

"And what might your name be, sir? I swear, it's such a pleasure to see a new face. We feel so isolated out here in the territory, you know."

Fergus rolled his eyes. Gracie pretended not to notice.

At last the stranger gulped, shook Gracie's hand, and stammered, "I—I'm—my name is William Chester Williams, Mrs. Trinidad. I just arrived in Diabolito Lindo today."

"And will you be staying with us long, Mr. Williams?" *Please say no,* her mind shrieked.

"Well, ma'am, I can't rightly say. I've been looking for a woman and a baby."

"A woman and a baby? Fancy that. Why, I don't think I've seen another baby since I left—"

Oh, God, where? She couldn't lie about the city, because she'd already told everybody she'd come from St. Louis. This was too small a town for her to begin mixing her lies up. Jake would hear about it, too, and wonder why she'd taken to lying. He'd drag the truth out of her then—maybe make her go back when he learned why she'd come. She'd run away again before she'd take Charity back there.

"—St. Louis."

"St. Louis?" Mr. Williams's expression sharpened. He eyed Gracie closely when he said, "It so happens the woman I'm looking for came from St. Louis."

"Really? Imagine that." Gracie wished she dared lick her lips. They'd gone as dry as her imagination.

"Yes. Really."

She didn't care for the tone of Mr. Williams's voice. To

offset his obvious skepticism, she said, "What's the name of the woman you're looking for, Mr. Williams? Perhaps we knew each other back home." Her smile was about to crack her face. She wanted to scream.

"I don't know."

Well, that was a blessing, at any rate. If he didn't know her name, maybe he wasn't after her at all. That would be some kind of luck. Gracie didn't dare let down her guard, but adopted a suitably puzzled expression and asked, "You don't know the name of the lady you're looking for?"

Williams brushed a hand through his sandy hair and looked harassed. "No, I don't. Whoever she is, she's got the baby of a woman named Martha Farthing with her."

So much for luck. Gracie's heart shriveled into an aching knot of fear; she suppressed her instinct to turn tail and run away from William Chester Williams as fast as her legs would carry her. Or pick up a barstool and batter him to death.

"My, my," she said. "What's this—Mary, was it? What's her baby's name?" The question sounded mechanical and dry. Gracie hoped it was only her ears, which were buzzing with the panic in her heart, which made it seem so to her.

"Martha. The woman's name was Martha. I don't know the baby's name."

Thank God. Making her eyes go round in an effort to appear dubious in her own right, Gracie said, "You don't know the name of the woman you're looking for *or* her baby? My goodness. That sounds a little strange, Mr. Williams, if you don't mind my saying so."

Williams's mouth kicked up at the corner, making him appear weary and cynical. His expression didn't lighten Gracie's heart at all.

"It *is* a little strange, I'm afraid, Mrs. Trinidad. It's also proving difficult."

Fighting an almost ungovernable urge to flee so she could sit somewhere and think, Gracie forced herself to stand pat and maintain her innocent pose. "Well, I hope you'll attend church services come Sunday, Mr. Williams. They're held right here in this saloon, believe it or not." She offered up a vague titter and hoped William Chester Williams wasn't as astute as he looked, because she was sure her good humor sounded false. It felt false. It was false.

"Thanks. I'll think about it." Williams turned back to the bar.

Exchanging one last look with Fergus, Gracie made her way to the piano. She got all the way to the bench before her legs gave out. She had to suck in several deep breaths and swallow three or four times before she could be almost sure she wouldn't burst into tears. She couldn't afford to fall apart. Now, more than ever, Charity needed her.

Knowing that the only thing that might save them both at the moment was an appearance of absolute normality, Gracie put on a deliberately jolly face for Charity as she settled her on the bench next to her.

"There you go, my sweet little girl. You sit right there by Mama, and I'll play us a tune before the choir shows up for practice."

Since they still had ten minutes or so before practice was scheduled to begin, Gracie plowed through three of Charity's favorite songs. Even in her rattled state, she took pleasure in the little girl's pretty, melodious voice as she sang along with the piano.

"Soo fie! Doh bodda bee."

Oh, God, please don't make this mean what I think it means.

"Soo fie! Doh bodda bee."

Why now, God? Why now? She's only just beginning to heal.

"Soo fie! Doh bodda bee, 'cause I beloh to Compee Gee!"

Can't you give us a little more time, Lord? I promise I'll tell Jake the truth, if you'll just give us time. I'm sure he'll be able to think of something to do.

"He'd fie froo da air wi' da gratess of eeezzz."

If you'll just let that man go away without learning who we are, God, I swear I'll never lie again as long as I live.

"Da daring young man on da fie-ing trapeeezzz."

You know her father will kill her if he gets his hands on

*her again, God. You can't mean to let Charity go back to
him to die. You can't.*

"An' my yuv he has purloined away!"

You can't be that cruel.

Gracie heard William Chester Williams thank Fergus for
his hospitality and walk across the plank floor to the
staircase. No matter how hard she strained her ears to hear
through the tinkling piano music and Charity's singing, she
didn't hear him continue on up the stairs. When she couldn't
stand the suspense another second longer, she slipped a
glance toward the staircase.

William Chester Williams stood at the foot of the stairs,
his hat in his hand, staring at her and Charity. Gracie's
courage very nearly failed her.

She was made of strong stuff, though, was Gracie Molloy.
By the time choir practice ended, she'd come to a conclusion.

"There's no way in the world that man can prove you're
not my own child, Charity," she muttered to the baby as she
walked back through the dust toward Jake's house. "I'll sure
as the devil never tell anybody—not even Jake."

Her resolution made her chest pulse with pain; it kept
time with the throb in her head. She knew what she had to
do, though, and she aimed to do it. Confession might well be
good for the soul; in fact, she longed to tell Jake everything,
and now more than ever. In this instance, however, confession might well get Jake hurt; Gracie would no more hurt
Jake than she would Charity, so she vowed to keep her
mouth shut.

"Even if that man asks around and finds out we just got
here a little more than a month ago, that won't prove a
thing."

With every beat of her heart, Gracie prayed she was right.

Several days later Jake said, "I don't know, Gracie. He
seems like a nice enough fellow to me."

"Well, I think he's sinister. Poking and prying into folks's
business the way he's doing." Gracie dumped her dough out
onto the floured board and gave it a good whack.

His chuckle grated on her nerves like fingernails on a slate. She clamped her lips together and didn't bark at him.

"Now why on earth do you think looking for somebody can be construed as sinister?"

"Depends on why he's looking, doesn't it?" she asked shortly.

There was a brief pause before Jake asked, "Are you sure *you're* not the woman he's looking for, Gracie?"

Peering over her shoulder, Gracie didn't like the look on Jake's face. Not that it was unkind; far from it. His expression was as gentle and loving as anything she'd ever seen, and its very goodness made her feel like an evil, blackhearted villainess.

Which wasn't fair, and Gracie resented it. She was trying to protect the baby from real evil. She almost told Jake so, but stopped herself in time.

Oh, God, I can't take much more of this. The thought shot through her brain as despair bloomed in her heart.

William Chester Williams didn't seem to be going away. To Gracie's mind, he hovered over the once-pleasant little community of Diabolito Lindo like a malignant thing, and she'd become jumpy as a cat on a hot stove.

"Of course I'm not," she snapped.

Jake didn't say anything for a second. At the moment, he was helping Charity walk across the floor. The baby had her tiny feet planted on his big boots, and she giggled with every step. The way Jake's eyes laughed almost made Gracie cry.

It wasn't fair. Things had just begun to go right. Charity was even overcoming her fear of men—well, she'd overcome her fear of Jake, at any rate, and that was a major victory considering how timid the child was.

"He says the woman he's looking for is from St. Louis," Jake said softly.

"Well, so what? St. Louis is a big city. Is it a crime to come from there?"

Gracie took a big breath and told herself to stop snapping and begin acting rationally. She didn't want to give Jake any more reason to be suspicious.

With a breathless laugh, she said, "I'm sorry, Jake. I didn't mean to sound so cross. I'm having trouble with these dratted biscuits again." She slapped the biscuit dough to emphasize what she hoped he'd take as her frustration about her culinary maladroitness.

"Well, everything else you've cooked in the last week or so has been real good, Gracie. I don't think you should let hard biscuits get you down."

She battered her biscuit dough the way she wished she could batter John Farthing's face. "But it's so silly, Jake! Thanks to Clara, I can cook everything else now, but I still can't make a decent biscuit. Makes me mad!" She gave the dough a particularly vicious punch.

Jake laughed, and she breathed a sigh of relief. Apparently, he'd accepted her act.

She tried to calm down and act natural. It wasn't easy, since she wanted to scream her frustrations to Jake's God—to ask Him why. Why, why, *why* was He making this so hard for her? For Charity? Certainly, Charity deserved some peace in her life, and that's all Gracie was trying to give her. Peace. And a chance.

As he watched Gracie's expression change from one of apprehension to one of solid determination, a pang of pain sliced Jake's heart. Why in the name of all that's holy wouldn't she trust him? She'd been edgy as a bear separated from its cub ever since William Williams arrived in Diabolito Lindo. Her nervousness was contagious; he'd caught it himself. Why only yesterday, he'd nearly jumped out of his skin when Fergus had asked him a question when his back was turned.

He shook his head, feeling something close to despair. She'd been living with him for nearly two months now; surely she knew he'd never do anything to hurt her or jeopardize her baby. If she was running away from something or somebody, he'd do his level best to help her. She kept promising to tell him the real story behind her inexplicable move to the Territory; he wished to blazes she'd do it and get it over with. The suspense, particularly in light of this new development, was like to kill him.

And he knew better than to pry further. She knew he wanted her trust; she simply refused to give it. Jake wasn't about to wrangle with her; he'd learned the hard way not to butt in where he wasn't wanted.

Her lack of trust hurt, though, more than anything else had hurt him in a long, long time. Hell, he loved her. He'd never hurt her.

Realizing that his mind had wondered onto an unproductive path, he gave it up and turned onto another. Picking Charity up, he sat on his chair and commenced giving her a bouncy ride. She giggled again.

"Want to visit the creek this afternoon, Gracie? Bart says there's a nest of robins up there in the willow tree. He says the nest is low enough that I can lift Charity up to see the baby birds."

Gracie peeked over her shoulder. "*Bart* saw a robin's nest and thought of Charity?"

Grinning, Jake said, "Astonishing, isn't it?"

"My goodness. I should say so."

Taking in Gracie's utter amazement, Jake's heart turned a somersault and went all gooey. "*You* did it, Gracie, you know that?"

Her big eyes blinked rapidly a few times, and Jake experienced a compelling urge to wrap her up and kiss those fluttering eyelids of hers until she squeaked and went limp in his arms. God, he loved her. He'd been having tormenting visions of her pretty blond curls spread out on his pillow; of seeing for himself the precious lushness of her breasts and body. Of feeling all of her passion directed at him. He sucked in a breath and told himself to stop thinking such things.

"Did what?" she asked in unfeigned puzzlement.

"You brought civilization to Diabolito Lindo. I didn't think you could do it, but you did. You were right."

"I did? I was?"

Her befuddlement was rapidly changing to pleasure mixed with embarrassment. Jake saw her cheeks turn pink and had to grip the seat of his chair to keep himself in it. He nodded. "I remember you telling me—in quite a huff, if I recall correctly—that it was men *and* women who civilized the stupid old world. Well, you were right."

His imitation of Gracie's vehement speech pattern was so accurate that her blush intensified. So did Jake's grip on his chair. Suddenly realizing that he'd better get the hell out of the house or he'd do something he'd regret for the rest of his life, he snatched Charity into his arms and got up so fast the chair legs bounced. Gracie's embarrassment shifted to surprise.

"Here, Gracie, will you watch Charity for a bit now?"

"Of course, Jake." She wiped her hands on her apron and reached for the little girl. "What's the matter?"

Raking his hands through his hair in order to keep them away from her body, he said, "Nothing. Nothing's wrong. I—I just forgot I have to see Fergus about something."

"Oh. All right."

Before he could weaken, Jake plopped a quick kiss on Charity's head, raced to the door, grabbed his gun and his hat, and hurtled outside. Just before he shut the door, he called over his shoulder, "I'll be back later to take you and Charity up to the creek." He was sure Gracie must be staring after him as if he'd lost his mind, and he couldn't fault her. He *had* lost his mind.

Once he got past his front gate, he dared to slow down. His flesh felt hot, his maleness was hard, and he wasn't sure how much more of this he could take. He needed the brotherhood of a good friend and hoped to heaven Fergus had time for a chat.

He supposed he could also use another heart-to-heart with God. The problem with talking to God, however, was that God didn't speak English. He spoke in emotional ways that were sometimes difficult for a poor, dumb sinner like Jake to recognize. Right now he needed some instant answers.

He shoved through the batwing doors and inhaled the thick atmosphere of the saloon with relief. Fergus stood behind the bar, lazily wiping a glass, and chatting with William Williams.

"Howdy, gentlemen."

"How-do, Jake."

"Good morning, Mr. Molloy."

In spite of Gracie's opinion of Mr. Williams, Jake had found him a personable fellow, a good deal better educated and informed than most of the citizens of the town Jake loved so much. He hadn't realized how much he missed intelligent conversation until he'd chatted with Williams for a few minutes. Not that Fergus and Bart were stupid; far from it. It's just that they hadn't done much reading in their lives, and Jake sometimes found himself thirsting for a good rousing discussion about books, like the one he and the newcomer had indulged in the other day.

"Any luck in finding that woman and the baby, Williams?"

"Not so far." Williams's discouragement was evident. "I wish to God I could find them, though."

"Well," Jake said with a grin, "I've never heard anybody say that talking to God hurt; you might try a good prayer or two."

"Don't mind him none, Mr. Williams," Fergus advised dryly. "He can't seem to stop hisself from preachin'."

Williams grinned, too, when Jake leaned over the bar and whacked Fergus on the back. "Now that's not true and you know it, Fergus. When's the last time I preached to you?"

Fergus scratched his whiskery chin. "Reckon that'd be the day afore yestiddy, Jake."

Fergus's audience laughed. "That's no fair. I always preach on Sundays."

"And you do a fine job of it, too," Williams said. "I don't recall ever hearing exactly that slant placed on the Twenty-third Psalm before."

Jake was so glad he'd run away from Gracie. He'd felt pretty foolish at the time, but he really needed this. After he'd stopped laughing, he said, "No, I don't expect you have, Mr. Williams. We fellows here in Diabolito Lindo might have a unique interpretation of a lot of the good Lord's words, but I don't expect you'd be able to find a bunch of men who appreciate them more."

Williams's smile appeared genuine. "I don't expect I could. As a matter of fact, it was refreshing to be sitting amongst a group of men who truly seem to believe in something. The last time I can remember believing in God was when the Rebels were shelling our ranks and I was cowering in the mud and praying I wouldn't get hit."

Jake felt a rush of pity when he saw what seemed like an involuntary shudder shake the fellow's shoulders. He clapped a hand on one of those shoulders in comradeship. "I've heard that tale more than once, friend. I feel fortunate to have missed the war, although I turned seventeen in sixty-five and tried to enlist. The conflict ended before I had a chance."

"Good thing, too," Fergus muttered. "You'd be a dead man sure if you had."

Jake felt his grin tilt as he stared into his best friend's compassionate face and knew he was right. "You're right, Fergus. I've always been grateful for my reprieve."

Fergus only nodded.

Williams continued, "You have a mighty fine choir here, too. I must admit it surprised me to see some of these fellows singing. They don't seem—well, quite the type. That sister of yours has them singing up a storm, though."

"Yes, she sure does. The way she explained it to me is, she has three basses, one baritone, two tenors, and a soprano—unless Harley Newton's still drunk from Saturday night. Then she's short a bass."

The thought of Gracie and her choir of misfits and lost souls tickled Jake and he chuckled. "She's always been like that, you know. Nothing ever seems to daunt her; I've seen her accomplish some crazy things before, but I have to admit I thought she'd fail with her choir." Which should teach him a thing or two about his own faith, he reckoned.

"She says she's from St. Louis, too."

Jake opened his mouth to answer, and shut it again. This man was fishing for something. Since he didn't know what it was—and since Gracie hadn't honored him with her full story—he guessed he wouldn't lie about this. After all, as

Gracie said, lots of people were from St. Louis. "Yeah. We both are."

"She been here long?"

Now Jake began to feel itchy. The man was not merely fishing; he was fishing hard. Some innate protective feeling in Jake's guts made him want somebody else to talk to the fellow about Gracie.

Turning to the one person who'd always rescued him in times of trouble, Jake smiled at Fergus. "How long's Gracie been here, anyway, Fergus? You remember?"

Fergus eyed Jake keenly for a second before he said in a voice that was more than normally expressionless, "About a month and a half, two months, I reckon."

Williams's face registered surprise. "That's all?"

"Yeah." Fergus didn't elaborate.

Jake, silently blessing him for it, gave the stranger a big grin and tried to turn the direction of the conversation onto a path that didn't make him so nervous. "It's been quite a time, hasn't it, Fergus?"

Fergus deliberately turned his head to eye the sampler behind the bar, the one that said "Judge Not, Lest Ye Be Judged." Then he let his gaze wander up to his painting.

Somebody had tacked two red bandannas over the formerly naked lady's more obvious attributes. One of the bandannas almost covered her upper pulchritude. The other provided more than adequate cover of her lower depths. Her plump thighs thrust tantalizingly out from under the brazen red cloth. Jake and Fergus had discussed the matter, and Fergus had agreed with Jake when he said he thought the bandannas made the painting more titillating than it had been before. Neither one of them had mentioned their conclusion to Gracie, who was convinced that Jake's flock was developing some morals.

Jake suspected that the Devil's Last Stop was probably the only saloon in the entire Territory to have frilly calico curtains covering its sparkling windows, too. He'd sure never seen pretty covers on any other barstools in his life, nor had he detected a faint aura of lavender in the air of any other saloon he'd been in. Gracie had tied little sachet pouches under all the tables, stools, and chairs.

After Fergus's glance wandered back to Williams, he said, with a sort of sigh in his voice, "Yeah, it's been a time, all right."

"I was under the impression she'd been here quite a while."

Williams's eyes had taken on a keen, questioning quality. Jake wished he could help him. Since he didn't know how, he shrugged and said, "Nope. Her husband died and she brought the body here because she wanted me to perform the funeral service."

Speculation faded into suspicion, and Williams said, "And what did you say her husband's name was?"

"Trinidad. Ralph Trinidad." Even though Jake knew better than anybody that Gracie was withholding a good chunk of whatever her truth was, he didn't like to see that look on the newcomer's face. A little tartly he said, "You can go up to Boot Hill and look at the name on the grave if you don't believe me."

"No. Oh, no. I didn't mean to imply anything."

Williams seemed startled, and shook his head. Jake noticed lines around his mouth and eyes, traces of weariness and worry, and acquitted him of subterfuge.

"I'm sorry, Mr. Molloy," Williams said. "I've just come a long way on what's beginning to look like a wild-goose chase, and it's wearing me down some. I didn't mean anything."

"It's all right. And I reckon you're right to be surprised about Gracie's move here." Jake grinned again, to show the man he was forgiven.

Fergus added, "Ain't that the truth. The rest of here in town were surprised, that's fer damned sure."

"Well, I'm sure the woman I'm looking for is around here somewhere, and I aim to keep looking. It's a hard job, though."

After a short hesitation while he weighed the wisdom of asking, Jake decided he might as well. "Mind if I ask why you're looking for this woman and her baby, Mr. Williams?"

Williams hesitated, too. "Well, Mr. Molloy, I don't reckon I'd mind for my sake, but I don't know that I should say anything. The reason I'm here involves other people, and their stories aren't mine to tell."

He looked as if he truly regretted the truth of his statement, and Jake guessed he could understand the man's sense of honor and discretion. Nevertheless, irritation flared in him. Damn it all, how many people and their secrets could one tiny territorial town handle, anyway? First Gracie wouldn't let on why she was here, and now this stranger showed up looking for a woman and a baby. From St. Louis. Was he looking for Gracie? Was it safe to talk about Gracie and Charity?

Jake would die before he knowingly jeopardized Gracie or Charity, but since nobody saw fit to tell him anything, how could he know who to talk to? Or what to say if he talked to anybody at all? This fellow sure seemed innocent enough. But, then, so did Gracie, and Jake *knew* she was keeping secrets from him.

He dragged a hand through his hair. He felt like stamping his feet and hollering for *somebody* to tell him *something*. Anything. All these secrets were threatening to drive him to distraction.

He wished Gracie would embroider herself a sampler about honesty being the best policy and study it awhile. Maybe give one of 'em to this fellow.

His frustration must have shown on his face, because Williams said, "I truly wish I could tell you, Mr. Molloy. God knows I'm sick of keeping everything to myself. I can't, though, because—"

"I know, I know. It involves somebody else."

"Yes. Yes, it does."

At the look of woe on Williams's face, Jake regretted his shortness of temper. Lordy, what kind of a preacher was he, anyhow, to get snappish with this poor soul who'd come all this way in search of someone obviously dear to his heart?

Even if it was Gracie.

He decided he'd better not start running around in *that* circle again or he'd lose his mind completely.

So he offered up another rueful grin. "I'm sorry, Mr. Williams. Your business is your own affair, and I have no right to pry." He had no right to pry into Gracie's affairs, either, and the knowledge made his stomach ache.

"Don't know why the hell not," Fergus mumbled from behind the bar. He'd taken to dusting off bottles now. "Shoot, I can't shut the boys up when they get to blabbin', wantin' to tell me all their damned troubles. They just about beg me to pry into their lives. You'd make a hell of a bartender, Jake."

"Don't I know it."

"Please don't apologize, Mr. Molloy," Williams said contritely. "I understand. And I'd take it as a kindness if you'd take a drink with me."

Jake caught Fergus's sharp look and gave his friend a brief shake of his head and a small smile. "Thanks, Mr. Williams. I'll take a cup of coffee with you. I don't drink any longer."

Williams's eyebrows shot up. "No? You're the first man in the Territory I've met who doesn't take whiskey, Mr. Molloy. Drinking against your religion?"

"Oh, no. My religion doesn't frown on much of anything." His anger forgotten, a tickle of humor began to grow in Jake's middle. He clapped a hand on Williams's shoulder yet again and started guiding him toward a table. "Come on and sit a spell. I'll tell you all about it."

Behind them, Fergus rolled his eyes and reached for the coffeepot.

13

"*WHAT YOU GOT* today?" Clara's scowl didn't seem quite as crabby this morning as it generally did.

Gracie was almost too nervous to notice, and she was certainly too worried to snap back. "Eggs wrapped in tortillas with cheese and chili."

Oh, great God, what are we going to do? The thought kept howling like a hungry wolf in her head. She had no answer.

"You make the tortillas?"

Clara's question jerked Gracie out of her desperate concentration. She glanced up sharply. "Of course not. Mine would break your teeth."

Ignoring Clara's expression of surprise, Gracie set her tray on the table and settled Charity in her chair. She'd brought along a small corncob doll she'd made for the baby, and gave it to her now to keep her busy while she tended Clara.

"Here. Fergus sent up some coffee, too."

"At least I don't got to drink no coffee you made."

"Right. That's something to be grateful for."

There has to be something I can do. If only I could think of something.

After giving Gracie a funny look, Clara seemed to understand that she wouldn't get a rise out of her today. She dug into her breakfast without slinging any additional barbs. When she'd eaten one of the tortilla rolls, she even offered a grudging, "It taste good."

"Thank you."

Please, God, give me a hint. Just a little hint. I'll take it from there.

"What wrong with you today?"

Clara's unexpected question made Gracie jump. She'd been sitting on the edge of the bed as she usually did. Today, however, she wasn't fussing with the baby or trying to get Clara to be friendly. She'd had her gaze directed blindly out the window while the unanswerable question rattled around in her brain: *Oh, God, what are we going to do?*

"What do you mean? Nothing's wrong with me."

Clara pointed her second tortilla roll at her. "You worried about somethin'."

Oh, Lord, was she that transparent? Gracie knew she'd always been a second-rate liar, if that. Subterfuge wasn't a part of her nature any more than idleness was.

Suddenly, a light went on in her brain. By heavens, Clara might be able to help her in spite of her nasty self. At least Gracie might be able to wheedle some information out of her. The prostitute already thought she was a fool; what did it matter if Gracie now confirmed her notion? Endeavoring to keep her expression blank so as not to betray her inner turmoil, she attempted a titter.

"Oh, I'm just being silly, I suppose."

Clara snorted. Since she was chewing, she couldn't agree with Gracie's conclusion, so Gracie continued.

"It's just that the stranger who's been living here and asking all those questions is making me nervous."

Clara's brown eyes opened wide as she swallowed. "That Mr. William? Him?"

Gracie pushed herself up from the bed in a rush, startling Charity. Inwardly berating herself for moving too jerkily, she patted the baby's shoulder and smiled down at her in apology. "Is that his name? Oh, yes. Yes, I seem to recall it now."

"Mr. William. Yeah. Why he make you nervous? That stupid."

"Do you really think so?" Gracie brushed her hands up her arms to smooth out the gooseflesh that had sprouted quite naturally in reaction to hearing Williams's name.

"Of course. He just stayin' here for a while. Lookin' for somebody, I hear."

Gracie made herself not glance at Clara. "Looking for somebody?" She tried for another titter, but it didn't come out right. "Who's he looking for?"

Out of the corner of her eye, she saw Clara shrug.

"I don't know. He don't talk to me. Fergus say he can't find 'em, though."

Gracie's heart leapt. Thank the good Lord and Fergus, Clara hadn't been told that Williams was looking for a woman and a baby! She knew good and well that the sly Clara would be able to put two and two together and come up with Gracie and Charity. "Really? Well, then, I guess he'll be leaving again soon, won't he?"

"No."

Gracie's heart fell again so fast, her stomach turned over. "No? Why not, if he can't find who he's looking for?"

Another shrug. "I don' know." Clara looked up from her breakfast. "Why you care?"

Flapping her hand in a gesture meant to convey nonchalance, Gracie said, "Oh, I don't. It's just that I've gotten used to the fellows here already. Mr. Williams doesn't seem to fit in. I suppose it's stupid of me, but he makes me nervous."

Since her mouth wasn't full any longer, Clara had no trouble saying, "Yeah, is stupid. Anyway, he more good-lookin' than anybody else in town."

"You think so?"

Gracie'd been so busy trying to avoid William Chester

Williams, she hadn't given a thought to his appearance. When she did think about it, she guessed Clara might be right. If a body appreciated that thin, sandy-haired, pale-skinned appearance in a man. On a personal level, Gracie went more for tall, broad-shouldered, rugged, dark men; men who had a lived-in air about them.

Oh, good grief, what was she thinking of? She loved Jake, for heaven's sake. Always had and always would; of course, his was the look she favored. She didn't honor Clara with her opinion because she didn't trust her not to come up with something too close to the truth regarding the relationship between Jake and herself. Instead, she said, "Hmmm. Maybe you're right."

"I'm right. He more—more—nicer, too. More like a gentleman I meet once in San Antonio. That gentleman, he treat me real good."

"Really?"

"Yeah. I seen Mr. William comin' up the stair yesterday an' he smile at me. Not like most of these ugly men, but nice-like."

"Hmmm. That's nice."

With a sigh, Clara pushed her plate aside on the tray and said, "Well, I think so. I think he the most handsome man I ever seen."

Daring to look at her patient at last, Gracie said, "You do?"

"Yeah."

Clara's opinion surprised Gracie. More than that, the way she'd offered her assessment had sounded the tiniest bit wistful. Wondering if she was out of her mind, impulse made her ask, "Would you like me to introduce you to him? Perhaps he'd be willing to—to play cards with you or something while you convalesce."

Hearing her own words, Gracie realized she'd just uttered an astonishing truth. Maybe she *could* introduce Williams to Clara, and maybe he *would* read to her. Or something. Anything. That would at least keep them both busy while Gracie pondered her fate and tried to think of something to do that might assure poor Charity's safety.

Turning her head away from Gracie, Clara murmured, "He won' wanna do nothin' like that."

"Why not?"

"He just won', is all."

"Now how on earth can you know that?" Gracie put her hands on her hips for effect. It wasn't wasted, because Clara turned her head again, sharply, and glared at her.

"I know 'cause I'm sick and can't do what men want. That's the only reason men like me, is 'cause of that."

Merciful heavens! Gracie felt her cheeks burn with embarrassment. But she refused to run away now; not when she perceived in Clara such a golden opportunity to keep Williams out of her hair for even a little while.

"Nonsense!" she said stoutly. "That's just where you're wrong, Miss Clara. Why, you said yourself Mr. Williams seems more gentlemanly than most of the fellows here in town. I'll bet when he hears about how you've been laid up, he'll enjoy coming up here and—and playing cards. Or reading to you. Or something."

She knew herself to be an unrepentant sinner when she realized she'd even favor Williams and Clara doing what Clara said was the only thing men liked her for. Even if it would hurt Clara's ribs and was an affront to God and the entire human race.

Clara said, "Humph."

Gracie said, "All right then, Miss Smarty Pants, I'll just show you."

And she swept Charity and her doll off the chair and ignored Clara's empty tray and the coffeepot as she swept toward the door.

Clara got as far as exclaiming, "Hey! What 'bout this dirty dishes?" before the door slammed behind her ministering angel's rear end.

Gracie made it to the head of the stairs before she stopped short and wondered if she'd gone completely mad. "But it doesn't matter, Charity," she muttered after a moment of thought. "He still can't prove we're who he's looking for, and if this works, it will at least keep him busy while I think of something for us to do."

She wasn't at all sure she *could* think of something to do, or how she'd go about doing it if she ever did. All she knew for sure was that she'd really like to have Mr. William Chester Williams occupied with something other than the search for a woman and a baby from St. Louis for as long as she could arrange it.

She found him eating breakfast at a table in the saloon. He looked up, surprised, when Gracie sailed over and plopped herself down in a facing chair.

"Mrs. Trinidad!"

She gave him one of her patented, never-fail, sunny-as-a-new-summer-day smiles. Then she laid her plan before him. He looked even more surprised when she was through explaining herself.

"So," she said, still beaming, "what do you think?"

He swallowed the bite of breakfast he'd been too astonished to swallow before. "You want me?" He poked his chest with a finger. "To sit with—with—with—"

"Miss Clara," Gracie supplied, unwilling to have him say the word *whore* if that's what he was struggling with. "Clara, who works for Mr. Fergus. She's damaged a couple of ribs and can't work for a while, and she's getting awfully bored. Since you're staying here, and I have to tend the baby and take care of my brother's house and all and don't have time, I thought perhaps you might find it in your heart to sit with her and read or play cards or something for an hour or so each day."

With luck, Williams would find Clara as fascinating as she did him, and the man would be occupied for a good deal more than an hour. And for more than a day or two.

"Well, er, Mrs. Trinidad, I'm not sure—"

"Oh, please, Mr. Williams. You look like a kindhearted man, and poor Clara is so weary of her invalid state." She made her eyes go round and pleading. Jake had never been able to resist one of her pleading looks.

Neither, apparently, could Williams. Gracie suppressed an incipient whoop of joy when, after a pause, and with a slight frown, he said, "Well, I reckon I could sit with her for a little while every day."

"Oh, *thank* you, Mr. Williams. You'll never know how much I—that is, you'll never know how much Clara will appreciate it." Inspiration made her add, "You know, she told me just today that she admires you."

He looked utterly astounded. "She did?"

"She did."

"My goodness."

Although his words came out sounding more bewildered than flattered, Gracie didn't abandon hope. Instead, she exacted a promise from Williams that he'd visit with the prostitute for an hour after breakfast each day. Then she gave him her most brilliant smile in parting before she went back upstairs to clean up Clara's breakfast dishes.

When she related the news to Clara, her patient didn't seem as pleased as she ought to, in Gracie's estimation. But she neither worried about it nor chastised Clara for her lack of enthusiasm. She'd already accomplished her purpose.

Williams had told her he didn't think being kind to the invalid would interfere with his search too much. Gracie hoped to God he was wrong.

Charity was napping after a full and interesting morning.

Gracie stood at the sink, her back to Jake, cleaning the radishes she and Charity had taken from their garden—the first fruits of their labors. Gracie had planted radishes deliberately because they grew so fast. It had been worth the effort, too, when Charity pulled the first dirty red round out of the soil and stared at it, initially with surprise and then with blossoming joy.

Since she knew Jake would hear about it from someone eventually anyway, Gracie had just finished relating the tale of how she'd lured William Williams into entertaining Clara. She really wished he didn't have to know about it at all. She tried to keep her tone casual, as if she were merely relaying an interesting tidbit of information.

"I can't believe you did that, Gracie."

He laughed as he said it, so Gracie guessed he didn't disapprove.

"Well, she said she admired him, and she gets awfully

bored lying up there all by herself without anything to do, so I figured it wouldn't hurt anything."

"I reckon you're right. My God, there's no end of your wiles, is there?"

Jake's choice of words struck one of Gracie's raw nerves. "And just what do you mean by that, Jake Molloy?" she asked sharply, shooting him a look over her shoulder. "What do you mean, 'wiles'? I'm not wily, and you know it."

Holding his hands up to fend off her irritation, Jake said, "I didn't mean anything. I just think you were pretty clever to recruit Williams to your cause. Plus," he added dryly, "playing with Clara will keep him from searching for that mysterious woman and child, won't it?"

Gracie's heart speeded up until her chest hurt. Oh, Lord, he knew! Her knees went weak. He knew!

He can't know, Grace Molloy. You're going crazy.

She said, "Don't be silly, Jake," and turned back to her radishes.

"All right. Didn't mean to tease." Jake went on about his business.

Gracie squeezed her eyes shut and thought with despair that she couldn't maintain this level of nervous tension much longer without losing her mind. She was frightened all day, every day.

Each time she left the house these days, she scanned the street for strangers, fearing she'd see the one man she dreaded, heading her way. Already she'd begun to undo all the good she'd tried to do for Charity. Her own anxiety was rubbing off on the baby, and Gracie had seen a hint of her old wariness cross Charity's face a number of times. She'd even awakened crying last night.

All at once she knew what she had to do. In truth, she'd known it ever since she'd seen William Williams talking to Fergus that day in the saloon, but she hadn't wanted to admit it. She dropped the radish she'd been washing and gripped the sink, in sudden danger of bursting into tears.

"What's the matter, Gracie?"

She must have jumped a foot when Jake's big hands

settled on her shoulders. "Nothing," she whispered, longing to pour all of her problems onto his strong shoulders.

That would have been wrong, though, and she wouldn't do it. If Jake had taught her nothing else in the short time she'd been blessed with his presence, he'd taught her that a body had to handle his own problems. Her own problems. And she would. No matter what it took.

And, as she stood there with Jake's hands comforting her, Gracie knew what it would take, and it nearly broke her heart. She and Charity had to leave Diabolito Lindo. They had to escape. Again.

"You sure?"

Suddenly Gracie's grit gave out. Knowing it might be the last time in her life she'd have the opportunity, she whirled around and threw her arms around Jake's broad chest.

"Oh, Jake, I love you so much!"

She didn't cry, which she later chalked up to a miracle of God. When Jake's strong arms wrapped around her, she didn't cry, and she didn't blubber or whine. Instead, she poured out her heart's longings.

"I'm sorry, Jake. I know there's nothing we can do about it because you were kind enough to take me in and lie for me. But I can't help loving you, and wanting more. I've loved you since I was four years old, you know."

"I know, Gracie." His voice sounded thick.

"And I expect to love you until the day I die. It's just so hard, living here with you and being unable to express my love in the way men and women have done since Adam and Eve. It's hard, Jake."

"It's hard for me, too, Gracie. My God, it's hard."

As she could feel the evidence of how hard it was for Jake, Gracie believed him. Her heart had never felt so heavy, nor her body so ripe. And she couldn't do a thing about either of them without ruining Jake's life and endangering Charity.

"I'm sorry I've been so unpleasant these last few days, Jake. I was worried that my late husband's brother might have sent that Mr. Williams out here to find Charity and me. I know he said he didn't know the name of the woman and baby he was looking for, but I'm not sure I believe him." It was as much of the truth as she dared tell him. She hoped it would help ease her conscience, even if only a little bit. So far it wasn't working.

"I understand, Gracie. I don't think you have to worry about Williams, though."

"I hope not."

They stood in the kitchen, wrapped in each other's arms, for another full minute or more before Jake spoke again.

"Gracie . . ."

"Yes, Jake?"

"Gracie, I don't think we'd better do this any longer."

Since she couldn't bear to release him, she squeezed him more tightly. "I don't want to let you go, Jake." She wanted him to make love to her, in fact. Right here. Right now. She wanted him to teach her body the secrets it was longing to learn.

"I don't want to let you go, either, love. In fact, if I don't do it pretty soon, I'm going to weaken. And Gracie, I really don't want to do that. I have too much at stake here. So do you."

Oh, Lord, didn't she know it! But she also knew this would be the last embrace she'd ever share with Jake, and that it was all she'd ever share with him. She wasn't sure how she'd be able to endure life without him. But she'd sworn she'd protect Charity, and she wouldn't go back on her word. She was still the only thing that stood between Charity and disaster, and she'd never fail her.

With an aching in her heart, Gracie guessed Jake's goodness must be rubbing off in spite of herself because she understood now, as she'd never understood before, that if she were to follow her desires, she wouldn't be failing only Charity. She'd be failing herself, she'd be failing every man in this town who depended on Jake Molloy, and, most especially, she'd be failing Jake.

"I know, Jake. I know." It almost killed her to drop her arms.

He stepped away from her, his distress plain to read in his eyes.

"I'm sorry, Jake. I know I shouldn't have brought that up again." But she'd had to at least hug him once more. She'd had to.

"It's all right, Gracie."

Sweat droplets had beaded on his brow and upper lip, and Gracie felt guilty. She could tell just by looking that she'd completely shattered his composure. Not that hers was all that solid. Pressure throbbed in her body, and she wanted nothing more than to wrap her arms around him again.

She clasped her hands behind her back and refused to compromise either of them. Or Charity. *Remember the baby. Remember the baby,* her brain shrieked, and she listened.

Jake continued, "But I reckon I'd better get the hell out of here for a minute or two, because I'm not sure I trust myself around you right now."

She lowered her head and whispered, "I'm sorry, Jake. I understand."

For the second time in as many days, Jake raced out of his house as if all the demons of hell, instead of one small woman with pretty hazel-green eyes and curly blond hair, were after him.

"You don't look so good, Jake."

Jake peered up from his dismal contemplation of the whiskey bottle before him and found Fergus observing him closely, his face lined with concern, his eyes worried. He was wiping a glass.

Sometimes Jake wondered if Fergus had one glass he kept just so he could pick it up when the saloon opened to wipe and wipe and wipe. Before his customers showed up, he did other chores around the place, but every time Jake had come in here during business hours, Fergus seemed to be wiping that same damned glass.

"I don't feel so good, either, Fergus."

"Sorry to hear it. Problems at home?"

If Fergus got any more discreet, Jake decided, he could be a spy. A wry smile twisted his lips. "You might say so."

"Anything the matter with Miss Gracie?"

Shutting his eyes against the compassion on his friend's

face, Jake wondered for the first time if Fergus suspected that Gracie and Jake's kinship was a sham. Since he'd promised Gracie to keep the secret, he did, but it cost him a lot. "No. She's fine."

Oh, God, she was fine. She was the finest woman Jake had ever known. His little Gracie. As recently as two months ago, he'd been taking out his memories of Gracie, dusting them off, and hugging them to his heart as another might hug a locket containing the tintype of a dearly beloved. Now she was here, and she was even more wonderful than he'd remembered.

Hell, she was a woman; an imperfect, pretty, darling, enticing woman, and he loved her. She was a lying woman, too, and manipulative, and he wished he could shake her so hard that the truth would finally fall out of her mouth and stop coming between them.

Not, of course, that the truth would change anything. He still couldn't marry her. The idea of living with her forever and being unable to touch her made his insides knot up. The idea that she might go away someday—and marry somebody else—hurt even more.

Sighing, Jake plowed his fingers through his hair and rested his forehead in his open palms.

"There's forgetfulness in that bottle, Fergus," he murmured, feeling more wretched than he had in five years. His voice came out ragged.

After a moment, Fergus said, "Reckon that's true, Jake."

"It might be nice to forget for a while."

"Who fer?"

Jake looked up, Fergus's question having jarred him. "Me."

"Ah." Fergus nodded, still wiping.

Everything in Jake's body cried out for a drink; even his hair and toenails wanted him to drown his problems in whiskey. "It's tempting," he murmured.

"Is it?"

"Yeah. I could drink that bottle and forget everything."

"For a while, I reckon."

Neither man spoke for a minute. Jake watched, intrigued,

as a streak of late-afternoon sunshine crept across the bar until it illuminated the rust-colored liquid in the whiskey bottle.

"It's pretty, in the bottle like that."

"It's a damned sight purtier in that there bottle than it ever was in you, Jake Molloy, if you don't mind my sayin' so." Fergus's voice had gone as dry as the glass he was wiping.

An involuntary chuckle leaked through Jake's lips. "Reckon you're right, at that."

"You know damned well I am. And don't you get to bellyachin' and whinin' at me, neither."

Fergus's glass hit the bar with a clunk, making Jake jerk back. He looked up, astonished, to find Fergus glaring at him. He'd never seen such a ferocious expression on his friend's face before.

"Goddamn it, Jake, I ain't never seen you like this, and I don't like it. Easy fer you to say you kin fergit it all in that there bottle, but it ain't likely I'd be so lucky, is it? Or Miss Gracie? Hell, you don't recollect the times I hauled your ass out of trouble and into bed, nor doctored you in the mornin'. Well, ain't that just lucky fer you. I sure as hell remember 'em. Every single goddamned one of 'em."

When Fergus's skinny finger poked Jake in the chest, he almost fell backward off his barstool. His mouth dropped open.

"Now, I'd do it again and I will if you suck up that there whiskey, Jake, but I won't like doin' it. No more'n I liked doin' it before. Goddamn it, I make my livin' off drunks, but I don't like 'em. I think they're the stinkiest critters God ever made. They're worse'n polecats and just as p'isonous."

"Fergus, I—"

"Shet your damned mouth, Jake. I ain't done with you yet." Fergus pressed his hands on the top of the bar and leaned over until he was talking right into Jake's face, his eyes snapping savagely.

"You was a stinkin', rotten, lousy drunk, Jake Molloy, and you ain't no more. Whilst you was drinkin', I kept tellin' myself there was more in your innards than whiskey, and you proved me right. I ain't about to set back and watch you turn around and make me wrong.

"Now, I don't know what the hell's got into you lately, and I ain't askin', but you know as well as I do there ain't nobody on this goddamn earth ain't got problems. Some problems is worse'n others, but there ain't no problem gonna be solved by drinkin' and if anybody should know that, it's you."

Fergus poked him harder this time. Jake rubbed the spot on his chest and gawked at his best friend. Fergus's mouth shut with a click of teeth. He grabbed his glass off the countertop and resumed polishing it. His ferocious expression did not abate, nor did he stop glaring at Jake.

"I ain't never took you fer no fool, Jake, but if you take a pull on that there bottle, I'll know I was mistook in you. Bad mistook."

Stunned, Jake didn't know what to say. It was just as well, as Fergus still wasn't through with him.

"And where the hell's that damned God you're always preachin' about, anyhow? He took hisself off somewheres? That why you're sittin' there, eyein' that damned bottle like it was salvation and whinin' about how bad things are? Shee-it, Jake, I ain't never saw such a pea-wit."

Jake couldn't recall ever having been called a pea-wit before. And he'd never seen Fergus give anybody a lecture, either. Fergus was the most self-possessed, easygoing man on the face of the earth in Jake's experience, and damned near impossible to rile.

That it had been Jake's ill-timed nonsense about starting to drink again that had riled him shook Jake to the soles of his well-worn boots. He'd always known Fergus as his friend. Hell, for years, he'd known him as his only friend since the others had drifted away, either disgusted by his behavior or driven off by their own demons. Until this moment, he hadn't realized how very much Fergus cared about him.

Gracie and Fergus.

Damn. He wasn't sure any man on earth deserved the love of those two people. Jake knew good and well *he* didn't. Instead of making him sink back into melancholy as it would have in years past, the knowledge goosed him in his own hard-won self-respect.

Damn it, everybody in the world deserved love. Love and respect. And knowing that he had somehow managed to secure the love of Fergus and Gracie made Jake sit up a little straighter. There weren't too many people who could boast of that much luck.

"Pea-wit. Good God." His mouth curled up at the corners.

Fergus eyed him hard for several seconds, his bushy eyebrows veeing over his eyes, before he apparently decided to believe Jake's grin. His features relaxed.

"You scared the hell outa me, Jake."

Jake laughed outright. "You scared the hell *into* me, Fergus."

Somehow, Gracie managed to get through the rest of her day. Her decision to leave Diabolito Lindo frightened her infinitely more than the decision to leave St. Louis had. After all, from St. Louis, she'd headed west to her beloved Jake.

In leaving Jake, she knew she'd be venturing into totally alien territory. Besides, she loved him. The very idea of leaving him made her stomach knot up, her chest hurt, and her eyes burn.

But William Chester Williams was looking for her, and one of these days he'd realize he'd found her, if he didn't know it already. One of these days, it wouldn't only be Williams here in town, sniffing out her trail like some demonic hound, it would be John Farthing, too. She couldn't risk being found by that devil, and she wouldn't wager Jake against him, either.

While Charity napped on, Gracie used her time alone in the house to pen a full confession to Jake. She wouldn't allow herself to succumb to tears as she wrote; she just wrote—doggedly, honestly, omitting nothing. She'd leave this note for him to find after she was gone. He deserved more than that from her, but it was all she had to give.

And when they got to—oh, sweet heaven, where would

they go? Gracie's determination to be strong almost deserted her when she contemplated the infinite number of places she could go—and how difficult it would be to cover her traces as she tried to get there.

The scarred face of the burly Bart arose in her mind's eye, and Gracie swallowed her weakness. Bart would help her; if not for goodness' sake, then for Jake's. She'd explain to him how she didn't dare ask for Jake's help and the reason for her reluctance. If anybody would understand, Bart would. He wouldn't want to jeopardize Jake either.

And Harley Newton. Harley would do anything for her. She was sure one of them would be able to suggest another town, too. And a way to get out of this one without being discovered.

At any rate, once they got where they were going, she'd write Jake and beg his forgiveness. Perhaps he'd give it; he probably would. Jake had the biggest heart in the world. If she were very lucky, perhaps he'd even join them.

It was far more likely, Gracie thought bleakly, that he'd thank his lucky stars she was finally out of his life. She'd never been anything but a burden to him, particularly these last couple of months.

On that daunting thought, she continued her missive, putting the decision about a possible destination out of her mind until she'd had the opportunity to discuss the matter with Bart.

When Charity awoke, Gracie had finished her letter. With every breath, she tried to remember to keep her manner cheerful; with every other breath, she failed.

Nevertheless, she managed somehow to scrape through the rest of the afternoon, feed Jake and Charity supper with a semblance of good cheer, and retire to bed. She held Charity close to her bosom and prayed. She didn't sleep at all.

14

"*Y*OU WANT ME and Harley to do *what?*"

Choir practice over, Gracie had cornered Bart Ragsdale and dragged him outside and around to the back of the saloon. Nobody could see them there, nor could they be overheard. Charity had gone to sleep on the piano bench during the last song. She now rested peacefully on a folded saddle blanket in the shade of the saloon's eaves.

Gracie wished she could rest so peacefully. Or do anything at all peacefully, for that matter. Her nerves were so ravaged by this time that her heart palpitated, her scalp tingled, and her skin felt as though it were too tight for her body. Panic filled her, never giving her a moment's rest, threatening to erupt; it wouldn't have surprised her much if she'd exploded from all the pent-up anxiety inside her.

From her vantage point at the saloon's rear, Gracie could see the garden she and Charity had been digging in yesterday. There were plenty more radishes in there to be pulled up, and the carrots were almost ready to pick. Her insides wept to know that neither she nor Charity would be here to harvest them. She wondered if Jake would do it, or if he'd avoid the garden as a too-painful reminder of things that might have been.

From here, Jake's backyard looked serene and peaceful and utterly scenic, framed as it was by the artistically broken-down wagon on one side and a huge oak on the other. Jake had propped one of the wagon's wheels against a fence post, and it reminded Gracie of pictures she'd seen of the West in dime novels and periodicals back home in St. Louis.

The chicken coop stood pristine and white, newly painted on the outside while on the inside, straw beckoned to the chickens scratching in the yard. Jake had fenced them off so they couldn't ruin her garden, bless him. The goat, tethered to the oak tree, chewed placidly on weeds at her feet. Jake had fashioned a watering trough and a grain bin. The silly goat always ate her grain first and then browsed on the sparse vegetation in the yard, considering the garden just out of her reach with an avid eye.

Today, terror all but consumed Gracie, rendering the beauty of her surroundings sadly inadequate to soothe her tattered spirits.

Bart stared at her as if she'd just asked him to climb the Alps. Although she hardly blamed him, her nerves had been rubbed raw during the past couple of weeks, and she felt perilously close to a shriek.

Refusing to give in to the urge to grab Bart by his massive shoulders and shake understanding into him, she strove to keep her tone pleasant but urgent. "Please, Mr. Ragsdale. I can't tell you why, but I can tell you that it's important. It might even mean Charity's life, because . . . because I think that man is after her."

Bart's eyes opened wide with surprise, and Gracie struggled to come up with a plausible excuse. Recalling the lie she'd told Jake on her first day in Diabolito Lindo, she rushed on. "You see, my husband's brother is trying to take the baby from me because . . . because his family is rich and he thinks he'll be able to offer her more material wealth than I can. But I can't give up my baby, Mr. Ragsdale. I just can't!"

"How can he do that?" Bart looked horrified, just as Gracie had hoped he would.

"Because he's rich and I'm not! Oh, Mr. Ragsdale, please, you have to understand. Please just do it. I'll pay you."

"I don't want no money!" Bart exclaimed, miffed that she'd even think such a thing. "But, ma'am, you can't just up and take off!"

"You know I wouldn't ask if it wasn't absolutely necessary. You care what happens to Charity, don't you? And me?"

"Yes, ma'am, I shore do." Bart's expression was mulish. "I care what happens to Preacher Jake, too, and he ain't goin' to like this. Not one bit."

"I know he won't." Gracie bowed her head and breathed deeply, trying to keep from bawling or bellowing. Both urges battled within her. When she looked up again, she placed her hand on Bart's brawny arm. He looked down at it as if he feared it might bite him.

"Mr. Ragsdale, I love my brother Jake. I love him more than anybody on the face of the earth, except maybe Charity. That's why I can't tell him about this. Surely you understand that if I asked him, he'd try to help me."

"Well, of course he would."

"But he *can't*! The man who's after me is a horrible, mean, vicious person. For all I know, he even has the law behind him. He's rich, you know, and rich men can do all sorts of things the rest of us can't."

Scratching his head, Bart muttered, "I reckon that's the truth."

"It is, Mr. Ragsdale! It is! Besides, he's truly evil. He'd kill Jake as soon as look at him."

Bart's expression altered and took on a skeptical cast. "Well, now, Miss Gracie, I ain't so sure he could do nothin' like that. I seen Preacher Jake take care of hisself more'n once. He ain't no pansy, and he ain't no seedy feller. He don't run from trouble, an' he don't run from fights. I seen him hold his own in more'n one. He's saved my bacon more'n once, too, and that's the God's honest truth."

"I know, Mr. Ragsdale. I know you've been friends for a long time."

Bart fingered his scars. "Damned right we have. He saved my damn life, Miss Gracie, beggin' your pardon."

"Yes, yes, I know. And I know he's strong and good and can take care of himself," Gracie said, nearly at the end of her rope. "But that's just the problem. Don't you see? Jake's *honest.*"

"Well, of course he is."

"And this other man—John Farthing—well, he's about as far from honest as a man can get, Mr. Ragsdale. He'd as soon hire somebody to shoot Jake in the back as breathe. I swear, this is the only way I can save both Jake and Charity! Oh, *why* won't you understand?"

Bart scratched his shiny, scarred face. "Well, now, if you put it like that . . ."

"There's no other way to put it. It's the truth."

Bart eyed her unhappily. "Well, if you're really sure this feller might . . ."

"I'm sure of it. How can I not be sure, with Charity's life at stake? And maybe Jake's?"

Abandoning strength for emotion, Gracie began to wring her hands. Tears she'd been keeping at bay for days now pooled in her eyes. "He's already almost killed Charity, Mr. Ragsdale! He's evil! He stops at nothing to achieve his ends. He—"

Bart reached out a huge paw and tried to pat Gracie's back. As he was obviously frightened and nervous, his touch was almost too light for Gracie to feel.

"Aw, Miss Gracie, don't cry. I'll do it. And I'll get Harley to help, too, afore he drinks hisself to sleep."

"Oh, Mr. Ragsdale, thank you! Thank you! You'll never know how much I appreciate this!" Gracie dashed her apron across her cheeks, wiping away tears. "Jake would thank you, too, if he knew."

"Well, now, Miss Gracie, I ain't so sure about that, if you don't mind my sayin' so."

"Oh, but he would. I'm sure of it."

"If you're so damned sure—beg pardon, ma'am, didn't mean to use no bad language—but if this man's so dadblasted bad, don't you think you or me or somebody should oughta tell Jake?"

Her face must have expressed her horror at Bart's suggestion because he hastened to add, "But I won't tell him, if you don't want me to, Miss Gracie. Swear to Jesus, I ain't a-goin' to tell nobody. Just like you asked me."

A wave of relief washed over Gracie so suddenly that she had to stick her hand out and brace herself against the side of the building. "Thank you, Mr. Ragsdale. Thank you so much. You'll never know how much this means to me. To all of us. You and Harley will have saved Charity's life by helping me. And maybe Jake's. And maybe even mine."

The truth of what she'd just said rattled her, and Gracie shivered in the warm late-May noontime.

"All right, Miss Gracie. We'll get on it right after sundown."

"Thank you," Gracie whispered. "I'll place a candle in the window as soon as I know Jake's asleep. And you'll have a wagon and somebody to drive and guard it waiting for us?"

"I expect I will, Miss Gracie." He didn't sound happy about it.

"Oh, thank you, Mr. Ragsdale. Thank you!"

"All right, ma'am." After heaving a defeated sigh, Bart slouched off. Gracie could hear him mutter, "Now how the hell am I gonna keep Harley Newton from drinkin' hisself into a ditch before nightfall, I wonder?"

Gracie prayed to God that Bart could do it.

As had been happening to her ever since she'd made her decision, the thought of leaving Jake made her want to cry. And, as she'd been doing for the same period of time except when talking to Bart, she clamped down on the impulse.

After she and Charity had made their escape, after she no longer had to fear for their safety, only then would she allow herself the luxury of tears.

You've changed, Gracie Molloy. You're not that flighty

*female you were when you first got here. Ever since you
made that promise to Martha, you've been strong, and you
do what you have to do. After you've done what you have to
do, you can succumb to your emotions.*

She prayed that she was right about herself, because
several lives hung in the balance.

Jake looked up from his half-finished sermon, his concentration jarred by the knock on his door. He still hadn't gotten
used to people knocking, although they did it more and
more frequently since Gracie had come to town.

Gracie. Smiling, Jake recalled her little emotional fit
yesterday and its aftermath as he rose and stretched.
Sometimes, he reckoned, an outburst cleared the air. He'd
survived two of them yesterday. Gracie's had sent him over
the edge, and Fergus's had yanked him right back the other
way with gusto. In fact, he'd landed on his butt so hard the
jolt must have rattled his brains back into place, because
he'd felt better ever since.

When he opened the door, he was surprised to see
William Chester Williams standing before him. He looked
nervous. And terribly sincere.

"Mr. Molloy, may I speak to you about something
personal?"

"Well, I reckon so, Mr. Williams. Care to step inside?"

"Er, would you mind coming to the saloon, Mr. Molloy?
I think we can be more private there."

More private in a saloon than in his house? Jake blinked
and tried to follow Williams's reasoning. Failing, he decided
he didn't much care where they chatted. If this man needed
him, it was his duty as a minister of God to be available.

"I'll be right with you," he said. And, after fetching his
hat, gun, and jacket and writing a note for Gracie, he was.

"Drat it all, where is he?"

Gracie's nerves, already stretched entirely too tightly,
threatened to snap. Jake had been gone all day long, and it
was now well past sunset. She'd just settled Charity in the
bed they shared, told her two bedtime stories, and sung three

songs, and she was now pacing the parlor, wringing her hands and wanting to shriek.

Snatching Jake's hastily scribbled note from the table, she read it yet again, wishing she possessed second sight and could read past the few brief words and discern what was in his heart.

Oh, Lord, what would happen if he didn't come back before she left? She thought she'd die if she couldn't see his beloved face one more time, even if she only watched it in sleep.

Worse, what would happen if he came home as she was trundling Charity out to the wagon Bart said he'd have waiting for her behind Old Man Ramirez's place.

Or—oh, good Lord—what if that man Farthing had sent him? Panic surged in her breast and tightened her throat. No. No, that hadn't happened. Bart had said Jake could take care of himself, and Gracie believed him. She *had* to believe him.

She pressed her hand to her bosom, feeling the paper she'd folded up and tucked into her bodice. It was the letter she'd written to Jake, and it contained her heart and soul. It probably held Charity's life, as well, and she prayed Jake would understand. If he ever came home.

Where in God's name *was* he? A clap of thunder rattled the house, and Gracie must have jumped a foot. She raced to the front door and yanked it open, only to encounter a spatter of fat rain drops. Even as she stood there watching, the rain thickened. In no more than several seconds, Gracie realized she was witnessing one of New Mexico Territory's sudden and drenching cloudbursts. The men in town had told her about them; this was the first she'd personally encountered.

"Oh, good Lord in heaven, why do You want to rain on us tonight? Aren't we in enough peril already?" She realized she was beginning to hold a real grudge against God, and hoped it wasn't a sign of moral decay.

At least the roll of thunder hadn't awakened Charity. Another tremendous crash and a gust of wind nearly tore the door out of Gracie's grip, and she shut it again, carefully.

Pausing to wipe up the water that had blown inside, she tiptoed into the bedroom and made sure that the latest thunderclap hadn't disturbed Charity's rest. It hadn't.

"Well, I don't dare wait any longer. If Jake comes home while I'm out, I suppose I can make up some excuse."

She absolutely hated leaving Charity in the house alone. If the baby were to awaken, she'd be frightened to death without Gracie there to comfort her. Unfortunately, Gracie didn't perceive an alternative. Where in the name of heaven was Jake?

First she set a candle on the windowsill to warn Bart and Harley that she was on her way. Then she grabbed a big burlap sack, tied a scarf around her head, slung a woolen shawl over her shoulders, picked up a sturdy lantern with a covered lid, and headed out the door.

Lord, she was sick of lying. Now, however, she was glad she'd kept up her pretense in front of Jake. If that awful William Williams ever did figure out exactly who he was looking for, at least Jake wouldn't have to lie again. He'd be able to say, honestly, that he hadn't known anything until after she'd left.

In the middle of the night, like a thief or something. The injustice of her situation rankled, and her grudge edged up an inch.

She almost slipped and fell flat on her face as soon as she stepped out the door. Her near-accident reminded her of what she'd been told about the quality of the soil hereabouts, and she made herself go slowly and carefully, even while every instinct urged her to run.

Trying to hold her skirts out of the mud—a hopeless proposition, she soon realized—Gracie picked her way through the slop, heading for the cemetery. With luck, Bart and Harley would have finished their task and be waiting for her. Without luck . . . no. She refused to think about it. Another shaft of lightning shattered the black sky, illuminating the top of the hill and making the grasping trees and cockeyed crosses stand out like some ghostly parody of a shadow-box pantomime.

The rain was coming down even harder now, and Gracie

found it difficult to see anything at all. She didn't dare tip her lantern for fear the pelting raindrops would leak inside and snuff out the fire. She wasn't sure she could find her way back to the house on such a pitch-black, rainy night.

She considered it nigh unto a miracle when she found the path to Boot Hill. The trail leading to the cemetery was as slippery as ice. If it weren't for all the rocks and pebbles and scrub brush holding the dirt in place, Gracie feared she'd never have made it to the top. As it was, she had to release her hold on her skirts in order to keep her balance. Not that it mattered much by that time; they were already soaked through and filthy. She did ultimately reach her destination, though, and could have kissed Bart and Harley when she saw them huddled near an open grave, shovels in their hands, awaiting her. A cross bearing the name Ralph Trinidad seemed to be sinking into the mud at Bart's side.

By the light of a solitary lantern perched on a nearby rock and sheltered by a makeshift lean-to, the two men looked miserable. If Gracie had been in a mood to be amused, she might have likened them to a couple of gents who'd been dunked in the weekly laundry kettle. She wasn't in such a mood, though, and the thought no sooner entered her brain than it slipped out again.

"Thank you so much, Mr. Ragsdale and Mr. Newton. I don't know what I'd have done without you. I'm so sorry you're getting wet."

"The weather ain't your fault, Miss Gracie," Harley told her graciously. Another clap of thunder made him jump. "You better git your work here done pretty quick, though, ma'am, or we're all likely to be struck by one of them lightnin' bolts and toasted."

Bart nodded morosely. "Harley's told the truth, ma'am. It ain't good to hang about on hilltops during a lightnin' storm."

"I know. And I'm sorry. Please, go on about your business. I can finish what I need to do here and then meet you behind Mr. Ramirez's house, Mr. Ragsdale."

"Don't you need no help, ma'am?"

"No." Gracie's heart lurched. "Oh, Mr. Ragsdale, I don't

know how to say this, but I don't want the two of you to know what I'm doing up here or what's in that coffin. You see, if you know, then that awful man who's after us might be able to hurt you. I've already jeopardized the two of you—and Jake. I can't bear the thought of endangering you any further."

Bart and Harley exchanged a glance. Harley said, "I reckon we appreciate that, ma'am, but we'd better pry the lid off'n that coffin for you. You ain't gonna be able to get it open nutherwise."

"Good God, I didn't even think about that." Which, Gracie thought glumly, just went to show how much she had yet to learn—in spite of the education she'd gathered in Diabolito Lindo during her time here. "Thank you. I'd surely appreciate it."

The two men had already lifted the coffin out of its soggy hole on two ropes. It now rested beside a heap of mud that seemed to melt like chocolate in the downpour. They slithered it forward and Bart picked up a vicious-looking metal implement. Gracie hadn't even noticed it lying on the boulder next to the lantern.

The rain was now coming down in sheets, and Gracie wondered how much longer the lantern could continue to burn, what with water splashing up all around it.

"Careful there, Bart," Harley said. "Damned ground's slick as a greased pig."

"Can't get the damned thing open. Hold the other side, Harley."

"Will do."

Harley slipped in the clay soil as he tried to make his way around the coffin, landing on his rear end with a loud splatter. Gracie pressed her hands to her cheeks, and wished she hadn't caused these dear men so much trouble. If her circumstances weren't so horribly insecure, she'd never have done it. Then and there she decided she'd be sending them each a bank draft. She already knew neither man would accept money from her if she handed it to them.

Bart helped Harley stand and then almost slipped himself

when he repositioned himself at the coffin's side. "Damn, this ground's like wet ice," he muttered.

Another flash of lightning followed by a tremendous crash of thunder made Gracie shrink back. As soon as her foot touched the ground behind her, it slipped from underneath her and she had to scramble to keep her balance, losing her shawl in the process. Small loss. It was sopping wet anyway and had ceased to afford any warmth or protection.

"I had no idea the ground would be this slippery," she said, feeling guiltier and guiltier with each passing second. "Jake told me what the dirt was like around here, but I didn't understand what he meant until now."

"Yes, ma'am," the game Harley said. "It's slipperier'n a whore's—" He looked up in horror when the words slipped out and he realized what he'd been going to say.

Bart said, "Harley!"

Ducking his head, Harley murmured, "I'm real sorry, Miss Gracie. I didn't mean no disrespect."

The very last thing Gracie was worried about at the moment was indelicate language. "It's perfectly all right, Mr. Newton." She stooped to retrieve her shawl, almost lost her footing again, and decided she could live quite nicely without it. She could always buy another one when she and Charity got to California.

She'd finally chosen California because it was about the closest thing to civilization the land west of St. Louis could provide. She'd have headed there in the first place but for Jake. Miserable as she was, thinking about Jake made her want to cry, so she cut off that line of thought in a hurry and resumed staring and shivering, wishing the blasted rain would stop.

Oh, Lord, getting back down the hill was going to be difficult. Well, she didn't suppose it mattered much; she could slide down on her bottom if she had to. She was already so wet and dirty that a little more mud and rain wouldn't matter.

"All right," Bart said when Harley finally got himself

around to the other side of the coffin. "Hang on, Harley, I'm a-goin' to pry this thing up."

"All set."

Gracie heard a screech of metal against wood and supposed it must be the coffin nails losing their grip on the mahogany box. Until this minute she hadn't considered purchasing such a well-made coffin a mistake, but she bet a plain pine box wouldn't have been as tough as this monster. Still, it had served its purpose well. At the time she'd had no way of knowing she'd have to disembowel its contents in the middle of a rainstorm in the middle of the night in the middle of the New Mexico Territory.

Oh, God, I hope all this thunder hasn't woken Charity up. The idea of the baby waking up in the dark and being unable to find her made Gracie's head throb. She wanted to shout at the men to hurry up and knew she was being irrational.

"Hell, Harley, it's slippin'."

Bart's comment jerked Gracie out of her worry, and she shot a panicked glance at the coffin. Sure enough, like a recalcitrant child bent on mischief, it appeared to be inching away from Bart. She saw Harley press down on the lid, but that only seemed to make it squirt forward.

"Oh, my God!" She tried to run over and help the two men who were scrambling to get a grip on the slippery wood in the slippery mud, and promptly fell on her face. She lurched to her knees, tried to wipe the mud out of her eyes with her muddy hands, and finally lifted her face to the cleansing rain, nearly hysterical because she couldn't see what was happening to the coffin. When she did manage to regain her feet and her sight, she was almost sorry she could see again.

"I can't hold on to the damned thing!"

Gracie could tell that Harley was doing his level best. On his belly in the mud, he clawed like a dying man at the sides of the coffin. It was heavy, though, and already perched on a downhill slope. Bart, struggling for all he was worth, crawled on his hands and knees in an effort to help his friend check the coffin's descent.

It was all to no avail. As Gracie watched, horrified,

Harley lost his battle with mud, rain, and polished mahogany. She saw the coffin shoot out of his hands like a bullet, a split second before his chin hit the mud with a thick splash.

Cursing like an artilleryman, Bart stretched himself out flat on his belly in the mud and reached, but he was an inch or so short of his goal. Even if he'd managed to touch the box, Gracie knew he would not have been able to hold on.

Her brain registered a moment of gratitude that neither man had been in the coffin's path when it shot loose. It was as heavy as a boulder. It might have caused even so burly a pair as Bart and Harley a good deal of bodily harm had it hit either of them. Slithering through the mud like an eel, she pushed herself to the crest of the hill and saw the glimmer of rain splattering off polished mahogany as the box thundered downhill.

Then she remembered what Charity had to lose, and panic seized her.

Wailing "Oh, my God, no!" she launched herself off the hill after the coffin. Scrambling to gain her footing, ripping plants up as she went, Gracie could barely see the box as it slithered along, picking up speed, careening this way and that over the slick clay, its path zigzagging as it displaced rocks and bumped over saplings and clumps of mesquite.

The scene was like something out of a maniac's dream. And it didn't end at the bottom of the hill. With horror, unable to stop her own downhill slide, Gracie watched the coffin, racing like the wind now, crash through Jake's rickety fence, slide past the wagon's skeleton, and speed directly toward the walls of the little adobe.

"Oh, my God! Oh, my God!"

Frantically grasping at vegetation as she hurtled down the hill, all Gracie ended up with were several handfuls of leaves and two badly scraped palms. Everything else felt scraped, too, but she didn't even care.

The coffin hit the wall of Jake's house just as a flash of lightning lit the entire sky above her. Virtually simultaneously, an accompanying blast of thunder ripped through the air. The cacophony of crashing wood and booming thunder nearly pierced Gracie's eardrums.

She finally came to a stop when her skirts became tangled up in the rails of the broken fence. Desperately, ripping cloth and breaking fingernails in her frenzy, she tore her skirts free and managed to get to her feet. Pains shot this way and that through her body, but she couldn't stop to worry about them now. Limping, slipping, falling, crawling, she groped her way to the coffin.

Thank God Bart had pried the lid loose before the box had slid out of his hands. It had slipped off in the crash, and by the light of the tiny candle still flickering in the window, Gracie could see the coffin's contents, spilled out like treasure in the mud.

Just as she reached her destination, she heard Charity.

"Mama! Mama! *Mama!*"

Gracie looked up at the window, her insides roiling. "Oh, Lord, oh, Lord!"

This was too much to bear. Her heart all but breaking, Gracie knew she had to leave poor Charity to her terror while she rescued what she could of the rest of their lives from the mud into which it had been dumped.

Somehow, she'd managed to retain a grip on her burlap sack in her crazy trip downhill. Without even pausing to consider the miracle that she was still alive, Gracie began gathering things up and stuffing them into the bag.

"Mama! Mama! Mama!"

"Oh, Lord, baby, I'm coming. Just wait another little minute."

"Mama! Mama! *Mama!*"

By this time, Gracie didn't know whether it was rain or tears that blinded her. Not even bothering to wipe the water away, she worked on.

Frenzied, in turmoil for Charity, who still screamed inside the house, Gracie didn't notice when another light joined that of the feeble candle, illuminating her activities. Her mind consumed with the need to rescue Martha's legacy and Martha's baby, she didn't think about anything but the task before her.

Until a huge hand came to rest on her shoulder. Then she screamed.

"It's all right, Gracie. You can quit now."

Time stopped. So did Gracie's heart. Releasing her sack and clutching her chest, she looked up, past the light of the lantern, and into Jake's face. His features were shadowed. She couldn't read his expression. She only knew everything was over.

Then she saw William Chester Williams standing behind Jake and realized Charity was still screaming. And remembered why.

"No," she whispered. "Oh, no. No, no, no. Oh, please God, no."

"Mama! Mama! Mama!"

But Williams wasn't looking at Gracie. He had raised his own lantern high. As if in a trance, he took a very careful step toward her. She flinched, but he still didn't look at her.

Instead, he knelt right down in the mud and reached past her as she shrank away from him. When he straightened, he held a packet of papers. By the light of his lantern, Gracie could see that they were envelopes, bound in a pink ribbon, sadly muddied and dripping wet now.

"Mama! Mama! Mama!"

Gracie stared at William Chester Williams, unable to comprehend anything except that she'd been found out and prevented from saving Charity from this monster's employer. Sweet heaven, she'd promised. And now she'd failed.

Then Williams said, "I sent these to her."

And suddenly, in a flash of enlightenment that nearly matched the next crack of lightning, Gracie understood. Her panic stilled, replaced by a cold, awful numbness. "Oh, my God."

"Mama! Mama! Jay!"

Numbness vanished, and her gaze whipped to Jake's face. He leaned over, gripped her elbow, and lifted her to her feet.

"She's calling for you, Jake," Gracie whispered.

"She's calling for both of us, Gracie."

Holding her tight, supporting her through the sucking mud, Jake helped Gracie to the house.

William Chester Williams finished the job Gracie had begun. When he'd filled the burlap sack, he followed them.

15

GRACIE DIDN'T LOOK as though she'd ever get warm. Jake shook his head, watched her shiver, and wished he could hold her.

He couldn't, of course, because at the moment he had Charity in his arms. The baby was still in distress, too, although she no longer screamed in terror. She clung to his shoulders like a barnacle, as if she'd never let him go.

Jake hoped she never would. He loved this little tyke; loved her all the more after having spent the afternoon and most of the evening with William Chester Williams, listening to his story, and piecing bits and snatches of Charity's tale together.

Williams had spoken to him for hours, pleading with Jake for understanding, asking for counsel and guidance. Jake had done his best, although he knew he couldn't solve this problem. They'd prayed together, however, and Jake had felt better after they'd finished. He wasn't sure if Williams did. And he still wasn't entirely clear on Gracie's part in the whole mess, either, but he knew she'd tell him as soon as she finished drying herself. At last!

At least he'd come to a personal decision. No matter how he sliced this particular pie, one of the pieces ended up mangled, but he couldn't fight his fate any longer. He aimed to marry Gracie and take care of Charity, even though it meant leaving the life and the men he'd come to love. It seemed a steep price to pay for having told his flock one small lie, but he reckoned he owed it, and he aimed to pay.

Maybe this was God's ultimate way of taking care of Charity. Jake didn't know. All he knew for certain was that every time he thought about leaving Diabolito Lindo, he felt as if somebody were carving on his heart with a knife. At last, though—at long, long last—Gracie was going to tell him the truth.

At the moment, she was toweling her hair dry. It had taken her nearly an hour to get out of her filthy clothes, clean herself up, wash her hair, cleanse her many cuts and scrapes, and join them again in the kitchen. She'd sprained her ankle pretty badly, and her foot now rested beside Jake on his chair, swollen and bruised.

Bart and Harley had appeared at his door shortly after Jake, Gracie, and Williams had entered the house. The two men looked as pitiful as a couple of drowned rats, and guilty as sin. They begged Jake's forgiveness for attempting to assist Gracie in deceiving him.

With a smile he figured was about as acerbic as any lemon, Jake had shaken his head. "Don't blame yourself, boys. It'd take a herd of rhinoceroses to resist Gracie when she gets her mind set on something. She can make the damnedest request sound reasonable."

After exchanging a look, Bart and Harley had agreed with Jake wholeheartedly, shaken his hand, and thanked him for his understanding. Then they apologized to Gracie for failing in their mission.

"Please, Mr. Ragsdale and Mr. Newton, don't blame yourselves. I guess—" She looked at Jake, a strange expression on her face. "I guess a higher authority took a hand in things tonight."

Bart had looked confused. Harley had nodded as if he, at least, understood.

"It's all right, boys," Jake had told them. "Everything will be all right now." The knife carved another nick out of his heart.

Bart seemed reluctant to leave. "You sure Miss Gracie will be all right, Preacher? We was only tryin' to help her."

"Thanks, boys, I know you were helping her, and I appreciate it. You did a good deed tonight, Bart. Harley. Everything will be all right now."

Finally convinced that Jake wasn't going to light into himself or Harley—or Gracie—Bart agreed to leave.

"Reckon Harley'n me could use us something to take the chill off," he said as he dripped on Jake's parlor floor, his teeth chattering.

"A fire and a towel and a cup of coffee might help, Bart," Jake suggested.

"Yeah," said Bart. "Sure."

"Thanks, Preacher Jake." Harley waved a farewell as he turned to go.

Jake watched both men slip and slide their way to the Devil's Last Stop and thanked God with every step the two men took that he didn't have to live like that any longer. Charity, still secure in his arms, waved good-bye to them.

No more than she could stop shivering could Gracie seem to stop crying. Jake sighed when he saw another trickle of tears drip down her cheek. He longed to comfort her. And have her comfort him. Maybe she could get that damned knife to stop digging into his chest.

"You going to be all right?" he asked her, for probably the fiftieth time.

Nodding, she sniffled and said, "Yes. Thank you." Then she said, also for undoubtedly the fiftieth time, "Can you ever forgive me?"

"There's nothing to forgive, Gracie."

"Yes, there is. Oh, yes there is, Jake. I've been so awful to you."

His grin kicked up. "Not so's I noticed."

"That's only because you're a wonderful man, and I'm just a horrible, deceitful, miserable sinner."

A chuckle sneaked past his grin. Charity, apparently concerned, took his face between her two chubby hands and turned it so that she could stare into it, solemn as a judge. From what he now knew of her past, Jake suspected she was scrutinizing his expression in order to evaluate the validity of his humor before she dared believe it.

Poor little girl. He hugged her. Even though his insides wept, he broadened his smile for her benefit. For the first time since he'd picked her up, her fearful mien eased up some. He guessed she didn't quite trust him enough to return his smile, but he'd give her all the time she needed. She sure as the devil wasn't going anywhere without him; he planned to make sure of that.

His decision hadn't actually been as hard as he'd expected it to be. Contemplating leaving Diabolito Lindo and his flock hurt like fire, but after the agonies he'd gone through tonight when he thought Gracie had left him, he knew it was the only decision he could live with. Life somewhere else seemed bleak to him; life without Gracie wouldn't be life at all.

"You weren't sinning, Gracie," he said gently. "You were just trying to save Martha Farthing's baby from a brutal life."

There went her tears again, falling faster now. She apparently didn't trust herself to speak; she only nodded miserably. With a big sigh, she finally thrust the towel aside and picked up her hairbrush.

Jake watched her for a second, loving her with every ounce of his energy. "Do you think you can tell us about it now? Bill and I would like to know as much as you're able to tell." After a pause, he added, "I think he deserves to know, too, don't you?"

Nodding once more, Gracie whispered, "Yes. Yes, I suppose he does."

She finished brushing her hair, looking about as dejected as Jake had ever seen a person look. She reminded him of himself some mornings after a battle with the bottle, only with a better cause. Gracie had fought a good fight. The only thing sordid or sinful about her battle was her enemy.

He decided to help her start the story by asking a question. "It really was Charity's father who broke her leg, wasn't it, Gracie?"

Her lips tightened. "Yes."

"He didn't just drop her, though, did he?"

When she looked up at him, her eyes held the same piercing clarity he remembered so well from when he was a boy. She used to see right through him with one of those looks; straight through his bluff and into his heart. It had bothered him then; tonight he only thanked God she was here to give him one of those looks. He'd never let her go again. No matter what.

"He tossed her down the stairs, Jake. As if she were a rag doll. I was there. I saw him do it."

"Good God."

"He did it to punish Martha. He was angry with her for some reason—God knows why. He never needed a reason, I suppose. He picked little Charity up out of her bed, dangled her over the banister, and tossed her. I picked her up."

The room was so silent for a minute, they could hear the clock ticking in Jake's bedroom. Jake pressed a hand over his eyes until he realized Gracie was shaking and he reached out to press a comforting hand on hers.

"He beat Martha too, didn't he?"

The hoarse question came from behind them. Jake looked over, blinking in surprise. He'd forgotten all about poor old Williams there for a minute. The man sat at the table, fingering a ring, looking tired and whipped.

Gracie said, "Yes. Yes, he did beat her. Nearly every time he got drunk, and he was drunk most of the time." Her voice shook still, but she didn't cry again. Jake was proud of her and squeezed her hand to let her know it.

Williams shuddered. He glanced up and lifted the ring, showing it to Jake and Gracie. It glimmered dully in the lamplight; a plain ring, obviously not expensive. Jake thought he saw some kind of pattern engraved on it: flowers or something.

"I gave her this." Williams's voice thickened and he looked down again.

Jake pretended not to notice when Williams mopped his eyes with his bandanna. Gracie, more naturally compassionate than he, Jake decided, had no such compunction.

"Oh, Mr. Williams, I'm so sorry. I thought John Farthing had hired you to find us and take Charity back. If I'd known who you were, I never would have tried to keep the baby from you."

"The only reason I tried to find you was to make sure Martha's baby was being cared for properly. If she hadn't been, I planned to see to it that she never wanted for anything, you see."

"I wish I'd known." Gracie's head drooped and she twisted her hands around her hairbrush, all but strangling its handle. "Oh, how I wish I'd known."

Williams only shook his head. Jake supposed his heart was too full for words.

Not so Gracie. "Charity's all that's left of Martha now, Mr. Williams, and she'd want you to know her. I guess you loved Martha as much as I did. I know she loved you."

Williams looked up again, his eyes shimmering with unshed tears, his expression almost painfully pleading. "She did?" he asked, as if Gracie's answer would be the most important one he'd ever hear.

"Oh, my, yes. She loved you very much. Why, she kept every letter you ever wrote her. And that ring. She kept that ring, even though it made John mad. She finally hid it from him."

His hand closed around the ring. Staring at his fist, he murmured, "But she didn't wait for me."

Gracie looked very sad. "No. She thought you were dead, you know. I imagine it's no good waiting for a dead man."

It occurred to Jake at that moment to wonder why Gracie had never married. She loved children. She was bright and vibrant and charming—when she wasn't being irritating. Any man alive would be proud to have her for a wife. It seemed a shame that she didn't already have a family of children and a husband to love.

It also occurred to him to wonder if she'd been waiting for somebody, and if he, Jake Molloy, might possibly be the man for whom she'd waited. She'd already told him that she'd loved him since they were kids, after all. Maybe she'd just never wanted anybody else. The notion offended his sense of modesty and he shelved it. Since the idea intrigued him, it kept falling off the shelf and rolling into his consciousness. He endeavored to ignore it.

"I wrote to her. I wrote to her and told her. I'd been captured and held by the Rebs in Virginia. They almost starved us to death, and I got the fever and ague and nearly died. I was too sick to know anything by the time the treaty was signed and they finally got us out of there. It took me two years in a hospital to learn my own name again, but I wrote her when I did. Then it took another three years to gain enough strength to get back to St. Louis."

"I'm so sorry, Mr. Williams. By that time, I suppose she was already married, and never even saw your letter. Her husband used to take the mail and go through it before he allowed Martha to see it. I know he threw out all the letters I wrote to her. I finally just went up to her door one day and knocked. That's how I found out everything."

"My God."

"She had a hard life, Mr. Williams. She would have loved knowing you were alive somewhere. Anywhere."

Gracie's words came out on a little sigh. Jake heard such regret and sorrow in them that he wished he could clasp her hand and offer her the comfort of his own strength.

Her hands were too sore to grab, though, and Charity was eyeing Gracie now, too, so Jake did the next best thing. He said, "Want to see your mama, Charity? I think she's dry enough now to hold you."

Gracie gave him a smile laced with such love that he had to fight back the passionate declaration suddenly swelling up in his throat. Charity nodded somberly and held her arms out to her mama. Gracie reached for her, too, and Jake winced when he saw all the scratches on her arms and hands.

"You've got to soak those hands, Gracie. As soon as Charity gets settled down again, I'm going to dissolve an antiseptic tablet in boiling water, and you're going to soak your hands for a good hour."

He sounded dogmatic and dictatorial and didn't care. He'd be damned if he'd let Gracie die of blood poisoning now. Not after what she'd been through and what he had planned for the three of them. In spite of his calling and his flock. Or anything else.

Gracie didn't object. She smiled at Charity, who snuggled up so close to her that she very nearly climbed up her chest, and then at him. "All right, Jake. Thank you."

"By the time I got back to St. Louis, I didn't want to bother her. I was afraid it would upset her to have me show up in her life again."

"She'd have loved hearing from you, though."

"I didn't know that, Miss Gracie." Williams sounded utterly beaten. He rested his head in his cupped hands. "Oh, God, I did everything wrong!"

"You didn't," Gracie said. "You couldn't have known anything about John Farthing. Or about Martha's marriage. Even Martha didn't know what kind of man he was until it was too late. Way too late."

Her pretty face puckered up into an expression Jake remembered from their childhood. It was her fighting-for-a-good-cause expression, and it made him smile even as his heart ached for all the years they'd had together. And all the years they'd been apart.

"When I finally began asking questions, the answers made me sick. I went away again."

"Where did you go?"

Williams shrugged. The gesture conveyed his hurt and helplessness in a manner Jake understood very well. He'd felt that way himself, far too often.

"I don't even know. Anywhere. Everywhere. I tried to get Martha out of my mind, but I couldn't, you see. I loved her."

"I understand," Gracie said. Jake realized she did, and his

curiosity about her having remained unmarried trampled over his reserve and galloped back into his mind again.

Lifting his head, Williams peered hard at Gracie. "Did he kill her, Miss Gracie? Did that man kill Martha?"

Gracie hesitated for long enough that she no longer needed to answer Williams's question. She answered anyway. "I don't know if you can say he killed her directly. Not so that anybody could call it murder, anyway." With a vicious frown, she added, "Not until they change the horrible laws to protect women like Martha, at any rate."

"Oh, God!" Williams buried his face in his hands.

"But every time he got drunk, he'd hit her. One night he beat her senseless and broke a couple of ribs. She never got over that. Eventually, she developed pneumonia. It was the pneumonia that finally killed her, the doctor said. But it was John Farthing who caused it, as surely as if he'd held a gun to her head and pulled the trigger."

Shaking his head back and forth in his hands, Williams uttered a wordless groan.

"It was when she was on her deathbed that Martha begged me to take Charity away from her father, to take her out of the city, out of the state, out of the country if I had to in order to protect her from that dirty bastard."

Jake's gaze jerked from Williams to Gracie. He'd never heard her utter a profanity in all the years he'd known her. He hadn't realized she possessed the ability until this minute.

"Martha was my best friend," Gracie went on fiercely. "She was my best friend all through teachers' school, even though she was older than I, and I loved her and Charity. I agreed to do anything Martha wanted, because I'd be damned to hell if I'd let that animal hurt Martha's baby another single time."

She seemed to have to recruit her resources, because she stopped speaking abruptly and fussed with the baby, taking deep, steadying breaths.

When she recovered her composure, she continued. "Martha had some money and jewelry of her own that she'd had when she married John. I suppose, technically, what was hers had become his when they married, but neither Martha nor I saw it that way. The laws are so unfair!"

She had to take another deep breath. Neither Jake nor Williams spoke. "John Farthing didn't deserve anything of Martha's—not her money, not her mother's jewelry, and especially not her baby. Besides, I needed every cent I could get my hands on in order to get Charity away."

"So that's why you bought that fancy coffin." Jake grinned, admiring her grit and spirit. His little Gracie. Always had been filled with grit and spirit. And daring. If he'd been in St. Louis at the time, he knew good and well she'd have recruited him to rescue Martha Farthing's baby. And he'd have done it, too. God save him, he'd have done it.

"That's why I bought the fancy coffin," she agreed. "I picked the prettiest one I could find and told everybody in St. Louis it was for my Aunt Lizzy."

She shot Jake a guilty look. He burst out laughing in spite of the solemnity of the occasion, the misery of William Williams, and his own bleeding heart. "Oh, Lord. When this is all resolved, we'll have to write her, Gracie. She'll love it."

A smile seemed to quiver at the corners of Gracie's mouth. "I suppose she will, Jake."

"You did a good job of covering your tracks. I had a terrible time following you."

An involuntary shiver shook Gracie's shoulders. "I almost died when I heard you talking to Mr. Fergus in the saloon that day."

Williams's mouth quirked up. "Sorry. I guess we were both trying to hide our motives—but it turned out our goals were the same."

"I guess." As if talking to herself, Gracie said, "I threw a piece of beefsteak in the coffin right before they hammered it shut. I figured everybody would think it was the body rotting. Lord on high, it stunk!"

Both men laughed. After a second or two, Gracie joined them.

Quiet settled over them. Charity yawned and rubbed her eyes.

"Do you want to go to bed, sweetheart?" Gracie asked gently.

Charity gripped her arms tightly and shook her head. Something tightened in Jake's chest.

"We won't go away and leave you alone again, Charity." He leaned forward and took one of her hands. It was as tiny as a hummingbird's wing in his big paw. "We're sorry we left you alone before. Something bad happened and your mama was trying to fix it. That's why she had to go outside and leave you alone, but it won't happen again. Do you understand?"

After staring at him with the intensity of a Texas Ranger interrogating a prisoner—Jake remembered that look all too well—Charity nodded. "Big noise," she said in her tiny baby voice.

Jake smiled. "And that big noise scared Charity, didn't it?"

She nodded again.

"Well, I reckon those big noises are over for the night, sweetie. But if they come back, your mama and Uncle Jake will be here to pick you up. Those big noises are called thunder, and they happen sometimes when it rains."

The baby's expression didn't change. She looked as though she were digesting Jake's explanation before she made up her mind whether or not to believe it and relax. Jake had the wistful thought that he'd like to see Charity smiling and happy, as unconcerned with the big bad world and its problems as children her age ought to be. Someday, God willing, maybe he would.

"Do you want to go to sleep on Uncle Jake's bed, Charity?" he asked. "It's close by, and you can watch us in here if you want to."

After considering the matter for what seemed like a long time, Charity nodded. "Unca Jay's bed," she said, pointing into the other room. They could see Jake's bed from where they sat. Under the circumstances, Jake considered her willingness to be left alone, even where she could still watch them, a brave one.

"All right, sweetheart," Gracie said. "I'll put you in your Uncle Jake's bed."

"No you won't."

Both Gracie and Charity stared at Jake, horrified. He tried to turn his smile into a facsimile of one of Gracie's winners—one of those heart-stopping smiles that nobody in the entire world could resist. He had a feeling he didn't quite make it.

"Your mama hurt her ankle, Charity," he explained.

"Oh, Jake, it's all right. I'm sure it won't matter."

"Look at it, Gracie," Jake requested reasonably. "And you take a look, too, Charity. Do you think your mama should be walking around on an ankle that looks like that? It hurts a lot because she sprained it."

Charity scanned Gracie's ankle, swollen to twice its normal size and black and blue, where it rested on Jake's chair. She said, "Spain?"

Jake, smiling, nodded. "Yep. It's bruised because it's sprained."

The baby's gaze went from the ankle to Jake's face to Gracie's and then back to the ankle again. Then she checked out her own ankle, lifting her little nightie and scrutinizing it with a frown. She found it pink and normal-sized and not at all odd-looking.

"So do you think your mama should walk on her sore ankle?"

After a careful investigation of her foot, Charity dropped the hem of her nightie, took another peek at Gracie's, looked into Jake's eyes, and shook her head.

"You know, Charity," he said solemnly, "you're about the best little girl I've ever met in my life. You're good to your mama and you're good to me. You're a really, really good girl."

Not even cracking a smile, Charity's gaze went from Jake to Gracie. "Charity good girl?"

Gracie hugged her, her eyes overflowing again. "Charity's a very, very good girl, sweetheart."

So, after kissing Gracie good-night, Charity allowed Jake to pick her up and carry her off to bed. She didn't flinch away when Jake plopped a kiss on her soft hair, either. Jake saw her watching them for a long time before her eyelids got heavy and drifted shut and she allowed herself to sleep. The knowledge that Charity trusted him—had even called out to him in a moment of sheer panic—gave him a funny, sloppy-good feeling in his chest.

He and Gracie and William Chester Williams talked far into the night. The feeling in his chest gradually resolved itself, and Jake realized this must be what fathers felt to know their children trusted him. He wondered if most fathers felt humbled, as he did, by their children's trust.

It was well past midnight when a knock sounded at Jake's door, interrupting Gracie in mid-sentence. The three of them looked at each other, surprised.

"Who on earth can that be?" Gracie wondered.

"Beats me," Jake said with a chuckle. "Maybe it's Fergus, come to see if I've succumbed to the lure of the bottle yet."

"Jake!"

He laughed as he stood and stretched. He hadn't told Gracie about that piece of foolishness yet. He would, though. He didn't plan to hold anything back from his Gracie again. Anything at all. Ever.

Williams stood and stretched, too. "Reckon I'd better be getting back to the saloon. It's been a rough day."

"Wait a minute until we find out who's here," Jake recommended. "If they've started shooting up the saloon, you won't want to go back there tonight. I reckon we can put you up here if this is Fergus with a warning."

Williams grinned very slightly. Jake realized he'd hardly ever seen the man smile. Shaking his head and thinking how sad life could be for even the nicest of people, he walked to the door and flung it open.

"For Pete's sake, who is it this ti—"

He got no further, because his words dried up as soon as he heard the click of a gun being cocked.

A voice snarled at him from out of the darkness. "All

right, you son of a bitch, where the hell's my money and my daughter?"

Jake heard Gracie's gasp as he raised his hands into the air.

16

"$\mathcal{Y}$OU BITCH," JOHN Farthing growled. "I ought to shoot you right here and now."

"Stop threatening my sister, Farthing."

Immediately, Jake regretted his angry words. John Farthing scared the daylights out of him, and Jake knew he had to keep his demeanor calm, even though his guts screamed out to kill the bastard. Unfortunately, it was Farthing who held a gun. He was drunk, too, and Jake had had enough experience with drunkards to know you couldn't trust one, particularly not with a gun. Guns were merciless; if a man made a mistake with a gun, it was permanent.

John Farthing was a tall man, and signs of dissipation had etched themselves deeply into his features. His skin was sallow and looked almost yellow by the light in Jake's house. His clothing was expensive, but dirty; he didn't look as if he bathed too often. Jake suspected the man preferred liquids other than water in his life. Farthing's hair was thin and dark, and he hadn't shaved for a while. His appearance conveyed an impression of dissolution, selfishness, and savagery. Jake wondered how any friend of Gracie's could have ended up with the likes of John Farthing. Then he recalled how, during his own drinking days, he could put on a good show when he had to, and his puzzlement lessened, even as his compassion for the dead Martha Farthing grew.

"Don't you tell me what to do, you bastard. This bitch stole my damned baby."

"Only to keep you from killing her," Gracie spat.

"Shhh, Gracie." Jake shot her a meaningful look and prayed that she'd keep her mouth shut. The man was as ugly a customer as Jake had ever seen. Anybody who would deliberately hurt a woman or a child was about as far from human as a body could get.

Gracie opened her mouth and Jake stiffened. Fortunately, she saw him before she said anything and, wonder of wonders, closed her mouth. *Thank God.*

"You stole my damned baby," Farthing repeated, slurring his words.

Gracie didn't say a thing. Jake saw her hands tighten over wads of her calico skirt and watched her jaw work as her teeth ground together, and he ached for her. He knew how much she wanted to vilify the man who had hurt Charity and Charity's mother.

William Chester Williams sat as still as a statue on a straight-backed chair, never taking his gaze off Farthing. Jake figured he was waiting for Farthing's attention to wander so he could kill him. Jake didn't guess he'd interfere. He wanted to kill the man himself.

"My sister was trying to help your baby after your wife died, Mr. Farthing," he said, keeping his tone mild, hoping to calm him down. Jake wished to God he'd quit waving that gun around.

"I'm gonna make you pay for stealing my baby."

Gently, hoping his words wouldn't make Gracie break her silence, Jake said, "Do you want Charity back, Farthing?"

"Course I do."

"But babies are a lot of work. You don't want all that work, do you?"

"What the hell do you know about it?"

"Nothing. Not a thing." Jake smiled and shrugged. Out of the corner of his eye, he saw Gracie open her mouth again and almost groaned. She must have understood whatever silent signals he was sending, because she just sucked in a huge breath, closed her mouth, sat up straighter, and remained silent.

Breathing deeply, wishing he knew what he was doing, since Charity's life depended on him, Jake said, "Well, you know, Mr. Farthing, maybe there's some way we can make amends without causing you the work of caring for your—a baby."

He was glad he'd caught himself before reminding Farthing that Charity was his child. If Charity's father could look upon her as a commodity, maybe they could strike up a bargain. The notion hit Jake as revolting, even as he mentally plotted his strategy.

A sly look crossed Farthing's face. "Maybe. Maybe there just is."

Gracie uttered a choking noise. Williams's back looked so rigid, Jake wondered if it might crack in two.

"Well, then," he said quickly before either one of them could get a word in, "maybe it would be best if we moved into the parlor. We can talk better in there."

"Good Lord, yes. If Charity wakes up and sees the man who killed her mother, the poor child's apt to die of an apoplexy."

Jake shut his eyes and prayed for patience. And for Gracie to shut the hell up.

"Don't you talk to me like that, bitch."

Farthing's thumb clicked on the hammer of his gun, and Jake saw Gracie flinch. He was about to throw himself at Farthing—and undoubtedly die for it—when Gracie shot him a guilty look.

"I didn't mean it," she muttered. After another second, during which Jake could see her struggling with herself, she said, "I'm sorry."

For a second, Jake wasn't sure if Farthing would shoot her or forgive her. When he released the hammer and lowered the gun, Jake's knees almost buckled. *Thank God. Thank God.*

"Here, Gracie. I'll carry you."

"Thank you, Jake."

He was so grateful that she was still alive that he almost squeezed her to death as he carried her into the parlor. He took the opportunity to hiss, "For God's sake, Gracie, keep your mouth shut."

She didn't answer, but he knew she'd heard him because she went stiff as a board and her lips pinched together. He settled her into a chair as far away from Farthing as he could get her.

Williams trailed behind them and sat next to Gracie. Jake wasn't surprised to see Gracie take his hand.

Farthing refused to sit. He swaggered around the tiny room, stroking his gun as if it were a woman. Jake felt almost sick as he watched.

"All right, what you got that'll pay for my kid?"

What did they have? Farthing's question stumped Jake, who had nothing but the remains of last Sunday's collection: two coppers, a plug of tobacco, three ribbons donated by one of the men for Charity's hair, a chunk of silver, a tiny sack of gold dust, and a small New Testament.

He was still contemplating the silver and gold and wondering if Farthing would shoot him for so paltry an offering, when Gracie's voice stopped his thoughts cold.

"I have Martha's money."

All three men turned to look at her. She was staring at her lap.

"I knew you took it," Farthing snarled. "You took it with the brat, didn't you?" He pointed his gun at her again.

Jake took an impulsive step toward him and the gun swung around and pointed at his belly. His heart went cold and he told himself that it was better he die than Gracie.

"I don't want the money," Gracie said quickly. "Take the money. Just leave Charity with me."

Farthing lost interest in airing out Jake's stomach and lowered the gun again. "How much you got?"

"Everything. Martha gave me everything."

"The jewelry, too?"

Jake saw Gracie's lower lip quiver. "Yes. Everything."

Farthing heaved a sigh that looked very much like one of contentment. "Good. Then give it here."

"Is that what's in that burlap sack, Gracie?"

Apparently she was too overwrought to answer Jake's question verbally. She nodded and looked as if she was trying not to cry.

"All right," he said. "I'll get it."

"Just watch it," Farthing warned him. "Don't you try anything. I still got my gun on you, y'know."

"Yeah," said Jake. "I know."

So Jake slowly and deliberately went back into the kitchen and retrieved the sack. Very carefully, he emptied its contents onto the table.

"There are a bunch of letters and papers and things in here, too. Why don't I separate them out, and you can take the cash and jewelry. You don't want to be carting around the rest of this stuff."

Jake hoped he was right. He also hoped that, somewhere among these papers, enough of Martha Farthing remained that her daughter might get to know her one day.

"Naw, I don't want that trash. I just want the money. And the jewelry."

Which went to show how much John Farthing cared about his child. Jake couldn't suppress a shiver of revulsion. If he ever had a daughter, sure as the sun rose in the morning she'd be worth more than a few paltry dollars to him. With each second he spent in John Farthing's company, Jake's understanding of Gracie's rash act in running away became clearer to him.

Without wasting any more words, he began separating the letters and papers from the jewels and cash. There was a horde of both in the sack; he was impressed. Martha must have brought a good deal in worldly assets with her into her marriage. It was a shame she'd ended up with the freak of nature pacing back and forth in the parlor.

"All right. I've put everything of value into this leather pouch." Jake held it up for general scrutiny. "All the papers and letters and so forth are in this stack right here. There's nothing but personal correspondence in the pile." He patted it to make sure Farthing saw what he was talking about.

At last, Gracie's stoicism deserted her. She cried, "Not everything, Jake! Save out a little something. Martha gave me the money and jewelry for Charity. It's not fair that he's taking everything. Poor Charity won't have a thing to remember her mama by. What about his child?"

"I'll take care of Charity, Gracie," Jake said quietly.

Feeling almost desperate, he tried to telegraph, _Shut up, Gracie_. Farthing was drunk as the proverbial skunk. Jake didn't figure him for a reasonable man under any circumstances. Drunk, he was worse. Drunk, everybody was worse.

He patted the stack of letters again. "I'm sure when she's old enough to understand, she'll be happier to be able to read her mother's words than wear her jewelry."

With a scathing look for Farthing which Jake prayed he didn't see, Gracie muttered, "I suppose you're right."

"I'm sure of it, Gracie. Don't worry about it anymore."

"Yeah," Farthing said, lurching over to the table. "Yeah. Don't worry about it. She won't want this stuff. She'll want the letters and such." Greedily, he picked up the pouch.

Right. Jake's stomach twisted. He'd seen all types of men in his day, but he'd seldom seen as despicable an example of the species as John Farthing. He said, "All right, then. Feel free to look inside that pouch."

Clutching the bag to his chest, Charity's father said, "No, I don't have to. I saw what you did when you did it." He smiled, evidently pleased by his own cleverness. "I saw what you did, all right."

His smile vanished and he pointed the gun at Jake again. "But if you try anything, Mr. Preacher, I'll be back. Don't you think I won't."

With those ominous words, he stuffed the leather pouch under his arm and turned toward the door. Williams made a move, but Jake had anticipated him and pressed him back in the chair.

"It won't do any good," he whispered.

Apparently realizing the truth of Jake's words, Williams sank back in his chair. His shoulders slumped in defeat.

The three of them watched the door slam shut behind John Farthing. Jake hoped they'd never see him again.

He heard Gracie's miserable "Oh, Jake," and reached for her hand.

"It'll be all right, Gracie. He's gone now."

"What if he comes back, though? What then? He's evil, Jake. He'll drink up all that money and come back, and what will we do then?" She began to chew the knuckles of her other hand. Jake suspected that if she weren't crippled, she'd be pacing back and forth like a lioness worried about her cub.

"We can't deal with what *might* happen, Gracie. We can only deal with things as they *do* happen."

"That filthy bastard," Williams spat. "That damned, stinking, drunken, filthy bastard."

"Don't expect either of us will argue with you there, Bill."

Gracie squeezed Jake's hand with both of hers. "No," she said on a stifled sob. "No. We won't."

They heard a horse whinny nearby, and Jake went to the window. The rain had stopped some time ago and a full moon now lit the scene outside. By its light, he could just make out John Farthing as he tied the leather pouch onto his saddle. Then he mounted clumsily and, without so much as a backward glance, rode off into the night, headed away from Diabolito Lindo.

"Now where in blazes do you suppose he's going at this hour? There's not another town in that direction except Hondo, and it's ten miles away and smaller than this one."

"I hope he gets lost on the desert and the buzzards peck his eyeballs out," Gracie said savagely.

Jake turned to look at her, his eyebrows lifting.

"Well, I do!"

A strange noise drew her attention, as it did Jake's. When he looked, it was to witness William Chester Williams, doubled over.

"Oh, God, Martha!" Williams choked out. "Oh, my dear, dear God!"

Gracie and Jake exchanged a helpless glance, and Jake's heart almost broke for the poor man who now knew for sure that he'd lost everything. And to whom.

17

"I'M NOT LEAVING these scratches unattended, Gracie. And I'm not letting you or Charity out of my sight for the rest of my life, either, so you'd better get used to it."

Jake uttered his declaration when Gracie tried to protest his bandaging her hands. She stopped protesting and stared at him, her eyes popping, wondering if he meant what she thought she'd just heard him say.

"You—you aren't?"

"Nope."

Almost afraid to ask, she stammered, "You—you mean you—we—I'm going to keep pretending to be your sister forever?"

Kneeling beside her, he looked up into her eyes and she knew the answer to her question even before he answered it. "No, that's not what I mean."

Joy exploded like a skyrocket in her middle. Because she couldn't quite believe it yet, she asked, "Oh, Jake. Do you really mean what I think you mean?"

Standing, he continued to watch her, a smile lifting the corners of his mouth and making his scarred face go soft. His eyes crinkled up around the edges, reminding her that this was Jake, her Jake, the Jake she'd loved her entire life. Gracie didn't think she could love him any more if she tried.

"Well, I'm not sure what you think I mean, but I plan to marry you, Gracie Molloy Trinidad Molloy."

"What about your flock?"

A small shadow of pain washed over his face. Gracie ached when she saw it.

"It will hurt me to leave Diabolito Lindo, Gracie, but it would kill me to lose you. I can't let you go again. We'll find somewhere else to live, I reckon; somewhere else that needs its own Preacher Jake."

"And you really think we'd have to leave?" she asked very softly, afraid she knew the answer; they'd been over this ground before.

He nodded. "I lied to them, Gracie."

She bowed her head. "I'm sorry, Jake."

"Well, I am too, in some ways. But, Lord above, Gracie, I can't let you go now. For years I thought I'd never see you again. Then you came here and . . . When I realized what you planned to do tonight and thought about what my life would be like without you and Charity, I knew I wouldn't be any good to anybody without you." He lifted his shoulders in a helpless shrug. "It seems I can't live without you, Gracie."

"I can't live without you either, Jake."

He knelt beside her again. Gracie's heart pounded as hard as God's thunder had rattled the sky earlier in the evening.

"And I don't hanker to wait until some other preacher ties the knot before I worship you with my body, either. It's been hell living with you and not being able to touch you. I don't want to wait any longer unless you tell me to, Gracie. If you want to wait, I will. Even if it kills me."

The pounding in her heart sped up until it rang in her ears so loudly she could scarcely hear herself think. She had to lick her lips. "I don't want you to, Jake."

"Well, then, I reckon it's time for bed."

Raising her arms to him, she whispered, "I reckon it is."

As if she were something precious, Jake lifted her out of the chair. She assumed he would immediately carry her to the room she'd been sharing with Charity. Instead, he peered deeply into her eyes. His own beautiful, dark brown eyes looked quite serious, and his expression made her nervous.

"What are you doing, Jake?"

A sweet grin softened his features again. She smoothed her fingers over his stubbly cheeks and wished the rest of her hand weren't bandaged, because she wanted to feel him with every inch of skin on her body.

"I'm looking at you, Gracie."

Gracie had known Jake since she was four years old; there was no reason on earth for her to suddenly feel shy with him, but she did. She felt heat burn her cheeks and nearly buried her face against his shoulder as Charity was wont to do against hers. "You've seen me before."

He nodded. "Yup. Not often enough in recent years, though."

"Well, I guess you'll see plenty of me from now on."

"I reckon."

"Have I changed all that much from when we were kids?"

"Yes. You're beautiful, Gracie. You grew up to be a beautiful woman."

That was too much for Gracie. Now she did turn her head and hide her burning face against his shoulder. "Oh, I'm not!" she cried, and wasn't sure whether she was more pleased than embarrassed or the other way around.

"Yes, you are." Jake twitched his shoulder, nudging her chin away. "Look at me, Gracie."

So she did, but she was still embarrassed. Then she felt her heart flutter like dandelion fluff in a breeze when she realized he was going to kiss her.

"I love you, Gracie," he said in the second before his soft lips covered hers.

The day's earlier lightning storm was nothing compared to the conflagration that ignited within Gracie at the touch of Jake's mouth to hers. Knowing that Jake loved her made her heart sing. Realizing that she was finally, after all these years, going to be physically united with him, this very night, in her very bed, made her body catch fire.

The sparks started where his lips touched hers. Then she felt them where his hands pressed against her back and bottom, and where her breasts flattened against his chest. The fire built to a flaming inferno in the place between her thighs. She'd always been taught that place was naughty. She could hardly wait to be naughty with Jake.

Against his lips, she cried softly, "Oh, Jake," and wriggled in his arms until the entire front of her body pressed against him.

His shoulders began to shake, and she realized he was laughing. He gave her only a moment to be offended, though. With three huge steps, he carried her into her bedroom, settled her on the bed, and sat beside her.

"Are you laughing at me, Jake Molloy?"

"Never."

He yanked off his boots faster than Gracie had known the operation could be performed. Then he turned around, took her in his arms and lay down with her, and she forgot about everything except the magic he began to create in her body.

He started with the pearl buttons on her bodice. In all the years she'd been unbuttoning buttons, Gracie hadn't realized that one could tease and tantalize with them. He opened the first three or four, and she gasped when she felt his long, strong fingers against her skin as he pushed the fabric aside.

"Your skin is like silk, Gracie."

"Oh, my land, Jake!" she cried softly when, a few buttons further along, his hand closed tenderly over her left breast. Although she wore her camisole still, the caress seemed incredibly intimate. It *was* incredibly intimate. Gracie hadn't realized until now how much touching the act of human procreation could entail.

"I've been wanting to feel you ever since the day you showed up at my door, Gracie."

"You have?"

"Mmmm."

Since Gracie, in her innocence, still wasn't absolutely clear on man-woman things, she was almost shocked by the feel of Jake's hand in such a personal place until she realized his hand was exactly what her left breast had been missing for so long.

Once she understood, she realized he seemed to be neglecting her right breast. She arched and slightly twisted her body to remind him. He caught on immediately, and began to lavish his attention there.

Gracie sighed with pleasure. Her nipples were hard as pebbles, and her breasts felt tight and hot and full. Lord above, she'd had no idea what a man could make a woman feel when he put his mind to it. Or his hands.

"Does that feel good, Gracie?"

If there were a contest for stupid questions, Gracie figured Jake's would win some sort of prize. How could he not know it felt good, what with her practically writhing against him? Since he'd asked, she said, "Yes." The word ended on a soft moan when his clever fingers found their way beneath her soft cotton camisole and his flesh pressed against hers, gently pinching her puckered nipples.

Oh, my Lord! Oh, my Lord! Nothing came out of Gracie's mouth.

"You're so soft," Jake whispered against her skin, sending a tidal wave of heat through her. "So beautiful."

Gracie didn't think she needed to respond. Which was just as well, since she couldn't think of a thing to say even if she could make her vocal cords work, which she doubted. She arched against his hand, pushing her breast into his palm. He knew just what to do with it, too. She uttered a stifled shriek when his mouth closed over her other breast and he suckled like a baby.

He swirled his tongue over her nipple, playing with it, blowing on it, loving it. Then he did the same with her other breast. Gracie wasn't sure she should be enjoying this so much.

All she'd ever heard about the physical side of marriage was that men and women slept together and made babies. As she was born and bred a proper female, nobody had ever explained the particulars. All she knew for certain at this point was that if this was how babies got to be, she expected the human race would last for a long, long time.

It did surprise her, however, that Jake, a minister of the Gospel, should be so adept at fleshly pleasures. She reminded herself that he'd been a sinner for longer than he'd been a preacher.

However he'd come by his skill, he had evidently learned a good deal of patience along the way. When they'd been kids together he'd always seemed to be in a hurry, especially when it came to her. Tonight, he took his time, teaching her new sensations every second or two.

By the time he'd unbuttoned all her buttons, carefully helped her out of all her clothes, and moseyed his hands and lips down to her thighs, he had reduced Gracie to a state beyond thought.

She seethed. She steamed. She quivered. The pressure inside her was so great she knew she'd explode—and the sooner the better. When he finally covered the mound of tight curls between her thighs with his hand, Gracie wasn't sure she'd survive. Then his fingers slipped inside to feel the hot honey of her most intimate secret, and she jammed her hand into her mouth so she wouldn't scream and frighten Charity.

It was too much. Or she'd anticipated it for too long. Or Jake was too skillful. Whatever the reason, Jake's fingers had no sooner found her slick nub and begun to rub than the sensations building in her spiraled out of control.

"Oh, my heavens! Jake!"

Forgetting all about her sprained ankle, her scraped arms, and the hand stuffed in her mouth, Gracie bucked on the bed as spasm after spasm of pleasure rattled her.

When the spasms subsided at last, she wrapped her arms around Jake and held on to him, vaguely afraid that she'd float away if he were to let her go.

She wasn't sure how long he held her, stroking her perspiration-soaked body with his big, wonderful hands and murmuring sweet nothings in her ear. Eventually his soft voice intruded into her wonderment.

"Gracie?"

"Y-yes?"

"You all right?"

She'd have told him what an idiotic question that was if she'd had her wits about her. The only thing she could manage at the moment was a tremulous, "Yes. Thank you."

"You're welcome."

He sounded amused again. Gracie was too stunned to take exception.

"Mind if I join you?" he asked after another few moments.

"J-join me?"

"Yeah. My turn now."

His turn. Her eyes popped open and she stared up at him. He smiled down at her with the sweetest expression she'd ever seen on his face.

Mercy sakes, she'd forgotten all about his pleasure. She'd known there was more to this act than her own feelings. Truly, she had. And she did want to share. It's just that Jake had rattled her out of her usual good manners. She said shakily, "Oh. Of course."

Although it was hard to let go, she managed to release his shoulders. She flopped back on the bed, still too stunned to properly control her body. From her vantage point, she had a splendid view of him as he stood to remove his own clothes. And he was worth looking at.

Apparently, he enjoyed the view of her, too. He took one look at her sprawled naked on the bed, groaned out loud, and began furiously working the buttons on his shirt.

"Someday I want to do that, Jake," she found herself saying. Then she was shocked that she wasn't shocked.

His smile was warm enough to boil water. "I look forward to it, Gracie."

Good grief, he was a strong man. Gracie stared at Jake's body as he revealed it to her, pleased that her husband would be such a model of manly perfection. She'd seen his bare chest before, when he and Bart were building the addition. It was as beautiful tonight as it had been then. It looked hard as a rock, but warm and smooth, covered with curly dark hairs. Although the one lamp in the room didn't afford much light, she thought she could see a few gray hairs interspersed with the dark ones. Right then, she decided she was going to investigate his chest at length one day.

His arms were works of art. In fact, at the museum back home, Gracie had seen just such musculature on ancient Greek statues.

He turned around to remove his trousers. Gracie watched his rear view, fascinated. My goodness, his hips looked so hard and narrow. Not at all soft and cushiony like her own wide female hips. His legs were like pillars of iron. She'd never seen an unclad male body before; those old Greek fellows always had something draped around them. She'd had no idea male bodies were so hard and hairy.

Then he turned around, and what really captured her attention was his stiff sex. She swallowed hard and whispered, "Mercy sakes, Jake. Will that fit?"

"Don't be afraid, Gracie. I'll try not to hurt you."

"I know you will, Jake." And she did, too, and in spite of her natural trepidation, she welcomed him with open arms. He came to her the way she'd always dreamed he would one day, in love.

Her Jake. His Gracie.

As they lay together afterward, with Gracie cocooned in Jake's strong embrace, she didn't think she could get any happier in this life. She snuggled against him, his love still warm and moist between her legs, the memory of him filling her etched in her brain. It had hurt a little when he'd entered her, but she'd felt completed by him somehow. In fact, she couldn't remember ever feeling so utterly fulfilled.

What an intriguing, wonderful act they'd performed. There was amazing pleasure to be had if one were in love with the proper person. She spared a moment to feel a stab of regret for Martha and William. They'd never experience this magnificence together. Sighing deeply, she guessed she had a lot to be thankful for.

She was teetering on the brink of sleep when Jake's soft voice nudged her awake again.

"Do you suppose Charity will ever think of me as her father, Gracie?"

She blinked, his question driving sleepiness away. "Mmmm? I don't know, Jake." Running her fingers through the hair on his chest, she added, "I hope so."

"Me, too." After another minute or two, he said, "I never thought about having children before. I guess my life was too unsettled, but I'd like to have children with you."

"I've always wanted children. With you."

He squeezed her and she could feel his smile. It seeped through him and into her as surely as if she could see his face with her eyes.

"Maybe by the time our children are old enough to call you Papa, Charity will think it's natural to call you Papa, too, Jake."

"Maybe. I hope so."

"She deserves a good father."

"Yes. Yes, she does."

"And you'll be a good one."

He twisted his head so he could look down into her eyes. "You think so?"

It was her turn to squeeze him tight. "I know so. You already are."

"Thanks, Gracie." He sounded as if her affirmation had touched him.

Gracie shook her head, wondering how Jake Molloy, the most perfect man God ever created, could possibly doubt his own goodness. No answer occurred to her before she drifted off to sleep, the comforting rhythm of Jake's heart thumping a strong, steady cadence in her ear, his arms warm around her.

18

$\mathcal{J}$AKE AWOKE THE next morning at dawn, with Gracie's soft bottom pressing against his stiff sex. His body was more than ready for another taste of her.

His emotions were in absolute turmoil.

Whereas yesterday his mind had been completely clear on the decision to choose Gracie and Charity over Diabolito Lindo and his flock, this morning doubts had managed to creep past the blockades he'd set up against them. They now niggled and stabbed at him with devilish little pitchforks, making his heart hurt, his head ache, and his brain whirl.

Taking his doubts and shaking them like the nasty little demons they were, he reminded them and himself that, however it had come about, he'd made his decision. There was no going back.

The problem was, of course, that when he'd made his decision, he'd still been suffering from panic induced by almost having lost Gracie. Again.

This morning his conscience tormented him mercilessly

over his having succumbed to the weakness of his all-too-human flesh. Also this morning, all sorts of alternatives to having taken Gracie to his bed and having to leave Diabolito Lindo occurred to him. He wondered where they'd all been hiding last night. Undoubtedly, his disgusting lust had obscured them.

You could have prevented her from leaving and still left her virtue intact, his ardent soul scolded. *But you didn't.*

The black heart that still resided at his core had tricked him, in spite of everything God had tried to teach him over the years. He'd violated Gracie, the only woman in the world he had ever loved—and ever would love—and there was no hope for salvaging his ministry here in Diabolito Lindo in light of that violation.

His insides gave a tremendous throb at the thought of leaving his town. Turning over so Gracie's succulent body couldn't distract him, Jake pressed his face into his pillow and prayed to God to help him be strong. He prayed and prayed. His prayers didn't do much to alleviate the craving of his body. He did, however, come to some kind of peace within himself about moving to another town.

It's the price you have to pay, he told himself. *You knew it when you agreed to lie for her in the first place. There's a price for everything in this life, Jake Molloy. If anybody should know that, you should.*

All in all, he reckoned the price God had exacted from him hadn't been too great. If he'd refused to take her in, John Farthing might have discovered her whereabouts more quickly. Now that he'd met John Farthing, he shuddered at the thought.

He didn't want to contemplate what might have happened to Gracie and Charity if he hadn't been with her when Farthing ultimately located her. Even thinking about it made him feel queasy.

Besides, thrashing over what he might have done or should have done or could have done paid no toll. Jake knew that as well as he knew the sun would set tonight. He now must deal with the consequences of what he had done, and that was that.

So he would marry Gracie—gladly—and try to be a father to Charity, and they would start over again elsewhere. And even though it would be difficult to restrain his animal lust, he wouldn't sully Gracie's purity again until the minister had united them in holy wedlock. The thought wasn't terribly appealing, but Jake had been trying to be a good man for the past five years. If he failed occasionally, he reckoned it was because he was a human being and not a saint. At any rate, he guessed a few more days wouldn't kill him.

Gracie, however, had another idea in mind. And, as had been happening since the first moment he set eyes on her, way back when he was as innocent as a new day, she won. He'd never stood a chance against Gracie.

"Aren't you sore?" he asked after a moment or so, by this time hoping she'd say no.

She shook her head and smiled, undoubtedly glorying in the effect she had on him, which was electric. He'd discovered she was awake when he felt her breasts rubbing up and down his back, her puckered nipples playing havoc with his self-control. Then her little swaddled hand had sneaked over his side to sift through his chest hairs. By the time her hand had wandered down his stomach to his groin, exploring every inch of the way, he was as stiff as an oak log and aching for her.

So he assuaged both their needs in the manner ordained by God before the Garden, and hardly felt guilty about it afterward. In truth, he felt relatively wonderful, at least physically. Slaked lust had numbed his conscience for a few moments, as well, and he wondered if there was truly any hope for him.

It was Jake who gathered Charity up off his bed when she awoke, since Gracie's ankle was too sore to walk on. And it was he who fixed and served breakfast.

"By gum, Jake," Gracie said, sounding utterly astonished, "I think I'm a better cook than you are."

He laughed. "I do believe you're right, Gracie. Never thought that would happen."

"Me, neither." Happiness gleamed in her eyes when she fed Charity a bite of tortilla. "I love you, Jake."

"I love you, too, Gracie."

Since Charity seemed a little confused by the emotional currents riding the air in the small kitchen this morning, Jake leaned over and planted a kiss on her cheek. She jerked and looked up at him, startled. "And I love Charity, too."

"And I love Charity, too," Gracie confirmed.

Charity seemed to accept the startling declarations of the adults in her life with composure. She nodded and chewed, her little face somber, as though she were mulling it all over and planned to pass judgment later, after she'd had an opportunity to think about it. Jake shook his head and offered up a silent prayer that, with Gracie and himself to love her, she'd heal completely one day.

What really worried him was John Farthing. Even though he'd told Gracie not to fret about Charity's father, he feared Farthing would be back. Jake pegged him for a man who didn't go in for long-term planning. Gracie had undoubtedly been correct when she'd said he'd drink up Martha's money and return for more.

Preachers didn't make much money out here in the Territory. And this particular preacher didn't even have a pulpit any longer.

He guessed he could always be a tinsmith. His head ached and his stomach churned at the thought of giving up his ministry, but he guessed he'd do what he had to do.

Yet another pain speared him when he contemplated moving away from Diabolito Lindo; God alone knew where they could go. Wherever it was, Jake expected Farthing would find them. He wasn't sure how they were going to fend off the old drunk forever.

The best thing to do, of course, once they got settled somewhere, would be to adopt Charity. He didn't know how on earth they could do that without Farthing's written permission, however, and Jake had a shrewd notion he'd never give it. Not while either one of them was alive to squeeze money from.

Even if he and Gracie laid out before a court of law every

single defect either one of them could dredge up about Farthing's character, Jake suspected it wouldn't matter. The court would pay a hell of a lot more attention to a father's rights than to those of a woman who might be said to have stolen that father's assets. And kidnapped his child. With Martha dead, there wasn't a soul left alive who could testify to Farthing's brutality except Gracie. If Gracie said she saw him throw his baby girl down a flight of stairs, the court would undoubtedly believe she said so for her own gain.

Lord, Lord. The problem wanted more thinking than Jake could give it at the moment. In the meantime, he had a job to do. It wasn't one he looked forward to. In fact, it made his stomach ache harder and his temples throb.

"Will you be all right here while I go to the saloon and talk to Fergus, Gracie? I'll take Clara her breakfast."

"What are you going to talk about?"

"Us." He smiled sadly down at her. "And leaving town."

Her own brilliant smile faded and he heard her breath catch. "Oh, Jake. I'm so sorry. I brought this on you."

Shaking his head, he said, "It's not your fault, Gracie. It's just circumstances."

He felt pretty low, though, when he pushed through the batwing doors of the Devil's Last Stop. He even stopped to finger their splintery finish, wondering if Gracie had had plans to repaint them. She'd sure done a job on the rest of the place. Chuckling ruefully, he climbed the stairs and gave Clara her breakfast, saving Fergus—and the hard part—until he'd done his duty.

"What you doin' here?" Clara asked ungraciously.

Jake's grin notched up. Small wonder Gracie found Clara a trying patient if this was the way she greeted her every day. As far as he knew, Gracie had never been impolite to anybody in her life, barring John Farthing and that long-ago whiskey-boat oarsman who'd abused that stupid mule.

Explaining that Gracie had sprained her ankle, Jake told Clara he'd be bringing her food for a day or two. She nodded, obviously unmoved, and he left her to her breakfast while he went downstairs to look for Fergus.

He found him, of course, behind the bar. This morning Fergus stood on a chair, occupied in dusting the frame surrounding the Devil's Last Stop's threadbare guardian seraph. The two red bandannas still covered her most tantalizing virtues.

Jake would miss that painting. His heart gave such an enormous lurch that a real, physical ache began to throb in his chest. A faint aroma of lavender lifted to his nostrils and mingled with the scent of stale tobacco, sweat, liquor fumes, and God alone knew what else. Jake speculated about how long Gracie's lavender scent would last. A year from now, would some footloose cowboy come in here, lift his head, and sniff, wondering if he was hallucinating?

He heaved an enormous sigh.

Fergus turned at the sound. "Mornin', Jake."

"Morning, Fergus."

Jake waited until Fergus had finished dusting the picture frame and climbed down from the chair before he told his story. Fergus listened silently. He nodded once or twice during the recitation, and his eyes opened wide at one point. When Jake stopped talking, Fergus didn't say anything for a minute, but only scratched his chin, pondering.

At last, he asked, "So how come you think you got to leave here?"

Fergus's question surprised Jake into stuttering. "I—well—well, hell, Fergus! I can't marry a woman the boys think is my own sister because I'm the one who lied and told them she was, and then go on as though nothing's wrong with it."

Fergus shrugged. "Don't know why the hell not."

"But I just told you. They trusted me. I lied to them. I violated their trust."

"All's you got to do is explain ever'thing to 'em. None of 'em are too dumb to understand."

"It's not that simple, Fergus. The boys trusted me, and I let them down."

Fergus rolled his eyes. Jake felt intensely frustrated.

"Hell, I figured you'd understand, even if nobody else did."

"What's to understand? You're bein' pigheaded, Jake."

"No, I'm not. Fergus, I lied to them! Can't you understand that?"

"Jake, ain't nobody perfect on this here earth, fer God's sake."

"Maybe not, but as a minister of God, I at least have to try. I failed, Fergus, and it's not fair of me to stay here and expect the boys to forgive me as if what I did was no worse than—than falling asleep in church. I flat-out *lied* to them!"

After shaking his head and rolling his eyes again, Fergus leaned over and patted Jake on the shoulder. "You just go ahead and do what you got to do, Jake. It'll all turn out all right. And I gotta say I'm right happy fer you. Miss Gracie'll suit you fine. Just fine."

This wasn't exactly the scenario Jake had had in mind when he headed over to the Devil's Last Stop. His own heart burned like fire at the thought of leaving Fergus and Diabolito Lindo and the rest of his friends. He loved these men. He loved this stinky, dilapidated, makeshift church. Leaving here was, to him, like cutting off an arm or a leg. He'd survive, but he'd bear the scar for the rest of his life.

He'd expected a little more show of emotion from his best friend, even though he'd known Fergus as a phlegmatic individual for thirteen years now. But at least Fergus hadn't kicked up a fuss. Jake guessed that was some kind of blessing.

"Thanks, Fergus." His throat felt funny, as if it were full of smoldering cinders or something. He had to clear it. "I reckon we'll have to bring in another minister to marry us."

"I'll send Ramón to Lincoln to fetch the one they got there. Then you can be married right here this comin' Sunday." He patted the shiny counter.

Well, that was easy. So how come Jake's throat still ached? "Thanks."

"No sweat."

"Well, ah, I guess I'd better be getting home, Fergus. Gracie can't do much until her ankle heals up a little more."

"I'll send Ramón over with some chow later on, Jake. I

know neither one of you can cook worth shit, even when she ain't laid up."

In spite of feeling low—and even faintly hurt about his best friend's casual acceptance of his own imminent departure—Jake chuckled. "Thanks, Fergus."

Kicking the dirt at his feet and feeling quite low, Jake meandered back toward his little house. Then he began daydreaming about how delicious Gracie's body had looked sprawled on the bed last night and his mood lifted.

In his mind's eye, she lay back against the pillows, spent from passion fulfilled, and staring at him with eyes that were huge and dark in the lamplight. He'd done a good job with her; he was proud of himself; he'd been so excited, he wasn't sure he could satisfy her and himself too, but he had.

And oh, Lordy, how she'd looked afterward! His Gracie. Mercy, mercy, she'd grown up well. He couldn't recall a woman who excited him more. Of course, he'd never been in love before. That undoubtedly accounted for at least some of his pleasure.

Still, she had a body any man would drool over. Her breasts were as plump and creamy as twin mounds of vanilla ice cream, and topped with the most delectably ripe cherries Jake had ever tasted. Her waist was small, and flared into hips as round and perfect as anything an artist could imagine. She was magnificent. That painting over Fergus's bar didn't hold a candle to his Gracie.

His sex had begun to respond to his fond thoughts when his attention was jerked back to the present most unpleasantly.

He stopped, appalled, at the specter of two strangers riding up the street toward them. One of them carried a body, discreetly wrapped in a striped saddle blanket and strapped to the back of his horse. The corpse's legs dangled straight out from under the blanket. They look weird, as the feet were bare and the body had begun to stiffen in death. Jake hurried over to the two men.

"Good God, what happened?"

The lead rider nodded and tugged his hat politely. "Can't

rightly say, sir. We found this poor bastard lyin' in the road not far from here and figured he must live here, since this is the closest town to where we found him."

"My Lord. Better take him into the saloon. It's the nearest thing we have to a funeral parlor in Diabolito Lindo." Fergus's place had had more corpses laid out in it than most formal funeral parlors, too, although Jake didn't honor these two gentlemen with the information.

"Thanks, mister. I'm not too happy about him hangin' around any longer than he has to."

"Interesting choice of words, friend," Jake said dryly.

The stranger uttered a surprised laugh.

"I'll go in first and clear off a table for the body."

"Thanks," the first man said. "We'll unstrap him and haul him inside."

Jake slammed into the saloon again, and Fergus looked over to see who had pushed his doors open with such energy. His right eyebrow rose when he saw Jake for the second time that morning.

"Howdy, Jake. Change your mind?"

Jake flashed him a rueful grin. "Nope. 'Fraid not. But some strangers just brought a body into town. They say they found it on the trail outside town, and I figured we'd better lay it out here and maybe try to figure out who it is before we bury it."

Nodding, Fergus said, "Best to have some kind o' name to carve on the cross, I reckon." With an audible sigh, he stepped out from behind the counter and helped Jake move chairs aside and push a couple of the scarred tables together. By the time the two strangers staggered into the saloon, puffing under the weight of their load, the tables were ready.

They heaved the corpse across the tables and stood back, panting.

Jake took one look at the dead man's face and felt as though somebody had punched him, hard, in his solar plexus. His knees actually gave out, and he had to grab the back of a chair in order to keep his balance.

Fergus eyed him oddly. "You all right, Jake?"

Was he all right? The second most pressing problem in

his life had just been laid out, dead, before him. Jake didn't know whether to laugh or cry. Or be totally appalled. Or do all three together.

"Farthing. My God, Fergus, it's Farthing."

Scratching his chin, Fergus said, "Who the hell's Farthing?"

"You know this man?" the man whose horse had borne him in asked.

"No. That is, yes. I mean, I met him last night."

"'Tweren't a long friendship," Fergus observed dryly.

Laughter was definitely winning this fight. It tickled Jake's innards and shook his words when he said, "No. No, it wasn't a long friendship at all."

While Jake stared at the body, Fergus turned his attention to the strangers and asked, "Find anything on him? Saddlebags? Hat? Gun? Pocketbook? Anything? Was his horse wanderin' around nearby?"

"Hell, no. He wasn't even wearin' his boots. I didn't find a pocketbook or anything. No identification anywhere. Not even a bandanna or a bottle."

Even though he already knew the answer, he had to ask. "I don't suppose there was a leather pouch lying around anywhere, was there?"

The man shook his head, and Jake's appreciation for the inevitability of some things made him grin. What a slick way God had of taking care of a fellow. Too bad Jake hadn't saved anything of Martha Farthing's when he was sorting through the contents of Gracie's coffin last night; at least Charity could have had something of her mother's. As it was, well. . . .

Fergus was peering closely at the body. "He's been cut up fer fun some after they shot him." He glanced at Jake. "See that there cross on his chest? That's the way Miguel signs his name. Figgered it was him anyway, 'cause they stripped his boots and took his horse and belt and everything."

Jake heaved a sigh. "Yup. I reckon it was." How ironic. How utterly ironic. Glancing from the body to the strangers he asked, "Where'd you say you found him?"

"On the road to this place, curled up on his side like a

baby with his arms folded acrost his belly. We had to pry 'em open."

Curled up like a baby. Jake caught Fergus's eye and knew he was thinking the same thing: John Farthing had not been blessed with an easy exit from life. It had taken him some time to die, and he'd felt it. If Miguel's bullet had killed him instantly, he'd not have had time to curl himself up, clutching at his belly in pain. No. He'd hurt a lot before he departed this green earth.

He knew himself to possess an evil streak when he realized he was glad. He hoped John Farthing's agony even marginally reflected the pain he'd inflicted on his daughter—the pain from which she might never recover. He had an urge to spit on the body and restrained himself. He reckoned his heart wasn't too black; at least he felt guilty about his impulse.

The two men who had been kind enough to spare John Farthing an ignominious finale as buzzard fodder shuffled and looked at one another. "Well," the first one said, "if you don't need us no more, reckon we'll be on our way.

Jake stuck out his hand. "Thanks for bringing the body in. Jake Molloy here. I'm the minister in this town."

The first man shook Jake's hand, smiling. "Reckon we asked the right person what to do, then."

The two men left the saloon.

"So you know this feller, Jake?"

Fergus already knew the answer; Jake could tell by the way he looked at him.

"He's Charity's father."

Both of Fergus's eyebrows lifted and he whistled softly. "No foolin'? Shit, and here I was feelin' kinda sorry fer the bastard, seein' as how runnin' into Miguel probably weren't no picnic. Now I'm kind of glad of it. Reckon he met a fittin' end."

"Reckon he did." Jake shoved his hat back on his head and gazed at John Farthing.

The man had traced Gracie and his own child all the way from St. Louis to Diabolito Lindo in the New Mexico

Territory and stolen his child's inheritance, only to lose it and his life within minutes of perpetrating the evil deed.

Every now and then, Jake's faith wavered and he wondered if there was any justice in the world. He had no doubt this time. This time justice had prevailed with a flair that almost took Jake's breath away. He hurried out of the saloon, anxious to tell Gracie her worries were in a way to being over.

He headed back to the saloon again no more than fifteen minutes later, grumbling and complaining and obviously worried almost sick about Gracie.

"You're being foolish to risk your ankle just to look at a dead man, Gracie."

His warnings were for naught. Although Gracie knew him to have only her best interests at heart, she wouldn't be stopped. She clung to his left arm like a vine as he balanced Charity on his right hip. She wasn't about to let that body be buried until she'd verified that it was, indeed, the body of John Farthing.

"That man murdered my best friend, almost killed his own child, and drove me from my home, Jake Molloy. I want to see for myself that he's as dead as you say." Her ankle was fairly killing her, but she knew that she'd believe John Farthing was dead only when she had seen his corpse, and not before.

She did. Standing one-legged like a stork and balancing herself by clinging to one of the tables across which he'd been laid out, she stared for a long time at John Farthing's cold, waxy face.

The face she'd once seen purpled with rage didn't look so terrifying now. The man who had battered his own wife, crippled his own daughter, and made Gracie's heart believe in evil for the first time now lay before her stiff and cold and way beyond human law.

"He's gone to his reward, Gracie," Jake told her softly.

"I only hope it's the one he deserves." Her voice came out as cold as John Farthing's body.

She was surprised that she didn't feel a greater sense of

relief. Instead, she only felt vaguely sorry that Miguel and his friends hadn't visited St. Louis before this creature had had the chance to do so much harm.

Oh, Martha, I can hardly believe it. Charity will have a chance now, even if her father stole all the money you set aside for her.

She looked up at Jake, an odd, heavy feeling in her chest. "What about the money, Jake? Did they bring that in with the body?"

He shook his head. "Sorry, Gracie."

She heard somebody on the stairs and looked up to see William Chester Williams descending. Jake turned, too, and gestured Williams to the tables. Williams smiled at the two of them.

"Good morning, Miss Gracie. Preacher Jake. I was just upstairs visiting with Clara and— My God."

Williams stopped in his tracks when Jake stepped aside and let him see the body. He walked slowly over and looked down at the face.

"So it's all over," he said softly, incredulously.

"Looks like it." Jake put a hand on his shoulder.

"Bandits killed him and stole everything he rode away with last night." Gracie couldn't make herself stop staring at Farthing's face. "First he stole everything from Charity, and then they stole everything from him." She shook her head. None of this made sense to her.

Williams looked stunned, and for several minutes the three of them stood there, gaping at the corpse like priests at some bizarre, solemn rite. Then Williams moved jerkily, as if coming out of a trance. He reached into his vest pocket.

"You can give this to Charity. Tell her it belonged to her mother." He handed Gracie the ring.

She stared at it in disbelief. "I thought he took everything."

"I stuck it in my vest pocket before he had a chance to see it. Will you please tell Charity that a man who loved her mother gave it to her?"

"I sure will."

"Tell her he gave it to her a long time ago, when they were both young and believed in things."

Gracie opened her mouth to assure Williams there were still things worth believing in, but she happened to catch Jake's eye before she could speak. In a gesture so small as to be almost imperceptible, he shook his head. She shut her mouth again, understanding for once that she couldn't fix everybody's problems. She hoped it was a sign that she'd changed for the better, although she wasn't sure about much of anything at the moment.

"'Spect we'll plant him this afternoon," Fergus said. His flat voice sliced into Gracie's reflections. "You aim to sing at the funeral, Miss Gracie?"

Her head jerked up. "No."

Fergus nodded.

Reaching for Jake, she said, "Take me home now, please, Jake." She made it all the way home before her tears leaked out, and was proud of herself.

19

*S*TILL FEELING GUILTY about having bedded Gracie
before the wedding, Jake was willing, if not eager, to remain
celibate until the minister from Lincoln married them.

He'd reckoned without Gracie, though, and guessed he
had a lot more traveling to go along the path of righteousness before he achieved true goodness. It didn't take much
persuasion at all on Gracie's part to make him see the
wisdom of her argument against celibacy that evening.

"But Jake," she said reasonably, "we might as well get
Charity used to sleeping by herself. It's not good for a child
to sleep with her parents. Mama used to say it leads to
unhealthy habits."

Borrowing a gesture from Fergus, Jake rolled his eyes.
"Unhealthy habits?"

Gracie frowned. In truth, she wasn't sure what her mother
had meant. She did know, however, that she wanted Jake to
herself, and as long as Charity felt secure sleeping alone in
Jake's bed, she aimed to have him. He'd begun to teach her

the joys of love last night and this morning, and she looked forward to another lesson. Eagerly.

So she sat Charity on her lap and told her bedtime stories. Then Jake explained to the little girl that while her mama's ankle was still sore, she had to put up with him tucking her in. She looked at him with big, grave eyes and nodded her understanding. Something tugged hard on Jake's heartstrings.

To the amazement of both of them, she reached for him, saying softly, "Charity seepy." To prove it, once she had snuggled into his arms, she knuckled her eyes. There went his heartstrings again. Jake wondered if he'd ever get used to this fathering stuff.

"Well, then, we'll let Charity sleep on Uncle Jake's bed again, sweetheart." He carried her in to bed after Gracie had kissed her good-night.

Gracie watched from the kitchen table, her heart too full for words.

Then Jake bore Gracie away to her own bed, and proceeded to love her until she was weak with it and he was, too.

"My God," Jake whispered afterward, his voice raw with emotion. "My God."

Gracie hugged him tight, loving the weight of him and the feel of his body on hers, and decided that that about said it all.

It took Jake an inordinately long time to write his sermon the next day. "It's the hardest one I've ever had to write, Gracie," he muttered more than once as he chewed the end of his pencil. He seemed to spend a great deal of time staring out his sparkling clean window at the bright spring day, and thinking.

She sat beside him on another chair, her leg propped on the table he'd drawn up for her. Charity was taking her afternoon nap, and the village of Diabolito Lindo seemed to be napping along with her. Outside the window, Gracie could see nothing stirring. Not even a breeze ruffled the leaves of the trees on top of Boot Hill. She wondered if the rain had melted that huge pile of mud back into the hole Bart and Harley had dug, or if it would take a few of the Territory's stiff winds to complete the job. Or maybe somebody would die before that happened and save Fergus and the boys the trouble of digging a whole new hole.

She'd made them dig a new grave for John Farthing. She didn't want even his remains residing in the same place that had housed the last remembrances of Martha's life.

And then there was that cross. Perhaps they could scrape off the "Ralph Trinidad" and use it for somebody who really needed it. A *real* dead person.

They'd marked John Farthing's grave with a big rock. Fergus had painted "John Farthing" on it. Jake said the paint would probably last about a year or so, unless they got a rainy spell. For the first time in her life, Gracie prayed for a hard winter.

As Jake contemplated his sermon, Gracie busily embroidered another sampler for the saloon. It would be her parting gift, and she intended it as a token of affection for all her friends in Diabolito Lindo. She felt foolish because she kept having to sniffle and swallow to prevent her emotions from spilling out. She hoped Jake didn't notice.

She felt so dreadfully bad for him. It was going to crush him to leave this place. She wished she could somehow help him cope with the loss. But the only thing she could think of to say was "I'm sorry," and her being sorry wouldn't help him one little bit. So she kept her mouth shut and worked on her embroidery.

Anyway, she was sorry, too. She didn't want to leave Diabolito Lindo. She loved it here. She loved the town and the people; she loved the little stream in the woods; she loved her choir; she even loved the difficult, demanding Clara because caring for Clara had helped Gracie grow.

And she'd fallen in love here. Really fallen in love. She'd always loved Jake, even when they were children, but the kind of love she felt for him now was deep, an abiding love that would weather any tests time threw at it. Now she loved him knowing who he was and knowing who she was.

Thinking about herself as she'd been when she'd arrived

in Diabolito Lindo, her mind's eye pictured a different Gracie altogether, a Gracie who'd always expected the world to mold to her expectations. She smiled when she considered how much she'd learned here. Mercy sakes, how arrogant she'd been. She wasn't arrogant any longer; she knew better. Life could get you when you weren't watching out. Even when you were.

And oh, how she loved Jake! She and Jake and Charity had already started to make a family together. Gracie longed to do it here, where they had all come together.

But they had to leave.

She felt as if the edges of her heart surrounding the part filled with Jake and Charity were being ripped away. It was a strange feeling, having half of her heart breaking while the other half glowed with happiness.

But she didn't share her sorrows with Jake. He had enough of his own to keep him occupied. So she silently continued her embroidery. She'd chosen the motto especially for her friends in town: "Make A Joyful Noise."

The motto appealed to her on two levels. She'd taught her friends to sing in a choir, and they'd taught her to judge a man by what was in his heart and not by how he looked. Besides, it came from the Sixty-sixth Psalm. They all loved the psalms.

Thinking about her choir made her eyes want to drip again. Since she'd forgotten to provide herself with a hankie, she yanked her apron out from under the sampler and wiped off her cheeks angrily. *Dagnabbit!* She kept telling herself she'd learned how to be a grown-up woman here; it was stupid to want to be crying all the time.

"You going to be all right, Gracie?"

Looking up from her needlework, she found Jake watching at her, an expression of sweet solicitude on his face. Lord on high, she loved him!

She reached over and took his hand. His shifted under hers until he was holding it.

"I'm going to be fine, Jake. Just fine. We all are."

His grin nearly broke the rest of her heart. "I reckon we are, Gracie. I reckon we are."

They completed their respective tasks at approximately the same time. Then Jake carried Gracie to bed.

He taught her more lessons in the art of love that night. Gracie, as ever, was an ardent student.

She felt as though she were going to her execution the next morning when she and Jake walked to church. She'd dressed Charity in her prettiest yellow checked calico frock and bonnet. She wore sprigged green muslin herself, and her best straw hat. She wanted on this, her last day in Diabolito Lindo, to show these men how much she loved them.

Jake had wanted to carry her to church but she wouldn't let him. She was going to walk if it killed her, and she was going to let Charity walk, too, in her pretty beaded moccasins Red Willie had so painstakingly crafted for her. Charity loved them because they were so bright and colorful, and they were made of soft leather so they didn't hurt her poor bent foot.

It was slow going, with Charity limping between them and Gracie limping, too, but Gracie didn't much want to get there anyway. Once they got to church, the service would start, and then it would be over, and then the minister Fergus had called from Lincoln would marry them, and then they'd have to leave town. Oh, mercy!

"Howdy, Preacher Jake. Miss Gracie."

"Morning, Bart. How you holding up?"

"Fair, fair. Got me a head."

Gracie experienced a powerful feeling of déjà vu. She remembered Jake and Bart exchanging a greeting very much like this on her first morning in Diabolito Lindo. Only on that morning, which seemed like years ago, she hadn't understood that Bart's interior powerfully contradicted his exterior. She hadn't know that he possessed a beautiful bass voice or that he loved to sing old hymns. She certainly hadn't guessed that Jake had saved his life or that his dreadful scars had been received in a fire started in a barroom brawl.

She heaved a big sigh. "Good morning, Mr. Ragsdale."

Bart tipped his hat, and Gracie smiled when the sun glinted off the knife he had stashed in its band.

"Morning, Miss Gracie. How-do, Miss Charity."

Bart swept Charity a low bow. To Gracie's astonishment, the child giggled before she hid her head in Gracie's skirts. Bart grinned. "She's gettin' used to me."

A wave of sorrow that she had to leave this wonderful man—and all the rest of the men who'd made such a difference in Charity's life—almost made Gracie wail out loud. But she was an adult woman now, and she swallowed her grief.

"She sure seems to be," she said politely, and was proud of her composure.

Then Jake leaned over and whispered, "It's all right, Gracie. Please don't cry. I'll feel terrible if you cry," and her tears welled up again.

Sighing gustily, she said, "I'll try, Jake." And she would.

The four of them—Jake, Bart, Gracie, and Charity—shoved through the saloon doors together, and Gracie blinked in reaction to the darkness, just as she always did. As soon as her eyes adjusted, she saw Jake's congregation: the same congregation of rough men and desperadoes who had greeted her on her first day in town.

Only today they didn't look like a herd of wild *banditti*. They looked like her dear friends, and she would miss them terribly. Smiling in an effort to banish her unhappiness, she said brightly, "Good morning, gentlemen."

Hats swept from heads, and they greeted her as they always did, muttering their good-days in a manner Gracie now understood as bashful. A stranger stood at the rear of the saloon, looking out of place and nervous. Gracie guessed he was the preacher from Lincoln. The six members of her choir stepped away from the group and gathered to one side of the piano, as she'd taught them to do. Since the establishment of the choir, Jake and Fergus had been assembling six chairs close to the piano, near the stairs.

This morning, there were enough men to fill them, too. Some Sundays, when Harley Newton had to be propped up against the back wall, the choir was missing a bass. Not today.

Gracie carried Charity over to the piano and settled her on the bench while Jake walked to the pulpit—this morning sporting a jar of wild mustard and Indian paintbrush that Gracie and Charity had picked especially for the occasion.

Her heart aching almost too much to bear, Gracie played the introductory chords of the first hymn. When the men joined her, right on time and in perfect accord, with the first words of "Shall We Gather at the River," her composure collapsed. By the time the song ended, her tears had run a river down her cheeks. She wiped them away with the back of her hand, since she'd forgotten her hankie again, and smiled sadly at her choir.

They smiled back, not sadly at all. *It's because they don't know yet,* Gracie told herself, and tried to be brave.

Leather creaked, chair legs scraped against the wooden floor, and fabric rustled as everybody settled back to listen to Jake preach.

"I've got another psalm for you today, boys."

Jake's voice was scratchy. He cleared his throat and started again, sounding stronger. "It's the Twenty-seventh. The first verse says, 'The Lord is my light and my salvation; whom shall I fear? the Lord is the strength of my life; of whom shall I be afraid?'"

He stopped speaking abruptly, and bowed his head. Gracie saw his knuckles whiten as he gripped the beer-barrel pulpit, and her heart wept for him. Mercifully, her eyes didn't for once.

A floorboard creaked overhead, and she lifted her head to see Clara peeking over the balcony. The prostitute's presence surprised Gracie; she'd never seen her take interest in one of Jake's sermons before. She didn't see William Williams anywhere, and was disappointed. Now that she wasn't scared to death of him, she kind of liked him. Martha had loved him; he must be a good man.

"Well, boys," Jake said at last, dragging Gracie's attention back to him, "I reckon I have no cause to be afraid of anything, because I know—as well as I know my own name—that God will be with me.

"The fourth verse of the chapter pretty much says it all: 'One thing have I desired of the Lord, that will I seek after; that I may dwell in the house of the Lord all the days of my life, to behold the beauty of the Lord and to inquire in His temple.'"

He paused again to gather strength, and Gracie's heart thudded painfully.

"I've got to leave here, boys. I've got to leave you."

A silence so thick Gracie could almost taste it greeted Jake's stark declaration. Not even a gasp of surprise drifted up from the congregation. She looked around, expecting to see shocked looks. Only one man did anything at all: Red Willie yawned.

Confused by their lack of concern, she returned her attention to Jake. He wasn't looking at the men he loved so much. He stared bleakly at his Bible, still clutching the pulpit as if to hold himself up.

He related Gracie and Charity's story, and his part in it, haltingly. It cost him dearly to tell the men he'd lied to them. Gracie wasn't sure she would have been brave enough to pay the price that Jake was paying now, and her conscience stabbed her. This was all her fault.

"We'll be leaving here, boys. I'm not sure where we'll go, but I reckon there must be someplace else on earth that'll have us."

Strange emotional currents zigzagged through the stuffy atmosphere in the saloon-church. Charity felt them. For the first time in a long time, she crawled onto Gracie's lap and scrunched back, pressing her head against Gracie's shoulder as if trying to hide from the world. Looking down at her tiny face, Gracie saw her watching Jake apprehensively and wished she could reassure her. With a sigh, she told herself that reassurance would have to wait. This was Jake's time, and Gracie wasn't going to interrupt him for anything short of a natural disaster.

Jake tried to smile and failed. "I'm not sure I'll ever find a congregation who loves the psalms as much as I do, though." With a tender look for Gracie, he added, "Or one that can sing so well."

As he continued to speak, the room was so quiet Gracie could have heard a pin drop. In fact, when one of Bart's knives fell from its mooring and struck the floor, it sounded as if somebody had shot a cannon into the room. Everybody jumped. Jake's head jerked up. Charity whimpered. Gracie squeaked.

When her startled gaze found Bart in the choir, he had bent down to retrieve his knife. He grinned sheepishly when he straightened in his chair, blushed, and murmured, "Sorry."

Jake gave him a brief smile. "It's all right, Bart."

His smile faded almost as soon as it began, and Jake looked at the men in his congregation as if he wanted to memorize every face. His last words came out thick.

"I'm sorry, boys. I lied to you."

Gracie saw him gulp two or three times. Then he blurted out, "God, I love you all!"

And that was all. He reached out his arm in a gesture Gracie recognized as one meant to beckon her and Charity to his side. So she limped over to stand beside him, and he put his arm around the both of them.

Gracie looked out over the congregation and tried to be strong for Jake and Charity. It was a tough assignment she'd set for herself. It got a little easier when things turned strange.

She saw Fergus, who was sitting in the front row, turn around and nod at the assembly. As if his nod were a cue, the men stood. Then, making almost no noise at all, they walked up to surround Gracie, Jake, and Charity.

For the first time in a long time, Gracie noticed the various attributes of this group of men. Bart's scarred face, which she had come to love, looked grim. If she were feeling fanciful, she might even have described it as sinister. She tried to curb her imagination.

Red Willie fingered the knife at his waist and grinned, his white teeth against his dark skin making the expression seem more like a grimace. Fergus stared at Jake, his gaunt features almost perfectly blank. Harley Newton spat on the floor, hooked his thumbs into his waistband, and waited. Chauncy Clifford leaned on his crutch and stared at them.

Gracie licked her lips and wondered what would happen if she bolted for the door. Then she told herself not to be ridiculous. She'd never make it. Besides, these were her friends. Anyway, she wasn't about to desert Jake. Not now. Not after everything he'd done for her.

She glanced up at him, hoping to read some kind of understanding of this odd occurrence in his face. He looked as ill at ease as she felt. She took that as a bad sign.

Bart shuffled his feet, and she whipped her head around to look at him.

"We don't like the idear of you leavin' here like this, Preacher Jake," Bart said.

Gracie swallowed. Oh, Lord. All the warnings Jake had drilled into her upon her arrival in Diabolito Lindo crawled back into her mind like ants at a picnic. These men were prone to violence. They lived rough and hard and thought nothing of perpetrating savage acts. This was an uncivilized town in uncivilized territory. Just because these men wore a thin veneer of civilization from time to time didn't mean they weren't primitive at heart.

There were two dozen of them and only three Molloys.

"A long time ago, you told us you'd be our preacher," Bart continued.

Jake didn't say anything. He tightened his grip on Gracie's shoulder.

"We ain't pleased about this."

Oh, sweet Lord have mercy. Grumbles and rumbles from Bart's friends began to make their way to Gracie's ears. She didn't like the sound of them one tiny bit.

"We ain't pleased at all." Bart turned suddenly. "Are we, boys?"

What seemed to Gracie to be an ominous mob of men shook their shaggy heads in the negative.

"We don't like it."

Gracie felt Jake take a deep breath. "Listen, boys, I'm sorry about this. Sorrier than I can say. I tried to explain the reason Gracie and I—"

"And that's another thing," Bart said, trampling Jake's explanation like chaff underfoot. "We ain't best pleased about your takin' our choir director off, neither."

Jake blinked and said, "I—your choir—"

"It ain't fair." He turned once again to gather support. "Is it, boys?"

Gracie's eyes followed twenty-four heads back and forth. A feeble light began to flicker on in her middle.

Bart poked Jake in the chest. "And another thing we don't like a-tall is you takin' our baby away."

Jake goggled. "Taking your bab—"

"It ain't fair. We ain't got no other baby to take this one's place." Bart jerked a thumb toward Charity.

"But—"

Gracie, her fear giving way to amazement, looked at the men again. This time she noticed twinkles in several sets of eyes. She noticed a suppressed grin or two, as well.

"And how the hell are we supposed to have us a choir without no choir director?"

"But—"

Gracie saw Red Willie lift his hand to scratch his nose. He wasn't quick enough to hide his smile. She craned her neck to find Fergus. She discovered him leaning against the banister, his arms folded over his chest, an expression of perfect peace on his wrinkled face, his blue eyes as benign as a cloudless sky.

"We don't like it a-tall, Jake Molloy. Not a-tall."

The light exploded in Gracie's chest, ignited her heart, and lit her soul. Thrusting an astonished Charity into Jake's arms, she cried, "Bart! Oh, Bart, thank you!"

When she threw her arms around poor Bart, he looked absolutely flabbergasted.

So did Jake when the crowd of men surged forward to surround them, reaching out to shake his hand, tweak Charity's cheek, and shyly accept kisses from Gracie. It took Jake a moment to catch on. Which only went to prove, Gracie told him later, that women were naturally much smarter than men.

His eyes almost popped from his head when he stammered, "You mean—you mean—"

Bart, having nearly recovered from Gracie's embrace, helped him out. "I mean you don't have to leave here, you damn fool bastard." Slipping Gracie an embarrassed glance, he murmured, "Beggin' your pardon, Miss Gracie."

As Gracie was too busy crying and hugging men to take exception to Bart's language, he continued explaining.

"Fergus told us what you planned to do before you showed up this mornin', Jake." He took Jake by the shoulders and shook him.

It was a testament to Jake's state of mind that the much smaller Bart could rattle him back and forth like a rag doll. The baby in his arms rocked back and forth, too, watching with great interest. She didn't seem to mind the ride at all. In fact, after a moment or two she smiled at Bart and began to giggle.

"How in hell did you come up with the idear that you had to leave here just 'cause you and Miss Gracie was gettin' married, Jake? What put that damn fool idear in your head, anyhow?"

Jake probably would have shrugged if he'd had possession of his body. Since Bart was still shaking him, he couldn't. "I don't know."

"Fer Christ's sake, Jake, did you really think we was dumb enough to take Miss Gracie fer your sister?"

This time Gracie blushed. Jake merely looked astounded. "Well, I—"

"Anyhow, Fergus says you figgered you had to leave 'cause you lied to us about the two of you bein' kin."

"I—"

"Well, shit, Jake, there ain't no man in Diabolito Lindo who knows you who wouldn't know that if *you* lied, it was fer a damned good reason. Ain't nobody in this whole territory less likely to lie than you are."

Jake stared at Bart, too overwhelmed to speak.

"Fer God's sake, it don't make no difference to us how you live. If you done taught us anything, Preacher Jake, you taught us that the only thing God cares about is what's in a man's heart, and that he at least tries to be good. You coulda lived with a passel o' whores, and we wouldn'ta give a shit."

When he realized what he'd said, he shot Gracie a horrified glance. She was too busy laughing to reprimand him. Jake still looked astounded.

"Fer God's sake, Jake, we don't want you to leave here. We don't want Miss Gracie to leave here, neither. Nor Miss Charity."

"I had no idea, Bart." Jake sounded stunned, undoubtedly because he was stunned.

"Jesus H. God, fer a smart man, you can sure be dumb as an ass sometimes," Bart told him affectionately.

When Bart finally let him go, Jake staggered back against his pulpit. Fergus had left his post at the stairway and was there to steady both pulpit and preacher.

"Told you so," he said expressionlessly.

Gracie had finished hugging everybody else. Now she aimed for Fergus, who ducked behind the pulpit, so she altered her trajectory and threw her arms around Jake. He hugged her so hard that Charity finally objected with a loud screech.

"Oh, poor baby!" Gracie took the baby from Jake's arms, and turned to look out over the sea of men. Her friends. Oh, how she loved them all.

Bart clutched his hat in his hands nervously when next he spoke. "And, Miss Gracie, I know we ain't the purtiest batch of fellers on God's earth, but we thought of a weddin' present for you, if'n you want it."

She could barely get out, "Oh, Bart, you don't need to give us anything but your friendship."

Shaking his head vehemently, Bart said, "No, ma'am. That ain't so. You done give us a whole lot here in Diabolito Lindo. Why, you give us music and purty pitchers on the wall and a saloon that smells like a funeral hall. We figgered we needed to give you somethin', too."

She could do no more than nod.

"If'n you'd like it, ma'am, we aim to rename the town."

Gracie's mouth fell open.

Jake said, "Rename the town?"

"Yep. We figgered since Miss Gracie come here—and what with your purty little gal livin' here and all—and mebbe who knows how many more kids to come—" Bart turned red and lowered his head. "Well, anyhow, we figgered Diabolito Lindo's a no-account name fer a town. We aim to rename her Angelito Lindo, if Miss Gracie likes it."

"Oh, Bart!"

Fergus dangled a clean bandanna over her shoulder, and she took it gratefully. After wiping her eyes and blowing her nose, she said, "Please, Bart." Her next look encompassed them all. "Please, everybody, don't rename the town." She looked up at the man who'd been willing to give up all this for her, and nearly started bawling again. "I love it just the way it is!"

"You do?"

"I do."

A new voice called out, "Good! That good!"

Everybody turned toward the stairs, from whence the loud affirmation had been delivered. Gracie smiled.

There was Clara, in her tattered robe, looking tousled and messy, clinging to the banister. William Chester Williams stood behind her, evidently not quite pleased about his role in this affair, but willing to catch her should she lose her balance and start to fall.

"Thank you, Clara."

Somewhat self-consciously, Clara murmured, "Thank *you*."

Then, at a signal from Bart, the men stopped milling about. They straightened their shoulders, sucked in their guts, and cleared their throats. As a group, they inhaled an acre of acrid air. Fergus, who had made his way to the piano—for a tall man, he could move remarkably quietly, Gracie noticed—plunked a key.

When the first sweet strains of "Amazing Grace" lifted to the rafters of the Devil's Last Stop, it was Jake Molloy who cried.

Epilogue

"PAPA JAKE! PAPA Jake!"

The door to Jake Molloy's sprawling adobe home crashed open, and Jake whirled around in his chair in time to catch Charity as she hurtled into his arms. Lifting her onto his lap, his heart registered a moment of pure joy at how well the past five years had healed her.

"What is it, sweetheart? I'm busy writing my sermon, you know."

"I know, Papa Jake," Charity said breathlessly.

Her smile was as warm as the weather. Jake had never known two females to possess such brilliant smiles as his wife and their daughter—and the two weren't even related, except by adoption.

"But Baby Jay just took his first steps and Mama and Aunt Lizzy and Uncle Fergus sent me to fetch you, because you've got to come and see!"

"He's walking?" Good grief. Their son, Jay, was only a year old. Their daughter Martha hadn't begun to walk until she was fourteen months. Figured. Boys were generally apt to act before they thought. His little Martha, now: She was a thinker.

"Yep." Charity's shiny brown braids bounced as she nodded. "They're all at the church, and Uncle Red Willie says if you don't come right now, he and Uncle Bart will come over here and speak to you by hand."

"Oh, boy," Jake said with a laugh. "That's a threat I'd just as soon not see come to fruition. I'd better get to the church right now."

Charity bounced off his lap, grabbed his hand, and tugged. Jake hurried along behind her, snatching his hat off the peg by the door. His old gun still rested there, too, but he no longer needed it. *Thank God.*

Charity skipped along ahead of him. Every time he saw her dashing about the village of Diabolito Lindo, his gratitude to the good Lord soared. She barely limped at all anymore. The doctor in Albuquerque said one of her legs would always be shorter than the other, and that her foot would never be completely straight, but she'd already managed to compensate brilliantly. Smart kid, Charity. Always had been.

The Diabolito Lindo Church he and his congregation had built four years before sparkled white under the noonday sun. Harley Newton and Bart Ragsdale had just finished adding another coat of whitewash to its walls. Jake smiled when he saw the pretty sign William Williams had painted hanging over the door. Williams was doing a booming business now, painting signs for Diabolito Lindo and the other towns in the area. Diabolito Lindo itself was growing by leaps and bounds. New businesses were opening up all the time.

Although he'd been ordained into the Baptist church, Jake's church boasted no denominational affiliation. He had decided, and his congregation agreed with him, that he didn't want to label it. As far as he was concerned, nobody should feel excluded from whatever good it might be able to offer.

He laughed when he saw the crowd gathered to watch the

phenomenon of his son taking his first steps. You'd think it was a national holiday, the way they were cheering him on. Lizzy and Fergus stood before the door. Jake shook his head when he saw them.

Gracie had been absolutely right about Aunt Lizzy. As soon as she got the letter telling her about their marriage and adoption of Charity, she'd descended upon them like a scourge of locusts. And, after Lizzy took one look at Pablo Fergus, poor old Fergus didn't stand a chance. They were married two months later. They seemed to be happy, too, what's more, and ran the Devil's Last Stop saloon together. Lizzy had opened a restaurant next door to the saloon. Unlike her niece, Lizzy was a wonderful cook. And, thank the good Lord, she delighted in sharing. Jake and the kids got to eat decent food at least a few times every week, thanks to Aunt Lizzy's generosity.

Sometimes Jake wondered whatever happened to Clara. She'd left town not long after he and Gracie were married. Last anybody'd heard, she was aiming vaguely west. Jake expected she was probably in California by now. He hoped she was all right.

A bright blond head caught his attention, and his heart swelled. Gracie. His Gracie. As if she sensed his presence, she turned around and waved, her smile as glorious as anything Jake had ever seen. Little Martha turned, too. Her hair was dark like his, but her eyes were as green as Gracie's. Her grin lit up his whole insides.

His steps sped up.

"Look! Look, Papa Jake!"

Jake took Charity's advice and looked. Sure enough, with the entire village of Diabolito Lindo watching, his son, Jay, stood on wobbly legs, looking mighty proud of himself. *And why shouldn't he?* Jake wondered, with all these people admiring his efforts.

As he watched, two-year-old Martha dropped her mama's hand and toddled over to her brother. She held out her hand, and Jay reached for it. He almost overset himself, but Martha was there to steady him. Then his two children set a course for him.

He picked Charity up. Gracie joined them and wrapped her arm around Jake's waist, and they watched their son and daughter make their slow way over, the surrounding crowd encouraging them along good-humoredly.

"Well, I never thought I'd see the day, Jake Molloy." Aunt Lizzy's voice, as loud and raucous as ever, carried over the cheerful buzz of the onlookers like a trumpet's blare. "But you finally did something worthwhile."

Jake took an encompassing look at his family and guessed that maybe Lizzy was right. Amazing. Utterly amazing.

FREE
Romance
(a $4.50 value)

Send in the Coupon Below

To get your FREE historical romance and start saving, fill out the coupon below and mail it today. As soon as we receive it we'll send you your FREE Book along with your first month's selections.

Our Town

...where love is always right around the corner!